PENGUIN
A VILLA

Dr Rahi Masoom Reza wa ... ct in Uttar Pradesh. He was educate ... igarh Muslim University where he took a ... Urdu, Hindi and Sanskrit, Dr Reza subsequent ... nd was a proponent of Urdu in the Devanagari script. ... o Bombay and became a successful screenplay writer and ... creenplays and dialogues for over 300 films including B.R. Chop ... elevision series, Mahabharat. Dr Reza died on 15 March 1992 in Bombay.

*

Gillian Wright is a journalist and author living in New Delhi. She studied both Hindi and Urdu at London University and has translated another of the modern classic novels of Hindi literature, Shrilalal Shukla's *Raag Darbari* as well as *Middle India*, the short stories of Bhisham Sahni. She recently co-authored *India in Slow Motion* with Mark Tully and has collaborated with him on a number of books including *No Full Stops in India* and *Heart of India*. Her other books include *An Introduction to the Hill Stations of India*, *Sri Lanka* and *Birds of the Indian Subcontinent*.

By the same author:

Fiction

- *Topi Shukla*
- *Himmat Jaunpuri*
- *Os Ki Boond*
- *Dil Ek Sada Kagaz*
- *Katra Bi Arzoo*
- *Muhabbat Ke Siva*
- *Chote Aadmi Ki Badi Kahani*

Poetry

- *Naya Saal*
- *Mauj-e-Gul, Mauj-e-Saba*
- *Ajnabi Shahr, Ajnabi Raaste*
- *1857*

Rahi Masoom Reza

A Village Divided

[*Adha Gaon*]

Translated from the Hindi by Gillian Wright

PENGUIN BOOKS

Penguin Books India (P) Ltd., 11 Community Centre, Panchsheel Park, New Delhi 110 017, India
Penguin Books Ltd., 80 Strand, London WC2R 0RL, UK
Penguin Putnam Inc., 375 Hudson Street, New York, NY 10014, USA
Penguin Books Australia Ltd., 250 Camberwell Road, Camberwell, Victoria 3124, Australia
Penguin Books Canada Ltd., 10 Alcorn Avenue, Suite 300, Toronto, Ontario M4V 3B2, Canada
Penguin Books (NZ) Ltd., Cnr Rosedale and Airborne Roads, Albany, Auckland, New Zealand
Penguin Books (South Africa) (Pty) Ltd, 24 Sturdee Avenue, Rosebank 2196, South Africa

First published in Hindi as *Adha Gaon* by Akshar 1966
This translation first published as *The Feuding Families of Village Gangauli* in Viking by Penguin Books India 1994

10 9 8 7 6 5 4 3 2 1

Typeset in *Sabon* by Mantra Virtual Services, New Delhi
Printed at International Print-O-Pac, Noida

I dedicate this book to my dear friend Kunwarpal Singh. But for him, I may well not have been able to write this story.

Contents

Translator's Acknowledgements

I am indebted to Dr Rahi Masoom Reza and Nayyar Reza for agreeing to my translating *Adha Gaon*. Unfortunately I could only meet the author once before he passed away. However, his family—that is Sarwari, Afsari and Baqri Begum, Professor Mehdi Raza, Shakeel and Deeba Abidi, Shamim and Dr Nadeem Hasnain, and Dr Shehla Raza—have been very helpful explaining to me the things particular to Gangauli and Ghazipur, which only they know.

I must thank Pratibha Arya for going through the draft with immense patience and enthusiasm, and Shah Ghulam Ahmed Ilmi who, in his own inimitable style, shared some of his immense knowledge with me. I must also thank Professor Kunwarpal Singh for the time and effort he spent in going through the translation. I am indebted to Asghar Wajahat, Sarwat Zahra Rizvi, Professor Mujeeb Rizvi and Dr Naiyer Masud for the enjoyable conversations I had with them, to Viqar Ahmad for sending me his excellent essay on divided families and reading the manuscript, to Qurban Ali for helping me out with some last minute queries, and to Avrille Turner for all her assistance.

I would also like to thank Begum Atiya Fatima Naqvi, Saeed Naqvi, Saiyid Ghulam-us-Saqlain Naqvi, Naheed and Shabihul Hasnain, Saiyid Mohammad Mehdi Adeeb—known to me as Mamu Jan—and all their family and friends in Mustafabad who welcomed me into their home and introduced me to the celebration of Moharram, and to the many people I met and who showed me such hospitality during Moharram in Lucknow in 1992.

Familiarity with Urdu has been of great use during this translation, and I must thank all those who gave me whatever I know, in particular Ralph Russell, the best of teachers.

David Davidar of Penguin India has again been most sympathetic about deadlines, and Zamir Ansari, who tells great stories of eastern UP with unbeatable humour, has been a great help. Sudha Sadhanand has been a most caring editor and has made me feel that my work has been worthwhile.

Last but never least I would like to thank Mark Tully, who has encouraged me throughout, and to remember Ambikanand Sahay, Ram Dutt Tripathi and Rajiv Saxena in whose company we made a very memorable visit to the area around Rahi Masoom Reza's Ghazipur, camping not in a village, or even in fields, but in barren land near Devsthali.

Translator's Introduction

Adha Gaon, Rahi Masoom Reza's semi-autobiographical novel about his own village, Gangauli, in eastern Uttar Pradesh, is, to my mind, the most outstanding achievement of his brilliant and varied career. Although he is most famous among the Indian public for his script of B.R. Chopra's much acclaimed television version of the Mahabharat, his talent is at its height as he recreates the world of Gangauli in all its complexities, and through it expresses his deepest convictions about India and his faith in its unique pluralistic traditions.

This is the story of a village divided, or more literally, of half a village—the half of Gangauli controlled by Rahi Masoom Reza's family. They are Shia Muslims, and the most important religious occasion of their year is the period of mourning during the Muslim month of Moharram, when for ten days they mark the anniversary of the martyrdom of Imam Husain, the grandson of the Prophet Mohammad, at Karbala in Iraq. During the course of this novel, as the characters fight or fall in love, the backdrop of Indian national politics is unfolding—from the beginning of the Second World War to the Quit India movement, from Independence to the land reforms abolishing large estates. This history changes the village—something of themselves is martyred too. The ten days of Moharram are reflected in the ten chapters of the novel. Given its centrality to the book, it is important to understand something of the customs and traditions surrounding this period of mourning in northern India.

To most non-Shias and non-Muslims, Moharram is synonymous with bloodshed, with an incomprehensible excess of emotion. Spectacular processions wind through the streets in which parties of young men beat their backs with chains ending with sharp blades, and young children cut open their heads with knives. This violence shocks and repels many, but it by no means represents the totality of Moharram. For the inhabitants of Gangauli to care about it so deeply, it has to mean more than this. For them Moharram is an occasion for mourning, but it is also a time of family gathering. It is the opportunity for concentration on things beyond the mundane level of daily life, for great pomp and poetry and ceremony, for beauty and simplicity and catharsis.

As Shias, the main characters of this novel are especially attached to the family of the Prophet. As Saiyids, they trace their ancestry back to the Prophet himself through his daughter Fatima and son-in-law Ali. As zamindars, they are the also the most powerful community in the village, controlling land, collecting rent from the cultivators and acting to a large extent as a law unto themselves. They also have the resources to celebrate Moharram grandly by village standards.

Rahi Masoom Reza observed this closely as a child, and he appears in the book as a young boy called Masoom—literally 'innocent'—lame as a result of tuberculosis. The Moharram he describes is one in which many of the traditions are localized, and others are influenced by the sophisticated culture of Avadh, the province on the fringes of which his village lies. Until annexation by the British in 1856, the rulers of Avadh were Shias, and their court at Lucknow drew poets, artists and artisans of the highest calibre. Moharram was an occasion in which all communities participated, and central to it was the institution of the majlis, assemblies of ritual mourning, which were held in imambaras, or houses of the Imam. In Gangauli too the assemblies held in the village imambaras relate every detail of the tragedy of Karbala. The stories become embedded in the hearts and minds of those attending and communicate profound truths about justice and injustice, life and death.

THE EVENTS OF KARBALA

After the Prophet passed away, he was succeeded in turn by three Caliphs who had formerly been his companions. I shall try to give a very simple outline of the main events. After the death of the Prophet, he was succeeded in turn by three Caliphs, who had been his companions. His son-in-law Ali was also considered a candidate, but he accepted those who were elected. After the death of the third Caliph, Ali succeeded although his position was challenged by the Umayyad leader Muaviya. Ali agreed to step down and was assassinated while saying his prayers in a mosque in Kufa in Iraq. His son Hasan was then made Caliph. However, Muaviya pressed his claim and Hasan either resigned, or according to an account that most Shias believe, was poisoned. Muaviya wished his son Yazid to succeed Hasan. In his *Spirit of Islam*, Ameer Ali sums up how most Shias, and particularly Shia poets of the nineteenth century, saw Yazid: 'His depraved nature knew no pity or justice. He killed and tortured for the pleasure he derived from human suffering.'

The people of Kufa, oppressed by the tyranny they lived under, sent messages to Ali's remaining son, Husain, to come and help them.

Husain sent his cousin Muslim to Kufa and he reported that there was great support for Husain. At that point, Ubaidullah ibn Ziyad, the Governor of Kufa, captured and subsequently killed Muslim, at which all the Kufans deserted Husain's cause in fear.

Husain with his seventy-two companions, many of them women and children, was already in Iraq when he discovered what had happened to Muslim. However, he resolved to continue his journey and to stand for a cause he believed to be just. At the beginning of Moharram, the first month of the Muslim year, he arrived at the arid plain of Karbala, next to the River Euphrates. Here he was surrounded by the forces of the Governor of Kufa loyal to Yazid. From the seventh of Moharram these forces prevented Husain and his companions from drawing water, causing great hardship particularly to the women and children. One by one his companions fell to the surrounding army, although Husain himself, armed with his sword Zulfiqar and mounted on his horse Zuljenah, was invincible. Husain refused to swear allegiance to Yazid, but, according to some accounts, did try to negotiate an end to the siege. However, the Kufan governor was implacable. On the tenth of Moharram, the remaining defenders fought to the death and Ameer Ali recounts the martyrdom of Husain thus:

> Wounded and dying he dragged himself to the river-side for a last drink; they turned him off with arrows from there. And as he re-entered his tent he took his infant child in his arms; him they transfixed with a dart. The stricken father bowed his head to heaven . . . . alone and weary, he seated himself at the door of his tent . . . . He lifted his hands to heaven—they were full of blood—and he uttered a funeral prayer for the living and the dead. Raising himself for one desperate charge, he threw himself among the Ommeyyades, who fell back on every side. But faint with loss of blood he soon sank to the ground, and then the murderous crew rushed upon the dying hero. They cut off his head, trampled on his body . . . .

The loneliness of Husain on the tenth of Moharram is the focus of a great poem which Rahi Masoom Reza quotes to effect in this novel.

Among those who were martyred at Karbala were Abbas, half-brother to Husain, who died in an effort to fetch water for the children of the encampment, and Hur, the head of Yazid's cavalry, who changed sides and joined Husain although he knew it would mean certain death. Then there were the children of Husain, eighteen-year-old Ali Akbar, the infant Ali Asghar, and Hasan's young son Qasim. Traditionally, Qasim is believed to have been married to Husain's daughter Kubara just before leaving for the battlefield to die. After the battle the only male child surviving was the ailing son of Husain, referred to in the novel by the name Sajjad, who became the fourth of the Shia Imams. Among the women and children at Karbala were Husain's sisters Zainab and Kulsum, his wife Bano, his young daughters Kubara and Sakina, and his cousin Muslim's daughter Ruqayya. They, with all the other survivors, were carried away to Damascus and the court of Yazid, only later being allowed to return to bury their dead.

All Muslims abhor the killing of the members of the Prophet's family, but Sunnis accept the first three Caliphs, the Prophet's companions, as legitimate rulers. Shias, in contrast, place faith in a line of twelve Imams, descendents of the Prophet, the first of whom are Ali, Hasan and Husain. Ali is especially seen as a solver of difficulties for the Shia faithful, and the villagers of Gangauli call on him for his help.

IMAMBARA, MAJLIS AND MARSIA

Wherever there were Shias in the province of Avadh, imambaras were built. In Lucknow today you find imambaras varying from the palatial ones of Asaf-ud-daula and Husainabad to tiny, richly decorated rooms in houses in the old part of the city. The imambaras of Gangauli share the main elements of those in Lucknow. At one end is the shahnashin, the seat of the king, a raised platform on which are kept the tazias, alams and tabuts which are carried in procession on the tenth of Moharram. Tazias are replicas of the tomb of Imam Husain at Karbala. They can be immense or tiny, made of paper stuck on a bamboo frame or of finely-carved wood. The wooden tazias of Gangauli are re-used every year, whereas cheaper paper ones are taken in procession and buried at the spot outside the village known as the Karbala.

Alams are standards. At the top of a pole is fixed a panja, or crest, often in the form of an outstretched hand representing the five pure souls of the Prophet Muhammad, his daughter Fatima and son-in-law Ali, and their sons Hasan and Husain. Down the length of the poles of the standards hang elaborately embroidered strips of fine cloth or patkas. Alams are also kept in memory of Abbas, who was the standard-bearer of Husain's companions at Karbala.

Tabuts are replicas of the biers on which the corpses of the martyrs were placed.

Imambaras are also richly decorated with glass candleshades of different design, which glitter in the evening majlises. The floor is covered with an immaculate farsh—or cotton sheet.

In front of the shahnashin, to the left of the congregation stands a mimbar, a stepped pulpit. These pulpits were developed from those in mosques, from which the imam leads the prayers. They became higher and were used as a stage by those declaiming marsias, poetic accounts of the events of Karbala.

At the beginning of a majlis drums were, and often still are, beaten outside imambaras to summon the congregation. Women have their own majlises, but also attend the men's, sitting behind a curtain or screen. The days of Moharram are passed in moving from majlis to majlis, hearing great poetry, moral lectures, meeting friends, and weeping in grief. As people come home for Moharram, the occasion strengthens family ties, and for women observing purdah it is also a great period of freedom as they are taken away from the normal routine of home and hearth. At a time of great illiteracy, a large proportion of Shia women were taught to read so that they could conduct their majlises. However, this did not always mean they could write. As Atiya Begum of Mustafabad told me, 'In the old days women could read but they [our elders] didn't want us writing in case we started sending letters to lovers.' Many of the women in this novel know only a rudimentary coded script in which they can make simple communications.

Although you are not meant to laugh during Moharram, there is great warmth and affection expressed within the gathered families, and, as Rahi Masoom Reza describes, a lot of gossip exchanged between majlises.

A majlis contains several elements. Nowadays in Lucknow the emphasis is on the zakir, the speaker who delivers a sermon on a moral theme, concluding with a vivid description of the afflictions of Imam Husain, at which the congregation weeps. There are zakirs in this novel too, particularly Maulvi Ibne Hasan, a celebrated speaker, who in real life was also an uncle of Masoom's.

In Masoom's Gangauli a majlis begins with soz, literally burning, in which a fragment of poetry about the events of Karbala is chanted to an Indian raag or raagini. Musical instruments are not allowed, as being contrary to Islam, and so the accompaniment too is vocal. Many of the Shias of northern India have been introduced to poetry and classical music through the majlis. Because of this musical element, soz never found much favour with the Shia ulema, but it was very popular with the common people and the rich zamindars.

Soz serves to draw the congregation's attention. Afterwards comes a salaam, a eulogy of Husain and his family, or a darud, a eulogy of the Prophet, and either a marsia or hadis, the former poetry and the latter prose.

Marsias are poems narrating the events of Karbala. The marsia developed and was brought to great heights by the poets of Lucknow, particularly Mir Anis (1802–1874) and Mirza Dabir (1803–1875), who wrote them in the form of six-lined stanzas, each stanza reaching a climax in the last couplet. The poems of Anis are particularly popular with the characters of this novel, perhaps because his eloquence enables him to use a great range of vocabulary and verbal conceits, while retaining idiomatic simplicity and pathos. In the words of Dr Mujeeb Rizvi, 'Every character is shown as a perfect Indian. The bride-to-be, for example, is described as an Indian Muslim bride—and like an Indian bride, she breaks her bangles when her husband's corpse is brought.'

Recitation of marsia is an art perfected by the poet Anis himself. As Abdul Halim Sharar writes in his *Guzashta Lucknow*, 'The art of making desirable changes in the sound of words, of adjusting one's facial expression to the subject, of moving one's limbs in a way befitting the discourse and of making it forceful through minute gestures is distinctive to Lucknow.' Gangauli represents the village, rather than the Lucknow tradition, but there too marsias are delivered with great feeling. As the poem reaches its climax the congregation weeps, reliving the trials of Husain and his family.

As the marsia-reader descends from the pulpit the whole congregation stands as a mark of respect, as when any dead body is brought home. They are mentally prepared for the nauha, a lament rendered to a raag, and nowadays to film song-like melodies, and to the rhythm of hands beating chests. Nauhas are composed in couplets rhyming *aa ba ca* and so on, the same form as the ghazal, a popular genre of poetry dealing traditionally with human and divine love. Nauhas are especially popular with women and young men. Groups of boys and young men gather beforehand to practice, as it is an art to perfectly match the rhythm of the hand beating the chest with the verse. The Husainiya Society of Gangauli is one such group. One person chants, and then the whole group repeats the same verse. After the nauha they perform matam—mourning by rhythmically beating the chest to the words 'Husain! Husain!' The fatiha—certain verses of the Qor'an—is also recited, as it is over the dead.

As the congregation disperses, tabarruk, or blessed food, is distributed to the congregation and to all who gather at the gate. To sanctify it, part of the tabarruk is kept near the tazias as the fatiha is read. To the Hindus of Gangauli this tabarruk is equivalent to prasad.

The distribution of tabarruk is only one of the customs which have grown up around Moharram. At the beginning of the month women take off their bangles and ornaments, and wear only black or green. No one chews betel-leaves, although betel-nut can be taken separately. The villagers of Gangauli believe that Imam Husain comes to India for the ten days of Moharram. Mannats are requested, a mannat being a favour asked at a tazia, or in the name of Imam Husain—for a child, for the safety of relatives, or for any need. In return for the granting of their prayers, believers promise next year to, for example, 'fill the pulpit', which is to place bowls of sweet pudding on the pulpit steps.

In Gangauli each majlis has its own traditions. Particularly mentioned is the *Sham-e-Ghariban* which after some thought I have translated as the Evening of the Bereaved. This majlis is held on the night of the tenth of Moharram in total darkness, in rememberance of the widows and children left behind in Husain's camp after he and his companions had been killed. Even their tents had been burnt and they had no food save a few charred grains.

It is also believed that listening to marsias, weeping for Imam Husain and mourning him all have great spiritual rewards.

TAZIAS AND PROCESSIONS

Although strict Sunni Muslims oppose the use of tazias, many Sunnis of north India still march with them in procession. Many of the customers who come from miles around to buy the tall, delicately made paper tazias from Kazmain in the old city of Lucknow are Sunnis. Previously certain guilds would prepare tazias, and in Gangauli it is the task of the Muslims of lower social status to prepare the tazias of the zamindars. According to local traditions, there are processions on various days—in Gangauli there is a big procession on the eighth night. The eighth of Moharram is traditionally associated with Abbas.

In some places an empty cradle symbolizing that of the infant Ali Asghar is taken out, and a horse symbolizing Husain's steed is wrapped in red-stained sheets. Standards accompany the processions, and crowds rush to touch the Imam's horse or cross beneath the tazias. Night is also the time for fire-walking over a bed of wood embers.

When not in procession, tazias are arrayed in imambaras, or set out on imam chowks, rectangular platforms in the open, often at crossroads, where women light small oil lamps at night.

The procession on the tenth of Moharram belongs especially to Imam Husain, and it is then that with nauha and soz and the self-flagellation, which many Shias themselves find hard to witness, that the tazias are taken to the Karbala, or graveyard, and buried. Men I have spoken to who whip themselves with knife-ended chains in this procession every year tell me that they feel no pain and believe it is a miracle of God that their wounds heal in only four or five days. In Gangauli there seems to be little blood-letting on the tenth of Moharram. There it is more a display of traditional martial arts. In Gangauli Shias, Sunnis and Hindus all form part of the procession. Till today in small towns and villages all over north India all communities take part in Moharram. For example, in Mustafabad in Rae Bareli district, Hindus crowd the back of the morning majlis, circumambulate and pray at the tazias, and turn out in huge numbers to witness the procession, while Sunni cooks prepare the special food for the occasion.

THE PEOPLE AND LANGUAGE OF GANGAULI

The zamindars of Gangauli may be Saiyids and Shias, but they are by no means saints. They live alongside the Muslim weavers and traders. The latter are predominantly Sunnis and known as Raqis. I am told by Ilmi Sahib, a learned man from Ghazipur, that the name may have originated from the word arq or essence, and that they may originally have been sellers of oils. The Raqis became more prosperous but the social status belongs to the Saiyids, who in north India are often compared to Brahmins. They form the topmost of the four noble communities of Muslims—the others being Sheikhs, Pathans and Mughals. The Brahminization of the Saiyids of Gangauli is clear in the Hakim Sahib's concern over ritual pollution, and the general concern over haddi—literally bone, that is to say purity of bloodline.

There are also Muslim Nais (barbers) in Gangauli and Hindu satellite settlements of Bhars, a low caste mainly of labourers, and Ahirs, whose traditional activity is looking after cattle. The Chamars, (untouchable leather workers) the remaining caste group of Gangauli, are those of lowest status.

The dominant Hindu caste of the area is that of the Thakurs, or

Rajputs, who are the zamindars in nearby Barikhpur. The officer in charge of the local police sub-district—a very important man—is also a Thakur.

Outsiders, notably political activists, when they visit Gangauli use languages alien to the villagers—Urdu or Hindi. One of the most fascinating aspects of this novel is the insight it gives into how the Independence movement appears to those away from politicized urban centres, and how decisions taken by those outside their control affect the villagers. Gangauli lies in Uttar Pradesh, the former United Provinces. As Viqar Ahmad writes in his essay *Lucknow's Divided Muslim Families—the Political Backcloth*, 'It was perhaps inevitable that the UP should play a central role in the shaping of Muslim politics in modern India. As well as being the Hindu heartland, it was the seat of the Muslim intellectual, cultural and political élite.'

Viqar Ahmad goes on to define the chief elements that determined Muslim political behaviour up to India's independence—'fear of democracy and of open competition on the basis of merit, loyalty to the British and, by the same token, an aversion to nationalist politics, and, above all, the sense of a separate Muslim identity. Paradoxically this ideal of a separate Muslim identity . . . could only develop in a province where the Muslims were in a minority, and especially in a province like the UP where political rivalry between Hindus and Muslims was compounded by linguistic and cultural chauvanism on both sides.' This sense of separate identity developed into the Pakistan movement. The intellectual centre for this movement was the Muhammadan Anglo-Oriental College at Aligarh. It was from Aligarh that young men came to canvass in Gangauli and found ideas very different from their own, and arguments which could counter theirs.

National level politicians do not come to Gangauli, but they are discussed there. The names of politicians from the United Provinces, like the Raja of Mahmudabad and Chaudhuri Khaliquzzaman, two key Muslim League leaders, are mentioned, as is Sarju Pande, a Communist leader who later became a Member of Parliament. Communism took root in areas under zamindari as a reaction against the old system and both Rahi Masoom Reza and his brother Moonis became communist supporters.

The language of Gangauli, as opposed to that of the urban political activists, is a mixture of Bhojpuri and Urdu, with the lower castes speaking a thicker dialect. Hindi or Urdu appears when men try to break out of their traditional roles, or practise social climbing. Village language is often crude—as army language is in Britain—and particularly around the time of Partition, when ugly events are taking place, the characters use some strong language. In English novels such language is not extraordinary, but some readers still remember *Adha Gaon* for its abuses. For people like Phunnan Miyan these abuses are natural and commonplace words, and is one reason why simply translating them into English just doesn't seem to work. Therefore, I have largely left them in the original, which retains the force of the sound, a flavour of the native language of Gangauli, and a very few words for the reader unfamiliar with them to learn. The translation of dialect is a problem which has no easy solution. As it is the natural language of the characters, I have left it mainly as colloquial English, leaving in the original some typical words, the non-translation of which does not detract from the general meaning, to give some flavour of the Indianness of the language.

Hardly any cuts have been made to the text. Only in a very few places has a phrase, sentence or paragraph been omitted when the editor and I felt it would help the English translation.

Another problem which I faced was that of characters' names, which vary in different parts of the book. For example, Wajid becomes Javad, and Abbu and Aggu Miyan both appear as Saiyda's father. I consulted those who know better than me, and have tried to name characters consistently.

The people of Gangauli also have full names and short, pet names, and it is the latter by which they are generally known in this book. Suffixes are added to their names to indicate their relationship with the speaker, -cha, meaning a relative about the age or generation of an uncle, and -da, a relative owed the respect of a grandfather.

In the second chapter of the novel, "My Village, My People", we meet a very large number of characters, some of whom are the subjects of stories later in the book. We meet so many characters in this particular chapter because the boy Masoom takes us to Gangauli, and we experience with him his return to his extended family. This is the most clearly autobiographical part of the novel.

However, in the course of time I have come to realize that many of the people of Gangauli have more fact to them than I had imagined. I have become very fond of them, and I have tried my best to translate them into English.

New Delhi — Gillian Wright

Some People of Gangauli

DAKKHIN PATTI

Dadda, or Akbari-bibi, mother of Shabbir Miyan, Bashir Miyan and Wazir Miyan

Shabbir Miyan (also known as Shabbu Miyan and to young Masoom as Bade* Abba Sahib), father of Tannu

Bashir Miyan, husband of Nafisa, father of Begum, Sarwari, Moonis, Masoom (the author), Maddu, Afsari, Ahmad Raza, Munni and Suraiya

Wazir Miyan, brother of Bashir, husband of Chachi

Abbu Miyan, brother of Rabban-bi, father of Aggu Miyan and Saiyda

Fussu Miyan, son of Rabban-bi, husband of Sakina, father of Salma (also known as Sallo) and numerous other daughters

Safir-va, a boy brought up by Rabban-bi

Phunnan Miyan, who carried off Kulsum, his children by her Imtiyaz, Mumtaz (also called Muntaz), Razia, Ruqayya and Maghfiya

Muhammad Husain, Phunnan's son-in-law

Hammad Miyan, son of weaver woman Naima-bi, husband of Kubara, father of sons Abbas and Mighdad and daughter Umme Habiba

Gaya Ahir, right-hand man of Hammad

Sulaiman Miyan, kept woman Jhangtiya-bo, father of Ali Akbar and Bacchaniya

Javad Miyan, kept woman Rahman-bo, father of Kamaluddin (also known as Kammo) and Fiddu

UTTAR PATTI

Husain Ali Miyan, brother of Ummal Habiba Ali Mehdi Miyan

Hakim Ali Kabir, father of Sa'adat (also known as Saddan)

---

* The 'd' in Bade is in fact a retroflex 'r', which is a common practice. We have shown it as a 'd'.

Deputy Collector Ali Hadi, younger brother of Hakim Ali Kabir

Maulvi Bedar Husain Sadrulfazil, uncle of Asiya

Ghulam Husain Khan, family retainer of Hakim Ali Kabir, brother of Karamat Ali Khan, whose wife was carried off by Phunnan Miyan

OTHERS

Anwarul Hasan Raqi, trader, father of Farooq

Najjan Mirasi, husband of Ghafooran, father of Sitara and Dil-Ara, from a community of musicians

Ashrafullah Khan 'Ashraf' of Salimpur, grandfather of Khairu, friend of Dakkhin Patti

Gulbehri, a maidservant of the above

Thakur Kunwarpal Singh of Barikhpur, friend of Uttar Patti and Phunnan Miyan, father of Prithvipal Singh, grandfather of Jaipal Singh

Thakur Harnarayan Prasad Singh, thanedar of Qasimabad police station

Gulabi Jan, his whore

Samiuddin Khan, his havildar, father of Moinuddin (also known as Moin)

Saifuniya, daughter of Mehruniya and Rahim, granddaughter of Jinti, all of the barber community

Gobardhan, businessman

Komila Chamar, one of the Hakim Sahib's men

Sukhram, father of Parusaram, the Congress supporter, and Balram, the Collector's gardener

Jhinguriya, lieutenant of Phunnan Miyan, and father of Chikuriya

The Dozing Town

Within the old fort of Ghazipur there's now a school, where the sound of the Ganga's waves reaches, but where the murmuring or cold sighs of history do not. No sentry now patrols the walls; nor even do schoolboys come to them to speak to, or hear from, the river shimmering in the light of the setting sun.

No one can guess how many stories the muddy waters of this great river must know. But mothers are absorbed in tales of jinn, fairies, ghosts and thieves, and for goodness knows how long this sleepy town on the banks of the Ganga has never even thought of sitting in the river's school to hear stories of its forefathers.

If anyone were to come and sit on these walls, and close his eyes, it's still not impossible for the villages and fields on the far shore to be transformed into dense jungle, for the huts of the rishis of the tapovan to appear, and for the young princes of Ayodhya, Ram and Lakshman, to emerge, bows slung over their shoulders, defending the sacred solitude of the forest.

But no one does sit on these walls because, when the age comes for them to do so, the young men of Ghazipur, their chests a yard wide, are yoked to the mill of unemployment to squeeze out the oil of their dreams, to drink that poisonous oil and quietly die.

A nudge of my bridal nosering sent
My love as far as Calcutta.

In the jute mills of Calcutta the dreams of this town are woven into the warp and woof of gunny cloth and sent to distant lands, leaving behind only empty eyes, desolate hearts and weary bodies, which lie in some small, dark room, constantly longing for footpaths, village ponds, and fields of paddy, barley and peas.

Calcutta!

Calcutta is not the name of a city. For the sons and daughters of Ghazipur it is another name for the yearning that comes of separation.

This yearning is a whole story in itself, in which the kajal lining the eyes of countless women has been washed away by tears, and then dried. Every year thousands upon thousands of men far from home send back thousands upon thousands of messages with the monsoon clouds. Perhaps that's why clouds burst over Ghazipur and, in these rains, seeds of yearning sprout in new and old walls, in the roofs of mosques and temples, in the cracks of school windows and doors, and the pain of separation awakes and begins to sing:

No one stirs out in the monsoon rains,
Only you would leave for a distant land.

Calcutta, Bombay, Kanpur and Dacca are the boundaries of this town. Far-flung boundaries. The people from here remain of here even after they leave. No matter how far balloons rise into the sky their link with the ground, where some child holds a fine thread, does not break.

But here for some time the threads in many children's hands have broken.

If the truth be told, this is the story of those balloons, or perhaps of those children who hold the ends of the limp threads in their hands and who are searching for their balloons, unaware of what befell them when the threads broke.

The Ganga constantly strokes the head and cheeks of this town like a mother caring for her sick child but when she senses no response to her love she begins to sob inconsolably, and the town is drowned in her tears. People say there's a flood. Muslims begin to sound the call to prayer. Hindus begin to make offerings to appease the offended Mother Ganga. The Ganga frets at this insult to her love and begins to strike her head against the walls of the fort and her bright, white tresses tangle and spread far and wide. We call it foam. When the Ganga sees that no one comprehends her pain, she wipes her eyes and then we say that the water is receding. Muslims say that the call to prayer is never without effect; Hindus say that the Ganga has accepted their offerings. No one says that the tears of the Mother have made the land even more fertile—for miles around a coverlet of soft earth has been drawn over the land.

But what can the Ganga do? The bullocks here don't have strength enough to bear the weight of the plough.

This town is heedless of its past. It doesn't even have the time occasionally to lie in the cool shade of a banyan tree and think about its history, which spreads from the time of the Ramayan to the present. As for the future, it doesn't have the courage even to consider it. There is a tiny hole in the pot of time, from which moments fall drop by drop. This town lives in moments, dies in moments, and then is reborn in moments.

Who knows when this great penance will end? Ghazipur is not on the caravan route of life. Sometimes, if the wind blows past here, it brings the dust of the caravans, and Ghazipur can find happiness in rubbing that dust into its clothes and body like attar of roses.

This is my town. Whenever I pass through its narrow lanes, it puts its hand on my shoulder. It meets me here and there on the roads of all my various stories. But I have not yet been able to grasp its whole reality; that's why I want to see it one more time.

This novel is in fact my journey. I have set out in search of Ghazipur, but first I will stop at my Gangauli. If I can capture the truth of Gangauli I will have the courage to write the epic of Ghazipur. This novel is really the prologue to that epic.

But I must say one thing more. This is not the story either of a few individuals or a few families. This is not even the story of the village in which the characters, good and bad, are attempting to fulfil themselves. This story is neither religious nor political, because time is neither religious nor political . . . and this story is actually about time. It is the story of time passing through Gangauli. Some old people die, some young men grow old, some children grow up and some are born. This is the story of the dreams and courage trapped in these changing ages of man. It is the story of the ruins where houses stood and of the houses built on those ruins.

And this story is as true as it is false.

I know the art of mixing truth with falsehood and falsehood with truth. Here and there I use the first person so that the story cannot go far from me, and I can touch it when I wish—to summon the courage to convince myself and you that I am like the story I am telling. Therefore, this is both an autobiography and a tale of others' experiences.

This age is like an unbound book lying in an open plain. Even the slightest gust of breeze sets its pages fluttering back and forth. In the pages the paragraphs advance and recede before the reader, sometimes he finds himself ten pages ahead, and sometimes is left ten pages behind. That is why I am making unreserved use of the first person—

so that the pages do not turn by themselves, so that order remains and I can see what was, what is and what is to be.

They say that on a dark night in the month of *Asharh*, at the start of the monsoon, a chieftain of Tughlaq, Saiyid Masood Ghazi, crossed the swollen Ganga and attacked Gadipuri. Accordingly, the town changed its name from Gadipuri to Ghazipur. The roads were the same, the lanes too, and the houses—just the name changed. Perhaps names are outer shells which can be changed. There is no unbreakable bond between names and identity, because if there were then Gadipuri too should have changed when it became Ghazipur, or at least the defeated Thakurs, Brahmins, Kayasths, Ahirs, Bhars and Chamars should have called themselves Gadipuris, and the victorious Saiyids, Sheikhs and Pathans should have called themselves Ghazipuris. But they didn't. They are all Ghazipuris and if the town's name had not been changed then they would all have been Gadipuris.

These new names are fascinating. When the Arabic 'fateh' or 'victory' is joined to the Hindi 'garh' or 'fort' it makes one unit—the town of Fatehgarh. That is why even after the creation of Pakistan I cannot comprehend its reality. If you take the 'Ali' from Aligarh, 'Ghazi' from Ghazipur and 'Dildar' from Dildarnagar, then whole towns will become desolate and nameless and if you take the 'Imam' from imambaras—the houses of the Imam—then how can you have Moharram?

The Ganga still holds Ghazipur to her breast, as she did Gadipuri. That is why it makes no difference whether it's called Ghazipur or Gadipur. Masood Ghazi's family would have been certain to seize the surrounding countryside in any case. This family, which chanced here from Delhi, would still have been sure to have split into several landowning families and I would still have written this story.

One son of Masood Ghazi, Nuruddin the Martyr (how and why he became a martyr I, and probably no one, knows) forded two rivers and conquered Gangauli, a village about a dozen miles from Ghazipur. They say that the name of the raja of this village was Gang and the village was named Gangauli after him. But even after Nuruddin Saiyid's family established its hold over the village, Gangauli did not become Nurpur or Nuruddinagar—and my Gangauli's name is no worse than my Ghazipur's.

But the amusing thing is that the tomb of Nuruddin the Martyr, which is newer than Gangauli, looks much older . . . . This small, brick structure must certainly once have had a roof but for the last thirty-five years or more I have seen it in ruins. Only on the tenth day of Moharram, when processions from both ends of the village come here, is there some kind of gathering. The men who learn lathi-work together congregate a short distance from the tomb, fencing with leather-covered wooden truncheons and shields, whirling long sticks, displaying how to fend off attack with a knife, and performing feats of swordsmanship. Then suddenly one man shouts, 'Bol Muhammadi!' and the whole village replies, 'Ya Husain!'

For some time now the residents of Gangauli have been dwindling in numbers and the percentage of Sunnis, Shias and Hindus has been growing. Perhaps this is the reason that there's no longer such a large crowd at the tomb of Nuruddin the Martyr and the air of Gangauli no longer resounds with the cry 'Bol Muhammadi!—Ya Husain!' as it did formerly. Perhaps this is the reason that today the tomb looks so forlorn and keeps searching with its blind eyes and asking, 'Where has my Gangauli gone?' But the foundations of this tomb are in the soil of Gangauli and that is why it stands alone, exactly where it always has.

Great trees do not move from their places unless they are felled or their roots grow hollow. Abul Qasim-cha, Baddan-bhai, Tannu-bhai, Tassan, Qaisar, Akhtar and Gigge are in Pakistan. But the tomb of Nuruddin the Martyr is still here in Gangauli and not even the Custodian of Refugee Property has laid a hand on it because he knows the tomb of Nuruddin the Martyr belongs not to the refugee Saiyids of Gangauli, but to Gangauli itself. The life of the banyan tree is rather long, and then several generations have enriched this memorial with their bones.

Apart from the tomb, the Saiyids of Gangauli also made a Karbala. This Karbala was to the south of the tomb and the tomb itself to the east of Gangauli. The Saiyids had also dug a tank on the western edge of the village. This tank must have been built by the heirs of Nuruddin the Martyr because there is no sign of any temple nearby. On the mounds of earth excavated from the tank are mango and jamun trees and on the tenth of Moharram the Saiyid gentlemen of Gangauli come to say their prayers here. West of this tank is a deserted, three-doored indigo factory made of brick and lime which we for some unaccountable reason call a godown.

This is a memorial to John Gilchrist, in other words a monument of yet another age. Now it comes in useful for the cowherds who sit here to suck sugarcane, or for lovers.

In between a decrepit tomb and a ruined factory lives this village. At two ends of the village are the homes of the Saiyids. All in all there must be ten houses. The ones to the south are called the Dakkhin Patti, or southern side, and those to the north the Uttar Patti, or northern side. In between are the homes of the weavers. From Sibtu-da's house the quarters of the Raqias, or Muslim traders start, and then a dirty, mud lane leads into Gangauli bazaar and, pressed beneath low shops and mangey, scratching dogs passes into the open area around the tomb of Nuruddin the Martyr, and draws a breath of relief.

Around the village are several settlements of thatched huts. In one live the Chamars, in another the Bhars and in another the Ahirs.

There are three main gates to Gangauli. One is in Uttar Patti and is called the Gate under the pakkar tree. This has a large, wooden door. Opposite is a pakkar tree. Just as you step down from the gate, on the right are several whitewashed platforms, on which beautiful wooden tazias are placed on the ninth day of Moharram, and then there is a large courtyard. These courtyards are of great social importance to the zamindars. Marriage processions from the grooms' side come here. Feasts of birth and death are held here. Subjects of the zamindars' domains are punished here. Land disputes are complicated and resolved here. Police officers, deputy collectors and collectors are entertained with dance and song here. If there were no such courtyards there could be no zamindars.

So there is one Great Gate in Uttar Patti and two in Dakkhin Patti. Of the latter one was built by my grandmother's family. This is called the Barka or Great Gate, and the other Great Gate, which is called Abbu Miyan's Gate belongs to Abbu-da's forefathers.

We have to pass through these gates and among the Saiyid families which live all around them.

And one thing more. This Gangauli is not an imaginary village, and the homes you will see in it are not fictitious. I have just emptied them of their owners and peopled them with the characters of this novel. These characters are such that they do not seem out of place in this environment, and perhaps you too will feel that Phunnan Miyan, Abbu Miyan, Jhangtiya-bo, Maulvi Bedar, Komila, Balram Chamar, Hakim Ali Kabir, Gaya Ahir and Anwarul Hasan Raqi and all the others too are the inhabitants of Gangauli. But I have mixed some real characters with the fictional ones too. These real characters are my own family, whom I have made the background of reality and due to whom the fictional characters of this novel too are on familiar terms with me.

Now let us go to Gangauli.

My Village, My People

I ran through Gori-dadi's courtyard and slipped into the Dakkhin Patti's room with three archways. I tripped and fell. My elder brother was running after me. The fact was that my sister had made some roast coriander mixture and hidden it in a chest. We saw her do it. The coriander mixture disappeared. My sister complained to my mother. Mother chased us—that's why we were running.

My brother had just rushed over and picked me up when I saw Mother's hand over my head. I wriggled like a girai fish and freed myself. Mother had caught hold of my brother's hair. I crept away quietly. Just opposite was the small door of Naima-dadi's private apartment. I slipped through it.

There was hardly room for anything besides the guava tree in the small courtyard of her apartment, two small string beds just managing to fit into the remaining space. On one lay Naima-dadi, telling her prayer-beads; two black kurtas, two pairs of black, close-fitting pajamas and two black dupattas were hanging out to dry on a clothes-line passing near her head. Black dye was dripping from the corners of one dupatta and soaking the string of her small bed.

I don't know what Manjhale-dada's father ever saw in this Naima-dadi that he left a good and fair Gori-dadi, and took in marriage this doll of black earth, and built for her these private quarters. In any case, Naima-dadi was a common weaver woman, and could not live in the same house with Saiyid ladies, descendents of the Prophet. People of the old school used to pay great attention to who could sit where and with whom. I didn't understand these things, but then there were many other things I couldn't understand either. I couldn't even work out why Manjhale-dada's only son, Gujjan Miyan, called more properly Saiyid Ghaznafar Husain Zaidi, and known to me as Chote-da, left a good, fat, round, soft and smooth Hussan-dadi and kept a prostitute called Zumurrad, or Emerald.

I've never seen Zumurrad, but I've seen Hussan-dadi from the time I opened my eyes to the time she closed hers. She was very tight-fisted, but very beautiful. Not one woman of Gangauli had ever seen Zumurrad, but they all thought that she'd cast some spell on Gujjan Miyan. As this was considered a Bengali art all the women of Gangauli were absolutely certain that Zumurrad was a Bengali. In fact, she was from Barabanki.

The women of the village had no complaint against Gujjan Miyan for taking up with a whore. There was no harm in keeping a prostitute. However, it was a sin to leave a beautiful wife like Hussan. After all, didn't Athar Miyan manage to get along with his one-eyed bride, that is Rabban-bi? And Athar Miyan was considered a handsome man. But, God bless him at every turn, he never let his one-eyed bride's heart be soiled, even though in those days that wretched Jinti, the barber's daughter, had so blossomed that the Saiyid men were going mad for her, and every wife dreaded the day a private apartment would be added to her courtyard. But Athar Miyan didn't give Jinti a glance because it would have hurt his bride's heart—that wretched Jinti was melting for him, but still . . .

In the same way that I didn't understand Naima-dadi and Zumurrad's stories, I couldn't fathom why, when Rabban-bi was one-eyed, and Athar Miyan was a real piece of the moon and sun, and Jinti, the barber's daughter, was melting for him too, he didn't take her in.

It wasn't considered wrong to marry a second time or put some common woman in your house, and perhaps there wasn't a single Saiyid family which didn't have its bastard boys and girls. Even in houses where there was nothing to eat the menfolk managed to indulge their fancies for grafted mangoes and grafted families.

Only Mir Athar Husain Zaidi had not done so. He spent the whole year eating opium and preparing for Moharram. He had spent his whole life preparing for Moharram.

The truth is that in those days the whole year was spent waiting for Moharram and the anniversary of the martyrdom of Imam Husain. The joy of 'Id was all very well in its place, but in no way did it dull the joy of Moharram. After the goat sacrifices of Baqra 'Id the preparations for Moharram began. Dadda, my father's mother, started to softly chant elegies about the martyrs. Mother set about sewing black clothes for all of us; and my sister took out the notebooks of laments knows as nauhas and began to practice them to new airs. In those days film music had not taken grip of nauha melodies. They were simple and at the same time deep, like the folk-music of villages and small towns, and when my sister, mother, or an aunt wore black clothes and stood up to recite,

Sleeping spoke out the dreaming Sakina,
The lord's breast's no more, so no more is Sakina . . .

the wrists supporting the books of nauhas were immediately transformed. It seemed to the listeners as if the lament was issuing straight from the jail in Damascus where Imam Husain's sister Zainab was trying to comfort his beloved daughter Sakina in a subterranean dungeon.

You can't buy simplicity.

I don't know about Lucknow—I don't even know about Ghazipur—but I certainly do know that among the Saiyid families of Gangauli, Moharram was nothing less than a spiritual celebration. The tunes of the nauhas were so carefully composed that the sweet, vermicelli puddings of 'Id paled in comparison. My brother started to practise beating his breast in mourning a whole month in advance. I didn't know how to beat my chest rhythmically with both hands, but my brother was a master of the art. He insisted that I should learn somehow, but I couldn't.

Matam, as we called this form of mourning, was no problem for the people of Dakkhin Patti. Uttar Patti couldn't compete with us—we had more boys and young men. As the ninth day of Moharram approached my uncle Wazir, and my other relatives Chachcha-Bachcha, Shabbar-da, Aggu-da, Hammad-da, Phunnan-da, Abbu-da, Sibtu-da, Hamid-da and—this was the limit—even Gore-da and Gujjan-da came forward and began to beat their breasts in mourning. And this matam used to be so powerful that the round and lotus-shaped glass candleshades and the crystal pieces of the chandeliers would tremble to its beat. And the silver-thread flowers embroidered on the hangings upon the platform where the tazias stood would melt into teardrops.

The only question to be settled concerned fainting—Uttar Patti's Masshu-bhai had perfected the art of falling unconscious during matam. Every year in the majlises, or assemblies, on the eighth and tenth of Moharram, he would collapse in an excess of grief. In our Patti there was no one who could do this, and so when Hakim Ali Kabir or Rashid Miyan or any elder of Uttar Patti sprinkled kevra water over the unconscious face of Masshu-bhai to revive him, the young men and boys of Dakkhin Patti burned with shame. They all reviled themselves for being unable to faint in their own majlis.

Immediately after the festival of Baqra 'Id, I would begin to practise fainting myself. But whenever I fell down I used to hurt myself, and so my brother and I would sit down and put our heads together to work out a way of fainting which wouldn't hurt. A full team of Dakkhin Patti boys would spend the whole year trying to work out such a formula. Apart from me and my brother, Tannu-bhai, Gigge, Addan, Phunnan-da's son Mumtaz, Hamid-da's son Chammu, his nephew Phuttu and Hasan-va, Javad-da's son Fiddu—all these boys rehearsed continuously. But still every year it was Masshu-bhai who fell unconscious and we were left gaping.

'What if we don't let Masshu-bhai faint?' I asked my brother.

'It would be a sin!' he said.

I had no reply to this and so I decided that I didn't care even if I did get hurt, this time I would definitely faint in the majlis on the fifth morning—thc honour of the Patti would be saved.

I was highly pleased to have reached this decision and impatiently began to await the day when the bus would drive to the gate of Bashir Manzil, our house in Ghazipur, and our caravan would set out for Gangauli.

Ultimately the day did come.

When the luggage had been loaded, and the passengers had taken their seats, my aunt, Chachi, passed my mother a betel-leaf and said, 'This year there's a bus going from Aggu-mamun's too.'

There was considerable sarcasm in this simple remark. At the time I didn't see it, but my mother did and she smiled. The fact was that in matters concerning Uttar Patti we were all one, but in Dakkhin Patti itself all was not well and there was a great deal of internal rivalry.

They say that Abbu-da, Aggu-da's father, had come into a lot of wealth after some rich zamindar's wife died. This happened a long time before I was born. But I heard from Dadda, and my great-aunt from Kamunpur, and from Muslim-da and Phunnan-da that when the Rani Sahiba died, Abbu-da had taught a sweeper woman her ABC and promised her the green garden of marriage—thereby prising a fortune from her basket of nightsoil. Gold bricks and coins belonging to the dead Rani Sahiba were first concealed in the toilet and then removed from the palace. Along with the pile of riches the sweeper woman too came to Gangauli. As is obvious, no Saiyid lady would have anything to do with her, and somehow the story leaked out. The police began to sniff around. Abbu-da hid his loot in the houses of his relatives. After the affair had been suppressed his relatives suppressed the loot, and poor Abbu-da could do nothing about it.

Even so he wasn't completely bankrupt. He still had a fair amount of the goods in his possession. Accordingly, he began to find it uncomfortable to ride in a horse cart, and bought a bus. Phunnan-da was made the conductor. After a while the bus broke down and never moved again.

Chachi's remark about his son Aggu-da's bus contained a veiled reference to this one, and that's why my mother smiled.

There was always some sort of competition going on between our home and Aggu-da's. If anything was made in our house the same thing would immediately be made in his. If any work was started there, hands went to work in our house too. So when we started to go to Gangauli by bus, his family was bound to do so. For some years they were held back by the fact that they couldn't hire a bus as smart as ours, and so they made do with palanquins and pony-traps. Then they found a new bus.

The fact is that they considered us inferior because my father used to receive a monthly allowance of five rupees from the state of Pirpur for his studies. It was thanks to this allowance that he had been able to complete his education. On the other hand Abbu-da himself had paid for the education of his son who had lived in great style at the Hewitt hostel. Aggu-da's wife was certain to mention the allowance whenever she had the chance.

As a result, although the men of these two households were on good terms, or at least seemed to be, there was obvious tension between the women.

Even then, at least Aggu-da's wife was quite a simple, honest woman. Her mother-in-law, Abbu-da's wife, was a spark of calamity. It was lucky that my grandmother was the eldest in the whole family, and Mother was very particular about holding her tongue, and so matters never went out of hand. Even my mother and Chachi didn't get on well, but neither of them would dare let anyone see it. Once a day Mother would go to Chachi's home, and once a day Chachi would come to ours, and they would both sit and chat as intimately as if they were real sisters. I came to know the truth years after they were both dead. My uncle's second wife was quarrelling with my elder sister and complained to my uncle. Then my uncle told his wife this story as a lesson. I was there and so I found out too. I don't think my brother and sisters know about it even now—perhaps Munni and Suraiya don't even remember Chachi, because they were both very young when she died.

Chachi was very small-built and spoke the extremely correct Urdu spoken in towns. We don't speak Urdu but as Father studied in Faizabad and Lucknow, he does.

My eldest sister married into a Lucknow family and so she too speaks Urdu occasionally, but the rest of us still speak the language our mother, Nasiba-bua and Matto-bua spoke, and which belonged to Idu and Raoof,* and still belongs to the Saiyids of Gangauli—that is Bhojpuri Urdu. My younger sister Afsari has been living in Delhi for nearly fifteen years but she still can't speak Urdu and remains loyal to the same Bhojpuri she drank in with her mother's milk.

But I used to like the way Chachi spoke very much. I would sit by her for hours just to listen to her. Because of her language, she remained an outsider to our home environment as long as she lived. Apart from Chachi, I had the chance to hear correct Urdu from Tami Bai. In her time she had been a famous courtesan. After she retired she became a devotee of the god Shiva and settled down to live outside the town in a mango grove which an aristocrat had given her in her youth. Her son had accused her of living off immoral earnings and started litigation against her. Tami had appointed my father as her lawyer, and would visit him regularly in connection with her case. She would bring with her a beautiful, silver betel-nut box, in which she used to keep little, folded, white betel-leaves. Before she ate a betel-leaf herself she would offer the box to Father. Father would refuse, and then she would put a betel-leaf in her mouth and begin to discuss her case. And I would stand holding the back of Father's swivel chair. I didn't understand what was being discussed. But Tami Bai had such an attractive voice, and there was such expression in it that it used to entrance me. Listening to Tami it seemed that words had no status of their own—even without being acquainted with them, meanings could be heard and understood.

One day I went and sat beside her.

She stroked my head and said, 'Bless you.'

I greeted her nervously. She burst out laughing. She had just taken out a betel-leaf for herself. She asked, 'Would you like it?'

I had been dying to taste one of her betel-leaves for ages, but still I refused. However, what significance could the refusal of a six-year-old child have for a woman who had spent her life turning the refusal of men of all ages into acceptance?

She fed me the betel-leaf. It was strange—the moment it entered

---

* family servants.

my mouth it dissolved completely.

Even so Tami was a whore and, tormented by the thought that perhaps I had been wrong to eat her betel-leaf, I ran away.

My brother was busy studying book-keeping. I sat down beside him.

'What is it?' he asked.

'I've eaten one of Tami's paans,' I whined. 'She's a whore, isn't she?'

'Ask Fatima-dadi.'

I crept like a thief out of our courtyard and into that of my father's sister's small house.

This aunt, Phuphu, was extremely fat and used to lie down most of the time. Even now she was lying down and Damri's wife was massaging her legs. My uncle, Rafi-phupha, was lying on a bed next to hers smoking a huqqa.

Because my aunt's mother, that is our great-aunt Chutki-dadda had brought up Damri, we used to call him Damri-cha, or uncle, and he called my father and uncle 'brother'. Chutki-da, our great-uncle, had set him to keeping a bookshop. One day a board appeared above it—Nadir Ali Tajir—Books. This Damri was very well turned out. He used to wear a long close-fitting coat over tight pajamas, and all his life only ever wore an Irani hat. That's why a short time later he became not only Nadir Ali but S. Nadir Ali and then Saiyid Nadir Ali Tajir—Books, elevating himself to the status of a descendent of the Prophet.

But Damri's wife, known as Damri-bo, remained as nameless as she was when she arrived. It is the fate of daughters-in-law to be nameless. The only difference is that in good families women are saved the disgrace of being called 'bo', or wife; they are either called, 'bahu', or daughter-in-law, or 'dulhan', which means bride. If the bride is wealthy she's given a title—'aziz dulhan', dear bride (even if no one in her husband's house will have anything to do with her), and 'nafis dulhan' or delicate bride (even if she is extremely coarse) . . . and so on and so forth. In short, you can either say that in our society the girl's family snatches back their daughter's real name in return for providing a trousseau, or that the boy's family cannot bear any name to be used in their home that they have not bestowed themselves. Whatever the case, the result is that girls who have for nine to seventeen years been called Rabya Khatoon, Rabban for short, or Kaniz Fatima, Kuddan for short, suddenly become 'Phoolan-bo' or 'bahu' or 'dulhan' or 'sultan dulhan'. They can also become sisters-in-law, aunts, and sometimes even grandmothers the moment they are married and then they are known by these names too. But they do not remain Rabya Khatoon or Kaniz Fatima. Perhaps that's why they restrict their interests to which ladies can attend the feasts of Fatima* and who is and is not permitted to share in the other affairs of the community. This is the one great privilege which no kept woman has, and perhaps for this privilege these respectable girls endure their anonymity.

Sometimes namelessness so sticks to these girls that they can't shake it off until they die.

That's what happened to Damri-bo. Even after her husband, Damri, died she remained the extremely black and ugly Damri-bo. She remarried twice but even now if we remember her, it's by the name Damri-bo. To each of her three sets of in-laws she was known by a different husband's name, and if all three families were to get together and talk about her, they wouldn't know they were discussing the same woman. In fact I don't know if even Damri-bo herself remembered her real name.

Damri-bo was also just Damri-bo because she had no home of her own to which she could go back from time to time, and where someone would call her by her real name. For example, when my father married my mother, out of respect for my mother's real name which was in fact Nafisa, in her family Father became known as 'nafis dulha'. In Father's family, where my mother lived, she became 'dulhan'. But when either of my mother's brothers visited us or when a labourer woman brought anything from my mother's village, or when any Harijan, Bhar or Ahir woman came from there to Ghazipur to take a dip in the Ganga, Mother became Nafisa again, and, refreshed, was able to face more days in the desert of anonymity. My mother was in any case somewhat fortunate because her nurse, that is our Mai, came with her to Ghazipur and all her life she called Mother Nafisa, and Father nafis dulha. Perhaps Father's mother, Dadda, was always cross with Mai because she had extended the boundaries of Mother's home territory. Perhaps that was the reason she always waited impatiently for Moharram, and perhaps, too, because in Gangauli that wretched, black Zumurrad's voice was drowned . . . so the moment my grandmother sat in the bus she heaved a sigh of relief and, after spitting in one corner when no one was looking, she wiped her lips with her long, tapering fingers and ran them through her short, extremely white

---

* Attendance was restricted to Saiyid ladies, and that too those who were not pregnant—the baby in their womb might have been male.

and silky hair.

Afsari slipped from my mother's lap and fell with a thud in exactly the place where my grandmother had spat her betel juice. My mother picked up her daughter automatically and put her back in her lap. She was busy beating Maddu but when she saw the red spittle stain on her banana-green collarless qamiz she thumped Afsari on the back—although she knew it wasn't her fault. She couldn't tell my grandmother off, after all! But Afsari didn't appreciate the delicacy of the situation, and began to howl. Then my elder sister gave Maddu a slap because he'd bitten her.

'Your whole qamiz is ruined!' said Chachi. With this she turned to my eldest sister who was busy reading in a monthly Urdu magazine how to make her complexion soft and glowing.

My aunt's comment reminded Mother of the red stain on her qamiz, but at that very moment the bus set off, rendering Afsari's screams practically inaudible in the part of the bus where the men were sitting. Even if they were heard they could be endured as additional squeaks from the vehicle's internal parts. The bus was squeaking and rattling simultaneously in several raags.

To take his mind off the cold breeze blowing through the vehicle, Father began to explain some fine point of the Qor'an to Maulvi Munavvar. My uncle Wazir began to cuddle his second son, Qaisar, who was sitting in the back seat and repeatedly sticking his hand out of the window and then touching his fat, red neck; and I was in Uncle's lap staring at Maulvi Munavvar and thinking that for at least a fortnight I would be rid of this lame cleric.

Our Maulvi took more pleasure in beating us than teaching us. He also used to take the one anna we were given as pocket money, which is why we passed our childhood in deprivation. Perhaps that's also the reason that neither I nor my elder brother are any good with money. We are in the habit of spending our money the moment we get it—perhaps in our heart of hearts we're still afraid of Maulvi Munavvar and think that if we don't spend it the Maulvi Sahib will pounce on us. Shehla, my sister-in-law, isn't aware of this, and that's why she sometimes scolds my brother for being a spendthrift.

But, unknown to the Maulvi Sahib, we would certainly manage to save up to eight annas a year so that when the Orphan's Share was auctioned at the end of the mourning assemblies of Moharram we could at least afford to buy it once.

At the end of every majlis one member of the Husainiya Society would bring out the 'Share'—blessed sweets called tabarruk—and auction it, crying, 'The Orphan's Share! The Orphan's Share!'

The bidding opened. If the tabarruk was good, Maulvis Bedar and Dildar both used to keep raising the bidding. I've never seen them bid for any ordinary tabarruk.

Every year on the eleventh day of Moharram at the Society meeting it was announced how much money had been collected for the orphans, and that sum was sent to the Shia Orphanage in Lucknow.

So when I put my hand in my pocket and felt the eight annas there, it seemed to me that the body and the parts of the bus began to sing. The stiff breeze blowing through the windows wrapped me round and I fell asleep against the soft pillow of Uncle Wazir's small pot belly.

When I opened my eyes the bus was crossing Bauri bridge. On the bank of the river stood a dilapidated temple, which had collapsed in places, but seemed pleased by the prospect of the green and prosperous fields roundabout. Just near the bridge were two or three heaps of lime mortar left over from building the bridge. The mothers of the neighbourhood used to give it to their babies to lick when they were teething and that's why these mounds were slowly disappearing. This mortar had been handed out by mothers since the time of the Mughals, and some people say that the Mughals did nothing for Hindustan! It's possible that P.N. Oak is right to think that they cannot be congratulated for building Fatehpur Sikri or the Taj Mahal. I can also accept that someone else might have built the Red Fort at Delhi, but for generations the mothers of Ghazipur have known that the Mughals definitely left several piles of material by the Bauri bridge and that it helps children with teething problems.

Startled by the bus' horn, a skeletal horse pulling a cart loaded with eight passengers reared and began to bolt towards the side of the road. But the weight of the passengers wouldn't allow it to gallop, and so the cart-driver got his chance. Jumping down, he managed somehow to control the animal. Content that he had done so, he turned and began to curse the bus-driver. I only think that he began to curse him because he was waving his arm as if he was. The bus-driver didn't hear him because at that point he himself was busy swearing at some children who had untied their loincloths and were swaying back and forth, displaying their nakedness.

'Don't they have any pajamas?' I asked my uncle.

'They're *haramzade*,' he replied.

'What's a *haramzada*?' I asked again.

'Ask your mother,' he said, playing with my hair.

'No, you tell me!'

'Eh, Masoom, look! Egrets!' cried my elder brother from behind.

I looked. A whole army of egrets had landed in a paddy field, and a sweet, young cowherdess, sitting astride a buffalo's back, was making her way down a narrow path through the crops.

In those days I used to envy any boy or girl I saw riding a buffalo and wished that my father would keep a buffalo instead of a horse.

I had no complaint against our horse, Moti, or Mathura, the groom, because whenever I wanted to play at being a prince, a switch broken from a bush tied to my side for a sword, Mathura would immediately put me on Moti's back, and Moti never objected. But we only had one horse and so my brother couldn't play at being a rival prince. Therefore I had to dismount, and then we both drew our swords as pedestrian princes. But it wasn't easy to be wounded and fall in the stable due to Moti's dung and urine and so we used to either come into the courtyard or go into the yellow house where Gori-dadi lived on her own. No one ever came near the yellow house in the afternoon because it was well-known that Gori-dadi had fallen under the influence of a yogi. By chance Mother and Latifan-bua had actually seen him. He was a bearded, elderly man, who used to squat on the ground with his elbows on the side of Gori-dadi's bed. But we never saw him.

Once it was my turn to be wounded and die. I had just fallen and drawn my last breath when my elder sister came and said, 'Eh, Masoom, just run off, will you, and fetch one paisa of green dye—God knows where that old servant has gone and died.'

I didn't stir. How could I? I was dead.

'He's dead,' my brother informed her.

'What!!'

My sister panicked and ran off to Mother. We two brothers quickly slipped outside. Later we found out that my sister, mother, Satto-bua, Mai, Chachi, Dadda, Chutki-dadda and Idu-bo the barber's wife, who was cutting my mother's nails at the time, and Madaran-bo the grocer's wife, who had come to sell lychees, and Latifan the bangle-seller—in short a whole troop of agitated women had streamed into the yellow house. It was a blisteringly hot afternoon and Gori-dadi had dampened her bed, sprinkled water on to the revolving fan she held, and lain down in her room exhausted. The hem of her muslin kurta was folded up to her neck and the swellings of her two flabby breasts clung to her stomach like two wet cloths. Seeing so many people coming into her home she sat up in bewilderment.

But neither was my brother to be found, nor my corpse. Therefore my sister had her first ever scolding.

She was such a favourite that she had even usurped my brother's share of affection, which is the reason my brother used to pester her. He was always on the lookout for an opportunity to tease her. My sister was always complaining about him, and my mother was always beating him, but that didn't stop him teasing my sister. Perhaps the spiritual satisfaction he found in teasing her outweighed the discomfort of being beaten, and so as far as possible my sister kept her distance from him.

She'd found a place for herself in the bus far away from him, but my brother crept up and was continuously making faces at her. Regardless of his mischief-making and the jolting of the bus, she was gently striking her chest in mourning, her eyes closed, and chanting a nauha. But perhaps she couldn't get the rhythm of the matam to match the words and so she was repeatedly stopping and adding new phrases.

My brother tied her dear little plait to the bar in the window and then when the bus jolted and dipped, my sister hung by her hair and screamed loudly. Now in domestic life there is no democracy, no referendum or investigation allowing the accused the opportunity to prove his innocence—and so Mother simply fell on my brother without a word of inquiry. He sat with his head bowed. He had learnt the art of keeping his head down and enduring beatings very well.

'I hope your hands break, you *matimile*, *jharumare* . . .' wailed my sister.

'All right, that's enough. Pipe down,' scolded Mai.

It was only Mai who time and again came to my brother's help. My brother was very fond of her too—and since he was I was as well. Apart from his wife, Shehla, I was an equal partner in all my brother's loves.

'You don't say anything to *him*!' retorted my sister.

'What should I say to him?' said Mai, 'Not the smallest thing happens without you opening your mouth and squealing. This Nafisa will spoil you so much you'll be fit for nothing. Come, son, come along to me!'

She called my brother to her and began to stroke his head with her small, extremely black and wrinkled hands. My brother dropped off to sleep.

Once the bus stopped I got down and climbed into the women's part of the vehicle. Dadda, my granny, sat me in her lap. Her complexion was so fair that I was scared to sit in her lap lest I made her dirty. I've heard that my grandfather was very ugly.

Nobody's seen the colour of an enemy's black heart, but there are still people alive who've seen Grandfather's well-cooked colour. I don't know how such a beautiful granny was married to such an ugly grandfather. He was not even particularly rich and my granny was the sister of Raja Munir Hasan. She was a virgin, while my grandfather was a widower. Grandfather seemed to have nothing apart from a good lineage. He held some insignificant post in the courts at Ghazipur. After her marriage Dadda went to her husband's home just once, and when she came back, she never even mentioned the possibility of returning. She said that her husband's home was a thick jungle of ugliness, and so we had no knowledge of our grandfather's village in Azamgarh at all. That's why we said we came from Ghazipur district, not Azamgarh, and that's why we would have given our lives for Dadda's village of Gangauli and our hearts didn't thrill at all at the name of Grandfather's village, Thekma Bijauli. We are our granny's grandchildren, and she never took to the people of Bijauli. But when Grandfather went mad and was held in chains and shut up in the room to the east of the imambara, I heard that delicate little Akbari Bibi, my grandmother, did him great service. She used to go to his room once a day—wash the filth from his body, clean out the room and dress him in clean, white clothes. Grandfather very quietly let her do all this; but the moment she left the room he would tear his clothes to shreds. Then, one dark monsoon night, he somehow managed to escape, and fell into a ditch near the pond and died. Granny wept a lot although he never had given her anything besides some children—but how can I say that! He'd given her the status of a wife.

Apart from Muslim-da, Phunnan-da, Kallu-kakka and Gaya Ahir, Grandfather feared no one. When he stood at the barred door of his room, swearing and exposing himself to the women passing down the lane outside, the poor things would blush with shame. Now he was the son-in-law of the village—who could say anything to the mad son-in-law of the Great Gate? But the moment anyone mentioned Muslim-da, Phunnan-da, Kallu-kakka or Gaya Ahir he would immediately shut up. He had driven his sisters-in-law up the wall. They would remark irritably, 'You don't say anything to Akbari-bu.' This sentence had greater power than the names of Phunnan, Kallu and Gaya. When he heard it, Grandfather would sit for hours in silence and, therefore, in Gangauli it was well-known that even lunatics respected Akbari Bibi. My granny too was well aware of her power—she was the seniormost Saiyid of Gangauli. What she said went, and she constantly reminded Mother of this fact. So when she saw that

Mother was not paying her proper attention she lost her temper and said, 'Eh, Dulhan, aren't you listening, I'm saying . . .'

'Eh, Mother! What's a bastard?' I interrupted Dadda to ask my mother.

My mother was so taken aback that she even forgot to scold me.

'Be quiet, *jharumare*!' said Dadda, hitting me on the back with her fan, 'Is that a thing to ask your mother?'

'Uncle Wazir told me to ask her,' I sobbed.

At that precise moment the bus turned off towards Gangauli and the conversation was brought to an end. I forgot my question and Granny her answer.

An extremely rough, mud road turned sharply from the indigo factory, ran along the banks of the pond and wound towards the village. Even now I still can't decide whether it's right to call it a road. It was in such a dreadful condition that the moment you were out of one pothole you went into the next. The driver did his level best to avoid them and the bus swerved right and left. Dadda was busy calling on the Prophet's son-in-law—'Ya Ali!'—and in between all the 'Ya Alis!' she was grumbling, '*Naooj*, and this is what that Bashir said was a comfortable way of getting here! This is a shameless wreck of a bus . . . Ya Ali!'

Gangauli must still have been two furlongs away when a crowd of boys began shouting and running in front of and behind the bus. The bus was proceeding so slowly that the boys overtook it as they ran. My brother and I began to kick up a noise in reply to the row the boys were making.

The bus turned left by Fussu-cha's house. Just opposite Hamid-da and Javad-da were stroking their white beards.

'Adaab, Javad-da!' my brother called out in greeting.

'Adaab, Javad-da!' I called out too, echoing my brother.

Javad-da must certainly have given us his blessing, but we didn't hear him because the bus had already passed on together with the procession of naked boys and girls of assorted ages.

The lane which headed east from the bamboo grove was lined on both sides with the houses of the weavers. The weavers were sitting on their bamboo bedsteads smoking huqqas. On one side a ten or eleven-year-old boy had hung large reels of different coloured threads on a wooden frame. Bamboo canes had been driven into the ground at a short distance from one another and the boy was winding the threads from the reels around them. He stopped when he saw the bus. The men on the charpoys smoking the huqqas stood up.

They bowed to offer the bus their salaams.

A girl sitting on the edge of a pond washing clothes hastily pulled down the hem of her sari and covered her wheat-coloured calves. Oblivious of all this the bus wound its way towards the Great Gate.

The moment it stopped I leapt down and ran off towards Phunnan-da's house.

'Eh, Miyan, don't go in there!' warned Gaya.

'Why shouldn't I?' I asked.

'Mother's come to the house!'

'Whose mother?'

I didn't wait for Gaya's reply because even if it was Gaya's mother herself who had come to Phunnan-da's house, what did it matter? For one thing the old lady wouldn't keep purdah, and even if she did, it would make no difference because she couldn't keep purdah from me.

I slipped into Phunnan-da's house. He wasn't there. But Kulsum, the mother of his children, was sitting in the courtyard chopping spinach. Their two elder daughters were lying in the arched room to one side practising nauhas. Kulsum looked up and smiled. Her big, black, kajal-full, deep-set, almond-shaped eyes smiled too and for a moment her face shook off the dust of misfortune and brightened. For that moment her duskily charming and extremely attractive personality spread through the courtyard like rain-washed moonlight.

'Adaab, Dadi!' I greeted her.

'Bless you. When did you come?'

'Just now.'

'Has your grandmother come or not?'

'She has.'

'Eh, Ruqayya!' she called out. Her daughter lifted her big, jet black eyes from the book of nauhas.

'Cut the vegetables. I'm just going to see his grandmother.'

'Where's Mumtaz?' I asked. The fact was that I was impatient to tell him that I'd been practising fainting this year, and was going to collapse so dramatically at the majlis on the fifth of Moharram that even Musshu-bhai would be astounded. I'd thought that the moment he heard the bus Mumtaz would come out of the house and I could take him to one side and tell him. But perhaps he wasn't at home.

'The Mother has come to him,' said Kulsum.

'Where from?' I asked. 'You're not talking about Gaya's mother are you?'

Kulsum-dadi burst out laughing. 'Listen to him! This Masoom seems to be completely mad . . . Mumtaz has got smallpox.'

'I'm really fed up. We've been eating nothing but vegetables for four days,' said Ruqayya.

Kulsum-dadi forbade me to go into the small room, but I didn't listen to her. I peeped in—Mumtaz was lying in bed and Phunnan-da was fanning away flies with a neem twig.

'Don't come in!' he said.

But I did. I had to! I had such a big piece of news to tell. I whispered it into Mumtaz's ear. He smiled and said, 'Phuttu has been practising . . .'

'No!' I said, 'I'm going to faint.'

'But . . .'

'No!' I tossed my head and said, 'I'll stab Phuttu in the stomach.' I left the room.

I was extremely angry about all this. It wasn't fair—I was the one to get hurt practising and then Phuttu would be the one to faint! Wonderful! I went straight to Hamid-da's house. Dulhaniya, his wife, was in the courtyard rolling out chapattis, and Hasina-dadi was lying on a bamboo cot humming a marsia.

Dulhaniya was the mother of Hamid-da's children, but we didn't call her 'Dadi' as we called the mothers of Muslim-da and Phunnan-da's children. All the Saiyids of the village knew her as Dulhaniya. And we didn't greet her with the respectful 'Adaab', as we did Saiyid ladies, but with the more commonplace 'Salaam'.

'Salaam!' I said.

She showered countless blessings on me and while she was doing so I greeted Hasina-dadi.

'Adaab!'

'May you live long,' she replied.

'Where's Phuttu?'

'He's gone down to the pond,' she replied. 'Sit down.'

But I didn't. I ran off to the pond. Phuttu was there bathing his goat. He was pleased to see me.

'I'm going to faint in the majlis on the fifth.'

'You can faint with me.'

'No . . .' I shook my head violently. 'This year only I am going to faint. You can do it next year.'

'Imam Husain is no servant of your father that you can . . .' began Phuttu irritably.

I had a stone in my hand. I lifted it and threw it at him. Phuttu screamed and fell to the ground. I ran off. I thought I'd killed him and that the police were sure to arrest me. Well, we'd see, I thought. After all Uncle Wazir was always saving murderers, so wouldn't he save me? And wouldn't Shabbar-da and Aggu-da argue my case for me too? So I didn't care a bit that I'd killed Phuttu! Still my heart trembled at the thought of going home and so I thought of hiding in the indigo godown.

I turned in that direction.

I had quietly crossed the ground floor and had just decided to climb to the second storey when I heard a boy moan. I was petrified—I remembered all the stories about the godown being haunted. I looked outside—there was not a soul in sight. And very far away in the west—even further than the mango groves—the sun was setting. My hair stood on end as that of frightened children does, and my heart began to pump away as madly as the engine of a mail train.

Then I heard a deep voice. I couldn't make out the words, but I recognized Taqqan-cha's voice! How could I fail to? Taqqan-cha always used to come to see Uncle Wazir every week about some case or the other. That's why I knew his voice off by heart.

'Eh, Taqqan-cha!' I called out nervously, as the ghost might have been imitating Taqqan-cha's voice to trick me. Then I climbed down from the godown so I could run away if a ghost put its head out instead of Taqqan-cha; but neither the ghost's nor Taqqan-cha's head appeared—the godown was suddenly completely still.

I thought I really ought to run away, and so I did, forgetting in my confusion that I had murdered Phuttu. But when I peeped through the Great Gate and saw beds and long cloth folding chairs set out in the area beyond, and the entire Saiyid community of the village assembled there, I suddenly remembered what I'd done. I looked around anxiously and saw my brother sitting in the three-doored hall of the imambara. He spotted me and came over. I took him outside.

'I've murdered Phuttu,' I told him.

'You've done what?'

'Murder!'

'When?'

'Just a little while ago . . .'

'But Phuttu is sitting at home with Hasina-dadi. She keeps complaining to Mother that, "If Phuttu hadn't ducked, the Lord preserve him, he would have been badly hurt for sure," said my brother mimicking Dadi.

I felt an enormous sense of relief.

'Is he alive then?'

'Yes.'

'So the police won't catch me?'

'No.'

I was so overjoyed I went over to watch some weaver children who were playing kabaddi.

'Want to play?' one of them asked.

'Yes!'

I joined one of the teams.

Holding my breath and saying 'Kabaddi . . . kabaddi . . . kabaddi' I crossed to the other team's half of the pitch. I was watching my opponents continuously out of the corner of my eye, but sometimes my glance would also stray towards the weavers who had gathered to watch a Saiyid playing kabaddi—as if it were unusual for the son of a Saiyid to play kabaddi. But it was an unusual event. That day for the first and last time I played kabaddi with the weavers' sons.

'Kabaddi . . . kabaddi . . .' I was saying. The circle of boys had begun to tighten about me. Then one boy bent down and caught hold of my leg. I fell. The boys all went for me. One had my legs, another was holding my arm. I was saying kabaddi and dragging myself towards my team's half of the pitch. My elbows were grazed, so were my knees. My white muslin kurta was in shreds, but I kept repeating 'kabaddi' and pulling myself towards the dividing line.

Then suddenly two large, rough hands pulled the boys off and scattered them in all directions.

'So you boys have got to be such lords that you think you can play kabaddi with a Saiyid's son?'

This was the voice of Gaya Ahir. The boys ran away in fear. I stood with my head bowed like a criminal. Gaya brushed down my clothes, filled my bleeding grazes with earth and took me in his lap.

'You are a Saiyid, you don't want all this,' he explained.

When Gaya brought me with him through the Gate, there was a great to-do. My wounds were washed with spirit. Ali Kabir-cha immediately wrote out a prescription. Ubbad-cha hurried off with it towards his dispensary. Phunnan-da rushed off to the houses of the weavers to bang his lathi and swear. Gore-da beckoned me to him.

'Where did you disappear after you got down from the bus?' he asked.

Gore-da had a lovely voice—as juicy as the sweetest mango. He was fair, just like Gori-dadi, his wife, but he was better looking. He had a good height, broad bones, and smiling, big black eyes. He was so fond of singing that in his youth he had run away to Calcutta and joined the New Theatre. When his family found out there was complete uproar. Relatives went to Calcutta and with great difficulty finally managed to persuade him to return. A brother of Raja Saiyid Munir Hasan working in a theatre! More appropriately the government appointed him tehsildar, and he was so content with the job that he never so much as thought of promotion. All his life he remained a tehsildar. He was a very good poet. He would hold people spellbound with his ghazals. After a year or two's absence he would come to Gangauli for Moharram. The year he came everyone else in the village was eclipsed. Their value fell and only he held court . . .

That's why I swelled with pride when he called me to him. But what answer could I give? I didn't want to let him into the secret of my plans to faint. I thought that when I dropped down unconscious it would make all the people of Dakkhin Patti happy and they would say, 'At last we've got a boy from our Patti who can give a fitting reply to Miyan Musshu's fainting.'

'I went up the pond,' I said in my Bhojpuri.

'No!' Gore-da corrected me in chaste Urdu, 'Say, I went up TO the pond.'

'I went up to the pond.' I repeated his Urdu as I was told, but all the words of the Urdu sentence seemed to me strange and extremely unpleasant.

'If we see the moon tonight you can read a salaam,' Gore-da continued in Urdu.

'Very well,' I replied.

'You can read Urdu, can't you?'

'Yes.'

'What class are you studying in?'

'The fourth.'

'Can you compete with Munna?'

I looked at Ali Mehdi-cha's son Munna. He looked back at me and smiled contemptuously. He was very skinny.

'Will you try your luck against him?' asked Ali Mehdi-cha.

'What, at wrestling?' I enquired.

'No, at English,' said Ali Mehdi-cha.

I looked at Munna again but I couldn't get the slightest idea from his face whether he knew more or less English than I did. I turned towards Maulvi Munavvar Sahib but his face was completely expressionless. He knew even less English than I.

'Eh, Uncle, what are we to do over this Ali Zaheer Sahib and Iqbal Suhail's election?' asked Fussu-cha, sticking his head up from behind Hammad-da's shoulder. I was immensely relieved that the competition had been postponed. Otherwise God knows what I would have done. I would have had to take my life in my hands and challenge him. After all it was a question of the prestige of my Patti.

'Iqbal Suhail is a sworn enemy of the Saiyids,' said Gore-da, 'but I think that there's no point in voting for the Muslim League either . . .'

I quietly crept out in case the matter of the competition was raised again after this discussion.

I went straight to the inner house. There all the women of the village had gathered to meet Dadda, my granny. My eldest sister was sitting surrounded by girls and telling them the plot of the film, *World of Deceit*. The girls accepted everything she told them but they absolutely refused to believe that pictures could move and talk. And as for singing songs, well, that was clearly out of the question. But there was no way my sister could be dissuaded. She said smartly, 'I swear by Allah, Babbo-ba'ji! I saw it with my own eyes!'

Now what answer could Babbo-ba'ji or Sallan-phuphu or Albuphu have to an oath in the name of Allah? These girls were still reeling when my sister saw me. I became a witness for her case.

'Ask Masoom.'

Masoom was asked.

And when I told them that Ba'ji was telling the truth, the poor things practically fainted away.

'These are all signs that doomsday is at hand.'

But the discussion stopped here as we heard shouts that the new moon of the first of Moharram had been sighted. Phuttu had seen the moon and without having seen it herself Hasina-dadi was supporting him. No one had said anything to me and so the moment the moon was sighted I sidled up to Phuttu.

'I'm going to faint!' I whispered. 'And if you faint, then I'll stick a knife in your stomach.'

Phuttu blenched and crept away towards Hasina-dadi.

All the women proceeded towards the zenana imambara.

There were some very strange things said about this imambara. It was common knowledge that every Friday night jinn used to hold gatherings there. That was the reason no one ever walked that way at night. But the moon of Moharram meant that Imam Husain had come from Karbala to Hindustan and the imambara had passed from the hands of jinn into the hands of men. Still, the moon had only just risen and I thought that some wayward jinn might have been left behind, or that in their hurry to go they might have forgotten something and one of them might have come back to find it, and so I began to walk between Mother and my granny.

The lamps had been lit in the imambara. Bade Abba Sahib was garlanding the crests of the standards and the biers with strings of flowers, and little Saiyda had climbed on to Tannu-bhai's stomach and was singing him a nauha. Tannu-bhai was lying on the floor of the imambara. Bade Abba Sahib was absorbed in his work, oblivious of them both.

They say that Bade Abba Sahib was once a great supporter of the Muhammadan Anglo-Oriental College at Aligarh. But I have only seen him as an ascetic. He used to live in Kanpur. No one knew what he used to do there, but he used to come to Gangauli for Moharram. He was so concerned with keeping himself pure and unpolluted that he even avoided kissing children. When sometimes he was overwhelmed by affection he would start making strange noises and touch the tip of the child's nose with the tips of two fingers. He didn't think there was anything pure in the world except for his prayer-mat. Even in winter he used to wear only a cotton shervani coat. When he sat on the stairs of the pulpit to address the Moharram congregations, the cold induced a pearl of mucous to hang from his nostrils like a nose ornament. And I used to sit and wait for it to fall. But it never did. As long as he lived no one else had the honour of garlanding the standards, tazias and biers.

As all the women belonged to the family, there was no question of them keeping purdah from him. He quietly went on with his work.

About twenty-five standards with silver crests, and hung with strips of cloth embroidered with gold thread, were standing against a wall. A silk dupatta was draped over them. Below the standards was a bier covered with sangi brocade. Around the tomb were some prayer-beads and sijdahgahs, small plaques made from the earth of Karbala, against which we touch our foreheads during prayer. Then there was a black curtain which ran the entire width of the imambara and which separated the raised platform of the shahnashin, where the tazias and standards stood, from the rest of the hall.

Besides pictures of artists' impressions of the encampments of Imam Husain, the River Euphrates, and Imam Husain's wounded horse, Zuljenah, framed pieces of calligraphy of verses of the Qor'an and quatrains by Mir Anis hung on the walls. Beautiful round glass candleshades suspended from the ceiling swung gently back and forth. There were no candles in them because the age of the petromax lamp had come to our imambara. Here and there hung large shiny coloured glass balls, in which the reflections of the people in the hall danced.

After Bade Abba Sahib had arranged the garlands and made an

offering of sharbat before the tazias, he left.

The ladies removed their glass bangles—black, fair, swarthy, middle-aged, old and young wrists became naked. My elder sister took out a sliver of neem twig from her nose where it had been pierced and put it on the pile of broken bangles.

Then she stood up with the book of nauhas. Her friends and several other women began to beat their breasts to the rhythm of the nauha. Dadda sat down and leant against the raised platform of the shahnashin. All the women covered their faces with their dupattas. My sister began to sing the lament. She had an extremely thin and reedy voice and then, to her mortification, she forgot the tune she'd been practising in Ghazipur. After two verses Gangauli put its own mark on that Jaunpuri air. My sister tried very hard to stick to the Jaunpuri but finally had to admit defeat.

My granny, my great-aunt, Rabban-dadi, Naima-dadi and the other middle-aged and elderly women were not pretending, they really were crying. They wept bitterly, repeatedly squeezing their nostrils, and wiping their fingers on the walls of the imambara. When Rabban-dadi's throat was dry with crying, she took some betel-nut and tobacco from her small bag and put them in her mouth, dipped two fingertips in lime and katha, licked first one and then the other, and then began to lament, 'Arre, my Lord . . . My Lady's darling child . . .'

Smallpox had robbed Rabban-dadi of one eye, and so she could only cry on one side of her face. She was very unhappy that everybody else cried with two eyes and she was forced to cry with one. So while she was lamenting the fate of Husain and his family, she used to add a few words about her own plight too.

'Arre, how can I weep with just one eye? Oh Lord . . .'

Their faces covered, the Saiyid ladies were condoling their Bibi—the Prophet's daughter. Some were condoling Zainab, Imam Husain's sister, others imagined they were holding Sakina, Imam Husain's four-year-old daughter, to their breasts, and yet others were imagining walking alongside Imam Husain's eldest son, the ailing Sayyad-e-Sajjad, captured at Karbala, holding up his chains. Who's to say why these Saiyid ladies never condoled Imam Husain's wives.

When I saw the tears flowing from Rabban-dadi's only eye I began to giggle. In the middle of her tears, my mother slapped my back, said, 'Wretch! Sit down!' and then continued weeping.

I was forced to straighten my face and sit still. My sister raised her voice. It cracked. Afzalun suffered a fit of giggles, while Sallan had to cover her dark, smiling lips with her dupatta. Meanwhile my sister paused, breaking off in the middle of a long, off-key note, corrected herself and resumed with the verse,

> *'Umme Laila wept and cried*
> *It's eventide, come home Akbar . . .'*

I looked up in surprise at the aunt I called Chachi. She was the only one in the family whose name was Umme Laila. But who could this Ali Akbar be? Why was she getting so upset about him? Of course I knew Imam Husain had a son called Ali Akbar, but there was no reason why Chachi should be calling out for him. I decided to get to the bottom of the matter.

'Who is this Ali Akbar, Chachi?'

My aunt didn't reply. When she kept weeping silently I began to feel worried. I thought that I should go out and ask Uncle Wazir and so I slipped away and into Gori-dadi's house.

'Let me be . . . someone will see!' This was the voice of Mehruniya, the barber's wife.

'No one will come . . . they're all in the majlis.' This was the voice of Sulaiman-cha. In my eagerness I came up very close to them. I saw Mehruniya swaying in Sulaiman-cha's arms. There was a kind of light burning in Sulaiman-cha's eyes. The moment he saw me he let go of Mehruniya. She ran off.

Sulaiman-cha had shared the same wet-nurse with my uncle Wazir. He used to live in Gangauli and must have been about thirty-six or thirty-seven then. He had a well-built, athletic body, was tall, with a light wheatish complexion, and large, deep brown eyes. People thought that he was fond of nothing besides prayer, fasting and exercise. And he used to run a mile from women. So even after Dadda's constant nagging and scolding he hadn't married. But since he couldn't entirely ignore her instructions, he'd put a Chamar woman in his house to take care of him. She was the mother of his three children. His entire household expenses were met by the zamindari treasury—that's to say that his year's supply of wheat came from Zaheer-da's lands. Responsibility for his clothes fell on Uncle Wazir. His son studied in Maulvi Qurban Ali's madrassa, and Father gave him a stipend of five rupees a month. His daughter, Bacchaniya, was learning to sew from one house and another. She was only eight or nine—just two or three days younger than me and I liked her very much. In short all was well with Sulaiman and his family. The only thing was that his untouchable woman could not sit on the floor-covering with the ladies of the family, although she was allowed to attend the majlises of Moharram. This was because she had a very fine voice. Sulaiman-cha had taught her two or three nauhas, and for years she'd been reciting them at majlises. Her tunes were so influenced by folk-music that, leave aside the ladies, even several of the Saiyid gentlemen would stand outside the zenana imambara to listen to her, and weep.

She didn't become a Muslim, and nor did Sulaiman-cha make any attempt to convert her. And she was known as Jhangtiya-bo. When she had married her husband, Jhangtiya, she had been eighteen and he had been four. Then Jhangtiya caught smallpox—she became a widow and Sulaiman-cha installed her in his house. They say that the Chamars came to attack him. And they also say that Phunnan-da managed to send them back with great difficulty after a good deal of persuasion and a monetary consideration. Sulaiman-cha said that the Chamars had settled for twenty-five rupees, but Gaya Ahir said that they only got twenty-three—the other two rupees going into Phunnan's pocket. Whatever the story, Jhangtiya-bo came to live in Sulaiman-cha's house.

This Jhangtiya-bo was very black but disastrously beautiful, as fragrant as parched earth after rain and sweet as fresh jaggery still steaming from the pan. Several Saiyid gentlemen were infatuated by Jhangtiya-bo's earthy fragrance. A few of them had also made her all kinds of promises but when she became Sulaiman-cha's, she remained his.

However Sulaiman-cha did have to face one problem. Since he was a strictly religious man, he couldn't make use of any wet substance which Jhangtiya-bo had touched. That's why even with a woman in the house, he had to make separate arrangements for food. He used to get dal and meat curry from Phunnan-da's or Javad-da's or Sumari-bua's house. As for chapattis, he could manage to make them himself. And after each meal, he drank a glass of water and gave thanks to God.

Jhangtiya-bo loved him very much, and that's why after Mehruniya ran off, Sulaiman-cha stood there, stunned, as if frozen.

'Her hand had been bitten by a snake!' he said to me, after thinking hard.

'Snake!' I leapt two steps backwards.

'It was a water snake,' he said. 'They're not poisonous.'

'Sulaiman-cha,' I said, coming to what was worrying me, 'Umme Laila is Chachi's name, isn't it? So why is my sister reading "Umme Laila, Umme Laila" in the nauha?'

I asked him because I had no idea of the significance of the scene of Mehruniya and his snake and didn't give it a second thought. Sulaiman-cha laughed when he heard my question.

'Umme Laila was Imam Husain's wife.'

'So is Uncle Wazir her second husband?'

Sulaiman-cha chuckled even more, 'Bhaiyaa, you'd better ask your uncle Wazir about that.'

'All right,' I said and left.

In the main imambara the preparations for the majlis were already underway. Gore-da, Abu Muhammad-da, Mukhtar Miyan, Dildar Miyan, Maulvi Bedar, Rashid Miyan, Ali Qadir-cha, Hakim Ali Kabir Sahib and Phunnan Miyan were in front of the pulpit. Then there was Father, then Uncle Wazir, Ali Mehdi-cha and Fussu-cha. Chachcha-Bachcha was stretched out leaning against the pulpit. Maddu was peeping out from under the cover of the pulpit, and my brother, Moonis, with several other boys, was sitting behind the pulpit. In a white kurta-dhoti, Gobardhan was explaining something to Muslim-da about the ups and downs in cotton prices. Muslim-da was listening, his eyes wide open in amazement.

The weavers were sitting in the part of the three-arched hall where there was no floor-covering. Chamar and Bhar boys were squabbling among themselves, squatting outside the hall on the ground, waiting greedily for the blessed food to be distributed.

Two petromax lights were burning. In their light sparkled the ornate tall candelabra, thc lotus-shaped glass candleshades, the round glass candleshades suspended from the ceiling and those set in the walls, and the crystal pieces of the chandeliers.

Near the Gate a short distance from the bathroom door, a large white pennant-shaped flag was billowing in the wind and the large crest fixed upon it made in the form of an open hand, was bending in the breeze. The menfolk were smoking a huqqa, sitting on the cotton floor-covering of the three-arched hall.

Hakim Ali Kabir Sahib was telling Abbu-da a story about a court case for arrears of land revenue. And Uncle Wazir was whispering something into Ali Hadi-cha's ear that was making it difficult for him not to laugh.

Maulvi Bedar was reciting to Gore-da a verse of a poem describing a wedding. Gore-da was amazed at its sharp satire and was swaying back and forth in praise. Sitting nearby, Sibtu-da was talking to Father about a match for Kajina-phu.

I went straight up to Uncle Wazir and sat in his lap. He rubbed his nose on the back of my neck and I giggled. Everyone looked at me in surprise. I quickly straightened my face.

'Who was the boy Taqqan-cha was beating in the godown today?' I asked. Uncle looked at Ali Hadi-cha. He smiled.

'He wasn't half crying,' I concluded.

'All right, we'll tell him off,' said Ali Hadi-cha.

'And was Chachi married to Imam Husain before she was married to you?' I asked.

Uncle Wazir and Ali Hadi-cha found it difficult to control themselves. They both tried very hard but finally burst out laughing. Aggu-da roared with laughter as well. Chachcha-Bachcha and Fussu-cha were some way away; but when they saw their Wazir-bhai and Hadi-bhai and Aggu-mamun laughing they knew there must be something to laugh about, and so they began as well. I couldn't work out what on earth was going on.

'Arre, Miyan Wazir, what's the matter?' asked Gore-da. With some difficulty Uncle Wazir managed to tell him the story. Gore-da smiled and then beckoned to me. I went over to him feeling like a criminal, and sat down with my head bowed.

'Hazrat Ali Akbar's mother's name was Hazrat Umme Laila,' he said in Urdu.

'But . . .' I began in my village language.

'No buts,' he interrupted, 'you're speaking like a peasant. Your Chachi was called after Hazrat Umme Laila.'

Since Gore-da said this, I had to believe it, although it was difficult to swallow. I wanted to escape from him too because my brother was sitting behind the pulpit gossiping and pulling faces at me. But it was as if Gore-da had resolved only to draw breath after he'd told me the entire story of Karbala.

And so I was soon absolutely exhausted with the comings and goings from Medina to Mecca, Mecca to Karbala, Karbala to Kufa, Kufa to Damascus, Damascus to Karbala and Karbala to Medina. I began to fall asleep. But my brother was signalling to me. When I realized what he meant, I looked round to see Kallu-kakka in an opium-induced stupor. His head was bending forwards nearer and nearer towards the floor. Saliva was dribbling from his open mouth and being absorbed into his dirty white beard. At that precise moment Bade Abba Sahib opened the green, folding door of the shahnashin. Everyone stood up to salute the standards. Javad-da pulled the headcloth from his shoulder, wiped his beard and prepared to weep. Chachcha-Bachcha cleaned his spectacles on the hem of his kurta.

Sujjan-da nudged Kallu-kakka, 'The majlis is beginning . . .'

'Arre, so am I sleeping then?' With this Kallu-kakka wiped his beard with his hands. His hands became damp, so he dried them on the cloth covering the floor.

Bade Abba Sahib put incense into the censer. Sweet-smelling smoke rose in waves—the copper, silver and mixed silver and gold crests, and the sangi brocade, velvet and poth silk hangings of the standards began to peep from behind the coverlet of smoke. In the centre was a beautiful wooden tazia with a round dome, draped with black velvet. On all four sides was a surround decorated with coloured pieces of glass which reflected light on to the small, white turbans placed on the biers and made them look as if they were coming to life. Pieces of banana-leaf shaped like amulets, and strings of oleandar flowers had been draped over the turbans and standards.

After casting a glance over the imambara from the platform of the soz-chanters and making sure he was in tune with his two companions, who gave the key, Bade Abba Sahib chanted a salaam, a poem in praise of Imam Husain.

Women's voices could be heard from the zenana gallery.

'Eh, girl, look where you're going. You've crushed my foot. To hell with those *matimili* English shoes of yours!' This was Hasina-dadi's voice. My sister had been told off—I could tell because afterwards I could hear her whining.

'But how could Hammad's wife have said that?' someone asked Abbu-da's elder sister Suggan.

'*Naooj*!'came the voice of another lady, 'Be quiet and let us listen.'

Meanwhile, Abbu-da had taken both books of soz poems from his pocket. After marking places in each he looked around, 'Eh, Hammad! Why are you sitting there, why don't you come up here!' Hammad-da came and sat to his right. Mushtaq-bhai took the left side. They began to give the drone. Abbu Miyan chanted the opening verse in the *Jogini* raag. Ever before he had finished the first line he gestured to Mushtaq-bhai to sit closer. Mushtaq-bhai slipped up very close, but there was still something wrong. As Abbu-da was reciting the second line he looked around the audience and as he began to lift his voice, he beckoned to Sujjan-da. Sujjan-da came and squeezed between Mushtaq-bhai and the pulpit.

Husain Ali-cha wanted to cry, but the tears wouldn't come. He and Uncle Wazir were pressing their eyes to make them water when suddenly Fussu-cha and Aggu-cha began to sob. Uncle Wazir and Husain Ali-cha too began to sound as if they were weeping but they still didn't succeed in producing tears. I kept trying to cry loudly, but I was able to produce neither sobs nor tears. Javad-da had begun to cry, his face hidden in his shouldercloth. Phuttu had buried his eyes in the wall opposite, and when he didn't let himself blink for a long time, his eyes began to water. He didn't try to wipe them, he just let the tears flow.

As the poem reached a tragic climax, the hall resounded with cries of mourning. Abbu-da was asthmatic, and so couldn't read the whole poem. The soz was concluded. Bade Abba climbed the pulpit. A poem in praise of the Prophet and his family was recited. The children's voices were the loudest. First Bade Abba Sahib recited a salaam. He didn't say who the author was. The people of Gangauli had become accustomed to hearing him read salaams composed by 'someone'. (After he died it was discovered that those salaams by 'someone' were in fact composed by Bade Abba Sahib himself.) By the time he had read two or three couplets he was in full flow. He put both hands on his chest and swayed as he recited. His voice was very bad, and he wasn't good looking either. When he became emotional his mouth opened even wider and his large, yellow teeth began to look very strange. Whenever I saw his teeth I thought of Kallu-kakka's beard. Both should have been white and the whiteness of both was stained a kind of dirty yellow.

But there was no wrinkle in his spiritual life—it seemed as though God had ironed him well before sending him down to earth—and added so much starch that even after a fairly long life it hadn't softened. When he addressed majlis congregations his listeners were swayed by his spotless character, and wept. Unlike professional majlis-speakers he didn't feed his audience flowery words and phrases in his speeches, neither did he speak for hours; he would address the audience for only three to ten minutes. Why should he senselessly spend hours telling Shias that God is One, Muhammad is the Seal of the Prophets, and Ali the First Caliph—they knew it already. And there was no point in making speeches to the women at all. When they had once accepted something, their faith was unshakeable.

One year the celebrated Hakim Murtaza Sahib of Allahabad had delivered his famous majlis address on the Oneness of God. This speech generally lasted some four-and-a-half hours. In the men's part of the assembly the Shia gentlemen were praising the speech until their tongues went dry, but among the ladies Dadda was saying to Chutki-dadda, my great-aunt, 'Has this wretched old maulvi gone senile? Don't we know that God is One? Even our grandchildren know that.' This was a reference to me. I was then about three-and-a-half. I heard this story from my uncle Wazir who had been told by Chachi.

What I mean to say is that Shia women only come to majlises to hear about the trials and tribulations of Imam Husain and his family. That is why Bade Abba Sahib was very popular with the women and recited in practically all the women's majlises in our Patti. And there used to be very great weeping and wailing in those majlises.

I cannot be sure about other Shia ladies but I do certainly know that the women of my family did not even need to hear about the afflictions of Imam Husain to make them cry. It was quite enough just to hear his name.

Once it was decided to hold the Bismillah ceremony of my eldest sister's son on the third day of the month of *Shabaan*—Imam Husain's birthday. Accordingly, our own poets were put aside and it was decided to call Khalu Miyan, more properly known as Maulvi Ibne Hasan Naunahravi, from Lucknow.

Khalu Miyan agreed. Now, in the first place this ceremony was being held at our house, and in the second, Maulvi Ibne Hasan Naunahravi was going to address it, and so there was a large gathering. First Qais Jangipuri read a panygyric in praise of Imam Husain in which there were many offensive remarks about the first three Caliphs accepted and revered by Sunni Muslims. A lot of Sunnis had also come to hear the chaste Urdu of the Maulvi, and naturally Father and other members of the family felt extremely uncomfortable. All the educated Sunnis began to fidget. Anyway, somehow or the other they endured the panygyric. The Shia weavers and men from the nearby locality of Nakkhas were leaping up in praise at the end of each verse, and so Qais-cha didn't realize the mistake he was making. He climbed down from the pulpit with the words, 'God is Lord,' and, stroking his thin beard, went and sat beside the Maulvi and began to examine the semi-precious stones set in his silver rings which were, like him, innocent and unaware.

Khalu Miyan stood up. He'd guessed the mood of the audience. He climbed the pulpit, adjusted the hem of his coat, very carefully spat out his betel-nut into a small inlaid metal spitoon placed on its steps, looked at his pocket-watch and recited the verse of the Qor'an which says poets are misguided and lead others astray.

The moment the Sunnis heard this, their faces brightened. They sat up happily. My family heaved a sigh of relief and Qais-cha looked at Khalu Miyan in a confused way, wondering what on earth he'd done.

As the Maulvi was criticizing poets, the name of Imam Husain somehow cropped up. From the ladies side came the sound of a woman's voice wailing, 'Oh, my lord!' This was one of my aunts. Father went across at once. My aunt had her face covered and was weeping bitterly. Father said, 'Sister! This is a joyful gathering celebrating the birth of Imam Husain.'

'Arre, if he weren't born then how could he have been martyred at Karbala . . . Oh, bhaiyaa . . . !' said my aunt in mid-wail. This argument completely silenced the best civil lawyer in Ghazipur. And so if the name of Imam Husain is sufficient to make you cry, it doesn't really matter what the majlis-speaker is saying. If the weavers, Chamar women and their children want to make a noise, they will, and the Shia ladies will keep on talking. But they will keep one ear tuned to the speaker, and the moment Imam Husain's name is mentioned, they will start to weep.

If the majlis-speaker wishes to make them cry more, he can raise his voice. And since Bade Abba Sahib was himself transported to Karbala as he read, he used in any case to raise his voice just to call himself back to reality.

If anyone else were to have spoken in the majlis of the new moon night of Moharram, perhaps no one would have wept as on that night you are not mentally prepared for mourning. But in the majlis I am describing, Bade Abba was speaking himself, and even Aggu-da was among those weeping. That's why you couldn't make out what Bade Abba was reciting. You could just see that he was gripping his shoulders, swaying back and forth in the pulpit.

Generally in Gangauli no nauhas were recited in the majlis of the new moon night. The congregation chants 'Husain! Husain!' several times, gently beat their breasts, and then a salaam is read. But on this occasion I saw that Shammu-cha was lining up the boys in two rows, and I ran over to join one of them. The older men had never seen such lines. Bade Abba Sahib had just begun the salaam when a thin, young man began to chant a nauha, the boys standing in rows repeating the verses after him. The young man was wearing a double-breasted coat over his wide pajamas. Bade Abba was startled and stopped reading. Everyone gathered round the group reciting the nauha.

'I have brought a cradle, oh dearest heart, rock in it,' chanted the unfamiliar young man, lifting his voice.

As Bade Abba too had spoken of the plight of Husain's six-month-old child, the moment the members of the congregation heard this lament of his mother, they began to sob. Even Uncle Wazir and Husain Ali-cha's eyes filled with tears. Aggu-cha made the young man recite each verse several times.

'Is this any occasion for nauha-reading?' grumbled Ali Kabir-cha, 'We've got at least two more majlises to go before that.' But Bedar-cha kept beating himself gently on his kurta, which he wore without an undervest, as if he hadn't even heard what Ali Kabir-cha had said.

'Eh, Masshu!' Ali Kabir-cha pulled the hem of Masshu-bhai's kurta. He was standing in line, his head bowed grandly to one side, and occasionally reciting with the others. This recital posed a personal problem for him.

Until now he was the only man in Gangauli to lead the recitation of nauhas, and so he was in charge of every tazia procession. He controlled every majlis. Now this young man was challenging his position as 'pandit' and he had to consider this. When Ali Kabir-cha tugged at his hem he had to turn and bend his right ear towards him. 'What nauha have you thought of reading for the majlis at the Gate then?' asked Ali Kabir-cha.

'*Ji*!'

'In fact you should read two . . . yes really you should.'

Ali Kabir-cha felt happier after issuing this order, and perhaps turned his thoughts to one of his patients in the neighbourhood.

The young man who had recited the nauha turned out to be one Muhammad Husain, a resident of Chavanpur who had some job in Calcutta. Phunnan-da immediately discovered this. As a matter of fact, Phunnan-da had begun to be troubled by a constant worry. It had been all very well to fall in love with Karamat Ali's wife and to go to jail for it . . . there was nothing wrong in making her the mother of his children either . . . but young girls grow up, and when they grow up they have to marry. There was no question of his daughters marrying anyone in the community, which was why right there on the floor of the majlis, he raised the subject of Muhammad Husain with Uncle Wazir and asked why his daughter, Razia, should not be married to him. Uncle Wazir approved the match and Muhammad Husain became Phunnan-da's guest.

In Ali Kabir-cha's majlis in Uttar Patti, Masshu broke with tradition and read two nauhas. The men of my Patti, like Phunnan-da and Javad-da, were furious. Javad-da loudly expressed his rage but Phunnan-da whispered into Muhammad Husain's ear, 'You read three nauhas in tomorrow morning's majlis—these Uttar Pattiwallahs have gone off their heads.'

I planned to faint in that very three-nauha majlis. I asked Phuttu's opinion. He raised no objection, but my brother thought that it would be better to do it in the big majlis on the fifth. My argument was that I should collapse so completely in the former majlis that Masshu-bhai couldn't dream of competing with me.

It was agreed.

After dinner everyone began to sort out their bedding and then a meeting began under the chairmanship of Gore-da. Alim-va Hujjam, the barber, filled the huqqas with tobacco and glowing embers.

From Uttar Patti came Maulvi Bedar, Ali Hadi-cha, Husain Ali-cha and Ali Mehdi-cha. Husain Ali-cha praised the muslin of Abbu-da's kurta. Abbu-da then began to relate how he had bought it, and then how the Raja Sahib of Pirpur had thought no end of his own kurta until Abbu-da had shown him his.

'What can I say, Mir Sahib? If the ship hadn't sunk, what muslin we would have been getting! Smooth as cream!' said Gobardhan, who was sitting on a tin chair.

'The whole ship sank?' asked Fussu-cha. 'Then there must have been a great loss?'

'What else, sahib! That's the risk you take in business.'

I went off quietly with my brother towards Kallu-kakka's room.

He used to live in the apartment behind the eastern room of the imambara. First there was a rather large room, three of whose arches opened on to the small courtyard of the apartment, and the fourth into the sideroom of the imambara. This room was full of wooden chests. In them, after Moharram was over, were put the trappings of Moharram. To the south of the courtyard was the small room where Kakka lived.

When we arrived he was making tea. His bedstead was standing in the courtyard.

Kakka poured tea into two earthenware cups and handed them to us. The cups were the sort that looked wet even when the clay had dried. As we held the tea, he stirred it with two small, broad, aluminium spoons to dissolve the cream. We sniffed the cups, and our nostrils were filled with the hot steam and the wonderful aroma of freshly brewed tea. We took a sip. Small lumps of cream came into our mouths and dissolved.

'Tell us a story, Kakka!' I said.

Kakka began to tell us tales of Amir Hamza. When I grew up I read these stories and found there were many things missing from them which Kakka used to tell us with such immense conviction that it seemed he'd seen them happen with his own eyes. I preferred Kakka's version; perhaps because he didn't tell it in the chaste Urdu of Lucknow but in Bhojpuri Urdu. And besides, he didn't just tell the story—he acted it out as well.

He showed all the tricks of battle, the expressions of the dancers. Sometimes he would nod off and his head would bow down and when we laughed the sound of our laughter would bring his head up with a jerk and he would continue the story.

'So Naushekhan's minister said, "Emperor! You did promise Amir Hamza that you would give your daughter Mehrnigar to him in marriage . . ."'

I imagined that even after we dropped off to sleep he would keep on telling his stories, until the opium lulled him into slumber too.

I don't know when I went to sleep but when I opened my eyes I was, as always, on Dadda's bed—and she had said her early morning prayers and was lying down telling her prayer-beads. The whole house was awake. Mother had already come back from majlises at Muslim-da and Phunnan-da's houses and the strong smell of breakfast was issuing from the kitchen.

I quickly ate breakfast and dressed, because we had to go to the majlis at Ali Kabir-cha's Gate. And then I had to faint in the majlis at our own Gate. But when I went outside, I saw that Father was happily smoking his huqqa. Two or three tenants were squatting on the ground, and there were a couple of Raqis, the village's Sunni traders. Naturally Gobardhan was there as well. He was telling Chachcha-Bachcha some tale of speculation. The traders were talking to Uncle Wazir about some court case. They were so wealthy that they could buy the whole village whenever they felt like it, but they couldn't sit on the cloth chairs. Wooden or tin chairs were put out for them.

There was a furious discussion in progress. Ali Kabir-cha was saying, 'Our forefathers lived here . . . our tazia platforms and imambaras are here . . . our honour and self-respect is here! Gangauli means something to us! If we don't care about it, then are some traders going to? Those who've earned their pile in Calcutta . . . I'm not stopping them, but . . .'

'Arre, bhai sahib, it's the fate of Muslims to be separated from their homeland. After all didn't the Prophet of God himself have to leave Mecca for Medina?' threw in Uncle Wazir.

'That he did!' said Kabir-cha, 'He certainly did, but then, we are not the Prophet of God.'

'Arre, Mir Sahib! This Congress is the party of the Hindus. Since the majority of zamindars are Muslims, they are bound to abolish zamindari. And where are the homes of Muslims in the countryside? They're like salt in dal,' said Anwarul Hasan Raqi, one of the traders.

'It's salt that gives dal its taste,' said Ali Kabir-cha. 'How many days have you tasted dal without salt?'

'It's the fate of Indian Muslims to suffer,' said Anwarul Hasan emphatically.

'In the first place, I'm not accepting that the British are about to leave us. And in the second place it's the fate of us Shias to weep. You Sunnis can stay wrapped up in your songs and qavvalis,' announced Ali Kabir-cha decisively. Everyone was speechless. I went up to Chachcha-Bachcha and began to play with his pot-belly.

'What are you doing?' he said, turning over.

'Let's be off to the majlis then,' said Gore-da standing up. The assembly dispersed.

Near the pond on the way to Kabir-cha's house we met Taqqan-cha.

'What boy were you beating in the godown?' I immediately asked.

He completely lost his composure and said, 'Don't you say a word to anyone . . . I'll give you an anna.'

'I told Uncle Wazir,' I said, 'but why were you beating him? It was Ainuddin-va, wasn't it?' I had finally recognized the boy's voice.

'I was comforting him, he'd been hurt!' With this, Taqqan-cha gave me two annas and it occurred to me that now I could afford to buy the Orphan's Share for ten annas. So I put the money in my pocket and, leaving Taqqan-cha, began to skim pebbles across the pond. A couple sank straight into the water. A couple more went just three or four yards. At that moment a weaver's lad came and stood next to me, picked up a stone and threw it. The stone skimmed across the pond right to the other side. The boy looked at me, smiled and walked on without a word. I was very ashamed. What was the point of studying in the fourth year, I thought, if I couldn't even skim stones like that weaver lad? In the end, what was the point of learning English?

Considering this important educational question I entered Kabir-cha's imambara. The majlis had already started. Husain Haidar-cha was chanting a soz. Everyone was sitting in their appointed places, except for Phunnan-da who for some unknown reason was sitting in Javad-da's place. Haidar-cha had just finished the second verse when Javad-da appeared. After saluting the standards, he said, 'What's this, bhai? How have you come to sit there?'

'Arre, sit somewhere else.'

'On what grounds should I choose to sit elsewhere?' said Javad-da in chaste Urdu.

'Well, look at that! You've started speaking Urdu . . .'

'What are you doing, Phunnan! Sit in your own place,' Gore-da scolded Phunnan-da.

Phunnan-da quietly moved to one side. Javad-da sat comfortably in the central archway and turned to face the pulpit. Haidar-cha began to recite. I wanted this majlis to finish soon so that it would be our turn. But Haidar-cha recited a long marsia, then Sajjad-da climbed the pulpit and began a marsia of Anis, 'Imam Husain is close upon the field of Karbala . . .'

People wept a great deal at this marsia. Then they began to beat their chests in mourning. Maulvi Qurban Ali had some sort of a fit. He began to beat himself like a lunatic. The men around him tried to restrain him by telling him that the nauha was about to be recited, but he didn't heed them. His steps became faster. Everyone began to beat their chests, and then to cry loudly. Already tired, my brother began to beat himself rhythmically with two hands. I was so exhausted I sat down. Then one after the other all the boys were exhausted. The cries of grief became even louder. Maulvi Qurban Ali's hands moved even faster. 'Husain! Husain!'

'Husain! Husain!'

'Lord Husain!'

'Master Husain!'

'Husain! Husain!'

And then the Maulvi stumbled and fell. I said to myself, 'All right, old man, you'll see. Just you come to our Gate and see our majlis . . .'

But Maulvi Qurban Ali had not just fainted. He had died.

I admitted defeat. By dying Maulvi Qurban Ali had broken my courage. I was not prepared to die as after death no one comes to life again.

The news of his death spread like wildfire throughout the village. The people of Uttar Patti began to make arrangements for his funeral. Our majlis ended in real rather than ritual mourning.

I went to the inner house.

My brother took advantage of this occasion to run off with the bundle of coriander mixture from my sister's box. We both quietly filled our pockets. We'd just made a plan to go to the pond and eat the coriander mixture in peace when my sister arrived. She shouted for Mother. Mother called us. We ran. Mother ran after us.

She caught my brother in the southern hall of Gori-dadi's apartment.

I slipped into Naima-dadi's room, hid under a bed and began to eat the coriander mixture as fast as I could. Mother came into the room beating my brother. She saw me and began to hit me with the bamboo handle of a revolving hand-fan. She was squatting down. The bed was very low. I was absolutely trapped.

'Now, let him go,' said Naima-dadi.

'I'll kill this *matimile* today.'

'Then I'll go to heaven like Maulvi Qurban Ali and never come back,' I said. I had heard from somewhere that Maulvi Sahib had gone straight to heaven.

'God forbid, my son . . . let your enemies go to heaven,' said Naima-dadi.

I thought that if heaven was such a bad place it was dreadful for the poor old Maulvi to be trapped there. Still, I couldn't think too much about this question as Mother grabbed me by the ear. She managed to drag me out, but at that very moment Dadda arrived, and I leapt into her arms.

'Bibi, pardon him just for today.'

I was content—I knew that Dadda wouldn't desert me.

The Source

The sky seemed washed as clean as after the monsoon, and as filled with stars as the earth is filled with the fragrance of mahua flowers in April. Even the branches of the kadamba tree in the courtyard of the ladies' imambara were smiling, holding their innumerable round, golden blossoms and joking with the breeze, like young girls waiting for their sister's husband to arrive.

Jhangtiya-bo was quite alone in the large courtyard of the ladies' imambara. She always was alone during the nights of Moharram as Sulaiman's piety awoke to such an extent that he wouldn't touch her even at night. She didn't mind this. As she said, 'After all one day he has to show his face to his Allah Miyan!' She had heard a lot from Sulaiman about his 'Allah Miyan'. In her heart of hearts she'd even begun to fear Him. As a result, although initially she'd resented the loneliness of Moharram, she'd now come to terms with it. And then it wouldn't have seemed right for Bashir Miyan and Wazir Miyan to sleep at the Great Gate and for Sulaiman to stay by his woman. So as soon as the caravan from Ghazipur arrived, Sulaiman would go to the men's quarters, and Jhangtiya-bo would move into the storeroom of the ladies' imambara. Her children, Ali Akbar and Bacchaniya, used to stay with Akbari-bi. Ali Akbar would carry messages between the women's and men's quarters, and Bacchaniya would massage Akbari-bi's feet, and talk about the town with Sarwari, Bashir Miyan's second eldest daughter. And occasionally, in some passageway or first-floor room deserted in the heat of midday, she would play mothers and fathers with Wazir Miyan's son Bikkan. He pretended to be the husband, and she the wife. And when one day a worm fell from her stomach, she softly whispered that she'd had a miscarriage.

No one in the house knew about this game. And Jhangtiya-bo was happy that her daughter was sitting with the Saiyid ladies, and playing with their children. She remembered very well how she had longed for these things when she was young, and how happy she'd been when for the first time Sulaiman had moved to one side and made her lie down beside him.

But there was something strange in the loneliness of Moharram this year. The people from Ghazipur had arrived, majlises were being held, but still the magic of the occasion was missing. Bashir Miyan, Wazir Miyan, Shabbar Miyan and Aggu Miyan hadn't come, and on top of that Phunnan Miyan, Hammad Miyan and Sulaiman had all left for Ghazipur.

The district court had referred a case against them to the sessions court, and on the say-so of Deputy Collector Ali Hadi the wretched judge had set the hearings during Moharram. The Great Gate didn't seem far away to Jhangtiya-bo, but Ghazipur did—so far away that in a house full of people, among throngs of standards and tazias, and the familiar sounds of nauhas and marsias, she felt alone. For the first time in her life she had to face the fact that the world she was living in was not her own. 'If, God forbid, anything should happen to Ali Akbar's father, then what will I do?' she asked herself. She longed to hug Ali Akbar and Bacchaniya tightly to reassure herself that she was not a thought blowing in the wind like a kite with a broken string waiting to fall to earth, that she was Jhangtiya-bo, that she was the mother of Sulaiman's children.

Suddenly from Kallu-kakka's old apartment came the sound of Najjan Mirasi softly singing a lament in the *Jogiya* raag:

He has taken land for the graves!
The Lord of the Faith is marking the ground for them!
The Imam of the Age is marking them!

Najjan's voice was even better than Jhangtiya-bo's. Most nights, with his daughters Dil-Ara and Sitara, he would sing laments to himself, and to the stars dropped in the sky and scattered like mahua blossoms, and to the breezes weaving over the earth, and to the shadows stuck to the walls. And when he sang Jhangtiya-bo awoke.

Najjan Mirasi belonged to the town of Jaunpur. He used to teach the courtesans of Ghazipur to sing, accompanying them on the sarangi. Bashir Miyan tempted him with an offer of four bighas of arable land, and he agreed to move to Gangauli.

This was how the apartment which had been deserted since Kallu-kakka's death had returned to life.

Najjan had brought his wife Ghafooran and his two daughters, Dil-Ara and Sitara, with him to Gangauli. Dil-Ara was quite grown up. Sitara was younger but somewhat more beautiful with a sharp bone structure, an attractive wheatish complexion, deep brown eyes and such long, jet black hair that she could wrap it round her like a shawl in the cold weather.

The people of Dakkhin Patti had settled these Mirasi women within their Gate to add splendour to the ladies' majlises. Najjan's daughters had inherited voices as poignant and expressive as his own. Najjan himself was an excellent chanter of soz and Dakkhin Patti was in great need of such skills. Abbu Miyan and Sibtu Miyan could move an audience to tears, but they were both asthmatic and couldn't cope with the thirty or forty majlises spread over the ten days of Moharram. That's why it was settled that Najjan Miyan would chant the soz in the congregations of Dakkhin Patti.

Najjan was oblivious of this. He was just singing away softly. In his voice the glow of faith was stronger than the glitter of professional virtuosity. Dil-Ara and Sitara were accompanying him, and the voices of the three were reminiscent of a dense, dark-leaved mango tree between two fresh, young corinda bushes—very different from one another but at the same time very close.

Dil-Ara was floating away in the deep ocean of the *Jogiya* raag, rising and falling on waves of high and low notes as she accompanied her father. But Sitara's mind was as lithe and flirtatious as her body and she was thinking about Hammad Miyan's eldest son Abbas, who was studying at Aligarh and only came to Gangauli during the vacations. To her, Moharram seemed to begin the moment he arrived. Dakkhin Patti yawned, stretched and came to life. All the deserted passageways began to breathe. Drowsy courtyards started to laugh out loud.

Sitara knew that Abbas came to Gangauli just to meet her, although he'd never told her so. It was just that if she wasn't there when he arrived, he was sad. When she did appear, he seemed indifferent to her but a ring came into his voice which made flower buds open in every vein of her body.

Abbas used to tell Ghafooran anecdotes about Aligarh and explain Jinnah Sahib's politics, mentioning the Raja of Mahmudabad, Chaudhuri Khaliquzzaman, Ghaznafar Ali, Nawab Ismail, Nawab Yusuf, Sir Sultan and goodness knows how many other unfamiliar names. He used to say that India's hundred million Muslims would give their blood for the sweat of the Great Leader, Mohammed Ali Jinnah. Neither Ghafooran nor Sitara understood these things. Ghafooran would say, 'Well, Miyan, you're educated, so you must be right.'

'Arre, Ghafooran-bua!' Abbas would say, 'Once Pakistan is created Muslims will have a great time . . . absolutely great!' He would get carried away and start abusing Khan Abdul Ghaffar Khan and other Muslims who supported the Congress. 'Bua, these people are bent on selling the Muslims out to the Hindus . . .'

Sitara had no interest in whether Pakistan was created or not, she would just listen to Abbas' voice. It engulfed her like the sweet smell of frying eggs. However, she did learn the name of Pakistan and she also became convinced that it must be a good thing. So when in Moharram the two Great Gates of Dakkhin Patti began to overflow with voices, and all the names Abbas quoted were on everyone's lips, sometimes Sitara would stand in the shelter of a doorway and be greatly astonished that, except for Wazir Miyan, no one in the Patti had a good word for Pakistan.

'. . . Since Imam Husain told Amar-bin-Saad that he would not swear allegiance to Yazid, and that if Yazid thought he would rebel he should allow him to go to India, therefore no one who is a follower of Imam Husain can wish India ill. After all the Imam Sahib must have had some reason for choosing this land of infidels.

'And it's not only that—a Kashmiri Brahmin was also martyred at Karbala along with Imam Husain. The descendents of that Brahmin call themselves Husaini Brahmins. They have a kind of red line around their throat like a ribbon. If you don't believe it take a look at Ghazipur's DrÿTrilokinath! He's a Husaini Brahmin and he's got that thread of blood on his neck.

'Imam Husain couldn't come to India, but we did. So we are not about to leave it now . . .' with this the conversation turned to the Shia Political Conference, Pride of the Nation Kalbe-Abbas, Husain Bhai Lalji and goodness knows what else. Sitara couldn't understand all this, but she could understand that Imam Husain had wanted to come to India. Perhaps Abbas didn't know this, but Sitara couldn't think how to tell him. She used to feel embarrassed even looking at Abbas.

And what sort of Shia was this wretched Mr Jinnah that he was against India? This was a question she wanted to ask Abbas, but there was no harm in asking Sarwari instead. After all she was always reading about some nonsense or the other.

'Ba'ji, what's Pakistan?' she finally asked Sarwari one day.

'It's a country that will be made for the Muslims,' replied Sarwari like a great scholar.

'What is a country, Ba'ji?'

This question completely stumped Sarwari as she didn't know what a country was either. She knew the advantages which Muslims would get from Pakistan. Her Uncle Wazir had already told her about them and when her brother Moonis came from Aligarh, he didn't talk about anything else. But so far no one had told Sarwari what a country actually was.

Just at that moment Abbas arrived. 'What's the matter, Ba'ji?' he asked.

'Sitara is asking what a country is.'

Abbas burst into laughter. Perhaps for a moment he forgot that his father was facing criminal charges and might be convicted.

'She's just mad, Ba'ji!' he said. 'One day she was asking Ghafooran-bua why when husbands are called "Miyan", Moonis, Masoom, Maddoo, Bikkan, Badda and all the other boys are called Miyan when they aren't even married!* Abbas began to laugh again. Sarwari laughed too. Even her grandmother, Akbari-bi, who was lying down nearby telling her prayer-beads, had to smile. Sitara turned bright red.

'I didn't say that, Ba'ji . . .' she told Sarwari.

'Should I call Ghafooran-bua?' threatened Abbas.

'Yes, do!' Then she started, realizing that in a courtyard full of people she was talking to Abbas. She was so overcome with embarrassment that she fled.

'Arre, daughter, what sort of note are you singing?' Najjan interrupted her.

Sitara jumped. She nervously looked at her father to see if she'd been found out. But Najjan was soaring high on the wings of the *Jogiya* raag. Without coming back to the first accented note of the raag, he rose high again—close to the clouds, higher than even the circling kites of midday . . .

Sitara once again began to put her heart into her accompaniment.

Lying in her courtyard, Jhangtiya-bo realized that Sitara had returned from her imaginary journey. Jhangtiya-bo knew the secret of daydreaming. She herself used to sing folk-songs and daydream about Sulaiman until some friend interrupted her thoughts. But, she asked herself, who was Sitara dreaming of?

---

* Miyan is used by Muslims to mean 'husband' and is also attached to names as a word indicating respect.

Sitara had no idea that she had been found out by Jhangtiya-bo. After the soz was complete she lay down and slept. When Ghafooran got up to drink water, she saw that Sitara's shalwar had ridden up, leaving the lower portion of her shapely, light brown legs naked, and that the stars were greedily staring at them. Ghafooran pulled down the hem of her shalwar. Perhaps at that moment Sitara was dreaming. Feeling the pressure of someone's hands on her legs, she said shyly in her sleep. 'Leave me be! What are you doing!', and then turned over and went back into a deep slumber. But this was enough to rouse Ghafooran's suspicion. She didn't sleep again that night. She knew that apart from the Miyans—the Saiyids—there were a number of Raqi trader boys and romantically inclined weavers who were madly in love with Sitara and Dil-Ara. She had no fear of the Raqis or the weavers, because they could never imagine that any girl who lived within the Great Gate could fall into their clutches. But who could restrain the hands of the Miyans? And now this lass had started seeing someone in her dreams and behaving bashfully.

Very early the next morning she told Najjan that the girls' marriages should be arranged.

'You good soul, is Moharram the only time you have for talking about weddings?' said Najjan, setting out for the assembly in Uttar Patti. Ghafooran too, chewing a paan from her betel-bag, set off for the women's quarters. There the women were still out in the courtyard. The beds had been pulled out of the sun. Refreshed by a night's rest, flies were intermittently launching attacks on the face of Umme Laila's infant child. He was stirring in his sleep and Akbari-bi was cursing the flies and waving them off with a date palm-leaf fan.

'Has this wretched, *matimili* good-for-nothing gone mad?'

Everyone heard her question, but no one bothered to reply. All the women were busy with their own work. Ghafooran sat down quietly at the foot of a bed and taking the fan from Akbari-bi's hand, began to wave the flies away from the infant's face. At that moment Abbas was attempting to lift young Afsari from Nafisa-bibi's lap, and Sitara was watching Abbas and blushing. Abbas could feel Sitara's eyes on his body and perhaps that was the reason his broad chest was stretched even broader. Then he had also rolled up the sleeves of his fine muslin shirt. His muscular arms were bare, and Sitara's eyes were stuck to them, fluttering like flies in thick syrup which half want to escape, and half not to.

Old Naima-bi followed Sitara's eyes and immediately guessed that her story was possibly about to be repeated. Some fifty-five years earlier when, like Sitara, she had been on the verge of adulthood and was known only as Naimuniya the weaver's daughter, her glance had fixed itself like that on the body of Abbas' grandfather. As a result, she had become known as Naima-bi. The young Saiyid boys had began to call her Nani and Dadi. They hadn't called her forefathers 'Grandfather'. So this was a great honour. And was this wretched, *mui* Mirasi girl, Ghafooran's daughter, worthy of such an honour? She was about to say something when the sky began to buzz. Everyone's eyes turned upwards. An iron bird came into view which was flying without moving its wings.

All the women began to point the aircraft out to one another. The children began to jump up and down in the courtyard. Qaisar kept on pointing to the aeroplane and then began to pee. Sitara and Dil-Ara, who were at that point looking at him, turned away in embarrassment.

Then the aeroplane suddenly came right over the courtyard and some women who observed purdah took shelter around the side, and with exclamations of 'Ooii!' and '*Matimili*!' ran stumbling into the hall. These women were convinced that the people in the aeroplane must be peeping at them.

In this melee Naima-bi had forgotton Sitara, and no one gave a thought to the fact that Abbas had tossed Afsari into Nafisa-bi's lap and gone off somewhere too.

The fact was that gazing at Abbas' arms had made Sitara so bashful that she had run off. Abbas knew that she must have gone off to her family's apartment. But he didn't cross the courtyard in that direction—the truth was that he left with no intention of going there. After Sitara had gone, his home had held no attraction for him, and so he'd walked out. The three-arched hall of the imambara was deserted, the green door of the shahnashin where the tazias were kept was closed. The flag planted next to the bathroom stood quietly, the crest surmounting it glittering in the sun. The petromax lamps hanging from pegs were lifeless. What interest could Abbas have in them? He would have gone to the majlis beneath the pakkar tree, but it occurred to him that it would be almost over, and Masshu-bhai must be boring everyone with a nauha.

So Abbas thought that he might as well take advantage of the Saiyids' absence to go and meet Farooq, the son of Anwarul Hasan Raqi, the trader. Farooq was his senior at Aligarh and Vice-Chairman of the All India Muslim Students Federation. In front of the Saiyids, Abbas couldn't go to his house without getting a shoe-beating . . .

'Miyan Abboo,' they'd say, 'you've got so big and you don't even know that no man of noble blood goes to the door of any descendent of an oil-seller.'

In this Gangauli of his he couldn't even call Farooq 'brother'. How could the son of a Saiyid zamindar call the son of some trader 'brother'?

After detailed consideration of all matters concerning high and low birth, Abbas turned into the alley which headed south opposite Phunnan Miyan's house.

'Eh, son, has any news-vews come?' came the voice of Phunnan Miyan's illegal wife, Kulsum.

He stopped. This was the first time in his life that Kulsum had called out to him. The fact was that from both parents' sides Phunnan was a pure-blooded Saiyid. And Naima, the mother of Abbas' father, Hammad Miyan, was only a weaver woman.

But Hammad Miyan belonged to the Great Gate, and Phunnan Miyan was just an ordinary zamindar. He was such an ordinary zamindar that instead of pajamas he wore a lungi—and that not even sewn down the side, but just a length of cloth wrapped round him like a butcher wears. That was all very well, but a Saiyid was after all a Saiyid.

Hammad was so proud of belonging to the Great Gate that he refused to have anything to do with Phunnan, and so for about the past twenty years they hadn't spoken to one another. That was why, though Abbas halted when he heard Kulsum's voice, he couldn't think how to address her.

'There should be some news by evening,' he replied.

'God rot those Uttar Pattiwallahs—how they bother everyone, *haramzade*!'

Abbas came to the conclusion that now she was addressing God, and so there was no need for him to stay. He walked on, happy at the thought of how pleased the Raqi traders would be to see him.

Muslims are all brothers. Islam does not accept the idea of high and low. Hadn't the Prophet himself reckoned Salmaan Farsi, a man from a different culture and community, one of his own family?

Inwardly he prepared a speech stating what he'd do if, heaven forbid, the Saiyids found out where he'd been.

When he'd hammered out the speech and taken a good look at it, he saw that he was in front of the outer door of Najjan's apartment, and the sacking curtain hanging across the doorway was pulled to one side. Beyond it he glimpsed Sitara's body.

He lifted the curtain and went inside.

Sitara stood up in confusion. She had been lying down using her dupatta as a pillow. But when she felt her body melting under the heat of Abbas' glance, she remembered that she was not wearing it. She quickly picked it up and wrapped it round her.

'Is Ghafooran-bua not at home?' Abbas said in Urdu, asking an exceptionally stupid question.

'No . . . She's gone over to your side.'

'And Najjan Miyan?'

'He's gone over to the majlis.'

'So you're all alone!' he said, reverting to the Bhojpuri tongue of his forefathers.

'Yes!'

'Why are you so beautiful?'

With this he left. He did well not to give Sitara a chance to answer his question, because what answer could she have given? She was tangled in the thickets of her breath and could hardly stand. After Abbas left she couldn't bring herself to her senses for a long time. She kept smiling, and blushing, and repeatedly rearranging her dupatta over her breast, and then she began to feel ashamed in front of the walls and doorways of the apartment, and the sacking curtain across the entrance.

And looking towards the empty bed, on which she'd been lying longing for Abbas, she died inwardly.

She peeped out of the doorway. The alley was deserted. From the direction of the imambara came the roll of drums, summoning the villagers—'Come, the majlis is about to start.'

She turned round again and looked at the bed, and then she folded her dupatta into a pillow as before and lay down. Her gaze fixed as unmovingly on the bed as Karamat's stubborn mare's gaze had fixed on the Bauri Bridge. The mare had shied and Sitara's father, who had been sitting holding the bamboo strut of the cart roof, had fallen out. And her mother had begun to recite a prayer to Hazrat Ali, and her elder sister had started crying out 'Oh, Ali! Oh, Ali!', and Karamat, the cart-driver, had begun to curse his mare with the dirtiest of abuses. The prayer-reciting mother, and the daughter accompanying her had both blushed in shame.

'What are you doing?' asked Abbas. Goodness knows where he had come from.

Sitara's heart began to beat hard.

'The majlis is about to start,' she managed to say with great difficulty.

In reply Abbas came up close to her and sat on the bed. He did so in such a way that his hand touched hers. Sitara's whole body resounded like the strings of a sitar, and the seven notes of the scale clung to one another in their confusion.

The beating of drums at the Gate stopped. Alim-va the barber removed the huqqa from the floor of the imambara. Shabbu Miyan opened the door of the shahnashin. The congregation stood up to salute the standards and tazias.

And then the unexpected happened. Shabbu Miyan looked at Najjan and said, 'Recite!'

Until Najjan had sat down on the platform of the soz chanters no one understood what was going on. But then the question arose of who would accompany him. No son of a Saiyid could be the accompanist of a common Mirasi, and in Gangauli no one except the Saiyids knew the art of soz chanting.

Najjan began softly:

The hour the camp of the Exalted Lord was pitched
upon the riverside,
And the Tormentors rose to oppose him there upon the
riverside . . . .

Husain Ali Miyan had thought that Najjan would just read some introductory verses, to create the correct atmosphere. But when he began to chant the entire marsia, first of all Husain Ali Miyan's little fists opened and shut several times, and then he stood up. Everyone was startled. Husain Ali Miyan caught hold of Najjan by the collar, pulled him down from the platform and began to curse him, his mother and his sisters. 'You dare to sit here and recite a soz!' he said.

The men of Dakkhin Patti were enraged but Husain Ali Miyan stuck to his guns.

'This is our majlis, and we recite here,' he said, addressing the imambara. Then he went and sat on the platform himself. Najjan sat quietly on the floor beneath him. Husain Ali Miyan began to recite the same marsia. But he'd only recited the first verse when Shabbu Miyan stood up and said, 'The Mourning of Husain.' This was the signal that the marsia had ended and now the nauha would begin. Everyone stood up and began to beat their chests in rhythm. Husain Ali Miyan climbed down from the platform and left the imambara without even reciting the salaam.

The women began to leave the ladies' gallery, cursing Husain Ali

Miyan. When Ghafooran came to the door of her apartment she found it bolted from inside. She called out to Sitara. The door opened, but a few moments later than it should have. Ghafooran was startled at Sitara's appearance because she was as deeply coloured as a ripe jamun fruit dripping with purple juice. Ghafooran went inside without a word. Abbas' handkerchief was lying on the bed—Ghafooran still said nothing to Sitara. But when Najjan came back she told him that it was no longer right for them to stay in Gangauli. Why should they get involved in arguments between the Uttar and Dakkhin Pattis? Najjan tried to change her mind, but she wouldn't budge. And when she didn't budge, Najjan was forced to accept her point of view. After all, Adam had left Paradise for Eve, and this was just a village!

By evening Ghafooran had bade farewell to everyone. All the women tried to make her change her mind, and all the men tried to change Najjan's. But Ghafooran was unshakable. Finally their possessions were loaded on to a horse cart.

When the cart was passing the indigo factory, Najjan saw Shankar Chamar approaching swiftly on a bicycle. Najjan called out to him, but Shankar didn't hear. The cart went on towards the main road, and the bicycle to Gangauli.

'The Miyans have been sentenced!' said Shankar the moment he came through the Gate.

A stunned silence descended within the Great Gate. No one could believe it. But Shankar told them that the police inspector had put all the pressure he could to get Phunnan Miyan convicted. If Phunnan Miyan hadn't been involved in the case they wouldn't have been sentenced. But because of one Phunnan Miyan they'd all been punished.

When this news reached the women, Jhangtiya-bo peered at the standards in the zenana imambara with eyes full of complaint, 'Hai, Imam Sahib! You shouldn't have done this!'

Then she collapsed on to the threshold of the imambara and began to weep. Naima-bi began to curse Phunnan Miyan, 'My son Hammad's been punished due to that matimile wretch!'

When Kulsum heard that Naima-bi was cursing Phunnan Miyan, she raised both her hands and began to curse Naima-bi and Hammad back.

In the middle of all this uproar who was going to give a thought to where the family which had been living in Kallu-kakka's apartment had gone and why? Abbas did think about them for a few days but then he forgot them too. One of the weaver girls began to appeal to him. But Ghafooran couldn't forget Gangauli. After all, she was Sitara's mother. She immediately arranged her daughter's marriage as there was nothing else she could do. A baby was born to Sitara after seven months of wedlock—a big, strong baby. Sitara's in-laws looked at this baby with suspicion. Sitara's husband divorced her. She came back to Ghazipur.

And she called her son Abbas.

The Miyans

After Moharram Gangauli seemed deserted. Most people didn't leave, but those few left whose presence brought the village to life. After Saiyid Ali Hadi Zaidi and Ali Mehdi Miyan had gone, dust began to blow through Uttar Patti, even though Ali Qadir Miyan, Ali Kabir Miyan, Haidar Miyan, Ubbad Miyan, Sajjad Miyan and Maulvi Saiyid Bedar Zaidi Sadrulfazil were still there. Uttar Patti was the name of an imambara and, after the tenth of Moharram, when Imam Husain was believed to return from Hindustan to Karbala, the imambara began to echo hollowly. The tazia platforms seemed to crouch like frail women, clutching the splendour of the delicate and beautiful wooden tazias to their breasts. And the platforms themselves seemed orphaned. The cloth-covering of the imambara's pulpit was removed. The floor-covering of the hall was taken up, charpoys were laid out to replace it, and the hall at once began to look like any ordinary room. Hakim Saiyid Ali Kabir would lie on one of the charpoys with a roll of bedding as a pillow, smoking his huqqa. He spent the time that remained after attending to his patients and taking part in the quarrels and disputes of the zamindars, in swearing at the boys of the village and dreaming about the future of his son Saddan, more formally known as Saiyid Sa'adat ul Hasnain Zaidi.

Many inhabitants of Gangauli had never seen a railway, because the nearest station was ten miles away from Gangauli, and Ghazipur twelve. So people generally travelled by pony-traps known as ikkas. And since in the eyes of the Miyans, the world extended no further than the Ghazipur courts, they had no idea what was going on in the rest of the world.

Hakim Saiyid Ali Kabir Zaidi was the first of them to travel by train, and that too because one year Gore Miyan had hurt him by mentioning, at the Uttar Patti's procession of the eighth night, that in Lucknow there was a silent procession of tazias which was much more splendid. This statement pierced the Hakim Sahib's heart like an arrow because he was immensely proud of his procession of the eighth. Several groups from surrounding villages came to chant nauhas for it. On one side of the great courtyard of Uttar Patti huge cauldrons of food were cooked, and Alim-va the barber put immense effort into making the most delicious tea. From Gangauli to Ghazipur no other procession had outside groups taking part, and so how could the Hakim Sahib accept that any procession in Lucknow could be bigger or better? To see for himself, one year he plucked up the courage to visit Lucknow, and was therefore obliged to travel by rail from Ghazipur.

For several years afterwards he would describe the railway and the carriages and the whistle of the engine and the rumbling of the train—and the people of the village would listen open-mouthed. Only the Raqis were not amazed by his stories, because they were traders and had long since grown accustomed to rail travel.

But the Hakim Sahib climbed once into a train, and the railway climbed into his brain. It even reached the stage where, when he dreamed of what his son would do when he'd finished his studies, he decided that first Saddan would become a thanedar, (because, by the grace of God, there was a great deal of extra income in running a police station), and then, when Saddan's income had grown sufficiently large, he would buy a train. This dream of the Hakim Sahib's didn't last long, however, as a train would have needed acres of land for its stable. That was why he chose a motor car for his dreams instead. He'd seen a motor car for the first time in Lucknow too.

'Arre, bhai, they're all as beautiful as young Jinti,' he exclaimed. He told Javad Miyan and Maulvi Bedar confidentially that the 'motors' wandered the streets swaying as seductively as Jinti and not turning to glance at those longing for them. As a car didn't even need a large stable, he imagined a shining 'motor' standing by the Gate. People were saying that there was an English elephant of iron at his door which, instead of sugarcane, ate strongly scented English kerosene, called by a very fine name . . . .

Not once did the Hakim Sahib ever dream of leaving Gangauli. It never occurred to him that he should build another Chattar Manzil opposite that famous mansion in Lucknow. The Great Gate of Uttar Patti was large enough to contain all his dreams and still have room left over. Especially after Moharram, when Ali Hadi Miyan's room was locked, there was more than ample space for his dreams.

If there was anything in Uttar Patti which could compare with the splendour of the imambara it was this room of Deputy Collector Ali Hadi. The imambara's standards, embroidered hangings, beautiful wooden tazias, wrapped bundles of poems, round glass lamps, lotus-shaped glass candleshades, incense burners and rosewater sprinklers all held their own attraction, but the grandeur of the various kinds of carved chairs, armchairs and three-legged stools in Deputy Collector Ali Hadi's room was also exceptional. In one cupboard were decoratively bound English books, some of them very old, and unwilling to mix with marsias. Several different styles of cigarette cases quietly smiled at the incense holders.

The Hakim Sahib was Ali Hadi Miyan's elder brother. He loved Ali Hadi very much, but he hated this room because the moment Ali Hadi arrived, it was unlocked and he began to hold court. There was more activity at Ali Hadi's court than in the imambara, the court of Imam Husain. His room was constantly packed with the young men of both Uttar and Dakkhin Pattis. And since one door of the room opened on to the imambara, cigarette smoke used to curl out into the imambara, and trouble the smoke of the fragrant incense which burned there. Occasionally even on the seventh and eighth days, peals of laughter from Abbu Miyan, Wazir Miyan, Fussu Miyan and Ali Hadi Miyan himself would lift the curtain over the doorway of the room, boldly enter the imambara and roll on the floor like children.

The Hakim Sahib couldn't even have the doorway closed off, because it had been made by his grandfather, Mir Najaf Ali Zaidi.

'Those were the days when sons of Saiyids did not roar with laughter on the seventh day of Moharram,' thought the Hakim Sahib: 'May God destroy the English and the study of their language! The faithless wretches have ruined everything!'

English education and the tension caused by this doorway gave birth to a desire.

During that memorable visit to Lucknow, the Hakim Sahib had also been influenced by the city's two great imambaras of Asaf-ud-Daula and Husainabad. As a result, he became anxious for Saddan to grow up and take charge of a police station as soon as possible, so that he could build a great big imambara like Asaf-ud-Daula's which would have a beautiful dome like Shah Najaf's, where Hazrat Ali was buried. The Hakim Sahib also planned to have the old copper crests of the standards replaced. All the crests in the new imambara would be made of mixed silver and gold, and each would be fastened to its pole with its own rope of gold and silver thread. The standards' hangings would be entirely covered with embroidery in gold thread and the flags would be of sparkling tamami cloth. The crests of the tazias would be golden, and the metal pots would be inlaid with gems. The imambara would be carpeted, and the pulpit would be of sandalwood—and at the procession of the eighth, on both sides there would be woven screens mounted with torches, and groups from far and around would come to recite nauhas, and to perform matam. Then he'd see how Gore Miyan could say that nothing could match the procession of silent tazias at Lucknow!

The Hakim Sahib had one more small wish in his bag. The tazia of rival Dakkhin Patti was known as the Great Tazia. It was decorated on the night of the ninth of Moharram, and then laid on the big platform in the part of the village where the Raqis lived—just like a nobleman! The Raqi traders would keep it company. As the men of Dakkhin Patti were the old zamindars of Gangauli, they didn't decorate their tazias themselves. The Raqis would decorate the Great Tazia. Some tazias were handed to the weavers, and others to the barbers.

In the early afternoon of the tenth of Moharram the Great Tazia held court. Dozens of wooden tazias came from their platforms to herald the arrival of the soz-chanters, and would be placed on the ground around the Great Tazia—like subjects around their king. Then the Great Tazia was lifted on the shoulders of eight bearers and the other tazias followed behind. Behind the wooden tazias came a whole army of paper tazias, offered by devotees whose prayers had been answered, and wishes granted.

In front of the Great Tazia walked Abbu Miyan, an embroidered belt around his waist, holding a rod with a silver handle and chanting. Phunnan Miyan, Bashir Miyan and Hammad Miyan would be on either side, accompanying him. They would stop after every two steps and recite two verses of a salaam. Behind came a crowd of five hundred to a thousand people. Women made children cross underneath the Great Tazia, and prayed for wishes to be granted. They sang songs of the tragedy of Karbala in Bhojpuri Urdu, and made offerings of sharbat. These women were not Saiyid ladies, because Saiyid ladies could not leave their homes except in a palanquin. These were the village's Raqi, weaver, Ahir and Chamar women. Indifferent to them, their prayers, and the anguish expressed in their laments, the Great Tazia proceeded like a stately elephant or an emperor.

In front of the soz-chanters went a group of Ahirs armed with lathis taller than themselves. The Great Tazia was so big that it couldn't pass through the alleys of Gangauli and so overhanging eaves had to be broken. The lathi-wielding group of Ahirs went ahead simply to knock down these eaves.

Preceding the Ahirs, marched the men who displayed stick-fighting and other martial arts, and in front of them went trumpets, horns, drums and cymbals.

With all this pomp and splendour the procession would make its way to the tomb of Nuruddin the Martyr. Then the Great Tazia, along with all the wooden tazias, was brought back and the rest of the procession took the path leading through the fields to the Karbala, where the paper tazias were buried.

Hammad Miyan returned with the wooden tazias and distributed money from the zamindari treasury for villagers to repair their roofs.

One year it so happened that due to a builder's error the eaves of a Brahmin widow's house jutted out a little less than they should have. The Great Tazia went by without them being knocked down. The widow began to sob, saying that the Imam Sahib was angry with her, and so some disaster was bound to befall her, otherwise it was impossible for the Great Tazia to go by without knocking down her eaves. She took both her sons with her to the tomb of Nuruddin the Martyr. Then she looked straight into the unseeing eyes of the Great Tazia and said, 'Oh, Imam Sahib! If anything happens to my two boys, it will not be well!'

Then she set upon Hammad Miyan, 'Please, Mir Sahib! Knock down my roof!'

Hammad Miyan thought she might be saying this for the money and so he replied sharply, 'If you want money go and take it at the door.'

'No, sarkar!' she began to wail, 'I don't want money, I want my sons' lives. Please have the eaves of my house knocked down! I fall at your feet!'

But no one heeded her complaint. And then it so happened that her eldest son was convicted in a murder case in which he'd been implicated. Abbu Miyan, Shabbar Miyan and Wazir Miyan all brought tremendous pressure to bear, but still he was sentenced to be hung by the neck until dead. The old woman went straight to Hammad and, to wipe out her anguish, took two wooden supports from her roof, arranged them like flower offerings on the frame of the Great Tazia standing in the courtyard, and, prostrating herself, cried, 'Oh, Imam Sahib! Don't do anything more to me . . . forgive my fault now.'

The government's case was somewhat weak. The High Court released her son. When Abbu Miyan asked for his fees, the old woman gave him short shrift because in her opinion the Imam Sahib had saved her son from certain death brought about by the lawyers' arguments.

After this curious happening at the Great Tazia, its popularity increased greatly. People began to come from Ghazipur to pray for their wishes to be granted. And the day that some twenty ladies left the Moharram of Lucknow to come to mourn and pray for favours at the Great Tazia on the ninth night, Hakim Ali Kabir's discomfort knew no bounds.

The lanes leading to the Great Tazia had to be closed off and the area around the Tazia surrounded by screens so that the women could weep and beat their breasts freely, and still maintain purdah. Because of the screens, the entrance to the Raqis' beautiful mosque was also closed, and those wealthy traders were forced to say their night prayers in a ruined mosque instead.

It was a great victory for Dakkhin Patti to have these women from Lucknow come of their own free will to the Great Tazia for matam. What did it matter that groups came from Chavanpur, Zahoorabad, Hainsi and Mata for the Uttar Patti's procession of the eighth? Ali Kabir Miyan used to pay their fares, feed them meat and pulao, and pander to their every wish. But it was the view of Dakkhin Patti that a tazia could be considered really great when ladies left the Moharram of Lucknow city and came all the way to Gangauli just for a sight of it—and paid their fares from their own pockets. The poor women also insisted on eating their own food, but the people of Dakkhin Patti refused to let them. It would have gone against the rules of hospitality.

This group of ladies from Lucknow proved one thing beyond doubt—that Imam Husain, who comes to India during Moharram, holds court on the ninth night on the platform of the Great Tazia in the Dakkhin Patti of Gangauli. This was more than the people of Uttar Patti could bear.

So it was the Hakim Sahib's great wish that somehow some miracle would take place at his Patti's tazia so that the pride of the Dakkhin Pattiwallahs could be broken.

It was a coincidence that while this thought was worrying the Hakim Sahib, a murder was committed in the nearby village of Barikhpur. The Hakim Sahib had a word with the thanedar of Qasimabad police station and had one of his own men, Komila Chamar, implicated. Since the Hakim Sahib was the brother of Deputy Collector Ali Hadi and one of the area's big landowners, his influence was useful to the thanedar in getting a lot of his work done. As a result, the thanedar only took one hundred-and-one rupees to have Komila named as an accused. It was settled that the case against him should be so weak that the judge would immediately order his acquittal. In a separate deal, the thanedar took eleven hundred rupees from the real murderers, so that after Komila's release the investigations should be dropped and they would get off anyway.

Komila was arrested. His mother Baburamva-bo (the wife of Babu Ram) came running to the Hakim Sahib. The Hakim Sahib called the thanedar. The thanedar vowed to try to save Komila. Then, through the head constable, he took one hundred rupees from Baburamva-bo to weaken the case against Komila. The Hakim Sahib consoled Komila's mother and sent her off home. By chance she met Ghulam Husain Khan at the door. This Ghulam Husain Khan was an old family retainer of the Hakim Sahib's. He told Baburamva-bo about the miracles of the tazia platform of Uttar Patti's Gate—how one day his wife had been bitten by a snake, and he had gone to the tazia platform opposite and prayed for her life, and the moment he'd finished praying the poison had left her body all by itself. As he related this story he omitted to recall that about thirty years previously his first wife had actually died of snakebite, and no snake had ever bitten his second wife. Baburamva-bo knew this but didn't remember it just then, because her son was accused of murder, and she immediately rattled off a prayer where she stood. Then it gradually spread round the village that Baburamva-bo had prayed for Komila's release at the tazia platform in Uttar Patti. Relatives living outside Gangauli were informed of this by letter, but in such a way that the readers of the letters would not guess that this was the purpose for which they had been written.

Slowly the news spread into the neighbouring villages and the residents of Uttar Patti sighed with relief.

But there was uneasiness in Dakkhin Patti. The people there may have tossed their heads and said that it wasn't every platform which could support a Great Tazia, but a fear stole into their hearts—if Komila were acquitted it would mean humiliation for the Great Tazia, and Dakkhin Patti would have its nose cut off in disgrace. Therefore, it so happened that in the same way that the thanedar of Qasimabad had been given a hundred rupees from the Uttar Patti's Moharram budget, he was given three hundred rupees from the Tazia Fund of Dakkhin Patti on the understanding that Komila would not be hung, but he would definitely be convicted. The thanedar, Thakur Harnarayan Prasad Singh, thought that he would come to no harm from this arrangement, and so this was also agreed.

Now, it was by complete coincidence that Komila's family had a longstanding quarrel with a comparatively wealthy Chamar family of the settlement called Chamtoli. Sukhram-va Chamar's elder son was the Collector of Ghazipur's gardener, and his younger son was a Congress supporter. The two brothers didn't speak to each other, but when this case came up, Sukhram-va summoned them both, and together they decided that this was the moment to take revenge on Babu Ram, Komila's father. So Sukhram gave up five mango trees and vacated half a bigha of land. The land was fertile. Hammad Miyan had not turned him off it because his son was the Collector's gardener. In return Sukhram-va received two hundred rupees. He took two hundred more from Chunnu Lal the goldsmith by pledging his house and his daughter-in-law's jewellery. His son Balram the gardener brought two hundred rupees from the town. When all together they had six hundred rupees, Balram took the bundle of money to Qasimabad. The moment the Thakur Sahib heard that the Collector Sahib Bahadur's gardener had arrived, he went out to meet him, although that was the time of day he relaxed with his whore, Gulabi Jan. (This Gulabi Jan was a very strict Muslim. The moment she left the Thakur Sahib's room she immediately bathed, and prayed to God to forgive her for being forced to sleep with a kafir to fill her stomach.)

Balram offered the bundle in the service of the Thakur Sahib and revealed what was in his heart. The Thakur Sahib made a calculation and came to the conclusion that twenty-two hundred rupees was a lot of money. Therefore he told Balram that there was no way the wish of the Collector Sahib Bahadur's gardener could be denied. At that moment the noose fell around Komila's neck.

The case opened. Several very good witnesses turned up. There was even one eyewitness. Komila was sentenced to be hung. When the Hakim Sahib complained, the Thakur Sahib replied that he'd tried his best, but the *behenchod* witness wouldn't be shaken, and so what could he do?

The men of Dakkhin Patti breathed a sigh of relief at the decision, and another Chamar woman told Baburamva-bo that she should have prayed at the Great Tazia because that was the one which had saved the Brahmin woman's son. Komila's sentence increased the renown of the Great Tazia even further.

It was exceedingly hard for the Hakim Sahib to endure this defeat. But he was helpless. There was nothing he could do. Still it wasn't easy to swallow the poison of disgrace. Therefore he thought of a way to bring the Dakkhin Patti's splendid procession on the tenth of Moharram into disrepute.

On the lane which led towards the Uttar Patti some ten to twenty yards west of the Great Gate, stood the house of Balli Sain, one of the Hakim Sahib's men.

At the instance of Ghulam Husain Khan, Balli Sain dreamed that a window opened in the sky, and a ladder of light came from the window down to the earth. A great man descended that stairway and said to Balli Sain, 'Unfortunate one! Prepare a tazia . . . death is at hand!' Balli Sain's eyes opened. It was the tenth of Moharram. He immediately built an earthern platform outside his door, put a four-anna paper tazia on top of it, had incense sticks lit on all four sides and himself sat down cross-legged on the ground next to the tazia.

When the men at the head of the procession reached the turning, they were amazed to see the paper tazia. It was like the Raja of Bhoj being faced with Gangua the oil-seller! A pathetic little four-anna tazia was challenging a procession of hundreds of beautiful wooden ones! In front of a four-paisa tazia, tazias escorted by embroidered hangings, silken ropes and golden standards were rendered helpless, because until that tazia was lifted from its platform, the procession could not proceed. Whether it's made of silver or gold, or of the paper used to make kites, a tazia is a tazia. Even in the intoxication of their power as zamindars, the men of Dakkhin Patti could not show disrespect to one. However, no one could stop them showing disrespect to Balli Sain. A three-paisa man who had the impudence to think he was equal to the Great Gate! Accordingly, Phunnan Miyan's hand shot out. Balli Sain staggered and collapsed on the ground. This is what Uttar Patti was waiting for.

Men armed with lathis were already standing in Husain Ali Miyan's doorway. They streamed out. This band of Ahirs, Chamars and Bhars leapt to the attack, invoking the name of the Monkey God and Imam Husain.

'Victory to Bajrangbali! Victory to the Imam Sahib!' Raising the cry, 'Ya Husain!', the Dakkhin Patti's stick-fighters stopped the assailants' staffs with their own, and then the roof-breaking Ahirs, who preceded the Great Tazia and had passed on ahead, came running back. There was fierce fighting. Aggu Miyan forgot that he was Saiyid Ali Asghar Zaidi, Advocate. Abbu Miyan forgot that it was beneath his dignity to indulge in fisticuffs. Wazir Miyan put aside all the laws of the Criminal Code. The boys of both Pattis began throwing sticks and stones. A clod of earth thrown by Mumtaz hit Ubbad Miyan, the marsia-reciter, on the nose. He wailed, and Mumtaz laughed at him. Gaya Ahir's lathi fell on Maulvi Saiyid Bedar Husain Sadrulfazil's shoulder. The Maulvi was hitting out with a stick, and cursing the

Dakkhin Pattiwallahs in Hindi delivered in a perfect Arabic accent. When Gaya shouted, 'Victory to Bajrangbali!' and hit him, the Maulvi exclaimed, '*Abeh, haramzade*! You dare to hit me!' But there was so much uproar that Gaya couldn't hear what the Maulvi was saying. The Maulvi panicked and bent down to avoid another blow, but the lathi still hit his shoulder again. This was enough for him. He collapsed.

Among the Saiyids, only Phunnan Miyan was wielding his lathi in a regular fashion. He had tied his waistcloth up around his loins, and wrapped his shouldercloth round his head, and his well-oiled, nine-foot-long lathi was working as fast as a shrewish woman's tongue.

When the terrified tazia bearers tried to turn back with the Great Tazia, Phunnan flew over to them like an arrow. He slapped the first bearer and said, 'Bastard! Where the hell do you think you're taking that tazia? Don't you know, you *madarchod*, that time may turn back if it wants to but this tazia's not bloody going to!'

The bearers lifted the tazia again.

The women of both Pattis went to their imambaras and began to wail and complain, 'Eh, Helper of the Prophet's Family! Come to our aid! Save us from calamity!'

But the Helper of the Prophet's Family didn't come to their aid. Who would he have helped? Both sides were Saiyids.

Then the police came.

But the news of the imminent arrival of the police came a little before the police themselves. The respectable individuals on both sides decided that it was not proper to involve the police in a domestic matter. And so the injured were at once removed. Abbu Miyan began to recite: 'What a world of loneliness lies upon Husain this day!'

From the other direction the Hakim Sahib approached chanting a soz and had Balli Sain's tazia picked up. By the time the police arrived the procession had moved on past Balli Sain's doorway and beyond the mosque. There were bloodstains on the ground, but what difference did that make? Not one man in the village would admit there'd been a fight. Because the whole village had taken sides either with the Uttar or Dakkhin Patti. Everybody's blood was boiling, but no one wanted the police involved in this religious and domestic matter.

No one except Anwarul Hasan Raqi. He was a Wahabite and opposed to the celebration of Moharram, as in his view the use of tazias amounted in a way to a type of idol worship. But even he couldn't escape taking sides. That's why he took the thanedar, Thakur Harnarayan Prasad Singh, and his subordinate, Samiuddin Khan, to his house. Over snacks he handed the thanedar five hundred rupees to at least register a criminal case against Mir Ubbad and Maulvi Bedar of Uttar Patti.

The thanedar, Thakur Harnarayan Prasad Singh, was troubled by the fact that he could find no witnesses. But still the sum of five hundred rupees was not so small that a thanedar would let it pass out of his hands easily.

So he kept the money and gave his word to Anwarul Hasan. Anwarul Hasan said that he would try to prepare some witnesses too.

When the Thakur Sahib went off with Samiuddin Khan in search of the procession, he found that it had come to a halt outside the Hakim Sahib's door. Very loud matam was going on. Most of Dakkhin Patti's lathi-wielding Ahirs had laid their staffs around the tazia and were slapping their chests to the beat. Only a few of them were standing in front of the Great Tazia with their chests pushed out like shields so that the men of Uttar Patti's heads could be broken if they tried creating trouble. With those four or five Ahirs stood Sulaiman Miyan. A shouldercloth was tied round his waist like an embroidered belt. He was standing slightly bowed with both hands resting on his well-oiled, nine-foot-high lathi. His son, Ali Akbar was with the stick-fighters, practising swordplay.

Generally the stick-fighters kept some way ahead of the tazias, but they were now keeping close to them to protect them. Intermittently, between their cries of 'Ya Husain!', rose the sound of Abbu Miyan's chanting.

Sulaiman Miyan was happy to see Ali Akbar's neat fighting moves. His eyes were leaping the walls of time and imagining him as a young man.

The Thakur Sahib came up with Samiuddin Khan and stood beside him.

'You people have had a good set-to today then!'

'Arre, if it hadn't been for the thanedar coming . . .' When Sulaiman realized he was actually speaking to the thanedar he fell silent, and again began to watch Ali Akbar's antics.

'It's a sin to conceal a crime too . . .' The thanedar's voice came to his ears from what seemed a long way away. '. . . I will certainly register a case, but no prosecution witness will be convicted . . .'

'Eh, Sulaiman Miyan!' called out Phunnan Miyan.

Sulaiman headed towards Phunnan without a word to the Thakur Sahib. When the Thakur Sahib turned to say something to Samiuddin Khan he found that he'd disappeared. Looking around in confusion, what did he see but Samiuddin Khan in his full belt and uniform standing with Phunnan Miyan's son-in-law Mohammad Husain and beating his chest in matam. This Samiuddin Khan was a Shia from Jaunpur. When he heard the sound of matam he couldn't control himself. The Thakur Sahib smiled. He was very fond of this subordinate of his.

Samiuddin Khan was a very strict Muslim. He was about as orthodox a Muslim as the Thakur Sahib himself was an orthodox Hindu.

Samiuddin would not eat anything touched by a Hindu, and Thakur Sahib would not lay his hands on anything touched by a Muslim. But Samiuddin Khan was an intelligent man. Since he had joined, the police station's income had greatly increased, and that's why he'd become as close to the thanedar as the hair in his nose. When the Thakur Sahib was alone with Samiuddin he'd really make fun of Islam—'Is this any religion? The Prophet Sahib himself married a full nine times, and all other Muslims have to make do with four.' Samiuddin would immediately answer back, 'Thakur Sahib, it all depends on the strength of a man's back. If that respected gentleman had wasted his strength in misdoings like us, he wouldn't have married more than four times. Arre, sahib, now it's become difficult enough to control one wife. But still we can't have do with one wife to five brothers like your heroes did in the *Mahabharat*. What sort of arrangement was that? My family's better off than that. We've a total of seven wives among four brothers. I've got one, my eldest brother three, and the one next to him three. The youngest's still unmarried. He'll have two or three wives at least. And that's on top of the earnings on the side . . .'

But there weren't many chances for this kind of carefree chat. The inhabitants of the Qasimabad circle were confirmed ruffians. There was either a murder taking place, or a dacoity. They were either fighting with lathis, or pointing guns. All the small zamindars were gangsters. They staged dacoities at night and fought legal cases during the day. Sometimes they evicted people, and at other times they put them in possession of land. There were fifty to a hundred crisp ones to be made from these changes of possession. The land was fertile. The moment the rains fell the black earth began to produce gold. That's why the people had so much time, and then they really were rough. The law was all very well in its place, but if anything was done to demean anyone's dignity the police station would be razed to the ground. Only some seven or eight years previously the then thanedar, Sharifuddin, had abused Phunnan Miyan, and Phunnan Miyan had raided the police station at night with some two hundred men and abducted the thanedar. Then they'd tied him to a tree and pulled out every hair of his magnificent, curling moustache one by one. Sharifuddin left the police station the very next day. He was succeeded by one Shivdhanni Singh. Shivdhanni Singh was much talked about. To prevent the public from losing all fear of the police, the Superintendent Sahib especially ordered him to see that Phunnan Miyan was punished. Sharifuddin, you see, had been considered a dauntless officer and his moustache was famous far and wide. It was the moustache of the government of British India.

The government had drawn the conclusion that Phunnan Miyan was a Congress supporter. However, the case of the insult to Sharifuddin couldn't be pursued as publicizing the incident would have brought disgrace to the government. It was a matter of deep humiliation for a thanedar to have been abducted from his police station. So Shivdhanni Singh had to take it upon himself to straighten out Phunnan Miyan. Soon after he took up his post, on the night of the Diwali festival, he made his first raid.

As he always did on Diwali, Phunnan Miyan was gambling, and, as always, was sitting for good luck under an image of the goddess Lakshmi, which looked towards an image of the elephant-headed god Ganesh in the shop of Nainsukh, the liquor-seller opposite. This gambling was taking place in Barikhpur. When Shivdhanni Singh left Barikhpur after arresting the gamblers, he forgot that the road to the police station passed through the Bhar settlement. The result of this forgetfulness was that he and his three constables were surrounded. The Bhars set the offenders free. Shivdhanni Singh was stripped of his belt and uniform. When he began to plead and grovel, Phunnan Miyan took pity on him. He said, 'Spit and lick it up!'

When Shivdhanni had done as he was ordered, his belt and uniform were returned to him. That moment he began to suffer dreadfully from kidney pains, and the next day he had to take medical leave. He never came back to Gangauli. As he left he gave the constables ten rupees each so that they would never mention the incident. The constables may not have mentioned it to anyone, but the very next day the story spread through all the neighbouring villages. Then the Thakur Sahib was posted to Qasimabad police station. The Thakur Sahib had had his eye on Phunnan for two years, but Phunnan hadn't given him the chance to finger him. It was no easy task to lay hands on a man who could steal his neighbour's wife, and then still go to his house every day to smoke his huqqa.

This was an incident which occurred some twenty years before the Thakur Sahib came to Qasimabad, but every outgoing thanedar was certain to tell it to the one replacing him. The story went that Phunnan Miyan's neighbour Karamat Ali Khan, (who was the younger brother of Hakim Saiyid Ali Kabir's family retainer Ghulam Husain Khan), married Kulsum in Tajpur and brought her home. This Kulsum was disastrously beautiful. Phunnan Miyan saw her once and, the moment he saw her, fell in love with her heart and soul a thousand times over. When the wedding procession of the Hakim Sahib's younger brother, Deputy Collector Ali Hadi, set out for his bride's village on horse carts, elephants and assorted palanquins, and both Pattis were deserted, Phunnan Miyan went to the wall of Karamat Ali's house. Karamat Ali's mother had also left with the wedding procession but Kulsum had not because she was pregnant. Phunnan Miyan carried her off by force. When the wedding party returned there was complete uproar. A criminal case was registered. Phunnan Miyan was arrested, but he didn't produce Kulsum in court. The whole of Dakkhin Patti was behind him. He was convicted. He served his time and was released. But from the middle of the court case itself his courage had won Kulsum's heart. And when he was released she upped and came to his house with Karamat Ali's infant child in her lap. Then gradually Karamat Ali grew used to the disgrace of it all, and Phunnan Miyan went back to smoking the huqqa outside Karamat's door like he always had.

No, it was no joke laying hands on a courageous and unpredictable man.

That was why the Thakur Sahib wanted to consult Samiuddin Khan. His idea was that if the Uttar Patti men were reminded now of what had happened to Kulsum—who was still in Phunnan Miyan's home, and was the mother of ten of his children—perhaps the sight of Karamat Ali would persuade Hakim Ali Kabir to register a case of rioting against the men of Dakkhin Patti.

But Samiuddin Khan was beating his chest in mourning.

'The Hakim Sahib is calling for you,' a Chamar boy told the Thakur Sahib.

'Really.'

The moment the Thakur Sahib entered the Gate, the Hakim Sahib and Deputy Collector Ali Hadi bore down upon him, saying that if the Dakkhin Patti's procession didn't move on for a week, they would have to remain shut up in their home. They insisted that the Thakur Sahib should have the procession moved on or the tazias of Uttar

Patti would force a way through with their lathis.

With great difficulty the Thakur Sahib managed to calm them down and then put forward his scheme. The Hakim Sahib was delighted with it and said in chaste Urdu, 'If God wills it, then so shall it be. I swear by the Chote Hazrat* that on no account will there be any dearth of men to bear testimony.' He then returned to his mother tongue with the words, 'Eh, Ghulam Hasan, go and call Ubbad.'

'The Government has been dying to call Phunnan Miyan for a long time,' said the Thakur Sahib into Deputy Collector Ali Hadi's ear.

Hearing of the government's longing, Ali Hadi became impatient himself. He said, 'That *haramzada* was leading the men with the lathis.'

'But we're not going to let Abbu, Bashir or Wazir get away either,' fumed the Hakim Sahib.

'Those are influential people,' replied the Thakur Sahib. 'It won't be easy to get them convicted.'

But the Hakim Sahib was beside himself and Ali Hadi Miyan had great difficulty in controlling him. Then a report was lodged that as prayers were being said at Balli Sain's door, Phunnan Miyan, assisted by Sulaiman and Hammad Miyan, had attacked Balli Sain with their lathis. 'When we, as a third party,' read the report, 'came to rescue Balli Sain, the accused also attacked us and Gaya Ahir, Raghunath Bhar and his two sons, Dina and Ghansham, attacked us with lathis . . .' Among the accused were all the most important men from the Ahir, Bhar and Chamar parts of the village. These were the men whose support made it possible for the writ of a small zamindar like Phunnan Miyan to run in Gangauli. Among those who signed this report, apart from Maulvi Bedar, Mir Ubbad Husain and Husain Ali Miyan, were several Bhars and Ahirs.

The news of this report travelled to Abbu Miyan at once, because Shakra Chamar was also present at the Hakim Sahib's gate, and he was Abbu Miyan's spy in the Hakim Sahib's camp.

Abbu Miyan immediately consigned the manuscript of the marsia he was reciting to his pocket. Consultations began. The procession moved on. All those named in the report were ordered to go into hiding. It was decided that they had been admitted to hospitals in Ghazipur and Muhammadabad, and that Phunnan Miyan had gone to visit his daughter Razia in Calcutta . . . .

---

* Hazrat Abbas, younger brother of Imam Husain.

That evening the Thakur Sahib stretched out the arm of the law to arrest the offenders. The poor man even went all the way to the Great Gate of Dakkhin Patti to find them. The moment he explained his mission, Abbu Miyan sent men to the homes of all the accused.

'But I think you've been misinformed,' he said after his men had left. 'Not one of them has been in Gangauli today. Phunnan might have gone to Calcutta, isn't that so Mohammad?' he asked Phunnan Miyan's son-in-law.

'Yes.'

'And Sulaiman has been in the Sadar Hospital for six days,' said Wazir Miyan. 'He's in great discomfort you know, Uncle.'

'Yes, bhai, what to say, the weather's been that odd,' remarked Abbu Miyan, 'I went to see him in hospital. The minute the civil surgeon saw me the poor man leapt to his feet and said, "Saiyid Sahib, why have you gone to such trouble?" I said, "Brother Mathur Sahib, I had to. He's very close to me." So then he said, "I've never seen a case like this one. He had practically recovered. By God, I still can't work out what's happened to him."'

'And poor Hammad met disaster on the night of the full moon. He slipped as he was coming down from his room and broke his right arm. He's lying in hospital in Muhammadabad,' said Shabbu Miyan, wiping a bead of mucous from the tip of his nose with his right hand. Actually Komila Chamar's elder brother Gharua had broken Hammad's arm with his lathi.

The Brahmin Matadin was sent for. He made sharbat for the Thakur Sahib. The paanwallah brought him betel-nut. And Bechu Halwai, the sweetmaker, himself came with fresh lakhte made with jaggery in a leaf cup. The Thakur Sahib realized that since the offenders had escaped his hand, there was no harm in taking refreshment. He looked over to Samiuddin Khan. He was sitting on the end of the bed on which Fussu Miyan was lying and smoking a huqqa. In one hand Samiuddin held a cup of tea and in the other a saucer. He was blowing on the tea he'd poured into the saucer. The Thakur Sahib clenched his teeth, thinking his subordinate was just about to noisily suck in his tea. The slurping noise he made put the Thakur Sahib's teeth on edge, and made his whole body shudder. He had already reprimanded Samiuddin for this, but why should Samiuddin change when nobody else did? Accordingly, the Thakur Sahib sat holding his glass of sharbat and waiting for the first slurp. By chance Samiuddin looked up and saw him in this condition. He drank his tea without slurping and then took a beedi from his pocket.

'Finish your damn tea, Khan Sahib!' said the Thakur Sahib irritably.

Everyone was startled at his tone as Samiuddin's cup was already empty and turned upside down on the saucer, near the leg of the bed, around and up and down which a troop of ants was busy at its work. The Thakur Sahib felt slightly foolish, and at that point the men sent off by Abbu Miyan returned.

'What happened?' asked the Thakur Sahib.

But the men were not servants of the British government. They didn't reply to the Thakur Sahib, but addressed their zamindars. They all bore the same news. No offender was present in the village.

'Mir Sahib!' the Thakur Sahib addressed Abbu Miyan, 'Maulvi Bedar's condition is serious . . . this business can't be hushed up. I'll produce two thousand witnesses to testify that those men were present at the scene of the incident.'

'By all means please do so, Thakur Sahib!' responded Abbu Miyan, 'How can we prevent you from producing false witnesses?'

'Just you be so kind as to bear in mind,' said Wazir Miyan, 'that there should be no dependent of Uttar Patti among them. I am saying this because I shall be conducting the cross-examination myself.'

The Thakur Sahib realized that this was a challenge. He knew several police officers who had been cross-examined by Wazir Miyan. He began to sweat profusely, but then collected himself and replied, 'Lawyer Sahib, our job is merely to put the case before the court.' He stood up. 'May I take leave now? You must be tired out after a long day too.'

The Thakur Sahib set off for Qasimabad, where Gulabi Jan was waiting for him. The moment he left, Abbu Miyan stood up.

'Let's go then, bhai, for the majlis of the Evening of the Bereaved.'

No one asked him what sense there was in attending a majlis in Uttar Patti after such a fierce fight, because imambaras belong to Imam Husain, and majlises are his as well. In Uttar Patti too no one considered a postponement.

After night prayers the congregation gathered in the imambara in Uttar Patti. Still enraged, Hakim Ali Kabir went and sat in Gore Miyan's place. But he felt strange there. So after exclaiming, 'Lord God Almighty, All-Controlling!' he returned to his own seat. The majlis of the Evening of the Bereaved is held in darkness and it was his duty as the eldest to order the removal of the lights. Everyone was watching him and wondering why he didn't give the order. The Hakim Sahib himself was amazed at his silence. The fact was that the empty places on the floor of the imambara were troubling him. He was just thinking of sending Alim-va the barber, to Dakkhin Patti, when the whole crowd from Dakkhin Patti, complete with numerous children, followed Abbu Miyan through the Gate.

They took their places without a word to anyone. The children of both Pattis sat behind the pulpit and began to chatter. The Hakim Sahib ordered the lights to be removed, but now the question arose of who would lead the majlis.

Until then, Dakkhin Patti's Shabbu Miyan had always done so. After the lights had been removed the Hakim Sahib's voice would echo through the darkness, 'Eh, Shabbu-bhai, recite!'

But could he say that now? This question troubled him. There was complete silence in the darkened imambara.

Then, as always, his voice boomed out, 'Eh, Shabbu-bhai, recite!'

Warp and Weft

Thanedar Thakur Harnarayan Prasad Singh had had no interest in seeing Hammad Miyan and the others convicted. He had only been interested in Phunnan Miyan. Even for Phunnan he had no personal enmity, and he also knew that the fault for the fight lay with the men of Uttar Patti, but he still made out a one-sided case. He had been successful in his efforts and, along with Phunnan Miyan, several men from Dakkhin Patti had been sentenced. In reward, four favourable entries were added to the thanedar's service record.

Immediately after the judgement he had his horse saddled and rode off towards Qasimabad.

Gulabi Jan was waiting for him in his quarters. Seeing the Thakur Sahib's face flushed with joy, she was certain that he'd succeeded in having the Miyans convicted. She at once sent Constable Dukhiram to call Havildar Samiuddin Khan. Apart from him there was no other Muslim in the Qasimabad police station. Gulabi Jan gave Samiuddin twenty annas and sent him to Hashmatullah the sweet-maker's shop so that a leaf-cupful of sweets could be offered to celebrate the Thakur Sahib's victory. Gulabi Jan had also promised to offer cloths to cover the tombs of the saints Fullan Shah and Chandan the Martyr—in short she had done everything she possibly could for his victory.

Not that Gulabi Jan had any personal enmity towards Phunnan Miyan either. She had only ever seen him once—in the nautch at the wedding of the young daughter of the great Khan Sahib of Bahadurganj.

Phunnan Miyan had been a member of the bridal party. Together with Gulabi Jan, the groom's side had also called the celebrated courtesan, Chanda Bai of Ghazipur.

In those days Chanda Bai's fame had spread far and wide. She made a grand entry, full of airs and graces. Gulabi Jan was already present in the gathering. Chanda Bai looked at her with contempt and sat down to one side. A short distance from these two sat a charming-looking young Chamar lad, his lips stained red with betel juice, smiling at both of them with contempt, exchanging swift repartee full of sexual innuendo with the men sitting around him, and moving his body like a flirtatious woman. Seeing his seductive behaviour, Gulabi felt that all the training she'd had in attracting men had been wasted. The eyes of the men sitting around that boy were burning with desire. The light of that fire was also rising in the eyes of the men sitting near Gulabi Jan and Chanda Bai, but the flames were not so high.

This was about six or seven years ago. In those days Gulabi Jan was about fourteen or fifteen, and although deflowered was still fresh. Phunnan Miyan was sitting in the place of respect, that is next to the bridegroom. Gulabi Jan performed first. She was familiar with the evening gatherings of the Miyans. After singing one or two folk-songs, she began a ghazal of the poet Ghalib. Chanda Bai listened with her head to one side, marking time with her right foot, but that boy kept joking with the circle around him, laughing and making others laugh. The voices of those near him grew increasingly moist with desire until Gulabi Jan felt that she and her voice might drown in this flood of lust. She glanced at her music master out of the corner of her eye, but what could the poor man do? The boy was one of the area's well-known dancers. And it was also well-known that the zamindar of Salimpur, Ashrafullah Khan 'Ashraf' kept this boy as carefully as he kept the handwritten volume of his grandfather's poetry, and that in his spare time he ruffled the pages of both back and forth. He had also forbidden the boy to dance, except on very special occasions. But obviously, even on these special occasions the boy could not sit next to him.

As the Khan Sahib of Bahadurganj was a close friend of the Khan Sahib of Salimpur, the boy had come to dance at his daughter's wedding celebrations, but was sitting at a distance from his master, teasing and being teased. Ashrafullah Khan was reclining on a bolster and talking to Phunnan Miyan about his grandfather's poetry. The lad was sitting on the floor-covering some way off. The Khan Sahib could hear the obscene sentences which were buzzing around that sweet, sugar-like boy like flies and repeatedly trying to land on him. The poor Khan Sahib could do nothing at that point, but he resolved to have the boy cut up and thrown into the jungle that stood between Bahadurganj and Salimpur as soon as the celebrations were over. He was unable to bear the humiliation.

The Khan Sahib's wrath was always on the tip of his nose, but he was a respectable man and couldn't display his anger everywhere. Of course it was well-known that he had been enraged when he heard that Gulabi Jan had put on her nose-ring* and the Thakur Sahib of Nasirabad had decided to be the first man to take it off. He said, 'How dare he think he can have her first? My late brother took the nose-ring from her elder sister, my late father took the nose-ring from her aunt and so I am going to be the one to take the nose-ring off her!'

As a result, Gulabi Jan's price went up. To deflower her the Khan Sahib gave one hundred-and-one rupees in cash and five bighas of revenue-tax-free land. The Thakur Sahib of Nasirabad lost hope. But fate so decreed that it should rain, and how on earth could Gulabi Jan come to the Khan Sahib in a downpour? First the Khan Sahib kept shifting in his seat, then he began to pace around the room. When the rain showed no sign of stopping he took out his double-barrelled shotgun and went outside. He banged two shots into the heavens. He was angry with God. Then God Himself perhaps decided to stop the rain. Gulabi Jan arrived and was robbed of her nose-ring. From that day on it became famous that even God was afraid of the Khan Sahib.

Now who wouldn't be scared of such a man? But that dancing lad was proud of his charms. He could say that the Khan Sahib of Salimpur had massaged his feet, rubbed his eyes against the soles of them and wept. If he ever smiled at anyone, the Khan Sahib would burn with jealousy. And the Khan Sahib gave him licence to taunt and abuse him like a woman. He would say time and time again, 'Torment me today, my cruel one! When I die, then you will miss me.'

And perhaps this was the reason that this lad was joking with people and laughing loudly, without a care for the Khan Sahib. In the middle of this noise Gulabi Jan was repeatedly picking up a note and repeatedly losing the thread of the melody. Chanda Bai was smiling contemptuously and whispering to her music master.

Phunnan Miyan suddenly stood up and headed for the Chamar lad. The boy looked at him and smiled lewdly. Phunnan Miyan gave him such a slap that it drowned out Gulabi Jan's music master's drum. There was pindrop silence. Phunnan Miyan returned to his place. The eyes of everyone present were fixed on the Khan Sahib.

'She was singing a ghazal of Ghalib, bhai,' said Phunnan Miyan. He was illiterate, but he knew by heart innumerable verses of the poets Momin, Ghalib and Dagh, just as he knew the marsias of Anis and Wahid. He couldn't bear any insult to Ghalib.

The Khan Sahib understood, and so he said nothing. Afterwards the thanedar, Shivdhanni Singh, and the zamindars of Uttar Patti

---

* The deflowering of a courtesan was known as 'removing the nose-ring'.

tried with all their might to persuade the Khan Sahib that Phunnan Miyan's slap had not fallen on the face of that Chamar lad, but on his own face. However the Khan Sahib refused to listen to them.

They say that hot compresses were put on the boy's face for weeks afterwards but the swelling didn't go down. When he recovered the Khan Sahib sentenced him to a terrible punishment. He sent him into a secluded apartment on some errand. In that apartment Sirajuddin Khan the wrestler and eight of his men were lying in wait. The next day the Khan Sahib threw the boy and all his community out of the village and he was never seen anywhere in the area ever again . . . .

But Gulabi Jan heard this story afterwards like other people. On the day of the nautch all that happened was that the lad was stunned into silence. He had never imagined that an ordinary zamindar like Phunnan Miyan would raise a hand against him in such a gathering. The boy didn't know that Phunnan Miyan may have been a small zamindar but he was also a Saiyid, and that the Khan Sahib's forefathers had come to the area with Saiyid Nuruddin the Martyr. Neither Phunnan Miyan nor Ashrafullah Khan 'Ashraf', disciple of the poet 'Nuh' Narvi, had forgotten this fact. So there was no need for Phunnan Miyan to say anything more to the Khan Sahib than that Gulabi Jan had been singing a ghazal by Ghalib.

Gulabi Jan sang for a long time. Then she danced a piece from the Kathak repertoire and sat down, and Chanda Bai, like a creeper of ishq-e-pechan, rose twining towards and up the string of the breeze, laden with the delicate little pink flowers of her own smiles. First she performed Kathak and Gulabi Jan had to admit that Chanda Bai did dance better than her. Then she began to sing the raag, *Darbari*. Her voice was good as well—as soft as the flowers of the harsingar and as far carrying as the scent of champa blossoms. But she was still singing the slow opening passages when Phunnan Miyan said, 'It would have been better to see that dancing boy dance than listen to this.'

When Chanda Bai fell silent in confusion, Phunnan Miyan looked at her and said, 'Your voice is good . . . but immature.'

Phunnan Miyan was no music expert. He didn't even know how many notes there were in a scale. But the tradition of soz-chanting had made him familiar with the way the voice should rise and fall, and keep to the required rhythm. He didn't know A from B, but he knew off by heart all the marsias in the bundles of manuscripts of Abbu Miyan and Husain Ali Miyan. As a result, when he sat to the side of the marsia-reciter to offer accompaniment, all he had to do was ask the reciter which marsia he was going to render. When he walked in the procession on the tenth of Moharram, he took a paper tazia in return for prayers granted to the tombs of each of his ancestors. Accompanied by Mumtaz and Phuttu, he recited marsias to the sleeping spirits in those tombs. As soz-reciters always carried the text of the poem they were reciting, he was always sure to carry a manuscript too, whether it was the same one he was reciting or not. One year Phuttu fell ill, and he made Shammu accompany him. Shammu began to read from the text. Phunnan Miyan dug him in the ribs and said, 'Don't read what's written. Recite what I'm reciting.'

More than learning it was matter of tradition. That's why Phunnan interrupted Chanda Bai, the celebrated courtesan of Ghazipur, and she swallowed the insult. The wealthy weavers, Banias and vegetable-sellers of Ghazipur didn't have the ability to distinguish between a mature and immature voice—their interest lay solely in the maturity of Chanda Bai's body.

In her heart of hearts Gulabi Jan was very pleased to see Chanda Bai disgraced like this, and she quietly offered a thousand prayers for Phunnan Miyan's well-being.

However, when she had become as permanent as dye in Thanedar Thakur Harnarayan Prasad's dhoti, she was compelled to wish Phunnan ill. She was doing very well with the Thakur Sahib, and didn't want Phunnan Miyan becoming a bone in the kabab. Therefore she had to pray for his conviction. She didn't keep these prayers a secret from the Thakur Sahib. They satisfied his male pride. When he went to the town and stayed in the police club, he would say to the other thanedars, 'Bhai, I suppose whores must be unfaithful . . . but my whore Gulabi Jan is the image of fidelity. Every Thursday she wards off the evil eye from me with an offering of black dal. And she has prayed for Phunnan Miyan to be convicted.'

It was ironic that the mother of Phunnan Miyan's children, Kulsum, had had prayers said at the very same shrines for Phunnan Miyan to be acquitted without a stain on his character. She had also prayed at the platform of the Great Tazia, yet when Phunnan Miyan was convicted her faith was not shattered. She thought that God was perhaps testing her, or perhaps that Damri-bo hadn't said the prayers at the shrines correctly, or that perhaps Fullan Shah and Chandan the Martyr were not in their graves when she did, and afterwards the angels of mercy had forgotten to tell them that Gangauli's Kulsum-bi had sent Damri-bo to make prayers on her behalf.

Kulsum didn't know that either Fullan Shah or Chandan the Martyr had granted the prayers of Gulabi Jan. Even if she had her heart may still not have been embittered. Prayers constantly clash with one another. Someone or other's prayers are always granted and that's why no typhoon blows through the world of faith. Those whose wishes remain unfulfilled are quietened with the thought that perhaps God is testing them.

When Samiuddin Khan arrived at the shop of Hashmatullah the sweet-maker he happened to find Hakim Ali Kabir's old family servant, Ghulam Husain Khan there as well. After greeting one another, Ghulam Husain Khan asked, 'Who are you buying sweets for, Khan Sahib?'

'For Gulabi Jan.'

Ghulam Husain smiled. 'What's this, bhai? Have you started eating Gulabi Jan's sweets along with the thanedar?'

'No I have not!' retorted Samiuddin Khan, 'The bitch had prayed for Phunnan Miyan's conviction. Now she's going to offer sweets, and have cloth-covers put on the tombs of Fullan Shah and Chandan the Martyr.'

In his heart Samiuddin Khan was not happy with the court's decision. It wasn't that he felt any sympathy for the people of Dakkhin Patti, but he did think that in this quarrel the mischief had been done by the men of Uttar Patti. This thought didn't prevent him from preparing false evidence, that was a completely different matter. Preparing false evidence was what he was paid a salary for.

'But what brings you here?' he asked.

'We're distributing five kinds of sweets today to celebrate their conviction. I've come to fetch them.'

Samiuddin went off to Qasimabad with Gulabi Jan's sweets. Ghulam Husain had his basket of sweets loaded on to the head of a labourer and sent him off to Gangauli. Then after smoking a pipe with Hashmatullah he set off too. He must have gone just about two miles when he was stopped by a fellow servant of the Hakim Sahib who was coming from the direction of Gangauli.

After the Hakim Sahib had despatched Ghulam Husain Khan to Bahadurganj it occurred to him that it was also essential to send sweets to the thanedar of Qasimabad, Thakur Harnarayan Prasad. He therefore instructed the servant to run off and buy some sweets from a Hindu sweet-maker and tell Ghulam Husain Khan to take them over to Qasimabad.

Ghulam Husain Khan turned back immediately. Since this wasn't a job for a Muslim sweet-maker, he had Jhinguri fill a small basket of fresh, hot imartis. He then had it loaded on to the head of another labourer and set off for Qasimabad.

The Thakur Sahib was extremely pleased with the basket of fresh, juicy, bright golden imartis. When Jhinguri had heard that the sweets were intended for the thanedar, he had sprinkled rosewater over them after arranging them, so that the basket became pleasantly scented.

Ghulam Husain Khan had seen the world. Consequently he brought up the fact that the sweets had come from Jhinguri's shop. Praising Jhinguri's style, he also mentioned that Jhinguri had arranged the sweets in the basket with his own hands—that was to say that neither he nor any other Muslim had laid a finger on them, and the Thakur Sahib could consume them without the least hesitation. The Thakur Sahib took his meaning. He himself was particular to call out for Samiuddin to make arrangements for Ghulam Husain Khan to be given food and drink. Ghulam Husain Khan's pony was especially sent to the Thakur Sahib's stable. His black stallion glanced at the pony with contempt and began to beat the ground with its hoof.

After bathing at the police station's well, Ghulam Husain Khan stretched himself out to dry on a charpoy beneath the neem tree opposite Samiuddin Khan's quarters. Samiuddin Khan joined him. His son Badruddin, Badrua for short, filled and brought a huqqa. The gold and silver thread which had been wrapped around the bamboo stem of the huqqa had come away and only the dust-absorbing red cloth beneath was left. Samiuddin kept drawing on the huqqa until the tobacco was properly lit, then he took hold of the huqqa where the mouthpiece joined the stem and turned it towards Ghulam Husain Khan.

The smell of the Jaunpuri scented tobacco mixture was making Ghulam Husain Khan long for a smoke. Samiuddin kept a little scented tobacco for special occasions, otherwise he made do with a cheap tobacco for everyday use.

Ghulam Husain Khan took two or three small puffs and then drew deeply on the huqqa. When he began to feel the effects of the tobacco, he started thinking what a good thing it would be if Samiuddin's eldest son Moinuddin were to be engaged to his niece Badrun. By the grace of God, the boy had been recruited into the army—last year he'd come to Gangauli during Moharram and Samiuddin had brought him to the majlis of the fifth day at the Barka Gate. He was strong, healthy and well-built and had surpassed even Phunnan Miyan's son-in-law Mohammad Husain at reciting nauhas. Having this match in mind, Ghulam Husain Khan had spent a whole year feeding Samiuddin all kinds of food and telling him that they were specially made by Badrun, and that after her marriage his kitchen would be completely desolate. It wasn't that Badrun couldn't cook—where could you ever find a home where the daughters couldn't cook—but as a measure of precaution he didn't give Samiuddin anything she had made. For example he had gram halva made by Fussu Miyan's mother, Rabban-bi, who was famous far and wide for this sweet. Forgetting the quarrels between the Uttar and Dakkhin Pattis, Ghulam Husain Khan would go to Fussu Miyan's house, call out from the doorway and, when Rabban-bi came to the door, would say, 'I need a little halva for Badrun's in-laws.' Now where it was the matter concerning a daughter of the community, how could there be any question of inter-Patti rivalry? And if there was rivalry then it was with the Hakim Sahib and Ali Hadi and Husain Ali, not with Ghulam Husain Khan who was just their servant. And so Rabban-bi would make the halva. It goes without saying that she didn't take any money from him for it. And anyway what did it cost! A pound or two of gram, a pound or two of ghee, a pound or two of sugar and some raisins. Beyond that there was the skill of the cook's hand, and who could ask money for that? . . . Forgetting all the fights and disgrace he'd gone through, Ghulam Husain Khan went to Phunnan Miyan's illegal wife, Kulsum for dahi-bade. Unlike Fussu Miyan's house, Phunnan Miyan's did not run with rivers of milk and ghee, but Kulsum too never took any money for the food she made. First it would have gone against the tradition of the zamindars, second Badrun was in any case her brother-in-law's daughter, and third Ghulam Husain Khan was the Hakim Sahib's servant and how can you refuse the request of a servant? So he used to get dahi-bade from Kulsum. Badrun was herself famous throughout the area for her sweet lentil-cakes. In short the whole of Gangauli was engaged in keeping Badrun's future father-in-law happy. Everyone took care of him.

Neither was Samiuddin Khan anyone's fool. He guessed the reason behind all this and so one day he sent a woman bangle-seller to the house of Ghulam Husain Khan. She returned with the news that, by the mercy of God, the girl's features were good and she was capable. This news had just arrived when Ghulam Husain Khan presented a bedcover embroidered by Sarwari, the lawyer Bashir Miyan's daughter, together with two pillow cases, to Samiuddin Khan, saying that Badrun had especially done the embroidery with her own hands. It was fortunate that Samiuddin's wife Bajjan was a simple village woman or the whole game would have been up. It was machine embroidery. Anyway, Samiuddin Khan too was pleased with this match. Ghulam Husain Khan had no standing of his own, but the Hakim Sahib's gate was large, and then Ali Hadi was a deputy collector. He could use his influence to have Moinuddin put in charge of a police station. After all Moinuddin had studied English up to the tenth standard. Bearing all this in mind, Samiuddin had decided to send out proposals for the match to all concerned from the thanedar to the Hakim Sahib on the ninth day of the month of *Rabi-ul-avval.** But Ghulam Husain Khan didn't know what was going on in Samiuddin's heart, and so, as he was puffing the Jaunpuri tobacco, he was also wondering why, when Samiuddin had sent the bangle-seller to see the girl, he didn't send a proposal. His wife and sister-in-law had shown the bangle-seller great hospitality. They immediately realized that she hadn't come to sell bangles (because first it made no sense to leave Qasimabad to trade in Gangauli, and even if she had done so, she should have gone either to the Barka Gate or the Gate beneath the pakkar tree. When she ignored these two great gates and the houses of the rich traders and headed straight for Ghulam Husain Khan's home, it was absolutely clear that she'd come on some other mission. And for what purpose could a bangle-seller from Qasimabad have come?) Therefore Badrun's mother found some excuse to make Badrun walk across in front of the bangle-seller several times, both fast and slowly, so that she might see that Badrun was not lame. Badrun swiftly threaded her mother's needle, so that the bangle-seller would know that her eyes not only looked large, they could see well too. And when a sale had been made (the Pathan lady, Ghulam Husain Khan's wife, also bought eight annas' worth of her wares), and the bangle-seller was about to leave, she had also slipped her a rupee to spend on paan.

In fact the real reason for Ghulam Husain Khan's worry was that his Pathan blood was somewhat less than pure. Upwards of four generations ago, the blood of his family had mixed with the blood of the Uttar Patti's Gate beneath the pakkar tree. Everyone in the surrounding countryside knew this. That was why no proposal had come to his family from the neighbourhood for four generations and their daughters had to find husbands from outside the district. If the in-laws found out after the match took place, they endured the blow to their honour in silence. Only the in-laws of Ghulam Husain Khan's aunt had refused to swallow the insult. Her husband had divorced her at once, and the poor girl had returned to her father's house. From

---

* The name of a month of the Muslim calendar. Shias observe mourning for two-and-a-half months. For them this period ends on the eighth of Rabi-ul-avval. No joyful task is undertaken during this period.

that divorce until now the question of arranging the marriage of any girl of the family had not arisen. Badrun was the first girl since then to have survived to adulthood. Therefore Ghulam Husain Khan's heart was trembling and therefore he had investigations made into Samiuddin's bloodline. He was considerably relieved to find that in Samiuddin's blood there was more than a drop from the non-Pathan Qazi locality.

But if only the proposal would come. They after all were the girl's family, they couldn't go barefaced and demand a proposal.

That day too Ghulam Husain Khan couldn't raise the matter, he just sat beneath the neem tree smoking the huqqa, listening to Samiuddin's old and new stories about the police force, recounting tales of the rivalry between the Saiyids of the two Pattis, thinking about Badrun's marriage, and eating paans prepared by Samiuddin's wife and served in cylinders of cigarette paper. Suhrab-va (Samiuddin's third son) would give the khasdan, full of paans, to Samiuddin. Samiuddin would lift the lid and offer the tray of paans to Ghulam Husain Khan. He would put a paan in his mouth, holding it in one cheek. Samiuddin would open the tobacco container inside the lid of the khasdan, and the fragrance of the glistening black tobacco of the manufacturers, Ahmad Husain and Dildar Husain, spread over the charpoy like a coverlet. Ghulam Husain Khan would put a pinch of tobacco into his mouth and rub his fingers clean on the edge of the charpoy. Then Samiuddin would take a paan and start another new story.

When the day began to draw to a close, and the Thakur Sahib, wearing only a dhoti wrapped round his waist, had ensconced himself in an armchair in the shade of a banyan tree and was having his legs massaged, Ghulam Husain approached him for permission to leave. Thanedar Thakur Harnarayan Prasad granted him permission and said, 'Please be so kind as to tell the Mir Sahib that there was no need to send the sweets. I am just happy that today the disgrace of Komila's hanging has been washed away.'

'What are you saying, Thakur Sahib?' replied Ghulam Husain Khan, 'The law is the law. The English Collector Sahib could never commit an injustice . . . he must have been a murderer.'

The Thakur Sahib smiled at this, as both he and Ghulam Husain Khan knew that it wasn't the Collector Sahib Bahadur who had sentenced Komila but the Indian judge, Girdhari Lal Srivastava, followed by Justice Khanna of the High Court. But the state belonged to the British. The Collector was British and so, without asking the

White Sahib first, Srivastava Sahib and Khanna Sahib couldn't have had the courage to sentence to death any man of Deputy Collector Saiyid Ali Hadi Zaidi, BA, LLB with a judgement which even the Privy Council would have upheld.

Ghulam Husain Khan also knew that the Thakur Sahib had fabricated evidence against Komila after being bribed by the Collector Sahib's gardener. But this was obviously not something that could be said. Hakim Ali Kabir and Deputy Collector Ali Hadi were acquainted with this fact as well. But they too said nothing to the Thakur Sahib as it would have been demeaning to have done so. The men of Dakkhin Patti might spread the news if they liked. Still, the Hakim Sahib had yet to forgive the Thakur Sahib and so it didn't please him to find Ghulam Husain Khan spending so much time at the police station. His son, Saddan, was going back again on the eleventh. It was already the fourth and still no preparations had been made. Even though Saddan told him, 'You're getting worried for no reason. For one thing there are still seven days before I leave, and for another what preparations have to be made anyway?'

'What would you know!' With this, the Hakim Sahib began to feel a patient's pulse. Then, without stirring, he called out to Ubbad Miyan, who was sitting in the imambara selecting a marsia for the evening's majlis. 'Eh, Ubbad, make up this prescription.' Then he turned to face the patient. First he cursed his sister, and then said, 'If you go and eat anything dirty from anywhere and peg it, there's nothing I can do to save you.'

He wrote the names of some medicines on a piece of paper and threw it in the patient's face. The patient went off to the dispensary. The Hakim Sahib went and sat by the tank and began to wash the hand with which he had been forced to touch the hand of an infidel—and that too a low caste one. And then he remembered that Saddan had said some thing to him, and took off from where he had stopped. 'These here Congresswallahs have turned the brains of the tenants downright bad, bhai. God knows what this Gandhi . . . .' Here the Hakim spent some time wishing ills on Gandhi and Nehru, '. . . now this *saala* Balram-va is the Collector Sahib's gardener and that Parusaram-va is a Congress supporter . . . so how on earth do you get the land revenue out of the bastards . . . and then you turn round and say, "You're getting worried for no reason" . . .'

He was about to go on, but then he saw the leading lights of the opposing Patti, Wazir Miyan, Aggu Miyan and Fussu Miyan coming through the gate. The Hakim Sahib had heard that the caravan from

Ghazipur had arrived that morning but was surprised to see members of it at his door.

'Adaab!' they all said together, bending low in greeting.

'May you live long!' replied the Hakim Sahib, 'When did you come?'

'We arrived this morning,' said Wazir Miyan. 'Where's Hadi-bhai?'

'In his audience hall,' replied the Hakim Sahib, gesturing towards the Deputy Collector's room. But hearing their voices, the Deputy Sahib came out himself to meet them. The children of the house brought the news to the women's quarters. Instantly anxious, the women rushed to the doorways of the zenana and began to peer from behind the curtains, fearing that, heaven forbid, something might happen. They even forgot the conventions in their anxiety.

Aggu, Wazir and Fussu went with the Deputy Sahib into his room. The Hakim Sahib recalled that his hand was not yet clean, and went down to wash at the tank, the water of which had been stagnant for months if not years and was stretched out in deep slumber wrapped in a thick sheet of algae.

But his mind was still on Ghulam Husain Khan.

Meanwhile, not far from Qasimabad, Ghulam Husain Khan was wondering why he shouldn't go alog to a majlis of the Khan Sahib of Salimpur. With this in mind he twisted his pony's reins round, and turned in the direction of the path which itself twisted a thousand times around field boundaries on its way to Salimpur.

The Khan Sahib used to say that his majlises began after midday prayers, and finished after afternoon prayers. So Ghulam Husain Khan thought that he could attend the Salimpur majlis and still get back in time for the evening majlis at his own gate. However, the majlis of Ashrafullah Khan 'Ashraf' did not even begin until after evening prayers. Still, once he got there, Ghulam Husain Khan couldn't leave without attending the majlis. Before evening prayers he did pluck up the courage to ask the Khan Sahib, 'Your honour's majlises generally begin after midday prayers?'

'I announce the majlis then,' replied Ashrafullah Khan, 'because if I announced it after evening prayers no one would turn up until morning prayers. In this village there is no other Muslim apart from me. People from Bhadi, Chavanpur, Gusainpur, Sunskri come over here once they've held their own majlises. The poor souls walk three or four miles to get here, that's why they can only assemble here by the time of evening prayers.'

After hearing this, Ghulam Husain went back to smoking the huqqa. After all, what else could he do? The tobacco mixture had been prepared in the Khan Sahib's house, and the pineapple flavour was very pleasant. But too much sourness had been added in the attempt to make it bitter-sweet, and so he pushed the huqqa to one side and took a bundle of Rafi Ahmad beedis from his pocket. First he offered the bundle before the Khan Sahib of Salimpur. When the Khan Sahib gave him permission to smoke, he lit a beedi and began to relate the story of the fight between the Pattis during the procession of the tenth of Moharram. It was no secret that the Khan Sahib of Salimpur was a friend of the Dakkhin Patti, and so he said, 'Ghulam Husain, I wasn't there or I would have driven a donkey-pulled plough through Uttar Patti.'

'You would have found the earth of Uttar Patti a little hard, sarkar!' replied Ghulam Husain Khan.

Ashrafullah Khan 'Ashraf' laughed so loudly that the man cutting fodder opposite suddenly stopped. The Khan Sahib said, 'You're a Pathan, aren't you! You can't stand any comment or criticism.'

'No, it's not that, sarkar!'

'Bhai, you know that I'm totally opposed to the custom of tazias. But my forefathers have always used them, and so every year I commit the sin so that their souls are not disturbed, and so that people won't say that the Khan Sahib's cut back because he had to give away free food. I hold ten majlises to stop people's tongues wagging. I have to distribute two thousand rotis every day. Up to my late father's time we used to have ten cauldrons of khichra cooked every year on the tenth. I've added two more and say, "Here, eat, you bastards, and understand that I care for my forefathers' good name more than my faith." I'm an old friend of the Dakkhin Pattiwallahs, and, bhai, I'm a Pathan. With us there's no other measure but friendship and enmity.

'Cross-bred antics are for the Sheikhs and low castes. Phunnan Miyan is a friend from long back. He used to have his poems corrected by my late father. I too learned wrestling, swordfighting and lathi-work from his late father and Amjad Husain, and so, Ghulam Husain, lathis will clash again, and the one who doesn't desert the field will be a man . . .'

As they spoke, the time came for evening prayers. Ashrafullah Khan went to the mosque opposite and said his namaz. The members of his family stood in a line to say their prayers. Ali Husain came to the front to lead them. He was a weaver, but the eldest among them, and so despite the fact that he was a servant in the house, he led the prayers because of his white beard, and the arrogant Pathans of that family had to stand behind him five times a day with their hands lifted in prayer.

Ghulam Husain Khan was a Shia, and so he performed his ablutions and said his prayers right there in the courtyard, kneeling on a wooden bed. The Hindus and Muslims of the area all began gathering there. The broad, long courtyard was packed full. Ali Husain recited the *Shahadatnama*—a very ordinary poem relating the story of the martyrdom of Imam Husain—but in the majlises of the fort of Salimpur the events of Karbala were of little importance. The important thing was the distribution of the roghani roti. Accordingly, uproar broke out over the sharing out of the rich bread, which continued for the next three hours. Then Ghulam Husain Khan was given a portion of the bread for the entire household of the Hakim Sahib and he mounted his pony and rode off towards Gangauli. Two labourers were carrying on their heads baskets of rotis for the families of both the gates of Dakkhin Patti. They set off beside Ghulam Husain Khan's pony too.

The new moon had already set. It was a pitch black night, so Ghulam Husain Khan considered it a blessing to have the two Chamars with him. He loosened the reins of his pony, dismounted and began to walk along.

Now it was entirely a coincidence that a group from the Bhar settlement on their way to 'a job' happened to pass by. Jhinguriya recognized Ghulam Husain Khan. All his sinews stiffened. The fact was that he was Phunnan Miyan's favourite disciple, and after him was going to become the chief of the wrestling-pit. He challenged Ghulam Husain Khan, 'Where do you think you're going, Khan Sahib, after getting our Miyan sent down?'

Ghulam Husain Khan recognized his voice. He was completely silent. It wasn't that he was a coward, but he was an old man and Jhinguriya's lathi was famous throughout the area.

The biggest problem was that he was alone and Jhinguriya had a gang with him. In fact the Khan Sahib did have two men with him, but they were both labourers from Salimpur, and what Jhinguriya said was true—Phunnan Miyan had been convicted on his evidence.

The Chamars from Salimpur both stood in silence as Jhinguriya's companions surrounded Ghulam Husain Khan. But when Jhinguriya grabbed the reins of his pony, they both put their baskets of bread on the ground and held their lathis at the ready.

'Eh, Jhinguriya bhaiyaa, don't do this!'

Jhinguriya tried to persuade them not to interfere as they were from Salimpur, and the Khan Sahib of Salimpur was Phunnan Miyan's loyal friend, but neither of them agreed. They argued that for the time being Ghulam Husain Khan was with them, and if they let him be beaten their Khan Sahib would have them flayed alive. And besides it was cowardly for ten stout-bodied men to pick on one elderly, weak one.

'That's enough . . . we're telling you, Jhinguriya bhaiyaa, if you know what's good for you, let go of those reins.'

But Jhinguriya was intending no good. He didn't let loose the reins but he did let loose his hand. The sleek twenty-two-or twenty-three-year-old lad stumbled. Then Jhinguriya and his companions went for them with lathis. The rotis were scattered, trampled, ground into the earth. The baskets were broken. Ghulam Husain Khan's pony galloped off riderless towards Gangauli. He began to defend himself with the three-foot-long stick he was carrying. The two Chamars from Salimpur were fighting very courageously, but still Jhinguriya was Phunnan Miyan's disciple, he wasn't attacking them but just warding off their blows and telling them, 'You people have gone mad. Once I grab hold of you you'll start twittering like birds.'

Jhinguriya's gang had surrounded Ghulam Husain Khan. Jhinguriya knew that he couldn't be hurt until he'd run out of breath. His gang also realized this, and so they were tiring him out like an angler does a hooked rohu fish. After half-an-hour's fierce fighting the Chamars from Salimpur began to lose courage. The Khan Sahib too was becoming disheartened. He was out of breath from the speed of the moves. In short, all three were on the point of defeat when a party of Thakurs appeared.

The Chaudhuri of Barikhpur had seen and recognized Ghulam Husain's pony as it galloped back to Gangauli. The Chaudhuri was the Hakim Sahib's friend. He immediately realized that Ghulam Husain Khan had been attacked, and so he came running with his seven sons and eighteen nephews. The Chaudhuri and Phunnan Miyan were disciples of the same guru. That is to say that the Chaudhuri too had learnt the art of lathi-work from Phunnan Miyan's father. For this reason Jhinguriya could not in any case raise a hand against him. The moment he caught sight of the Chaudhuri he stopped fighting. The Chaudhuri said, 'You've turned out a real man, Jhinguriya! Found a poor old man all on his own and suddenly become a hero—just try hitting out at me . . . let's see what Phunnan has taught you.'

The two Chamars and Ghulam Husain Khan began to wipe the blood from their bodies. When Jhinguriya didn't reply, the Chaudhuri challenged him again. Then Jhinguriya had to say, 'It's just a matter of two years, Thakur Sahib! Just wait for our Miyan to be released . . . then we'll see . . .'

He went off with his men without waiting for the Chaudhuri Sahib's reply. If the Chaudhuri had wanted he could have had them surrounded but he thought it beneath his dignity to lay a finger on any disciple of Phunnan Miyan. He thought that if he were to attack Jhinguriya now he wouldn't be able to look Phunnan Miyan in the eye again, and so he let them go.

Ghulam Husain Khan went with the Chaudhuri to Barikhpur. Both the Chamars returned to Salimpur. They immediately sent word of what had happened to the Khan Sahib's residence. The Khan Sahib had not yet gone to bed and came out immediately. He was incensed to see his labourers wounded. 'Who is the hero born around here who has dared to lay hands on men of mine?' he asked.

One of the Chamars told him the whole story, not omitting to say that Jhinguriya had avoided hitting them as far as possible. The Khan Sahib gave them a reward of a rupee each from his special pocket, ordered that they be given an eighth of a seer of tobacco each and went inside.

Once inside he lay down again and two female servants began massaging his head. On the bed next to him under a mosquito net his begum, Khairunnisa or Khairun for short, was feeding her infant child. Her wheaten-coloured breasts were visible, but she was in a deep slumber. When the infant cried, she put its mouth to her breast in her sleep. The child stopped crying. For a short while she kept patting it with her right hand, and then her hand too fell to one side under the weight of sleep.

Khairun was five years older than the Khan Sahib and very ugly indeed. But she was his first cousin and his father's brother's only child. To prevent the division of the family property Ashrafullah Khan's father had consulted Khairunnisa's father and Ashrafullah had been married to Khairun. He didn't object to the match as his interests lay elsewhere, but he had not displayed any meanness in his role as husband either. Khairun had borne eighteen children one after another. The youngest son was just over a year old and the eldest daughter thirty-six, she herself being, by the grace of God, the mother of eight children. Her only son was about twenty-two and in the army. He was named Khairuddin after his grandmother, but was known as Khairu. He was a very good-natured boy, attractive of face and limb. The Khan Sahib loved him dearly, even more so since he'd joined the army. And so he was worried because when he went to Ghazipur to hear the decision in the case between the two Pattis, the first news that Bashir Miyan gave him was that Germany had attacked. Europe was already finished. Now the government of Britain was engaged in battle, and the government of Britain's position was weak . . . Khairuddin was a lieutenant in the army of the British government, and so the Khan Sahib had good reason to be worried. His grandson was the only boy in the whole family, the Khan Sahib himself having had seventeen daughters and one son who was so young that he couldn't be counted. He was still lying sucking his mother's milk. He had already had ten of his daughters married who had given him a total of thirty-four granddaughters and one grandson. Therefore it was obvious that Khairuddin, or Khairu, was the star in everyone's eyes. All his aunts wanted him to be married to one of their daughters, and there had already been several altercations between them on this issue.

The Khan Sahib of Salimpur was against taking up employment. Did any son of a man of noble blood ever become an employee! One of the reasons he looked askance at the men from Uttar Patti was that for years the Saiyids there had been taking up employment. Whether you are a Deputy Collector or a Collector—a job is a job. But the men from Khairu's paternal grandfather's family had maintained a centuries' long tradition of military service. They said that Pathans should stay in the army, because they knew how to play with nothing save death. This was the reason Ashrafullah Khan couldn't oppose Khairu joining the service. His daughter's in-laws were great zamindars, but they regarded it as a matter of pride to add a soldier's salary to their income. Guldar Khan Tokhi, Khairu's great-grandfather, was one of those who'd been through the Revolt of 1857. Guldar Khan Tokhi's eldest son, Hijab Ali Khan Tokhi, became a colonel in the British Indian army before he died, and his grandson, Ghaznafar Ali Khan Tokhi, gave his life in the war of 1914 and won a Victoria Cross.

When he heard about the war, Guldar Khan Tokhi stroked his white, curling moustache, and stuck out his chest. But the same news upset Ashrafullah Khan 'Ashraf'. Khairu was staying with him. When he heard the news he was pleased too and said, 'Grandfather! Now I'll take a Victoria Cross!'

Ashrafullah Khan walked out without replying. But yes, Khairu's grandmother did try to persuade him otherwise. For a while Khairu discussed the matter with her but then he grew bored and went outside as well. The Pathan woman, his grandmother, immediately got up, went to the mosque, and promised to spend a whole night awake praying, if only he were kept safe. When this did not provide her sufficient consolation, careful that no one should see her, she went up to the tazia which still remained to be decorated, glanced around and then said, 'Oh, Imam Sahib! Don't tell Khairu's grandfather that I came.to ask something from you. But stop Khairu going to war . . . next year I'll give you a new cloth!'

Having secretly made her prayer at the tazia she ran home. But she was still not fully at ease. She gave her old servant Nasiba one-and-a-quarter rupees and sent her to the hermitage of a Hindu holy man to offer sweets there.

But Ashrafullah Khan couldn't make such prayers because he was a Wahabite and for him they were sinful. But he did add a prayer at the evening namaz, 'Lord Almighty! If Khairu returns from the war alive, next Baqra 'Id I will have three cows slaughtered and send two poor Muslims on Haj . . . and give up tazias at Moharram!'

He was lying there wondering if his promises had been substantial enough, and the two girls kept pressing his feet, unaware of his thoughts and fed up with the massage because one of them was to meet Khairu in the deserted mosque behind the house, and the other was her confidante and had already met Khairu in the very same mosque the night before.

Salt

Sulaiman was like a spreading tree, under whose shade Bacchaniya had no opportunity to grow. But when Sulaiman went to jail for a year, she suddenly blossomed. She had inherited the charm of her mother along with the fair complexion of her father. She didn't use kajal, but her eyes were such that they looked as if the moment she got up in the morning Jhangtiya-bo very lovingly lined them with collyrium. She had also grown to a good height. Her waist was so tiny that one's hand automatically longed to hold it, and the curves of her broad hips beneath it resembled the fresh, new earthenware bowls used for making offerings. Her dupatta could not contain her breasts. Her lips were fresh and full like pieces of dasehri mango, and the voice which came from them dripped with sweet juice. And her coil of hair was so large that Naima-bi's head looked small in comparison.

Naima-bi was very jealous of her, and Jhangtiya-bo had begun to be afraid of her beauty. There was no girl to compare with her in the entire village. She was so gorgeous that even the body of Maulvi Saiyid Bedar Husain Zaidi Sadrulfazil, began to itch for her, and he began to think that there was no reason to ruin one's life by worrying over ancestry. One day he told the Hakim Sahib, 'I'm getting old, bhai Kabir, and the house is so empty it's frightening.'

The Hakim Sahib gave him the proper reply, 'I'm telling you, get married.'

'I'm also thinking the same thing. How do you think Sulaiman's daughter Bacchaniya would do?'

The Hakim Sahib was not pleased with this match, because he didn't want any part of the property of Uttar Patti to pass into the hands of Dakkhin Patti. But when, after wasting his whole life, Maulvi Bedar Husain Sadrulfazil began to think about marriage, the Hakim Sahib couldn't be so insensitive as to bring up matters of inter-Patti rivalry.

The fact was that Maulvi Bedar had been living alone in his house for some twenty years. Forty years previously his sister-in-law had died. He had one niece, Asiya. She had been married to one Ali Akbar of Naunahra. Only a few days after her marriage the Maulvi's elder brother also passed away, and he was left quite alone in the house.

The Maulana didn't marry because his father was a maulana to the nth degree. He was also a great student of geneology. His investigation of the family trees of all the Saiyid families of India led him to discover that not one had the spotless ancestry essential in a wife for his second son. As a result, Maulvi Bedar Husain Sadrulfazil was left to live life alone in his beautiful house. He managed to get through the days but the nights bothered him. His cowherd and two servants slept in the outer part of the house, but he kept up the custom of sleeping in the zenana or women's quarters, which was a zenana only in name. Deep into the night, the curves of the archways there seemed to mock him.

The zenana of the Maulana's house was of a very fair size, as it had never occurred to the founder of the family who built it that a time would ever come when there would be such a dearth of Saiyids that Bedar couldn't find a wife. And Maulvi Bedar passed his days in the deserted zenana, a prisoner of loneliness. After Gaya Ahir hit him with his lathi the pain of that loneliness had increased to such an extent that Dulariya the sweeperess began to melt before the heat of his glances. But when he didn't do anything except look at her, even she began to loathe him. Dulariya's husband, Mahabir, was twelve years younger than her. She was a shapely girl of twenty-two or -three. Since she had come to Gangauli after her marriage four years previously, she had laid the foundations if not for thousands or hundreds, then certainly for dozens of minor rivalries. Wherever she carried her basket, thousands of eyes opened like buds on the branches of the lanes of Gangauli, doorways became arms opening to embrace her and pulses began to beat fast in bedsteads. Some traders and weavers had even gone to the extent of having lavatories built in their houses so that she would come to clean them. Otherwise all the women, apart from the Saiyid ladies, formed a group and went off to the fields with their lotas, sat down together and complained about their mothers-in-law, or whispered about their dreams and the things lacking in their lives. Occasionally a girl would slip some distance away in the dark and a new, unspoken story began.

Only the feet of the Saiyid ladies were not bound in the chains of such stories, because they didn't go to the fields but to dirty, stinking drop lavatories in their homes. But that didn't mean that no stories fell to their lot . . . such and such's wife had fallen for her nephew . . . such and such a woman had become the kept woman of her brother-in-law . . . . However there was no doubt that due thought was given to status in such stories. That is to say that no one's wife ever fell for a trader or a weaver.

No story ever fell to the lot of Maulvi Bedar Husain Sadrulfazil for the simple reason that there wasn't a single woman in his zenana. Because Asiya's mother had died when she was a child, she had been brought up by her maternal grandparents. No woman has any excuse to visit a house in which there are no women, and so even when Dulariya did come there, besides staring, poor Maulvi Bedar didn't know what else to do.

That's why Dulariya began to loathe him and somehow or other transferred her cleaning duties to her widowed sister-in-law who was an extremely ugly woman about fifty years old.

The Maulvi Sahib was dreadfully depressed until one day he noticed Bacchaniya peeping out of Phunnan Miyan's home, watching some boys playing kabaddi just opposite. It was obvious that the Maulvi couldn't turn and stare at her, and so he walked on. But for several days afterwards the thought of Bacchaniya crawled over his body like red ants.

The Hakim Sahib was unaware of these details but he hadn't been born yesterday. When he saw that this fifty-year-old maulana was talking about a non-Saiyid, bastard girl, he realized that there was something black in the dal, and didn't answer the Maulvi immediately.

'Bhai, she's a bastard!' he finally said, managing to raise one objection.

'What fault is that of hers?' replied the Maulvi.

'It's not her fault but what will folk say?'

'Nowhere is it written that it's sinful to marry a bastard . . . after all I didn't waste my time at the Sultan-ul-Madaris in Lucknow. I studied the Qor'an and the Hadith.'

'So isn't it written anywhere not to marry bastards? . . .'

The Hakim Sahib knew that it wasn't written anywhere but he still asked because, whether it was written or not, it certainly didn't look good for a son of a Saiyid to marry a bastard girl, and that too a bastard girl whose mother was an untouchable, and on top of that an untouchable from Dakkhin Patti! Since the Hakim Sahib couldn't actually say all this, Maulvi Bedar Husain Sadrulfazil managed to gain his consent. It was settled that the proposal should be mooted with Sulaiman's maternal grandparents. Accordingly, when the Hakim

Sahib went to Para to attend the majlis of Rajjab Ali Miyan, he took the opportunity to mention to Sulaiman's uncle, Ali Murtaza Khan, that it didn't matter if Bedar Miyan was on the old side. He owned such a large property, and then there was no possibility of getting a boy from a good family for Bacchaniya. Accordingly, when Ali Murtaza Khan went one Friday to visit Sulaiman in the district jail he mentioned this proposal. Sulaiman said he could do nothing without consulting his brothers, that is Wazir Miyan and Bashir Miyan, and so Ali Murtaza Khan mentioned the matter to Wazir Miyan. Wazir Miyan said he had no objection provided the sum of fourteen thousand in the currency of the realm was offered as mehar. Ali Murtaza Khan came back to Gangauli and repeated his reply to Maulvi Bedar who, despite opposition from the Hakim Sahib, agreed to the condition. It was settled that the marriage should take place in a few months' time after Sulaiman was released from jail. There was no way this matter was going to be kept quiet; it flew off to Asiya's in-laws' roof and began to shout out its presence. The moment she heard it Asiya sent for her palanquin.

The palanquin came to a halt inside the Great Gate of Dakkhin Patti. There was no one there besides Naima-bi and her daughter-in-law Kubara. It was clear that a pure Saiyid lady like Asiya couldn't be the guest of women of such low blood and so she walked through Aggu Miyan's empty house to Fussu Miyan's.

It was morning. Rabban-bi was sitting in the sun drinking tea from an enamel cup. And Fussu's wife Sakina-bi was sitting quietly in the kitchen thinking of her mother's house while her eldest daughter, Salma, was rolling out chapattis.

'Phuphu, adaab!' said Asiya, greeting Rabban-bi.

'May you live long!' replied Rabban-bi, putting her cup down on the bed, 'Eh, girl, you've altogether forgotten your own family.'

'What can I say, Phuphu, someone or the other is always ill. And then who do I come to here?' said Asiya. 'The only one I have here is Chacha, and I hear he's marrying Bacchaniya.'

'*Naooj*!' said Rabban-bi, putting a finger to her nose, 'Has he gone senile or what?'

'And what else do you expect the poor man to do, all alone in the house?' interrupted Sakina from the kitchen. 'Now the poor soul is old, his body and heart must both be aching.'

'I'm not joking, *Bhauj*,' said Asiya, 'if he really does marry her what will the community say?'

'And will the community massage his body . . . make sure he gets his meals? And if you're so worried about him why don't you take him to live with you?' Sakina went on, so to speak, to separate the milk from the water, 'Why don't you admit that you're thinking that if he gets married and has a son, you'll lose the zamindari.'

Asiya began to seethe.

'Let those that have a zamindari worry about it.'

'Eh, sister, I'll have you know I don't come from any pauper's family . . .'

Sakina thought that the distance between them was too great and so she left the kitchen and entered the courtyard. But Rabban-bi interrupted. It had been a long time since a typhoon had stirred the becalmed life of Gangauli. Fighting and fisticuffs didn't count; they went on all the time. If there are men they will eye women and keep mistresses. After all, Gore Miyan kept Yaqoot and Zaheer Miyan kept Pukhraj. Phunnan Miyan had carried off Karamat Ali's wife, but as yet no Saiyid had ever sent a formal proposal of marriage to the child of a kept woman. Something like this only happened once in several generations. Accordingly, Rabban-bi scolded her daughter-in-law, 'Eh, Dulhan, this is nothing to fight over.'

Sakina returned to the kitchen, inwardly cursing Rabban-bi. She hated her mother-in-law with a vengeance. The old woman just refused to die. She kept all the house keys with her and Sakina had to beg for every pice. She had to wear whatever Rabban-bi gave her to wear; she had to eat whatever Rabban-bi chose that she should. Fussu kept quiet because the property he depended on to allow him to act like an aristocrat, smoke his huqqa and curse his tenants, actually belonged to his mother. And in any case Fussu was not too happy with Sakina. He had no complaint about her ugliness—it wasn't at all necessary for a wife to be beautiful, prostitutes were the ones who had to be good-looking. Fussu Miyan's complaint was that she'd given birth to seven girls on the trot, and he was dying for a son. After each new daughter was born Fussu Miyan went and prayed at shrines for a son, and then, tightly grasping charms and amulets, began trying afresh until Sakina started to get morning sickness and to crave food from fresh, new earthenware pots. Fussu Miyan anxiously endured the time until another girl was born.

Then his face fell and his mother raised her hands again and again to berate Sakina.

'She's producing one girl after another—but there's no money in the house to pay for their weddings.'

Sakina endured these insults. If she had been alone she would have cried and cursed herself. She too had said innumerable prayers at saints' shrines for a son. Unbeknownst to Rabban-bi she had sold her ear ornaments to have forty days of prayers recited. This led to the birth of her third daughter and Sakina losing her faith in prayers and amulets. She had even given up saying namaz, and then two more daughters came her way and she reached the conclusion that whether a baby was a girl or a boy was not a matter that concerned the Lord. This thought again brought peace to her spiritual life and she was mentally prepared for her eighth daughter. She went back to the kitchen and began to watch Salma, who was making chapattis, and to consider that there was only a difference of seven or eight days between her daughter's birth and Bacchaniya's.

This was a fact also known to Rabban and Fussu. Fussu was also worried about a match for her, and Rabban-bi had put her mind to it. But these days you were scared to accept proposals. May the Lord destroy these wretched Germans for starting the war! The army was recruiting. A recruitment office had even opened in Gangauli by Hakim Ali Kabir's gate. Men were queuing to sign up.

'This is the time to hold your daughters close to you. Eh, sister, who knows who'll be off to the front next?'

Rabban had said this to Aggu Miyan's wife when she brought a proposal for Salma's hand for her son, Qasim. And her remark cut Aggu Miyan's wife to the quick, because Qasim was her first-born son, and had joined the army against Aggu's express wishes.

'Well then, sister, don't get her married!' she had replied, 'Keep your beloved granddaughters put away safely!'

And Rabban-bi really had done so. Several times she had quarrelled with Sakina on this matter, as Sakina believed that it was a parent's job to arrange her daughters' marriage. As for the future, only the girls knew, or their fate did, no one else. 'Will this war ever end or not? Everything's been set on fire. My shoulders have begun to ache with wearing a dupatta of sackcloth. You can't get sugar to make offerings at shrines. Last year I had to fulfil my promise for prayers granted and I couldn't get the cloth to do it. And there's just no sign of this war finishing.'

'You're saying this to me?' said Rabban-bi. 'So do you still want to get your child married even though you'll have to send her to her in-law's house dressed in sackcloth?'

Sakina had no answer to this. But when she looked at Salma she worried because, whether times were bad or not, people's tongues were still a yard long. It would be appalling if anyone said anything against her daughters. Therefore she took her anger against her mother-in-law out on Salma, as if she, not the Germans, had started the war. When she set foot in the kitchen the unfortunate Salma was making dolls out of dough for her youngest sister. That was enough to make Sakina's blood boil.

'So you're making chapattis, are you?'

'She was crying!'

'Just you hold your tongue,' said Sakina, absolutely beside herself, 'you'll need a maund of flour to make toys for the litter of girls in this house!'

Salma began to make round balls of dough for chapattis, but Sakina wasn't happy in the kitchen and so she went out again, sat down on a child's cot and began to make paan. She had decided to take no part in Rabban and Asiya's conversation.

'And is he likely to listen to us?' Asiya was saying, 'Why don't you try persuading your Jhangtiya-bo to see reason.'

'Are you listening, Dulhan?' Rabban addressed Sakina, 'Do you think she'll take notice of me?'

As luck would have it, at that precise moment Jhangtiya-bo arrived. She greeted Rabban, Sakina and Asiya and sat down on the ground. She was in need of four annas. She was always borrowing small amounts from Rabban-bi. Once she had absolutely no money to have the bracelets made at Moharram to keep her promise for prayers granted,* and so she left a thick, silver bangle with Rabban and took cash from her. Rabban-bi possessed a small wooden chest, in which she kept her pen-box, an almanac of religious festivals and auspicious and inauspicious dates, a copy of five important chapters of the Qor'an and a Shia religious book—in short, all essential things. And in a bag of red cloth she kept money. Rabban-bi didn't know how to read and write. But her husband, Mir Athar Husain, had taught her a simple coded script in which she could write letters and keep a diary.

'What is it, *re*?'

'I just thought I'd come to give my salaams to you.'

'Would you like paan?' asked Sakina.

Jhangtiya-bo gave no reply. She just held out her hand and Sakina dropped a betel-leaf on to her open palm, which unfolded as it landed. Jhangtiya raised her hand to her forehead in thanks and ate the paan

---

* If prayers are granted then these bracelets and anklets are worn in rememberence of Sajjad, Imam Husain's ailing son, who was taken from Karbala in shackles.

while Sakina busied herself making one for Asiya.

'Now things have come to such a pass, *re*, that your Bacchaniya is going to get married to my uncle!' remarked Asiya, going into the attack. Jhangtiya-bo glanced at Rabban. There was a terrible sparkle in her eye.

'Eh, sister, why are you getting angry for no reason, we didn't go to him with a proposal,' said Jhangtiya-bo.

She had a point. Asiya was momentarily floored, but then she flexed her claws and went after Jhangtiya-bo again. Jhangtiya-bo listened in silence, but when Asiya had dealt with Ali Akbar and Bacchaniya and began to curse Sulaiman, the chains of her eternal, submissive silence snapped.

'Eh, Bibi, that's enough!' she said. 'If you say any more, there'll be no end to it. And anyway I don't eat your bread. May the Lord preserve Wazir Miyan and Bashir Miyan. Why should I be scared of you?'

Asiya was flabbergasted that Jhangtiya-bo could answer her back on equal terms.

'Will that whore be married into our house!'

'She is not a whore. In fact we live in a zenana. And if I say anything, you'll run yelping and whining back to Naunahra.'

Rabban thought that matters were going out of control. In her heart of hearts she was pleased that Jhangtiya-bo was giving such a good account of herself. But she didn't want any fingers pointing at her in the community for sitting quietly and watching while an untouchable woman cut Asiya's nose off with her shoe.

'That's quite enough for now!' she scolded Jhangtiya-bo, 'Don't go too far!'

At this, Jhangtiya-bo went off railing against herself. In fact for the first time in her life she was angry with Sulaiman. Had she raised her champa-flower-like Bacchaniya just for Maulvi Bedar? What was there to him now? But in the end Sulaiman had agreed. As she thought this the reins of her anger turned towards Sulaiman and for the first time she regretted that Sulaiman had carried her off. If he hadn't Bacchaniya would have been married to the Chaudhuri's son.

Bacchaniya had no idea of the storm that was raging. She was lying on a bed, murmuring a nauha because it was almost Moharram. She was very happy because she knew that when Sarwari-ba'ji heard this tune she would be thrilled. Then from Sarwari-ba'ji her thoughts turned to Masoom and she began to wonder whether he would bring her that pearl necklace. She didn't know whether or not he'd remember the promise he'd made her six years ago. She liked Masoom the best of all Bashir Miyan's and Wazir Miyan's sons, although he spared her the least time. The boys from this family seemed to her in any case to be a little different from other boys. They were so absorbed in their own circle that perhaps they hadn't even noticed that Bacchaniya had grown up. Moonis was always busy tearing open the legs of Sarwari-ba'ji's dolls and being beaten by his mother, and Masoom did nothing besides roam around following Moonis. Five years of illness and confinement to bed had left him lame. But how on earth could you call him lame! He ran from one tiled house to another and Barki Bibi (Akbari Bibi—Bashir Miyan's mother) ran after him, scolding him and praying for his welfare. As she recalled this scene Bacchaniya smiled. How was she to know that Jhangtiya-bo would return that moment.

'Smiling are you!' said Jhangtiya-bo landing her two slaps, 'I'll cut off your lips and throw them out, do you understand?'

Bacchaniya didn't understand the reason for this outburst in the least.

'It couldn't happen that you'd sweep the house and make it clean! Here you are just lazing around. Your father will be back soon. Just let him come back. I'll make sure you have such a tanning that the smile will be wiped off your face.'

Bacchaniya endured the beating in silence. When she was small she used to run away, but blossoming youth and beauty are heavy weights to carry. Jhangtiya-bo beat her for a long time. When she was tired out, she began to cry and curse herself instead. She began to long for Ali Akbar, whom Wazir Miyan had taken with him to Ghazipur, and who played there with Wazir Miyan's motherless children and did odd bits of work about the house.

Seeing Naima-bi approaching she dried her tears. Naima-bi was a weaver woman but in front of Jhangtiya-bo she pretended to be a real Saiyid lady, and took revenge on Jhangtiya-bo for the contempt with which she was herself treated by the other Saiyid ladies. In any case she was superior to Jhangtiya-bo first because she was a weaver and not an untouchable, and second because Hammad's father had not just put her in his house, they had been married by Maulvi Dildar, Maulvi Bedar's father, in a regular fashion. Jhangtiya-bo's son could never be a 'Khan', but her son, Hammad, was a real Saiyid. That's the reason she did not regret at all that her son was in jail. She could have cut her head off for the sake of her Lord, Imam Husain. Like other Shia women she too longed to have been at Karbala so that she could have sacrificed her son for the Lord.

'Just you grind this dal!' said Naima-bi, holding out a small basket of channa dal to Jhangtiya-bo. 'I'm thinking I'll make a little channa halva, God knows what Hammad is getting to eat over there.'

Jhangtiya-bo took the basket. Naima-bi went back to her apartment and Jhangtiya-bo began to think what she said was true—what on earth must Ali Akbar's father be getting to eat in jail? Sulaiman's father had served a term for digging through the mud walls of village houses to steal. He knew what jail food was like—chapattis made of dust, dal full of stones. Sulaiman must have shrivelled like a dry stick. A wave of such pain stirred in her heart that she lost her composure. Her big, deep black eyes again filled with tears because she couldn't cook anything for Sulaiman. First she didn't know how to cook the sort of food made in the Saiyids' houses, and second it would have made no difference if she had. Sulaiman would not touch any food she made.

'Why don't you cook something, *re*?' she asked Bacchaniya, because Bacchaniya did know how to cook all the things which were made in Rabban-bi's and Abbu Miyan's houses and in the Barka Gate. But as she said this, she remembered that she had originally gone to Rabban-bi's to borrow four annas.

'Just go up to Rabban-bi's and bring me back four annas,' she said to Bacchaniya and then began to grind the dal.

Bacchaniya never hesitated to go to Rabban-bi's house because she very much liked the smile of Safir-va, or Safir Muhammad, who had been brought up there. Perhaps Safir-va knew this because the moment he saw Bacchaniya he started smiling. One day he had held her hand in the zenana corridor running at the back of Rabban-bi and Aggu Miyan's houses. It had so happened that there was some important majlis being held. Rabban-bi, Sakina and Salma—in short, the whole household—were out at the Barka Gate. Bacchaniya was husking rice and so she had been left behind on her own. When she'd finished her task and set out for the majlis she had met Safir-va coming from the direction of Aggu Miyan's house. His body was very beautiful. Phunnan Miyan thought that he would bring as much glory to the name of his wrestling-pit as Jhinguriya had. Already he could throw a wrestler one-and-a-half times his size up in the air like a ball. So how could Bacchaniya resist him? She had been unprepared for whatever happened. Every limb began to ache. This was about four months previously. Since then Safir-va's smiles had been full of meaning. He began to come to Jhangtiya-bo's house whether he had an excuse to or not. His visits became so frequent that one day Naima-bi said to her daughter-in-law, 'Just you wait and see, Dulhan, that Jhangtiya-bo will run off with Safir-va one of these days.'

Jhangtiya-bo didn't run off, but when Bacchaniya reached the corridor on her way to borrow four annas she ran into Safir-va again. He caught hold of her hand. As always, Bacchaniya felt a thrill going through her body. Safir-va dragged her into Aggu Miyan's deserted zenana. She told him a thousand times that she was on her way to Rabban-bi's on an important errand, but he didn't listen. 'D'you know you're being married off to Maulvi Bedar?' In reply Bacchaniya told Safir-va something that made every one of his hairs stand on end. A new sparkle came into his small, sparkling eyes. His chest became even broader and his glance fixed on Bacchaniya's body. She blushed. And to Safir-va this shy little Bacchaniya was even more beautiful than the Bacchaniya he had held four months ago in the adjoining zenana corridor.

'Does your mother know?' he asked.

'No!'

'But this can't be hidden. And now we can't stay here. Come with me, let's run away to Calcutta.'

But Bacchaniya was not prepared to run away. All Safir-va's persuasion came to nothing. He lost patience with her and went off. Bacchaniya was left alone in Aggu Miyan's wide, empty zenana.

Running an errand to Rabban-bi's house, Hammad Miyan's wife Kubara saw Bacchaniya sitting there quietly. Afterwards when all the fuss started she said that she should have suspected something then, but that day she sensed nothing at all.

'What are you doing here?'

'Nothing.'

Bacchaniya had forgotten that she was on her way to Rabban-bi's to borrow four annas and so she went back home. Kubara went to Rabban-bi's. Rabban-bi was sitting down on a bed having some snacks with Asiya. The smell of savoury bread fried in ghee and fried eggs came to the door to invite Kubara in. After greeting Asiya, Kubara sat down on one end of the bed. Rabban-bi asked her if she'd like something to eat, but she refused. Salma began to make a paan for her.

'I heard that Ba'ji was here so I thought I'd come to pay my respects,' said Kubara.

Then they began to talk about how everything was going to rack and ruin. Nothing was available. And was it a sign of the Almighty's wrath or not that wheat was now four seers to the rupee! You had to get a permit to buy a shroud, and to get a permit you had to bribe someone. These were all things that Rabban-bi, Sakina and Kubara knew too. But Asiya revealed an astonishing fact.

'Parusaram-va, Sukhram-va Chamar's son, was wearing a khadi cap and going round making such speeches that Maulvi Ibne Hasan didn't know what to do!'

'May God strike down those *matimile* Congressmen for giving the untouchables ideas above their station!'

'They're not untouchables any more . . . they're Harijans . . . they've stopped eating the meat of animals that are found dead and about a month ago a group of Chamars led by Parusaram-va attacked the Brahmins' well and drew water from it.'

At this Rabban-bi's single eye opened wide in amazement. In her opinion this was all the fault of the Germans. Otherwise Chamars could never have had the courage to do that. It was also her opinion that all the finest Dacca cotton was being sent to the front.

Her only problems were that she couldn't get fine fabric for her dupatta, and it was difficult to get sugar for tea. On the last Shab-e-Barat* she had had to make an offering of halva made with poor quality sugar. For the whole year she was in a quandry—God alone knew if the souls of the dead had accepted the halva or not. When the year passed without any mishaps she was reassured. But the gossip about Parusaram-va was even sweeter than the halva.

'I hear that there's trouble brewing,' said Asiya, putting a paan into her mouth and holding it in one cheek.

'Eh, sister, what more trouble can there be? And how will Bedar Uncle get sugar to send for the marriage?'

The conversation once again came around to the matter of Maulvi Bedar's marriage.

'Drown Uncle, and drown the wedding too!' said Asiya. 'I'm not going to come to Gangauli again if I have to call that black-faced Bacchaniya "Chachi"!'

Soon afterwards Asiya left.

Maulvi Bedar knew that she had arrived in Gangauli. He was very upset. To speak to Hakim Ali Kabir about his marriage was one thing, and to face his niece was another. He was just trying to decide what to do when Asiya's palanquin arrived.

---

* The night of the fourteenth of the month Shuban when special prayers are said for the dead and food distributed to the poor.

'Adaab!'

'May you live long. When did you come?'

'Just now. I was wondering how you'd make the arrangements for your marriage all on your own. I'm telling you, Chacha,' she said, 'you've gone completely senile! Is Jhangtiya-bo now so acceptable that you're going to take a wedding procession to her door?'

'Islam recognizes no difference between the great and the small.'

'You're saying so, and so how can I disagree?' she replied, 'But our forefathers weren't mad to discriminate between them. Your own father, my grandfather, was a scholar of Islam, was he not? It's not enough just to quote Islam . . . the world also counts for something, does it not?'

Maulvi Bedar knew that the world did count for a lot. If he'd just been a zamindar he could have kept whom he liked in his house. But he was a maulvi too. He knew that Wazir had laid the condition of a fourteen thousand rupees' mehar to the marriage simply to disgrace Uttar Patti, as Saiyid girls themselves were not married for a lesser consideration. But Bedar was in the hands of his emotions. He wanted to win Bacchaniya even at the cost of having to bear such disgrace.

'I'm not stopping the marriage—people here have started saying that I'm after your property. Do as you please, get married, not once but four times over. Who am I to stop you? But there's no way I'm going to call that daughter of Jhangtiya-bo "Chachi"!'

'But, beta . . . .'

'There's no need for you to try to talk me round.'

Asiya covered her face and began to cry. The sound of her weeping reached the zenana of Hakim Ali Kabir. His wife immediately called for her palanquin. Gradually all the women of Uttar Patti gathered in Maulvi Bedar's house. All their sympathies were with Asiya. They were all criticizing Maulvi Bedar. Several widows were inwardly grieving that they'd been passed over for Bacchaniya! Husain Ali Miyan's sister, Ummul Habiba, had been wearing white for around twenty years. She'd been widowed on the third day after her marriage. There were just three days between Asiya's wedding and her own. Now, by the grace of God, Asiya was the mother of six children. And Ummul Habiba was treated as an outcaste at weddings and marriages. Her shadow was not allowed to fall on the floor-covering of the feasts of Fatima. She couldn't touch bridal garments. Her hair even turned prematurely white from constantly listening to the songs sung at other girls' weddings. Husain Ali Miyan took very good care of her. But still a brother is just a brother. He couldn't give her a married life.

Neither did her sister-in-law trouble her. But when any of her daughters had their ear-piercing ceremony or any of her sons read their first words from the holy Qor'an, Ummul Habiba writhed in anguish. It's obvious that she couldn't cry on such an occasion. But when a feast of Fatima was held on the occasion of Husain Ali's eldest daughter, Asghari's marriage, and Ummul Habiba was asked to leave the place, she burst into tears and for the first time her sister-in-law spoke to her sharply.

'What sort of time is this to cry, Ummul!'

Ummul didn't take this to heart. The fact was that until then no one had ever told her what things a widow shouldn't do. Then gradually she became accustomed to her widowhood and gradually she also learnt its duties too.

But she was still troubled by one thought. As the Prophet of God had taken a widow to be his first wife, did this mean that by refusing to do so these noble-blooded men set themselves above him? But of whom could she ask this question? And now when even old Maulvi Bedar had thought of marriage, it was Bacchaniya who had attracted him.

Only one or two of the women observed purdah in front of Maulvi Bedar, and so he couldn't run away. The ones who did were sitting chattering continuously, their faces concealed behind their dupattas. The portent of their words was that it had been a waste of time educating Maulvi Bedar if he didn't even know that it could no way be right to marry the bastard child of an untouchable woman.

In short, the ladies of Uttar Patti were arrayed against him in battle formation. Foremost in the attack was Ummul Habiba.

'After all, family honour still counts for something!'

Maulvi Bedar was not deaf and so couldn't help overhearing these remarks. But he was obstinate and refused to accept defeat.

But he had weakened somewhat in his purpose. When some ladies from his niece's in-laws' family began to pressurize him he came to the boil and told Asiya, 'Beta, this house is yours, whenever you like you can come here and stay as long as you like. But you shouldn't interfere in the matters of your elders. I have never criticized your father-in-law for keeping a whore in Ghazipur and neither have I ever asked him to explain his relationship with her. And I'm not keeping a whore, I'm getting married.'

At this, Asiya wept a great deal and then called for her palanquin and set off for Naunahra. After she left the Maulvi's zenana again became deserted and the inhabitants of the Saiyid houses accepted that the match was impossible, but that the impossible was happening and there was nothing to be done about it. It was obvious that Bacchaniya wouldn't be allowed to sit with the ladies of the community. Whether the Maulvi Sahib married her according to *mutah* rites or in a regular wedding ceremony, the ladies of Gangauli would consider her no more than a kept woman, and now the Maulvi Sahib was prepared for this.

But Safir-va was not prepared for it. The day that Bacchaniya told him that she was carrying his child, he changed. His playfulness disappeared. He became preoccupied. If Rabban-bi or Sakina spoke to him, he looked startled. Fussu Miyan's little girls, who were very attached to him, began to complain. But what could he do? His entire attention was turned towards the baby taking form in Bacchaniya's stomach. What would it look like, what would it be called? Thinking this, Maulvi Bedar came to his mind. And he would ask himself whether his child would be born in the house of Maulvi Bedar. He'd heard from several people that it was easy to get work in a jute factory, but Bacchaniya wasn't willing to elope.

Two days before Sulaiman was due to be released from jail, Jhangtiya-bo noticed the change that was coming over her daughter. She was stunned, and then her blood began to boil. She caught hold of her by the hair, slapped her several times and said, '*Markinauni*! Who's given you this stomach? Tell me whose is it?'

Bacchaniya was amazed that her stomach could belong to anyone else. 'It's mine, who else's?'

'It's yours, is it?' Jhangtiya-bo slapped her two or three times more. 'How can I show my face to your father? What can I say to him, you *matimili*?'

Bacchaniya endured the beating in silence, and didn't tell Safir-va's name. But that night she lay pretending to sleep. Jhangtiya-bo, tired out with cursing her, had also fallen asleep. Then Bacchaniya got up and quietly walked past the zenana imambara into Aggu Miyan's house. She didn't once remember that the imambara was inhabited by jinn. Safir-va slept in Aggu Miyan's zenana. She softly shook his shoulder. Safir-va leapt up, sprang to the far side of the zenana, grabbed hold of his lathi and turned round. Then he saw Bacchaniya and laughed.

'You frightened me,' he said putting his lathi on the ground. 'Come, sit down.' He took her by the hand and sat her down on his bed. She began to cry. Safir-va knew the art of comforting small children when they cried, but didn't know how to comfort a weeping young woman.

Goodness knows what he said to her. Finally, bit by bit, Bacchaniya told him everything.

'So is that anything to be worried about? Let's leave for Calcutta.'

Bacchaniya agreed. Safir-va thought that if they left immediately for Yusufpur, they would be able to catch the early morning local passenger train.

In the morning when Rabban-bi opened her chest, the almanac and the other religious books were there. Everything was there except for one thing—the red cloth-bag in which she kept her money.

The news that Bacchaniya had run off with Safir-va spread like lightning.

Every hair on Maulvi Bedar's body seemed a tongue of lamentation and he felt his life had been destroyed. He was as humiliated as if his wedded wife had run off. Ummul once again grieved inwardly as she couldn't bear the elopement any more than the engagement. Amjad-va, the lad brought up by her grandmother, used to look at her and smile, but she was busy carrying the load of her family's honour like a forced labourer. She could have, but never did, relieve her weariness by coming to him.

Rabban-bi was the most upset. She was sorry that the boy she'd brought up was separated from her, but she was even more sorry about the loss of the red bag. In fact there were no more than fifty or sixty rupees in it, but she thought there was no point in admitting the theft of such a small amount. So she started by saying one hundred-and-twenty-five rupees, and by the evening the sum had grown to three hundred.

At first she couldn't believe that Safir-va could do such a thing.

'What will he do, he's still a child?' she asked Sakina.

'The things you say . . .' railed Sakina. 'If you had got him married he'd have been the father of a whole basket of children by now.' Sakina was particularly irritated because now there was no one to look after all her little daughters. The youngest was so attached to him that she'd been crying her eyes out since morning.

Rabban-bi was about to reply when Kubara entered and said, 'I had a feeling about this, Ba'ji, the day I saw her sitting on her own in Aggu bhaiya's house. But I never dreamed she'd run off so quickly. I'm sure there must be some reason behind it.'

Rabban-bi and Sakina also suspected as much. Accordingly, Rabban-bi immediately found some pretext for sending Salma away so that she could express herself openly on the subject. 'Go and get a reel of black cotton from Naima,' she said. When Salma had gone she ordered her next eldest sister Sughra, or Suggan, to take her younger sisters into the kitchen and give them something to eat. After she had left and the field was quite clear, Rabban-bi gave vent to her opinion on this particular matter. 'I say that Jhangtiya-bo must be stone blind. She sits there with eyes as big as waterpots and has no idea what's going on in her own home!'

Kubara agreed in stronger language, but it was Sakina who put her finger on the nerve.

'Sulaiman is coming out the day after tomorrow but now the poor man's not fit to show his face.'

Jhangtiya-bo was also worried as to what she could say to Ali Akbar's father. Finally she took a straight way out.

The whole day no one noticed. But in the evening when Naima-bi poked her head through the door on some errand she was startled to find the house in complete darkness. She softly called out once or twice to Jhangtiya-bo. When no reply came she told her daughter-in-law that it looked like Jhangtiya-bo had run off too. Then Kubara hurried off to Rabban-bi's. Rabban-bi was lying down telling Fussu Miyan's youngest daughters the story of the pomegranate fairy. The prince had just picked the pomegranate and all kinds of strange noises were coming from behind him. The story had not lost a bit of its magic despite the fact that the children had heard it hundreds of times. The girls' hearts were pounding in fear that the prince might look behind him and be turned to stone.

'Jhangtiya-bo's not at home!' said Kubara.

'What?' Rabban-bi sat up.

The girls frowned and sat with long faces. Kubara's arrival hadn't pleased them at all. But what could they do?

'Dadda, then what happened?'

But the old lady was not about to listen to them.

By morning it had spread throughout the village that Jhangtiya-bo had also run off. Bacchaniya's elopement was not such a big event, but Jhangtiya-bo's disappearance was a mystery. The question was who had she run off with? None of the village men were missing. As a result, the whole of Gangauli held its breath and awaited Sulaiman's return.

Sulaiman arrived in the evening. Fussu Miyan was the first to meet him. Sulaiman greeted him but Fussu turned his eyes away, and went indoors as if he hadn't seen him. Hamid Miyan didn't wait to greet him either. He disappeared indoors too. All the weavers avoided his glance, but one child, wearing just a shirt, came running up, said,

'Bacchaniya has run off, and Jhangtiya-bo's run off too!', and ran away again like an arrow. Sulaiman didn't understand, but his heart began to beat hard. He entered the Great Gate. Labourers were repairing the tiled roof and whitewashing the walls as Moharram was coming round again. When they saw him the labourers began to work faster.

'When's Hammad Miyan being released?' asked Gaya Ahir's son, who was looking after the work in Gaya's absence. He really wanted to find out when Gaya was coming out.

'Tomorrow,' replied Sulaiman, 'Gaya has come out . . .'

'So I'll just go home for a while and come back.'

'Go.'

He went. The labourers busied themselves with their work again. Sulaiman went inside. There was complete stillness.

'Bacchaniya!' he called out.

No reply. However Kubara put her head round the door of her apartment.

'Eh, *Bhavaj*! Where has Bacchaniya's mother got to?'

'How do I know?' said Kubara, 'She's been missing since yesterday.'

'Missing?'

'Yes, Bacchaniya has run off with Safir-va, you see.'

'What are you saying?'

'That *nikaundi* girl was so plagued by the fire of lust in her loins, that don't ask,' said Naima-bi, also coming to the door, 'but now there's nothing you can do but be patient.'

Naima-bi gave the advice she should have done. If the truth be told she was in fact happy in a way because it was now clear that Maulvi Bedar intended to get married, and if he'd agreed to marry a bastard like Bacchaniya then what was wrong with her granddaughter Umme Habiba? Agreed, she wasn't beautiful like a whore, but she would make a good housewife. So if the matter was approached properly, a match could be arranged. Despite this it was her duty to show sympathy with Sulaiman and she fulfilled that duty. But it was obvious that Sulaiman couldn't follow her advice. His head hung down, he walked through Gori-bi's courtyard into the big courtyard.

There were three beds laid out. On each was a bedroll. Sulaiman recognized them. One was Bacchaniya's, one was Jhangtiya-bo's and one was his. After sweeping and cleaning the house, Jhangtiya-bo had laid out his bedding too. His eyes filled with tears. There was a bundle under the bedding. Jhangtiya-bo had taken off every last one of her ornaments. Only one silver bracelet was missing. Sulaiman knew that it was with Rabban-bi.

Sulaiman suddenly felt immensely old. He lay down exhausted. From her apartment he could hear Kubara reciting the nauha,

'Rudely forcing their way indoors came the foe,
Fatima's home has become a bazaar, oh Husainaa . . .'

Late into the night he felt like washing his hands and face. He took a bucket and rope to the well in the zenana imambara. When the bucket got caught in something, he looked into the well. But the well was in any case deep, and it was night. He couldn't see anything and so he lowered a hook into the well. The hook caught hold of something heavy. He knocked on the door of Naima-bi's apartment and asked to borrow Hammad Miyan's torch. Its battery had run out, and so he tied a lantern to his waist and climbed down inside the well. He was right. The hook had caught in Jhangtiya-bo's corpse.

'So this is where you're hiding, *re*.'

Sulaiman lived some days after this, but he was always repeating the same thing—to grown up and respected people, to children, and to walls and doors.

'I knew that she hadn't run away! She was hiding because she was afraid. But the bitch must have been mad. I would never have hit her.'

Then one night as he searched for Jhangtiya-bo he disappeared down the same well as she had, and three days later Kulsum received a letter from her daughter Razia in Calcutta. She wrote that she'd gone to the cinema and had happened to meet Bacchaniya. She was very happy. Safir-va was working in a jute mill. Bacchaniya had said that Moharram was about to start and Imam Husain was not likely to come to Calcutta. Where would she get the halva of the eighth and special tea there? As she had talked about Shabbu-cha's majlis she had begun to cry, but for fear of Sulaiman she hadn't had the courage to come back to Gangauli.

Razia didn't tell her that there was no longer any reason for her to be afraid because she had begun to relate her own woes—Zaigham was ill, Dabir was studying for his exams, and so she couldn't get there before the fifth. For the first four days her body would be in Calcutta, but her soul would be there in Gangauli.

On the fifth morning when Razia stepped down from the train at

Yusufpur the sun had not yet risen. It was a slightly chilly April morning. The breeze saw her and embraced her. Her husband, Mohammad Husain, quickly put up the purdah around the sides of a horse cart. He didn't want to miss the majlis of the fifth because he had prepared a nauha which would absolutely astound Masshu Miyan.

Even so by the time he helped Razia down from the cart in Gangauli, the huqqa had already been removed from the floor of the imambara, Husain Ali Miyan had already sat down on the platform of the soz-chanters, and the folding green door to the end of the imambara where the tazias stood had already been opened. Mohammad Husain saluted the standards and sat down in a corner, but Phunnan Miyan saw him. Perhaps he would have called him over but at that moment the soz-chanting began.

The children stopped talking. Masoom noticed that Moonis, Maddu, Tannu, Gigge and Hassana, and all the other boys of their group, who before would sit beside or behind the pulpit, were now sitting on the main floor of the imambara, knee to knee with their elders, and other children had taken their places. No one had told the former that they should no longer sit behind the pulpit, and nor had anyone told the latter to sit there. This change had occurred by itself.

Masoom had come to Gangauli after six years, but all this while nothing had changed. Husain Ali Miyan was reciting the same marsia. After him Wazir Miyan would no doubt recite the same marsia which had been recited in the majlis on this day for generations. The picture of the blood-covered horse of Imam Husain was still in the same place. The quatrain of Anis and the verses from the holy Qo'ran were still where they had been five years—or perhaps fifty years ago. The standards on the platform of the tazias were arranged in exactly the same way. The dupatta spread across them was the same. So were the drapery of the pulpit and the floor-covering—black flowers printed on a yellow ground. And the people sitting on the floor-covering were the same too. They were in the same places they had been occupying for the last five or twenty years. The only difference was that those by the pulpit and away from the pulpit had changed—and several places were empty. The places of Gore Miyan, Abu Mohammad Miyan and Rashid Mukhtar were empty. Or rather they seemed so. Because had they really been empty it would have meant that these gentlemen had been delayed for some reason. Their places had been filled, but the men sitting in them were uncomfortable because their seats weren't really their own . . . . That is to say that the men who used to sit there would never do so again. Looking at this congregation, Masoom became convinced that Gore-da, Abu Mohammad-da and Rashid Miyan had really died. Abbu Miyan had taken Abu Mohammad Miyan's place. Shabbu Miyan had taken Gore Miyan's and Deputy Ali Hadi had taken Rashid Miyan's, as Hakim Ali Kabir had refused to sit in the place of any dead man. Then these men's places had in turn been filled by more junior men, until revolutionary changes had taken place over the whole floor, but the floor remained basically the same.

After the soz was finished, Wazir Miyan recited the marsia, 'Oh pen, once again scatter pearls o'er the paper's hem . . .'

People had heard this marsia for generations. Wazir Miyan read the first half of the couplets, and the audience supplied the second half. The same happened with practically every marsia. These poems, describing the afflictions and heroism of Imam Husain and his family, were the ones which both Phunnan Miyan, who was completely illiterate, and Aggu Miyan, who had studied at university, knew by heart. In unhappy and lonely moments they would both murmur these marsias. It was seated on the floor-covering formed of the words of these poems that the Saiyid ladies and gentlemen of Gangauli had learnt to live and die, laugh and weep, and love and hate. The whole pattern of their entire life was established upon these marsias, inscribed in beautiful calligraphy on large sheets of paper.

Husain Ali Miyan tried to cry at the description of the leave-taking, but was unsuccessful. But as the time for Imam Husain's martyrdom approached, he managed to summon moisture to his eyes. Fussu Miyan was weeping loudly and bitterly and the boys behind the pulpit were amused to see him so upset.

After Wazir Miyan finished his recitation, he wiped the sweat from his face with a handkerchief and climbed down from the pulpit.

'Masha Allah!' said Abbu Miyan.

'Well read, bhai!' said Deputy Ali Hadi.

'Vah!' exclaimed Husain Ali Miyan in praise but in a tearful tone, wiping his dry eyes with the hem of his kurta.

Wazir Miyan bent low to offer his salaams to each of them. At this juncture Mohammad Husain took a notebook from his coat pocket and Moonis began to line up the boys.

'Husain! Husain!' the whole group said together and the imambara began to tremble to the rhythm of hands beating chests.

'Husain! Husain!' the elders joined in with their soft voices too.

'Husain! Husain!' Moonis' voice rose above the rest.

'Husain! Husain!' all the boys' voices rose.

The matam took on a steady rhythm. But Masoom felt that the matam of Dakkhin Patti was weaker than before. He cast his eyes over the regiment of men. Many familiar faces were missing. Abul Qasim wasn't there, neither was Ali Saiyid or Amjad-va, or Bakrid-va or Shammu . . . . The group of young men had shrunk by half.

'Where have they all gone?' he asked Phunnan after the majlis.

'They've signed up for the war,' replied Phunnan. He then turned to Ashrafullah Khan 'Ashraf' and said, 'This is Masoom. He knows a lot of ghazals by heart.'

Ashrafullah Khan smiled.

Masshu Miyan, the joint secretary of the Husainiya Society, began auctioning the Orphan's Share. Balushahi sweets were distributed at this majlis, and Maulvi Bedar Husain Sadrulfazil always used to buy them. Bashir Miyan had been careful to ensure the sweets were pure, and had with great difficulty managed to obtain a sugar permit to have them made. So when Masshu Miyan's voice boomed out, he smiled and looked towards Maulvi Bedar, but Maulvi Bedar made no bid.

'What's this, bhai Bedar? Aren't you going to buy the Share today?' Bashir Miyan couldn't help but ask.

'These days his stomach is upset,' said Phunnan Miyan.

Everyone laughed. Shabbu Miyan objected to this laughter and quietly walked into the adjoining room.

'Two annas!' bid Fussu Miyan.

'Chi, chi, chi! Is that any price to offer?' said Deputy Collector Ali Hadi. 'Just remember that sugar's not available and bhai Bashir must have gone to great lengths to have these sweets made. With this problem in mind, I myself had a word with the supply officer in advance, and the good soul had three sacks of sugar sent over on the night of the new moon.'

'Two rupees!' bid Deputy Collector Ali Hadi's son. When Ali Hadi Miyan stared hard at him he was taken aback. He had thought that he would praise his spirit, and Bashir-cha would also be pleased that someone had appreciated the fact that you couldn't get sugar in wartime.

'Why are you staring?' asked Wazir Miyan, 'I'll add an extra four balushahis for that. Eh, Nana!' he called out to Hamid Miyan who was distributing the blessed food, 'Ali Hadi's son has made a bid. Put another four balushahis in the Orphan's Share.'

In fact by this gesture Wazir Miyan had given a fitting reply to Ali Hadi Miyan's boast of three sacks of sugar sent by the supply officer.

'Just you keep quiet!' Hakim Ali Kabir scolded Ali Hadi Miyan's son. 'Don't go and bid so high that Bedar will be stifled into silence.'

'You're talking as if he can't afford to give two rupees for the orphans!' said Husain Ali Miyan.

'I'm an orphan myself,' said Maulvi Bedar.

'Two rupees for the Orphan's Share!' announced Masshu Miyan.

'Tannu, why don't you join the army?' Deputy Ali Hadi asked Shabbu Miyan's eldest son, who had just completed his FA examination and come back straight to Gangauli. 'I can get you a commission.'

'Why don't you get Saddan one, then?' said Phunnan Miyan. 'Are our sons the only ones left to be killed?'

'Who are you to send Saddan or not?' thundered the Hakim Sahib.

'I was thinking that I don't know what exams he's passed but he's better built than Tannu.'

Hearing himself praised Saddan looked at Tannu. He was proud of his height and body. He was as gleaming and firm as an image of copper. In comparison Tannu was a rather skinny young man. Tannu was keenly aware of this because Saifuniya, the barber's daughter, had rejected him in favour of Saddan.

Jinti's granddaughter and Mehruniya's daughter had turned out to be stunning.

Tannu had fallen in love with her two years ago. He had come to Gangauli in the hot weather to eat mangoes. There was no one at the Great Gate and so he got down at Fussu Miyan's house. In Gangauli Fussu Miyan was famous for his mangoes. In his mango groves grew green langras from Ghazipur, elongated dasehris and large, yellow safedas from Malihabad, samar-bahisht from Rampur, and grafted alfonsos from Bombay. There was no counting the small seed mangoes. In the largest room in the house, Fussu Miyan had mangoes laid out between layers of paper to ripen under his own supervision. Then when the mangoes were ripe he sent one basketful each to Bashir Miyan, Wazir Miyan, Aggu and Abbu Miyan, and then tied up his lungi and got stuck into them himself.

Tannu had seen Saifuniya's ripening youth in that room full of mangoes. She was bending over picking out the ripe fruit. Her dupatta had fallen down and her thin kurta, damp with sweat, clung to her like a black skin.

Sensing a shadow in the doorway, she had started. She had thought that perhaps Fussu Miyan had come, because she'd been noticing for a month or more that his eyes seemed to drool after her. The thought of it made her nauseous. When she saw him, she felt an unpleasant stickiness, but she couldn't do anything about it because . . .

She had been startled by the shadow because she knew that Rabban-bi and Sakina-bi were not at home, Salma was in the other apartment with her younger sisters, and she was in a room with only one door.

In these circumstances she would never have come here except for the fact that Safir-va had told her that Fussu Miyan had gone to Yusufpur. She was very annoyed with Safir-va. That son-of-a-bastard didn't even look at her and even if he did he would joke, linking her name with some Miyan.

But when she saw Tannu she was greatly relieved because it was well-known throughout the village that Shabbu Miyan and Bashir Miyan's boys were growing up with no idea about the purpose of youth, absolutely clueless. They didn't even know how to smile at a girl! So when Saifuniya saw it was only Tannu what need was there for her to wrap her dupatta around herself or pull her clinging kurta away from her body? She bent down again and began sorting the mangoes. Tannu himself was speechless. But beneath her fine kurta her breasts were slipping out of her bodice like ripe langra mangoes, and the red drawstring around the top of her green pajamas and the portion of her torso above it were all visible. Tannu's throat turned dry.

'Here, take these!' she said, putting two mangoes into Tannu's hands. Tannu backed away nervously. Saifuniya burst into laughter. 'You even beat girls at shyness, Tannu bhaiya.'

Tannu's blood rushed into his earlobes.

'I'm going,' was all he said, and ran out. Saifuniya kept smiling at Tannu's cowardice for some time. Then some days later in the Hakim Sahib's house, also in a room where mangoes were ripening, Saddan arrived. But Saddan didn't run away with the words, 'I'm going.' He came in. At that time he was just wearing a length of cloth wrapped around his waist. Saifuniya was amazed by the sight of his broad chest. Then his chest came so close to her that it became impossible for her to see. As far as her eyes could see there was just Saddan's broad chest.

Saddan told this story to his circle of friends. Naturally one of these was Tannu. As a result, Tannu couldn't look Saifuniya in the eye. The moment he saw her his earlobes turned bright red, his throat went dry and his brown eyes began to glance here and there. Saifuniya guessed this weakness of his and used to tease him. Then Bacchaniya and Suggan and Habiba and Sallan and Billo—in short, all the young girls and women of Dakkhin Patti began to tease him too. Even Sakina and Kubara and occasionally Naima-bi too weren't averse to throwing a few remarks his way. And the dreadful thing was that Saifuniya even told Saddan about him, and so Saddan started teasing him as well.

So when Saddan looked at him and smiled on the floor of the majlis, Tannu's body became tense. That very evening he ran away to Yusufpur and, stating he was a year older than he really was, signed up to join the army. This news reached Gangauli when a group of Sunni mourners from Yusufpur arrived to take part in the matam on the eighth of Moharram.

Even Saifuniya didn't know that Tannu had joined the army solely because of her.

Akbari-bibi prayed at the pulpit on the eighth of Moharram, vowing that if Tannu came back safe and sound she would fill its steps with offerings of sweets. And Tannu's father, Shabbu Miyan, described the martyrdom of the young Ali Akbar so graphically at the ladies' majlis that the audience cried and beat their breasts for a long time. Rabban-bi made a whole length of the wall wet with the tears she wiped on it, and Naima-bi beat herself so forcefully that she knocked over the spitoon and a long streak of betel-stained spittle spread over the floor.

'Have you turned senile?' Akbari-bi rebuked her.

'It's not as if I did it on purpose,' replied Naima-bi.

'Oh, Lord, how did you lift the corpse of your young son!' Akbari-bi began to lament.

Shabbu Miyan completed his recitation and left, but the women continued to weep for some time. Kubara even had a kind of fit, her teeth clenched together, and the matam that began then was long remembered in Gangauli. After the majlis was over, the girls went into lonely corners and held up their kurtas to examine their breasts, which were covered with black bruises of coagulated blood.

'. . . Ali's daughter was displaying the courage of one born of Fatima. She had sat her young sons, Aun and Mohammad, beside her and was explaining, 'Beta, you represent the memory of your grandfathers, Ali-e-Murtaza and Jafar. Tomorrow you must lead the jihad. And if you even look once towards the river I will never free you before God from the debt you owe me for the mother's milk I fed you . . .'

The imambara was resounding to the sound of Shabbu Miyan's recitation of the Hadith. Every tiny hair on the listeners' bodies seemed witness to the scene, and it appeared as if Dakkhin Patti would be washed away in a flood of tears. Each of the women standing near the doorway had for a while become Zainab. They were all in Karbala advising their sons to sacrifice their lives for Husain.

'Arre, Lord! I was not there. If I had been I would have sacrificed my Abbas just like that!' lamented Kubara, although a part of her was afraid that Abbas too might somehow run off and join the army like Tannu.

A little removed from these scenes of grief, Gaya Ahir was swearing at the young boys sitting at the door of the bathroom to keep quiet. The great white flag was billowing in the breeze. It was torn in several places and Gaya was thinking that the war had robbed Moharram of its splendour. Otherwise could a torn flag ever fly at the Barka Gate?

When he saw Maulvi Bedar returning from the majlis he stood up. This was the first time he had come face to face with the Maulvi since he went to jail. A fight was a different matter. If there was another, he wouldn't hesitate to attack Maulvi Bedar a second time, but the Maulvi Sahib was, after all, a zamindar. Gaya bent down and touched his forehead in greeting.

'How are you, *re*?' asked the Maulvi Sahib.

Gaya grinned and replied, 'I'm well, Mir Sahib.'

The Maulvi Sahib walked out of the Gate. Inside uproar broke out over the distribution of the blessed sweets. Javad Miyan was swiftly distributing several foul abuses and one share of sweets to each boy.

The night was good and chilly. Maulvi Bedar wrapped his quilted shawl well around himself. The lane was deserted. Even the stray dogs were crouching somewhere out of sight. The doors of the weavers' houses were already shut, and the darkness was deep. The Maulvi Sahib thought he'd take the way around the back of Phunnan Miyan's house. But the ground there was uneven. He stumbled and fell. By chance Saifuniya came by on her way from Husain Ali Miyan's to Phunnan Miyan's, carrying a tray piled with shares of sweets from the majlis. She put the tray on the ground and helped the Maulvi Sahib to his feet. The night suddenly became so warm that the Maulvi Sahib began to sweat. Maybe not for the first time since his mother had died, but certainly for the first time since Asiya had grown up, he felt the warmth of a woman's body. And what a woman—Saifuniya—who was no less than a red hot stove. His body began to tremble.

'Take me home!' he said.

How could Saifuniya object? None of the women in the village counted the Maulvi Sahib as a man. She balanced the tray on her head and began to support him with her other hand. When Kulsum saw them, the Maulvi Sahib's hand was on Saifuniya's shoulder and he was entering his house through the back door.

'Eh!' she said sharply, 'Bedar bhaiya! Have you gone senile? Don't you know that it's the night of the ninth tonight?'

The Maulana could have died of shame and Saifuniya suddenly realized how things can get blown out of proportion.

She freed herself with such a violent jerk that the Maulana staggered, and then, without a backward glance, she walked off with swaying hips and the tray balanced on her head towards Phunnan Miyan's house.

Kulsum said nothing to her, because her young daughter Ruqayya was present. Saifuniya attempted to say something in her own defence, but Kulsum just scolded her. Taking a quarter of a seer of rice in return for delivering the share of sweets, she left. Kulsum waited up for Phunnan Miyan.

But Phunnan had no idea of what had happened. He was wandering off towards Salimpur talking to Ashrafullah Khan. The fact was that the Khan Sahib wanted to discuss something in particular with him. The story was that three months after his grandson Khairu had left it became apparent that one of his maidservants, Gulbehri, was pregnant. When she said Khairu was the father, the Khan Sahib gave her a beating and threw her out of the house. This news reached Hakim Ali Kabir. He had a word with the Thakur Sahib of Barikhpur who had one of his agents keep her in his house. Now the bitch had put in a claim for maintenance. She was saying that Khairu had married her.

'And Thakur Harnarayan Prasad is supporting her too,' concluded the Khan Sahib.

'That's nothing to be surprised about,' remarked Phunnan Miyan, 'I have some things to settle with him too. And I've heard that the Thakur of Barikhpur, Kunwarpal Singh, has got very courageous lately. Jhinguriya would have given him a thrashing but out of regard for me he kept quiet.'

'But what can be done about this? The child is Khairu's.'

'Arre, what does that matter? If there's a baby, there's a baby. Don't you worry yourself. When there's no bamboo, there'll be no bamboo flute to play.'

When Phunnan Miyan returned he was surprised to see that Kulsum was still awake and dumbfounded when she told him about Saifuniya and Maulvi Bedar.

'But he's not capable of taking Saifuniya into his house and doing anything with her.'

'I know nothing about that,' said Kulsum, 'I haven't seen it. But what I have seen, I've told you.'

'Accha! Eh, Muntaz!' Phunnan Miyan called out to his son, who was in a deep slumber. He only woke up after he'd been called several times. Then Phunnan Miyan said, '. . . Go and call Rahim-va.'

Mumtaz bestirred himself. The moment he pushed off the quilt he began to shiver from the sudden contact with cold air.

'Is this any time to go?' he complained.

'You roam around as you like the whole day and when there's any work to do you say, "Is this any time?" This is the time, so get moving!' retorted Kulsum.

Mumtaz wrapped around his shoulders the old military overcoat which had been kept in the house for such occasions since God knew when. No one but Phunnan Miyan knew where it had come from. He had won it from a havildar in a game of Diwali cards.

Phunnan Miyan paced up and down until Rahim the barber arrived. He hadn't realized that there would be an opportunity to take revenge on the men of Uttar Patti so soon. Accordingly, after Moharram, the barbers' panchayat met.

Rahim stood up—

'I'm standing up to ask just one question of the elders. In the end do we have any honour or not . . .' He told the whole story from beginning to end. The elders listened, shaking their heads. The problem was somewhat complex because the elders knew that they didn't have any honour. The only people who did were the zamindars, who were mother and father to the rest. But it's obvious that the elders couldn't say this, and that when this matter had been raised on the jute-cloth floor of the community they would have to reach some decision.

'The thing to consider,' said the Chaudhuri or headman of the barbers, after long consideration, throwing a beedi stub to one side, 'is what should be done in these circumstances.'

'What should be done is that the Maulvi Sahib should come here with a wedding procession and Saifuniya should be bade farewell to and he should take her away,' said Rahim.

'But how can this be . . .' said the Chaudhuri.

'Why shouldn't it be?' said Rahim, becoming annoyed. 'Aren't our daughters, daughters?'

Now who could say that Rahim's daughter was not a daughter! There was total silence. The Chaudhuri thought many things. He had to think of the fields which had been given by the zamindars. The fields the Chaudhuri himself ploughed had been given to him by Maulvi Bedar. His uncle farmed some of the Hakim Sahib's land. His son-in-law's land had been bestowed on him by Husain Ali Miyan. The plot on which their mud houses stood had been donated by the zamindars. And so on one side was a matter concerning a daughter of the community, and on the other houses and lands. It was obviously a difficult decision.

A visitor from the city of Benares, Abdul Alim, wearing a silk lungi and a mixed silk and cotton kurta, and wrapped in a shawl, was sitting to one side smoking a Scissors cigarette. He was the son of a distant relative of Rahim's. A guest had come and accordingly Rahim made his final assault, 'I have been disgraced in front of a guest.'

At this the guest tapped the ash off his cigarette.

'I would like to say something . . . ,' he said. Naturally no one could stop a guest's tongue. He was given the opportunity to speak. He had heard the speeches of Pandit Nehru, Subhas Bose and Maulana Abul Kalam Azad. The tones of Ram Manohar Lohia, Jayaprakash Narayan and Acharya Narendra Dev were also resounding in his brain. Apart from all these the voices of Chaudhuri Khaliquzzaman, Zaheeruddin Lari, Maulana Shabbir Ahmed Usmani and other magical orators of the Muslim League were embedded in his ears. Therefore, for a short while he became Pandit Nehru and Abul Kalam Azad and Chaudhuri Khaliquzzaman and Acharya Narendra Dev—in short, he became them all. These people didn't speak any sloppy dialect and so he cleared his throat and began in pure Urdu, 'Brothers in Islam! Assalaamalaikum . . .'

'Valaikumassalaam!' the barbers replied in unison.

Abdul Alim the barber was thoroughly taken aback because no speaker in any meeting at Benares had ever been met with such a concerted and loud reply to a customary greeting. He straightened his high-sided cap and went on, 'I want to say . . .' he cleared his throat, 'I want to say that we people are not animals for the Miyans to herd us wherever they like. This is not just the matter of one Saifuniya, it's a matter of the honour of the whole community. In such matters keeping quiet is like drowning yourself. Nara-e-takbir!'

He thought that in response to his call 'Nara-e-takbir!' the whole community would shout 'Allah-o-Akbar' at the top of their voices, but the audience was completely nonplussed. They weren't familiar with this—apart from Moharram's 'Bol Muhammadi—Ya Husain!' they knew no slogans.

'It is for the sake of the honour of we poor brothers-in-Islam that the Qaid-e-Azam is concerned about the creation of Pakistan, and the Raja of Mahmudabad is touring the villages. Just four days ago Chaudhuri Khaliquzzaman came to speak. He said . . .'

'Eh, bhaiyaa, who told your Chaudhuri about Saifuniya?' interrupted the headman of the barbers. He was not at all pleased at having some other Chaudhuri poking his nose into his affairs.

'Hahn, that's right! Our Chaudhuri is Khalifa Nurul Hasan,' piped up another young man, who wanted to marry the Chaudhuri's granddaughter. Being a guest certainly didn't mean that you had the right to interfere in the matters of the community.

Abdul Alim sat down in confusion, and the Chaudhuri was so angry he dismissed the meeting. Rahim was left gaping at his community, because this was the first time in the history of the panchayat that a meeting had ended without a decision having been reached. He took Abdul Alim off home. Saifuniya was draining the water off some cooked rice and her mother was warming herself in front of the fire.

'What did the elders say?' asked Saifuniya's mother.

'The elders said nothing,' replied Rahim. 'Thanks to this bastard girl I'm not fit to show my face anywhere any more.'

He began to beat Saifuniya. When her mother tried to protect her, he began to beat her too. Both women began to curse him. During the time he beat them, his corpse was taken out on a bier dozens of times, dozens of times worms ate his body . . . in short, he was in a bad way. But he kept on beating the two of them. Abdul Alim tried to interrupt him once or twice, but Rahim wouldn't let him speak. So he lit a Scissors cigarette, sat down on a bed in the arched room and began to watch Saifuniya, whose kurta had been badly torn . . .

When Rahim was tired of beating Saifuniya and her mother, he left the house, abusing them roundly. For some time after he went, Saifuniya cursed him and seven generations of his forefathers. When her store of abuses ran out, or had begun to seem stale due to too much repetition, she felt the penetrating glances of Abdul Alim. She immediately covered herself. Abdul Alim began to look the other way. Saifuniya went inside, and her mother began to tell Abdul Alim imaginative tales of the loose ways of her mother- and sister-in-law, concluding by saying of her husband, '. . . And now that *harami* must have gone straight from here to Phunnan Miyan. Don't you know that he is Phunnan Miyan's son?'

However her words didn't carry conviction because Phunnan Miyan was only six or seven years older than Rahim.

Still, whether or not he was Rahim's father, Saifuniya's mother was right in saying that Rahim had gone to Phunnan's house. He wanted to inform him that his guest had ruined everything. But he didn't find Phunnan Miyan at home. Mumtaz told him that Phunnan had gone somewhere.

The night was very cold and so Phunnan had put on the overcoat he'd won at cards and buttoned its brass buttons up to the neck. With him were Jhinguriya and twelve of his men. Jhinguriya had taken his men ahead.

In Barikhpur the deep stillness and dark of a night in the country spread all around. Jhinguriya and his men stopped in front of a neat, clean tiled house. No one in the area could dig a hole in a mud wall like Jhinguriya. In a short time he had made a very neat, clean hole. One of his men slipped through it into the house. Then a dog yelped. But its yelp was cut dead. The door of the house opened. Jhinguriya and the rest of his men entered.

Thakur Kunwarpal Singh's agent, Sher Mohammad, was asleep, completely unaware of them. Two men took position on either side of his charpoy. Jhinguriya began to look for the maidservant whom Phunnan had described to him. The girl would have a small child with her, and so Jhinguriya didn't pay much attention to the description. There was a young woman sleeping with a baby.

Jhinguriya covered her mouth and carried her off so smoothly that she couldn't make a sound. But as he left the house with her and his men, the baby woke up. When no one patted its back, it began to scream loudly. Another woman got up and went over to the baby. She took it in her lap and when it didn't quieten she fed it milk from her own breast . . .

Three days later when a woman's body was fished out of a well, there was an outcry in Barikhpur. Thakur Harnarayan Prasad Singh immediately left his Gulabi Jan, mounted his horse and rode there. Behind him came Samiuddin too. Sher Mohammad identified the corpse as that of his missing sister. He was relieved by the sight of the corpse as it had been spread round the village that she had run off with someone.

Phunnan was stunned by the news. He didn't regret that Sher Mohammad's sister had been mistaken for the maidservant and murdered. He regretted that his mission had failed and now the date for the court hearing on the Gulbehri case was on top of them.

'Now what do we do?' asked Ashrafullah Khan.

'That's what I'm wondering,' replied Phunnan Miyan. 'Look, why don't you go to Bedar and tell him to tell Hakim Ali Kabir to drop the case or Saifuniya will file one against him.'

'I can't go to his door.'

'Who is saying that you should go in person?' said Phunnan Miyan, 'I'll go . . . I still have scores to settle there.'

Ashrafullah Khan said, 'Bhai, it's all up to you. If this matter isn't buried I won't be fit to show my face to my daughters' in-laws.'

'The things you say!' replied Phunnan, turning the mouthpiece of the huqqa to one side, 'The matter will certainly be buried. And, bhai, that Lakhna Chamar came to see me yesterday. Why aren't you giving him that land by the well? He's offering you five hundred rupees for it.'

'That *saala* is a cunning bastard. He took Thakur Kunwarpal Singh to court. After the Thakur lost he thought he'd evict Lakhna from the land he was on, but he went there to cut the crop and the Chamars turned up too, with their lathis. These Congressmen have really gone too far. Now these low caste people want to look you in the eye when they talk to you. Why should I give him land?'

'Shall we make it eight hundred?' asked Phunnan Miyan.

'I was thinking of handing it to a sharecropper.'

'Come on, bhai, since when has the Khan Sahib of Salimpur been reduced to giving out land to sharecroppers?' Phunnan Miyan stroked his moustache, and added, 'The matter can be settled for up to a thousand rupees.'

Ashrafullah Khan agreed because a thousand rupees was not a small sum. Phunnan Miyan too made two hundred rupees profit as he had settled with the Chamar for twelve hundred.

'I've heard Jhinguriya's been arrested.'

'Yes,' confirmed Phunnan Miyan, 'but what does that matter? He was in the lock-up in Yusufpur when it happened. Two days later he was released and the Thakur Sahib arrested him.'

'But . . .'

'Bhai, haven't I told you? There's no point in mentioning these small things! I gave the thanedar of Yusufpur, Abdullah Khan, three hundred rupees. And then the work was done.'

'But why should you give the money?'

'What's mine is yours.'

Ashrafullah Khan tried hard to persuade him but Phunnan refused to take the money. The Khan Sahib, poor chap, was silenced. After smoking one pipeful, Phunnan made to go as he'd left Lakhna Chamar waiting at his house. When he reached home he found Lakhna squatting at his door just as he had left him.

'Salaam, Mir Sahib!' he said, standing up.

'Your work's been done. But the Khan Sahib's not willing to settle for a pie under fifteen hundred.'

'That's all right. There's not much difference between twelve hundred and fifteen hundred. So I'll be off. Tomorrow or so I'll have the money delivered here.'

'Yes!'

Lakhna Chamar left.

Phunnan Miyan went inside and called out to Kulsum, 'Fetch me something to eat and then I'll go over to see Miyan Bedar for a moment.'

He sat down cross-legged on one end of a charpoy. Ruqayya spread out a cloth before him on the bed. Some Persian verses were printed in black on a yellow background. Phunnan Miyan began to look at these letters of the alphabet which became meaningful when joined together, but which were alien to him despite his having spent his life in their company. He was still staring at the letters when his third daughter, eight-or nine-year-old Maghfiya, brought a tray of food. In one bowl was some beef curry. In another thin arhar dal, with hot ghee and a fried clove of garlic floating in it. On a plate was some reddish rice and to one side eight chapattis, folded in pairs. Ruqayya brought some drinking water in a copper bowl.

Phunnan Miyan had eaten and washed his hands and face, and was just wiping his moustache dry with his shouldercloth when Samiuddin's voice came from the doorway. Maghfiya took shelter behind the door.

'Is Phunnan Miyan at home?'

'Yes.'

'Tell him that the Thanedar Sahib is calling for him at the Hakim Sahib's gate.'

'Eh, Abba! The Thanedar Sahib wants you to come to see him at the Hakim Sahib's gate,' Maghfiya called out loudly from where she stood.

'Tell the Thanedar Sahib that I have a gate of my own,' said Phunnan Miyan.

'You want me to go and tell him that?' asked Samiuddin.

'Yes, I do. Go and tell him. I don't depend on your Thanedar

Sahib for my bread.'

'What's the point of making things worse for no reason?'

'Things haven't got worse yet!' said Phunnan Miyan, cleaning his teeth with a toothpick. 'Have a paan before you go. Eh, mother of Razia, send a paan to the Khan Sahib.'

Kulsum began to make a paan.

'I was just saying, Mir Sahib, that . . .'

'There's no need to say anything,' interrupted Phunnan Miyan. 'If I want to meet him I'll go to him. If he wants to meet me he has to come here.'

Samiuddin took the paan from the hand Maghfiya stuck out from behind the door. Putting it in his mouth, and loudly bidding farewell to Phunnan Miyan, he returned. From the moment he had engaged his son, Moinuddin, to marry Ghulam Husain Khan's daughter, the people of Dakkhin Patti had lost all sympathy for him. It had been settled that the marriage would take place as soon as the war was over. If Moinuddin returned on leave before that then the wedding would be conducted immediately.

Ghulam Husain Khan had even begun making the wedding preparations. In his words, there was no saying that you get something for the same price tomorrow that you could today. Therefore, slowly and surely, you should start making arrangements. There was no money tree in the house whose fruit of rupees could be ripened like mangoes. Accordingly, cloth for five suits of clothes had been arranged on paper for display, stitched in place and put away in a chest. Gold jewellery enough to be given on three trays, and silver jewellery sufficient for five had also been made. Copper and brass pots had been bought too. For the rest they relied on Allah.

Ghulam Husain Khan was at this moment sitting on the edge of the tank smoking a beedi oblivious of what was about to take place in the courtyard.

Thakur Harnarayan Prasad was seated on a chair which had been brought from Deputy Collector Ali Hadi's room especially for him, and all the wealthy people of Gangauli were sitting either on the ground, or on stools or on iron chairs, as befitted their status. The Hakim Sahib was leaning on a bedroll smoking his huqqa. His daughter's three sons were busy playing hopscotch in the courtyard. The married ladies were peeping out towards the outer house where the men were sitting. Saifuniya was standing outside with her hand on her waist watching Anwarul Hasan Raqi's son Farooq, who had returned to Gangauli at his grandfather's death and had come with his father to offer his respects to the Thanedar Sahib.

Once or twice Farooq looked back at Saifuniya and the entire Muslim League programme slipped from his mind.

The Thakur Sahib's eye fell on Saifuniya as well. He stroked his moustache and pushed out his chest. A thought entered his mind, writhed and lay still, like the worm some young girl had spat betel juice on in play. He thought that Gulabi Jan no longer held any charm.

'Mai-baap! We can't give that much,' said Gobardhan the Bania, slipping forward a foot. He was squatting on the ground just by the Thanedar Sahib.

This Gobardhan was very wealthy. It was well-known that he had buried several pots of valuables under his hearth. Once Jhinguriya had tunnelled a hole through his wall, dug up the ground under the hearth and found nothing, but this didn't lessen people's belief in his riches. Jhinguriya attacked him seven times, but every time returned empty-handed, and every time the villagers became more convinced that Gobardhan was immensely wealthy but also very clever. They imagined he had hidden his money in such a place that even the likes of Jhinguriya couldn't find it. These remarks wounded Jhinguriya's pride, and so the eighth time he robbed Gobardhan he tied him up and beat him badly. But Gobardhan told him absolutely nothing. Jhinguriya had to return empty-handed once again.

Gobardhan was not a native of Gangauli. Gangauli was the village of his wife's family. He lived with them, but because he was the husband of an only daughter he was thoroughly indulged. He used to wear a silk kurta and sit at Anwarul Hasan's door talking about lakhs of rupees—such and such a thing's price was falling but why not invest twenty thousand rupees in it? Then despite opposition from Anwarul Hasan he would invest the money, and after three or four weeks start talking about the ten or twenty thousand profit or loss that he'd made. But not a paisa did he bring into the house, and so one day his father-in-law went and took a quiet look at his book of accounts. The old man's eyes opened wide in amazement. Gobardhan's business was worth lakhs. He had spread his net over Bombay, Calcutta, Chittagong, Rangoon, Hong Kong and goodness knows where else. His father-in-law came to the conclusion that he only looked good-for-nothing. Accordingly, Gobardhan went up further in everyone's esteem and began to strut around the village, his chest thrown out. Traders came to seek his advice, and there was no doubt that his advice always hit its mark. And so his renown spread. After his father-in-law died, he inherited his entire business too and became one hundred per cent part and parcel of Gangauli.

When he came to see the Miyans he was given a seat on the foot of a bed. This was a privilege which had never before been accorded a non-Shia in Gangauli. When he had first come to the village he had been a very young man. Now he'd become old. But his eyes still had the same sparkle. Of his six sons, four had joined the army, and one was studying in Allahabad. Gobardhan himself was much inclined to study. He used to worship Saraswati, the goddess of learning, at the same time as Ganesh, the elephant-god who removes all obstacles. Accordingly, he took no notice of what some villagers said, and gave all his sons an education. The government had sent his sixth son on a scholarship to England to study. And it was well-known that he'd married a Memsahib there. Gobardhan had pronounced that there was no longer any place for this son in his house, and had even had him cut from his will.

In short, his life was passing very comfortably when the Thakur Sahib undertook to raise a lakh of rupees for the war effort, and asked Gobardhan for ten thousand. Gobardhan jumped at the mention of such a sum, leapt up from the foot of the Hakim Sahib's bed and squatted down on the ground near the Thanedar Sahib. At that point the Thanedar Sahib was watching Saifuniya, but still the sound of Gobardhan's objection came to his ears . . .

'What are you saying, Sethji?' replied Thakur Harnarayan Prasad, 'Your business is spread over many countries. You're a man worth lakhs if not crores. Isn't that so?' he said, addressing Haji Bulaqi, from whom he'd already collected a thousand rupees. 'Tell me if I'm wrong.'

'There's no doubt about that, sahib, you'd be hard pressed to find a man as rich as him except for one or two in the town.'

'Look here, Seth, there's a war going on. Four of your sons are in the army. I don't want to put your name down as a Congress supporter.'

'Arre, Ram-Ram, how could you ever think it?' said Gobardhan, thoroughly upset. 'I'm not in any Kangress-Angress. No, no, what are you saying, sarkar!'

'Any man who won't help the war effort must be a devotee of Gandhi.'

'It's not so, sarkar!'

'How is it not? Now, you tell me, Hakim Sahib!' the Thanedar Sahib continued, 'What does ten thousand matter to Seth Gobardhan?'

'Arre, give it and finish the matter,' said the Hakim Sahib.

'Where will I get it from to give?'

'Arre, only yesterday you were saying that you'd made eight thousand in some deal,' said Ghulam Husain Khan.

'Look here, Gobardhan! I'm telling you for the last time . . .' He had just got this far when Samiuddin arrived. 'What did Phunnan Miyan say?'

Samiuddin thought it inadvisable to repeat Phunnan's reply out loud and so he whispered it into the Thanedar Sahib's ear. The Thakur Sahib's face turned bright red and his hand automatically felt for his moustache.

'The rope has burnt, but it hasn't lost its twist. If I don't set him to work at the jail grinding stones for four years, I'll change my name!'

'So what order do you have for me?' asked Gobardhan fearfully.

'Bring the full amount to the police station within the week.'

The sparkle which had been in Gobardhan's eyes for the last sixty years was suddenly extinguished.

As he entered his sitting-room he folded his hands in respect before the images of Ganesh, Lakshmi and Saraswati, and then fell on to his mattress like an old tree. When one of his daughters-in-law came to light the lamps in the evening he was startled, and then folded his hands before the lamps and sat up.

The daughter-in-law told this news to his other daughters-in-law in the inner part of the house. His eldest daughter-in-law came out, her face veiled.

When she'd heard the whole story from Gobardhan, she too thought that ten thousand was no great amount. Gobardhan lost his temper. Ten thousand was such a great amount that for want of it his eldest daughter had drowned herself when she began to grow old. That was what ten thousand meant! He scolded his daughter-in-law and then sat quietly. When his daughter-in-law asked him if he wanted his dinner he said no. Finally, when it became difficult to sit quietly he locked the door of the sitting-room and went off to the Hakim's Sahib's house. But his shoulders were breaking under the weight of his accounts book.

The Thakur Sahib had decided to spend the night in Gangauli itself. He had collected donations for the war fund of five thousand rupees with receipts and eight thousand without receipts. He sent the sum covered by the receipts off to the tehsil office and the sum with no receipts off to the police station with Samiuddin Khan.

The Thakur Sahib was sitting in an armchair smoking a cigarette. He had changed out of his uniform.

Dressed in a lungi and wrapped in a blanket, he was talking to the Hakim Sahib about current affairs. The Hakim Sahib was enquiring as to who would farm the land when all the young men were being forced to serve in the war, and complaining that it was impossible to extract one-and-a-half or double the land revenue from cultivators against whom you were always having to put in claims for arrears of revenue at the old rates. And even if the government started taking the grain from the fields of half-dead crops, which were thirsting for young hands to tend them, then they would face the danger of an uprising in the countryside. And with all the army engaged in fighting the Germans and the Japanese, it would be difficult to contain a revolt.

'And how far is it true that Hitler is out to rape Turkey? When I went to Ghazipur the day before yesterday people were praying for his victory in the Sana Mosque.'

The Thakur Sahib tossed the stub of his cigarette into the courtyard. 'The fact is, Mir Sahib, that if land revenue rates don't go up, and if grain isn't collected directly from the fields or donations are not extracted by force, then where will the money come from to pay for such a big war? And if young men are not recruited how will the war be fought?'

The Hakim Sahib had no answer to such logic. He said, 'You're right there but . . .'

'Salaam, Mir Sahib!' said Gobardhan as he entered. 'Salaam, Thanedar Sahib!'

'Have you seen, Hakim Sahib? He's straightened out,' said the Thanedar. He turned to Gobardhan and said, 'Give it here.'

'Yes, sarkar!'

The Thanedar Sahib gathered his thoughts. He'd decided to give Gobardhan a receipt for only one thousand rupees. He was inwardly extremely pleased with Gobardhan because now his calculations would come out correct. He had decided to collect twenty thousand for the war fund and thirty thousand for his own fund. Gobardhan's donation would complete his thirty thousand and take the war fund up to eighteen.

'Sarkar, I have brought whatever I have,' said Gobardhan, presenting him an accounts book and a bag. The bag was very small. The accounts book was very fat. The Thanedar Sahib frowned, 'What do you expect me to do with the ledger?'

'My whole business is contained in it, sarkar!' said Gobardhan, 'And my capital in the bag. Altogether four hundred and eighteen rupees. What more can I say?' He fell silent, waiting to hear the crash of his personality collapsing like a wall weakened by seepage. His business was a dream. A poor dream, which had never harmed anyone except his daughter. He used to transact business in his dreams and record the details in his accounts book. He would spend hours looking at these magical, lifeless sums and be happy. When he suffered some imaginary loss he would be miserable for weeks, and when he followed a hunch which proved right, and made an imaginary profit, he was happy for weeks. He would play with his grandsons and granddaughters and exchange pleasantries with his daughters-in-law. He told all this to the Thanedar Sahib, but every sentence was like a noose round his neck. He began to feel suffocated and to cry like a child. He melted like a wax doll.

'So what order have you for me now?'

Thakur Harnarayan Prasad was a human being, after all. He returned the bag of money. Gobardhan touched his feet and left. And about nine o'clock the next morning the Thakur Sahib heard that Gobardhan had left Gangauli. The villagers said that they had never seen such a fly-sucking miser.

Only the Thanedar Sahib and the Hakim Sahib knew why he'd gone. But they both kept quiet as there was no point in saying anything without reason. And there was also the fact that they were both busy in their own work. The Hakim Sahib was concerned because Saddan had studied a lot. By the grace of God, he'd passed his tenth standard. His name had been entered as an assistant tehsildar and so now he should be married. The Thanedar Sahib was concerned about Phunnan.

As the head of the family, Abbu Miyan should have been present. But he was in Ghazipur. So Hammad Miyan, who had been entrusted with the power of attorney for the ancestral estate, was fulfilling the duties of host. He had made a great deal of money by disposing of land here and there and was now thinking of leaving his small apartment and building his own house. Accordingly, he'd had the foundations of a two-storey house marked out opposite the Great Gate. And since he'd become suddenly rich, he no longer had any time for Phunnan Miyan. Phunnan Miyan, however, was a pure-bred Saiyid, and so the relations between the two houses had soured.

'How can I tell you, Thakur Sahib!' Hammad Miyan told the Thanedar Sahib. 'We are sick and tired of Phunnan Miyan's behaviour.

But we have to carry the load of our family honour. He has dacoities carried out. He gets robberies done. He's the one who carried off Karamat Ali's wife. He's like a young bull! He keeps grazing in the fields.'

'But he's crossed all limits by giving the Thanedar at Yusufpur money to put Jhinguriya in the lock-up,' said the Thakur Sahib, 'and the same night that incident took place. And what an incident! Murder! But I can't understand what he had against that woman.'

Hammad Miyan laughed, 'You're a fine one, yourself! Arre, sahib, Jhinguriya went to kill Gulbehri.'

'Gulbehri!'

'Arre, that Ashrafullah Khan affair!'

'Ooh! So that's the story!' The Thakur Sahib nodded his head. 'So that child really is Khairu Khan's.'

'It's obvious.'

'Now I'll get my hands on Ashrafullah Khan too,' said the Thakur Sahib and inwardly began to wonder how much Ashrafullah Khan would part with to get himself out of this particular case. He hadn't reached a conclusion when Phunnan Miyan arrived. He looked at Hammad Miyan, then at the Thakur Sahib and, without greeting either of them, sat down on a bed with his legs hanging down.

'What is it?' he asked.

'Mir Sahib, I wanted to have a word with you about Jhinguriya,' said the Thanedar Sahib.

'Go ahead.'

'He dug through that wall in Barikhpur.'

'But I heard he was in the Yusufpur lock-up then.'

'I know you gave the officer-in-charge at Yusufpur three hundred rupees.'

'Is he going to give a statement saying that?' Phunnan Miyan stood up. 'I don't have time to waste.'

'No one can take on the government and win, Mir Sahib!'

'I suppose not. But you're not the government, Thakur Sahib!' said Phunnan Miyan looking the thanedar straight in the eye. 'And at this moment you are a guest at my Gate, otherwise there's no mother's child who could threaten Phunnan Miyan and get away with it. You can show off your thanedary to Hammad-Ammad and the likes.'

'I've heard that you give donations to Sarju Pande.'

Phunnan Miyan smiled, but the smile was very poisonous.

'So far I've not. But if you say so I'll start. Is it written anywhere in the law that you can't give money to Congressmen? Have you been banging your drum to announce it?' he asked Dukhran-va the chowkidar. 'I haven't heard it!'

'You haven't donated to the war fund.'

'There's no land revenue left!' replied Phunnan Miyan, 'I've given one son as a donation. It's been six months since there's been any news whether Imtiyaz is alive or dead. If you like I'll send Muntaz too. War fund . . . a war fund for what? Did I ask them to fight the Germans that I should give to the war fund? You can't get cloth. Eh, bhai, everything to eat has disappeared from the bazaar. I couldn't get sugar to make offerings. Kerosene has become like the water of paradise. Only certain special people get it. I'm not giving an anna to the war fund. Do whatever you like.'

'Hold your tongue!' The Thanedar Sahib's tone became harsh.

'Eh, Thanedar Sahib,' said Phunnan, turning like a wounded cobra, 'no one speaks to Phunnan Miyan like that. What do you want from me?'

'Is it not correct to say you gave the officer-in-charge at Yusufpur three hundred rupees?'

'Tell him to state that in court. And tell him to tear up the police station records of Jhinguriya's arrest, and to come and snatch the copy of the First Information Report from me.'

'Why do you have a copy?'

'This is no court that it's my duty to answer every question of yours!'

'Gulbehri is now in police custody.'

'Really? And who else is in police custody?'

'I feel like arresting you for treason.'

'If you have the courage, try it.'

'Don't make the mistake of thinking that Bashir Sahib or Wazir Sahib or Aggu Miyan will be able to save you!'

'You just ask Thanedars Sharifuddin and Shivdhanni Singh who it is that saves me.'

The Thakur Sahib's body was on fire, and words were melting in its heat. Phunnan Miyan waited for several moments but when the Thakur Sahib failed to reply he left by the Great Gate. He had no worries about Jhinguriya. The Thanedar of Yusufpur must have admitted what had happened in private, but he would never state it in court as that would mean being caught himself. Only one question was troubling Phunnan. Maulvi Bedar had rejected his suggestion about the withdrawal of Gulbehri's case because the Hakim Sahib had successfully won round the Chaudhuri of the barbers on the matter of Saifuniya, and Saifuniya herself had stated that there was nothing between her and the Maulvi.

Rahim had no choice but to keep quiet; he couldn't take on his community. The Chaudhuri had offered to have Saifuniya married to his own grandson if there was any problem in finding a match for her. In reward for this, the Chaudhuri received half a bigha of land, and Maulvi Bedar gave Rahim one hundred-and-five rupees, and a promise to bear the entire expenses of Saifuniya's wedding. Phunnan Miyan discovered all this very late, which was why he was astounded by the vehemence of Maulvi Bedar's refusal. But he spoke to Rahim on his way back from the Maulvi's house and then all became clear.

'So you sold me out for a hundred-and-five rupees?'

'What else could I do, Mir Sahib? The Chaudhuri went and spoilt everything.'

'Very well. It's not as if he's left the village. I'll see to him.'

Phunnan's head was echoing with all that had happened. On his way to Salimpur he had to pass through the Chaudhuri's fields in which stood a good crop of gram and barley. He smiled, gave the meandering path a kick, and walked on.

When he reached Salimpur, Ashrafullah Khan was busy shouting abuse at a man who cultivated fields within his zamindari. When he saw Phunnan Miyan he stopped swearing and said, '*Saala*, if the land revenue and loan complete with interest are not delivered to me by the day after next, I'll auction your land complete with livestock. And you can take this Lord Sahib of yours and teach him how to speak to zamindars!'

Opposite, a well-built, good-looking young man was squatting down like a chicken and holding his ears in penitence. A tower-like pile of bricks had been placed on his back. When the tower was removed he was unable to stand upright for some minutes. Even after he could stand, he rubbed his back.

'Salaam the zamindar!' his father whispered to him, nudging him with his elbow. The young man salaamed the Khan Sahib, and then went off with his father. For some time after they departed the Khan Sahib kept pouring out invective against them and against the whole class of cultivators.

'Bedar Miyan didn't agree,' said Phunnan Miyan.

'He didn't?' said Ashrafullah Khan in surprise.

'No, the fact of the matter is that the *saala* Chaudhuri is a man of the Hakim Sahib's.'

'Then?'

'Arre, then what? As long as Phunnan is alive, who can touch you! Today I've given that *saala* Thanedar of Qasimabad a real piece of my mind. And I can see now that Hammad is the next one heading for disaster.'

'And what will happen to Jhinguriya?'

'Why are you worrying yourself over that? It's my job to get him out. But I have to think about this Gulbehri. As I see it we're left with one alternative—to get hold of her baby, and to get a warrant issued from another district saying that she's someone's wife, she ran off, it's been discovered she's living in the house of Sher Mohammad of Barikhpur, and that therefore she should be brought back. Once this case gets underway, then we'll see.'

After some discussion they decided that this case should be filed by Ghaznafar Ali Khan of Mattopur, district Faizabad.

'Very well, so now I'll be off.'

'Have some food before you go, and hear a new ghazal I've composed.'

Betel-nut was sent from the inner house. The Khan Sahib's daughters sent their salaams. Phunnan Miyan put the paan in his mouth and settled down to listen.

'Bismillah!'

The Khan Sahib began to recite his poem. Phunnan Miyan swayed from side to side, and praised it. But he was startled by the twenty-first verse and said, 'Please take the trouble of repeating that.'

Thc Khan Sahib did so.

'Vah!'

'What is it?' asked the Khan Sahib, surprised by Phunnan's tone.

'Sahib, I'm not an educated man, but I didn't really follow the idiom about "raising one's head for the beloved". A lover can have himself beheaded for his beloved like Mansoor or Sarmad. Or he can be crucified like Christ. But a man in love cannot raise his head. By raising his head he proves the immaturity of his love, as if he were boasting about it.'

Ashrafullah rolled up his sleeves to contest the point, but in the end he was persuaded, and the verse was deleted from the poem. Then food was served. Egg qorma, meat curry, peas pulao, and, for the sweet, carrot halva covered with a thick layer of cream.

Phunnan Miyan had finished his meal and had set out on his way home when he came across Thakur Kunwarpal Singh of Barikhpur.

The Thakur Sahib came to a halt when he saw Phunnan. They began to exchange a long list of complaints against one another.

Then the point was put that Jhinguriya had not acted wisely by surrounding Ghulam Husain Khan. That was enough to put Phunnan Miyan's hackles up. 'Let that matter rest,' he said, 'just let it be. I wasn't there and so you attacked Jhinguriya.'

'Because of you I'm keeping quiet, otherwise . . .'

'Otherwise, what? Anyway, that's a matter between you and me. We'll work something out. You're the disciple of my father and I've inherited his position as head of the wrestling-pit, I'm the Khalifa. But you shouldn't have taken Hakim Ali Kabir's side against me.'

'I was certainly the disciple of your father, but let's leave aside the matter of who's the Khalifa. It's never been decided whether it's you or me. That leaves the matter of Hakim Ali Kabir. He's my friend, so don't go bringing our ustad's name up there.'

'Why not?' asked Phunnan Miyan. 'And another thing, Thakur, if you're a man, don't go bringing the police into a matter between us, and have Gulbehri brought to the court the day after tomorrow.'

'Very well! I'll go with her myself.'

'Agreed!'

This plan had not been part of Phunnan Miyan's scheme of things, but by now he'd shaken hands on it.

'Good. It'll be settled then once and for all whether I'm your father's successor, or you are!' said the Thakur.

'So do like this—you come alone, I'll come alone. If you win Gulbehri stays here, if I win I can do what I like with her,' said Phunnan Miyan.

'Agreed! I'm thinking of setting out with her tomorrow night.'

The matter was settled, and they both began to talk about the harvest, and inflation, and the excesses of the government. Phunnan Miyan even stopped a while in Barikhpur. The Thakur Sahib's sons and grandsons gathered round him. Home-made jaggery which smelt strongly of cardamom and which had been prepared with home-made ghee, was sent to him from the inner house. Phunnan Miyan then drank some water and after chatting about this and that set off again for Gangauli. On the way he crossed the fields of the Chaudhuri of the barbers and smiled again.

That very night the Chaudhuri's crops were cut.

The hearts of all the cultivators roundabout began to tremble, because crops are never cut in isolation. So the watch on the fields was increased, and the next night about one o'clock in the morning a Chamar guarding the fields near the indigo godown saw Phunnan Miyan striding along towards the road carrying his lathi. A short while before he had also seen a bullock cart which, contrary to his normal habits, Thakur Kunwarpal Singh was driving. There was definitely a woman in the cart because the Chamar clearly heard the sound of a baby crying. And before that he'd seen Jhinguriya heading that way.

Phunnan Miyan was proceeding alone when, about a full mile from the village, he saw that Thakur Kunwarpal Singh had stopped the bullock cart and was waiting for him.

'I've been waiting for you a long while,' he said.

'Yes, I got late.'

Gulbehri recognized Phunnan's voice. Her heart began to pound, and she held her baby tightly to her breast.

'Take guard!' said the Thakur Sahib.

'Ya Ali!' said Phunnan Miyan.

They both began to fight, shifting their stances. They had no audience but the mud road, the mango, tamarind and jamun trees on either side and the stillness of the night. Gulbehri had closed her eyes and was praying to the great Pir Sahib.

Their staffs clashed. So far neither was badly injured. They were both trained in the same pit and they were both favourites of the same ustad. Their moves were measured, and their hands experienced. Their well-oiled lathis gleamed in the light of the setting moon.

'Ya Ali!' Phunnan Miyan launched an attack. The Thakur Sahib's head split open. His beard turned red with blood.

'Jai Bajrangbali!' he shouted, attacking Phunnan Miyan. Phunnan's left shoulder drooped.

Gulbehri screamed. Phunnan Miyan pushed the Thakur with his lathi. The Thakur stumbled and fell. Jhinguriya stepped out from behind a tree.

'Are you badly hurt?'

'Take Gulbehri away.'

'But . . .'

'Haven't I told you,' Phunnan said sharply, 'take her!'

Jhinguriya dragged Gulbehri away. Phunnan Miyan saw that the Thakur Sahib's bullocks were licking his wounds. Phunnan was injured in several places himself, and his left arm was useless, but he began to clean the Thakur Sahib's wounds. The Thakur opened his eyes.

'Congratulations, Khalifa!' he smiled.

With great difficulty Phunnan lifted him into the cart, and then sat in it himself. He was still sufficiently in his senses to turn the cart towards the village. What happened after that, he couldn't have known.

But the bullocks knew their way.

When the bullock cart approached the indigo godown, the Chamar standing guard saw that an empty cart was passing by.

When he raised the alarm, several other watchmen ran from the fields with their lathis. They saw that there was no one in the cart apart from two unconscious, wounded men. Barikhpur was nearby. The cart was taken there. One man ran off to Qasimabad.

Samiuddin was sleeping next to his penbox wrapped in a blanket. First he woke up, then he wrote a report. Since the matter concerned Thakur Kunwarpal Singh, he woke up Thakur Harnarayan Prasad, officer-in-charge Qasimabad, who was tired out and sleeping with Gulabi Jan. He was dreaming about his very ugly wife who lived with his parents, and was quite happy to be woken as the memory of his wife was always painful. He hurriedly adjusted his uniform, but by the time he reached Barikhpur, Alim-va the barber-cum-surgeon had dressed the Thakur Sahib's wounds and Hakim Ali Kabir had reached the conclusion that he couldn't survive.

'Bhai, as far as I can see there's no one but Phunnan that could have done this,' said the Hakim Sahib.

Everyone thought the same. But Phunnan was himself injured and had himself brought the Thakur Sahib home. So no one could understand what was going on and in all that confusion no one gave a thought to Gulbehri. When the Thanedar Sahib arrived, and the first question he asked was about Gulbehri, bedlam broke out. The Thakur Sahib opened his eyes and said, 'Thanedar Sahib, write down my statement. The time has come for my last journey.'

'No, Thakur Sahib, you . . .'

'No!' interrupted the Thakur Sahib, 'I don't fear death. I was taking Gulbehri to the court when half a dozen men attacked me. At that moment Phunnan Miyan was with me, we fought them together . . .' Having dictated his statement the Thakur Sahib breathed a sigh of relief and said, 'Jai Krishna! Jai Krishna!' He looked towards his son, 'Come, the time has come for you to lay me on the ground . . .'

He was laid on the ground.

'Where's Phunnan?'

'I'm right by you!' said Phunnan, who had managed to make his way up to him with great difficulty.

'I'm going, Khalifa . . .'

Phunnan Miyan's eyes filled with tears and he began to sob like a child.

At that moment it didn't occur to anyone that the Thakur Sahib alone was capable of dealing with half a dozen men, and therefore it was impossible for he and Phunnan Miyan to fight side by side and be beaten by them. But after the wailing over the Thakur Sahib's death subsided, people began to consider this point.

Thakur Harnarayan Prasad Singh was also of the above opinion. But neither could he say that Thakur Kunwarpal Singh's statement was false . . . and Gulbehri and her child were missing. Years later a man from Salimpur saw her at a house of ill-repute in the red light area of Ballia. Then the story broke that on that very night the Thakur had fought Phunnan Miyan, and after the Thakur Sahib had been wounded Jhinguriya had spirited Gulbehri away. This news didn't cause any sensation because people had suspected something of the sort since the day it happened.

However, at the time Thakur Harnarayan Prasad, Thanedar of Qasimabad, felt thoroughly humiliated. He brought the full might of the law to bear, but no one knew anything. He didn't touch Phunnan Miyan because he was quite badly injured. But still Phunnan's insulting behaviour stuck in his heart like a thorn.

'How can I deal with that Phunnan Miyan?' he asked Gulabi Jan. It's obvious that Gulabi Jan could have no answer to such a question. Even Samiuddin had no answer, despite being asked the same question by the Thanedar Sahib every day. His worry was that he didn't want to do anything by half measures, he wanted his blow to be so effective that Phunnan would be broken for good.

'Why don't we get Saifuniya to put in a claim against him?' suggested Samiuddin one day.

'Didn't you see what happened when we made Gulbehri file a petition?' replied the Thakur Sahib, 'If it hadn't been for Bashir Miyan, Wazir Miyan, Shabbar Miyan and Aggu Miyan, we would have crushed Phunnan Miyan long back. But what to do—they're well in with the officials in the town, and now I've found out that they're even trying to have me transferred from here.'

Samiuddin would certainly have expressed his sympathy, but at that moment the post came. There was a letter for him too. It carried very varied postmarks. His heart began to beat hard, because only his son's letters came marked like that. The Thakur Sahib also noticed the envelope.

'Here,' he said, handing it to Samiuddin, 'it looks like a letter from Moin.' Moin had written that he was coming home on the fifth of August. He had also written that he had been discharged from the army and his pension papers were being prepared.

Samiuddin ran with the letter to his quarters. He called out to his wife, 'Arre, do you hear, Moin is coming home! He's been discharged! He'll be here on the 5th of August!'

'What day of August is it today?' asked his wife.

'It's the 25th of July today.'

'You do one thing—go to Gangauli and fix the date for the wedding.'

'Arre, servant of God, what's the hurry? We've made no preparations yet.'

'How do you know whether things are prepared or not? I've got everything prepared. All the clothes for the bride are ready. Her ornaments have been made and kept in the trunk. And yes, write to our people in Jaunpur and let them know that the date is fixed. Don't forget to write to Ghafooran the singer, or she'll leave no stone unturned to eat my life. And I think we should invite Idu-bo. She's an experienced barber woman. She'll work well, and she has a great desire to see Moin as a bridegroom.'

'Let me go to Gangauli first . . .'

'You and your foolishness . . . is Ghulam Husain Khan likely to object?'

'Still, is there any harm in asking?'

Samiuddin took his shervani out from the very bottom of the trunk. He had no opportunity to wear it except on the festivals of 'Id and Baqra 'Id. He had to wear his uniform even in Moharram. He had only one complaint about his job, and that was that it made him miss the Moharram of Jaunpur. What pleasure there was in making the great drums ready.* Daggers were cleaned for the matam where people would cut themselves in grief. Thin chains, terminating in tiny sharp knives, with which the mourners used to beat themselves on the backs and chests, were washed. Samiuddin himself used to be one of the foot soldiers in the procession on the eighth of Moharram. A black string round his waist, wearing a green kurta tied round with black and white strings . . . . He still did march as a foot soldier, but it felt very strange to have to wear the khaki shirt of his uniform on top of his green kurta—and in such circumstances there was no question of him wearing a shervani. So after Baqra 'Id, Moin's mother would put the shervani away in the trunk of warm clothes, where it stayed until the next 'Id. But Samiuddin didn't want to go and fix the date of his son's marriage wearing his uniform. Moin's mother ironed out the

* The Shias of Jaunpur use a large number of great drums in Moharram.

creases in the crumpled shervani with a hot enamel bowl, and Samiuddin put it on. His wife then quickly fed him a paan and Samiuddin said, 'Bismillah . . .' and left his quarters.

'Where are you off to?' asked the Thakur Sahib, seeing his shervani.

'Moinuddin is coming home on the fifth. His mother thinks the wedding should be on the sixth or seventh. So I'm going to Gangauli to set the date.'

'Congratulations!' said the Thakur Sahib. 'And, bhai, since you're going there, go and meet the Hakim Sahib and tell him that Monroe Sahib praised him for the help he gave in procuring the grain. The honours certificates will be coming in a few days. The word is that he might even be made a "Khan Sahib".* But let him know that if ten thousand more comes in from this area, he's not going to lose that title either.'

'That's very good news.'

Samiuddin Khan climbed on to his bicycle.

The monsoon had begun. There was a dampness in the air, the wind was blowing strongly and clouds were gathering from here and there. Samiuddin looked at the clouds and guessed that he could reach Gangauli before it rained. But to be on the safe side he called for an umbrella which he tied to the crossbar.

In Gangauli bazaar Samiuddin caught sight of Phunnan. Phunnan also saw him and so the havildar was forced to greet him and climb off his bicycle. Phunnan Miyan had almost recovered, but his left shoulder still drooped, and he still didn't look his normal self.

'Tell me, Mir Sahib, how are you?'

'Huhn, there's nothing wrong with me!' said Phunnan Miyan, as if he had resolved not to speak politely to policemen. 'How come you've make the mistake of coming here? Whose house have you come to loot? No one in Gangauli has money now except the traders.'

'Adaab, Chacha!' Anwarul Hasan's son Farooq greeted Phunnan Miyan.

'Eh, bhaiyaa, how is your Pakistan doing?'

'It's being made.'

'Of course it is, bhaiyaa! You said it would be so it must be. But will Gangauli go to Pakistan or stay in Hindustan?'

'It'll stay in Hindustan. Pakistan will be made up of the Frontier Province, Punjab, Sindh and Bengal. And we're trying to get the Aligarh Muslim University in Pakistan too.'

---

* The name of Pathans and also a title bestowed by the British.

'You're not trying for Gangauli?'

'There's no question of trying for Gangauli.'

'If there's no question, then what is it to me if Pakistan is made or not.'

'There'll be an Islamic government.'

'Is there true Islam anywhere that you can have an Islamic government? Eh, bhai, our forefathers' graves are here, our tazia platforms are here, our fields and homes are here. I'm not an idiot to be taken in by your "Long live Pakistan!"'

'When the British go, the Hindus will rule here!'

'Yes, yes, so you say. You're talking as if all the Hindus were murderers waiting to slaughter us. Arre, Thakur Kunwarpal Singh was a Hindu. Jhinguriya is a Hindu. Eh, bhai, and isn't that Parusaram-va a Hindu? When the Sunnis in the town started doing *haramzadgi*, saying that we won't let the bier of Hazrat Ali be carried in procession because the Shias curse our Caliphs, didn't Parusaram-va come and raise such hell that the bier was carried. Your Jinnah Sahib didn't come to help us lift our bier!'

Farooq laughed.

'In reality the "sincerity" of the Hindus is a deception,' he said using an English word.

'Their what is a deception?'

'"Sincerity" . . . I mean that . . . Arre, sahib, that is to say . . .'

'What is it, bhai? Have you forgotten the language of your forefathers?'

Farooq began to scratch his head.

'So, Mir Sahib, I'll take my leave,' said Samiuddin Khan.

'I forgot about you with all this talk of that *susar* Pakistan. Where are you off to?'

'We've had a letter from Moinuddin saying he's coming on the fifth. We're thinking of having the rites read on the sixth and so I'm going over to see Ghulam Husain Khan.'

'Congratulations, bhai!' Phunnan Miyan smiled although he remembered with anguish that Imtiyaz would probably never return. He had already received the news that his son was missing, presumed dead, after fighting courageously at the front. When the SDO of Yusufpur had told him, he'd said, 'The things you say, Deputy Sahib. Is it any surprise that the son of Phunnan Miyan should die after fighting courageously? It's not as if he was the son of Hakim Ali Kabir!' But now when he heard of the return of Moinuddin he was sad, because he had had great hopes of Imtiyaz's marriage.

He had even chosen Hammad Miyan's daughter, Umme Habiba, as his bride—he knew that such a marriage could never take place but what was the harm in imagining it could? He had never mentioned his idea to anyone because he knew that Hammad would refuse, but he had been confident that when Imtiyaz returned he would certainly find some girl or other. The real question in life was about girls. After all, hadn't God made man and woman? Razia and Ruqayya were settled in their own homes. That left Maghfiya and God must have made a match for her too. But then news came of Imtiyaz. The loss of Thakur Kunwarpal Singh had extinguished something inside him, and now Imtiyaz's death spread utter darkness all around. That year he didn't even go to sit with the Diwali gamblers, and when Harnarayan Prasad raided them, solely with the intention of catching Phunnan Miyan, his effort was wasted. He stripped the other gamblers of their money and let them go. It was a major event for Phunnan Miyan not to gamble at Diwali. Phunnan Miyan had not stopped at this, he had even begun to say his prayers regularly. Before Imtiyaz went missing, he had begun to pray for only three things, 'Pure Protector of the World! In the name of Muhammad and Muhammad's Family, forgive Thakur Kunwarpal Singh, send a husband for Maghfiya and send Imtiyaz back safe from the war!'

Now who's to say whether or not the Almighty forgave Thakur Kunwarpal Singh, but no proposal had come for Maghfiya and there was no question of Imtiyaz returning safely. Phunnan had only one son left—Mumtaz—and he was still very young. Phunnan Miyan wondered what would happen if, God forbid, the war dragged on and Mumtaz grew up. And so, contrary to the wishes of the Muslims of Ghazipur and the traders and weavers of Gangauli, he began to add one more request to his prayers.

'Pure Protector of the World! In the name of Muhammad and Muhammad's Family, forgive Thakur Kunwarpal Singh, send a husband for Maghfiya and defeat the Germans and end the war . . . Amen!'

No one in the village knew about these prayers. Only Phunnan Miyan and God, if there is a God and He heard them—that is to say if no angel intercepted them.

But after each time he prayed, Phunnan began to ask himself who had killed the Thakur—the Phunnan who was the friend of Ashrafullah Khan, or the Phunnan who was his father's successor, the Khalifa of the wrestling-pit. He was no philosopher to consider the enigma of life and death.

Neither was he a maulvi, or any Sheikh Saadi to extract any moral lesson from the Thakur's death. He was just Phunnan Miyan, a zamindar of Gangauli and apart from Moharram he had no treasury of moral and philosophical history. As he pondered, he remembered Muhammad Ibne Abu Bakr, the son of the first Caliph who was politically opposed to his father, and took solace from the thought that if the Thakur had been killed by the Phunnan Miyan who was the friend of Ashrafullah Khan, then there was no need for repentance. But still he couldn't get the Thakur's last words out of his head—'I'm going, Khalifa!' This sentence again and again told Phunnan that perhaps the Khalifa Phunnan also had a hand in his murder. That was why, when there was a difference of opinion between Hammad and the Thakur Sahib's eldest son, Prithvipal Singh, over some land, and it came to a fight, Phunnan Miyan told his men to side with the Thakur. As a result, he came under a lot of fire from within the Patti. When he could bear listening to it no more, he lost his temper and said, 'If looking after the Patti's lands just means that Hammad can cause whatever disasters he likes and everybody should support him—I'm having none of it!'

As a result of this Phunnan Miyan was even cast out by his community in Dakkhin Patti. That hadn't happened when he'd carried off Karamat Ali's wife. Then all that had happened was that Kulsum hadn't been given the right to sit with the other Saiyid ladies. And that was as it should be. Phunnan Miyan had no complaint about it. But when Phunnan Miyan once sided with Prithvipal Singh, he was put beyond the pale. He felt no particular remorse over the *huqqa-pani bund*, which meant no one from his community would share their huqqa with him or their food or water. He knew that now he would have to look for spouses for his children from outside the community. But it was painful for him to think that there was a *huqqa-pani bund* against him, Muntaz was still young, Imtiyaz had died fighting courageously at the front, and Samiuddin was setting the date of his son's wedding. He shook his head, 'Eh, bhai! If that's what's written in your fate, what can you do?'

When he told Kulsum about Moinuddin's marriage, it brought back all the memories of Imtiyaz, and she began to cry. When she saw her mother crying, Razia also began to weep, and Ruqayya too. Razia's six-year-old daughter, Kaniz Fatima or Kaddan, saw her mother weeping and began to cry as well. Seeing her cry, Razia's five-and-a-half-year-old son, Saiyid Dilshad Husain Abidi, or Dullan, also began to sob, followed by four-year-old Sultan Fatima, or Fatto, who started to scream. Razia had miscarried the child she conceived after Fatto, and the one after that, Parveen Fatima or Pammo, was still only a year old and oblivious of the difference between laughter and tears.

For the last six or seven months Razia hadn't been keeping good health. She'd begun to feel weary in the evenings and to run a slight temperature. Her large, shining, black eyes were clouded, and the light of laughter which had always played on her lips was extinguished. And on top of this she was three months pregnant again.

Kulsum had been furious.

'Is this the only thing Mohammad Husain can find to do? Whenever you see her, she's pregnant! They're coming out one after another as fast as if they're following a timetable!'

She could say this in her anger to her daughter, but she daren't say a word to her son-in-law. Since the climate of Calcutta was not suiting Razia, she had come back to Gangauli so that she could spend Moharram there and about the same time give birth to her child.

When Naima-bi heard about Razia's condition, she made no bones about what she thought. 'Now Razia won't survive, and just you wait and see, Phunnan will marry off Maghfiya to Mohammad Husain.'

'Never!' said Ummul, putting one finger to her nose, 'Phunnan's not senile. Mohammad Husain got married late, otherwise his daughter would be as old as Maghfiya. In any case there's not much difference between them. I don't think Maghfiya can be more than three or four years older.'

'So where is Phunnan going to get a suitable son-in-law from, then?' asked Naima-bi tartly.

'From the same place he got one for Razia and Ruqayya! Why, don't you think Allah Miyan has made a husband for her?' asked Kubara.

'Do you always have to interrupt?' said Naima-bi irritably because after Abbas, Kubara too had produced a string of daughters—Umme Habiba, Sughra, Azra, Najma and Firoza. There was something of a riot over the naming of Sughra because one of the Hakim Sahib's granddaughters had the same name. The child's mother was upset that Hammad had given his daughter the same name as hers. Names were incredibly important for women.

Bashir Miyan's father's name was Muhammad, and his mother, Akbari-bibi, was so particular about not referring to her husband by name—which ladies did not do—that despite spending more than half her life in Ghazipur, up to her dying breath she always referred to the village of Muhammadpur as 'that-pur'.

And when her eldest granddaughter, Sarwari, was married to Ibne Ali, it caused great discomfiture because the words Ibne Ali—which mean the Son of Ali, that is Imam Husain—cropped up repeatedly in marsias and nauhas. During the first Moharram after she was married, when Sarwari stood up to recite a nauha as usual, she came across 'Ibne Ali' in the second verse. Since Sarwari had been a regular student of Urdu, and had gone through some books of preliminary English with Mrs North, she was no longer alive to the delicacy of the situation. She read the verse. Akbari-bibi was so infuriated that she leapt up from the floor of the imambara to say, 'I told Bashir never to bring that Christian into his house! But he was so keen to have English taught! Now see the results of this English! She can't stop taking her husband's name!'

Everyone tried to explain to her that Ibne Ali was a name of Imam Husain, but she wouldn't listen. Her logic was strange, 'Don't you think I know all that? But is Ibne Ali the name of her husband or isn't it?'

No one could counter that, consequently Akbari-bibi didn't speak to Sarwari for months. In such a world, who could ever dare give themselves the same name as someone else? But Naima-bibi endured the naming of Sughra. Somehow she also managed to endure the names Azra and Najma, although she was wont to say, 'What on earth sort of names are those?' But she drew the line at Firoza. In her opinion Abbas was finding names for his sisters like the Christians had. She was enraged and said, 'These names are all thanks to Bashir and Aggu Miyan.' Still, Abbas was obstinate and she had to admit defeat. But nothing could prevent her being annoyed with her daughter-in-law, and so she began to be as constantly irritable with her as Rabban-bi was with her daughter-in-law, Sakina.

Therefore, when Kubara made her remark about Phunnan being able to find a son-in-law, Naima-bi became annoyed. Kubara went off grumbling into the kitchen and Naima-bi began talking to Ummul. She insisted that Razia was going to die and Phunnan Miyan would marry off Maghfiya to Mohammad Husain. Ummul had no great objection to accepting this theory.

'I've heard that a proposal came for Fussu's daughter Salma from Faizabad. The marriage was being arranged, but then the boy's family broke it off because the girl was bad-looking.'

'So were they wrong?' said Naima-bi, 'We've got a whole clutch of girls to marry off. But there's no doubt about the fact that Salma is no beauty.'

'Do you think Salma's the only one? Who can say that either Kubara, Saida, Umme-Laila, Kaniz, Rabab and . . . what's the name of the baby . . . yes, Mahjabin are anything to look at? The whole tribe of them are baked in the same kiln. It says something for the strength of Fussu's heart and kidneys that he loves them all.'

'And I've heard the date's set for Badrun's wedding.'

'Ye-es. The singing of wedding songs has started.'

'Ghulam Husain Khan has prepared a very big trousseau for her.'

'I've heard he's giving her five trays with gold and ten with silver jewellery. But the cloth's a worry. It's suddenly disappeared completely from the market. He couldn't get any permit-ermit. But let's see, whatever he gets is a blessing. What times we're living through!'

But Ghulam Husain Khan had done everything humanly possible and somehow had eleven suits of clothes stitched. Badrun was after all the only daughter in the family, because after Kulsum was carried off, his brother Karamat Ali hadn't remarried. And Ghulam Husain Khan was the favoured servant of Deputy Collector Ali Hadi. He even lived in his house. So there was a large amount of additional income, and there was not one paisa expenditure. Ghulam Husain Khan didn't see any reason for saving money for anyone. Accordingly, he entrusted his post office savings book to his elder brother. His account contained 840 rupees and thirteen annas.

Ghulam Husain Khan went well beyond his means in making arrangements for the wedding. However, the Hakim Sahib and Deputy Collector Ali Hadi helped him too. They donated a set of clothes each. The Hakim Sahib's daughter gave eight silver bangles. Deputy Collector Ali Hadi's wife gave an old pair of earrings which were cleaned by the goldsmith and came back gleaming. Finally, Badrun's own mother gave her all her ornaments and jewellery. Thus was the trousseau prepared. Hands began beating the wedding drums, and Badrun was straightaway made to sit on a charpoy where Saifuniya's mother began to massage her morning and evening with a paste of mustard, sesame, chiraunji and other herbs and spices. Badrun was made to fast and the pallor this caused enhanced the glow on her skin from the paste, and she began to dream about all kinds of strange things. Her married friends, and the sisters-in-law of the village began to tell her all sorts of stories. Sometimes her heart pounded and sometimes she blushed shyly and gathered up her paste-stained clothes about her, like a delicate lajwanti plant, folding up its leaves at the slightest touch.

The Chamar women began to sing songs full of obscenities. The other women—respectable ladies—listened to them. Sometimes a lady would give a four-anna bit so they would sing obscenities about someone in particular. Sometimes someone would give eight annas for the same. As a result, it seemed as if everyone's sister had been carried off by the thanedar, and that all the women, married and unmarried, were cow-elephants whom a hundred men couldn't satisfy. And the ladies listened to the insults and laughed and laughed, and ate paan after paan. And they pounded their foreheads with despair at the times they were living through, with wheat four seers to the rupee.

On the seventh of August it began to rain from early morning. The girls began to tease Badrun.

'We told you not to eat out of the pot. Now what will you do if Miyan-bhai slips over in all this mud?'

Badrun was sitting on the charpoy with her legs bent up in front of her. At the mention of her husband she hid her face in her knees.

When the wedding procession from the groom's side arrived about eleven that night, it was discovered that one of Moinuddin's legs was made of wood. From inside the house came the sound of women and girls singing:

With lots of noise and drums, here he comes, ri,
Down the alley of the potters, here he comes, ri.
He's got his mother up to dance, so he has, ri,
He was fathered by a potter, so he was, ri.
With lots of noise and drums, here he comes, ri,
Down the alley of the sweepers, here he comes, ri.
He's got his granny up to dance, so he has, ri,
He was fathered by a sweeper, so he was, ri.
With lots of noise and drums, here he comes, ri . . .

But the moment the news of the wooden leg reached them the singing suddenly stopped.

The news spread through the village. The men said that Samiuddin Khan had not done well by concealing it. The women beat their foreheads and said that Badrun was ill-fated. The whole village considered it an outrage, and said the wedding procession should be sent back. But Ghulam Husain Khan wasn't prepared for that. Karamat

Ali Khan, his brother, even went so far as to raise his lathi. But Ghulam Husain Khan was the father of the girl and couldn't risk dishonour. He said, 'Don't you forget, we are from the girl's side.'

'So what if we are, bhaiyaa? Is our daughter lame or cripple? To hell with Samiuddin Khan! I'll knock his police *officery* out of him this minute. Bhaiyaa, there's no shortage of boys for Badrun.'

'If this cripple is written in her fate, who are we to interfere with the will of God?'

The people of the village had forgotten their differences over caste, community and property and were all set for a fight to the death. The men from Jaunpur in the groom's procession were preening themselves in their shervanis.

'Arre, let's throw out this son-in-law and take care of these *susaran* . . .' said Gaya Ahir.

'You stand aside, Khan Sahib! This is a matter of the honour of the whole village,' said Sukhram-va the Chamar.

'Who do those *saale* think they are bringing a wedding procession like this?' said Phunnan Miyan to Kulsum.

'I didn't expect this of you,' said the Hakim Sahib to Thakur Harnarayan Prasad.

'Mir Sahib, what can I say? I was sure Samiuddin must have told you. In fact I was surprised that you people were knowingly throwing the girl down a well.'

'The poor girl has been plagued with misfortune. For one thing . . .' The Hakim Sahib couldn't complete his sentence because at that moment Maulvi Bedar Husain Sadrulfazil came out of the house bringing word that Badrun had given her assent to the marriage. Inside women began weeping and wailing. Badrun's mother was crying and no one was paying attention to the women who had come with the groom's procession.

'What I'm saying is are you marrying the girl to the boy's leg or to the boy?' asked Moinuddin's mother, burning with anger. She was not in the least pleased by all this crying at her son's wedding, although when Moinuddin had first come hobbling into the house on his wooden leg she had let out a scream. She had never imagined that such a thing could happen. She had stood bare-headed in her courtyard facing the direction of Mecca and cursed the Germans and British for the war that had cost her son his leg. That had been one thing. But when the Maulvi Sahib was asking the girl, 'Do you agree to marry Moinuddin Khan, son of Samiuddin Khan, on the provision of five hundred and eleven rupees and five gold ashrafis?', there was no occasion to weep. No mother could bear such a thing.

Badrun's mother swallowed what Moinuddin's mother had to say. She also thought that what had to be had happened. What was the point of crying? And so she began to make paan for her daughter's in-laws.

But when the boy came hobbling in on his leg for the jalva ceremony, when bride and groom sit beside one another and are shown each other's faces in a mirror, the village women couldn't restrain themselves. '*Naooj*! It would have been better for Badrun if Ghulam Husain Khan had pushed her down a well!'

But the Mirasin singers saved the day. They began to sing insults.

Taller than the roof is our young bridegroom
The mother of the groom is a Bareilly bamboo
The father of the groom is a fighting cockerel
Taller than the roof is our young bridegroom.

Then the Mirasi women conducted the jalva ceremony and Ghafooran from Jaunpur sang obscenities for the women of Gangauli. The women gave her rewards for it. The time came for the salaami, when the bride's side gives money to the bridegroom. An aunt of Moinuddin put the end of Badrun's mother's dupatta into his hand and said, 'This is your mother-in-law. Hold on tight to her dupatta!'

Badrun's mother gave him eleven rupees. He didn't let go of her dupatta. She gave five rupees more. He still didn't let go. The women began to whisper that this was too much, what did the boy want? The boy's aunt said, 'The boy wants a bicycle.'

'A bicycle for a wooden leg, *naooj*, what a peculiar idea!' Ummul blurted out. Saifuniya burst into giggles. The aunt was annoyed and the argument was threatening the future of the marriage, until Badrun's mother pleaded for forgiveness and the aunt was mollified. Otherwise she'd made up her mind to leave the bride to rot in Gangauli.

Anyway, with great difficulty, the boy finally took his leave.

Sleeping arrangements for the members of the bridegroom's party had been made at the Great Gate of the Hakim Sahib. Beds had been laid out in the courtyard. For the groom there was a bedstead with red legs strung with cotton tape. For everyone else there were beds strung with string made of cotton or munj grass. One of the guests was given a bedstead made of bamboo. He asked irritably if this was the sort of hospitality you got in Gangauli.

The Hakim Sahib swallowed his pride, and another bed was

brought for the gentleman.

Packs of cards were taken out, and coatpiece, gun, black queen, twenty-nine, mang-patti, pairs and flash began to be played. The older guests smoked huqqas and ate paan until they were tired out and went to sleep. Thakur Harnarayan Prasad's bed was near the Hakim Sahib's. The Thakur Sahib was congratulating the Hakim on his new title 'Khan Sahib', when somehow the topic of the Hindu holy man who had taken up residence in the deserted temple at Murdarpur came up.

'Bhai, I've heard he's a man of standing,' said the Hakim Sahib. 'Night and day he sits before the idol reading from a fat, red-coloured book. He doesn't speak to or have anything to do with anyone. He eats whatever people give him, and if they don't give him anything he goes to sleep on an empty stomach.'

'I've heard that he grants people's prayers. One man didn't have a son, he blessed him. Now I've heard his wife's with a child.' This came from Maulvi Bedar, and there was no shade of contempt in his tone.

'I know a thing about him too,' said the Thakur Sahib.

'Gulabi Jan went to him without consulting me to ask for my promotion. The poor soul had no idea that a Circle Inspector is a promotion only in name, the job's worthless. Am I mad to want to be promoted? But when I went to Ghazipur fifteen days after she approached him, the Superintendent Sahib congratulated me on my forthcoming advancement. I think I'll find some work to do in Murdarpur, go over and touch the saint's feet and request him to let me stay a thanedar. I don't want any promotion.'

'And if you are promoted?'

'I'll leave the service. What enjoyment is there in being an inspector once you've been a thanedar? I've got myself a bit of a zamindari, and a hundred bighas I'll cultivate myself. I'll go there and take up farming.'

'That's the best thing, sahib,' said the Hakim Sahib, and then stopped when he saw Rahim the barber. 'What is it, *re*?'

'Phunnan Miyan's eldest daughter's taken very ill. The poor Miyan went running off to Ulavalpur, but the Dagdar Sahib* had gone to Ghazipur. The house is full of weeping and wailing,' said Rahim, picking up the bowl of the huqqa and blowing on the embers. When it was burning properly he put it back in its place. The Hakim Sahib

---

* Doctor Sahib.

began to take short and frequent puffs on the huqqa. For a short while he tried to put off doing anything about the news of Razia's illness, but after five minutes or so he said 'Ya Ali' and got up.

'I'll just go and take a look at her,' he told the Thakur and then turned to Rahim. 'Did Phunnan Miyan send you here?'

'No,' Rahim replied, 'Bibi begged him to, but he said let her die. I'm not going to salaam Hakim Ali Kabir . . .'

The Hakim Sahib smiled.

'You go on ahead. Who knows if Saifuniya might not come out from somewhere and you'll call a panchayat meeting and give a speech against me. Why don't you get the girl married? The *haramzadi* is flaunting herself all over the place. Do you want to ruin our boys' characters or what?'

Rahim grinned, as if the Hakim Sahib was not talking about his own daughter.

When the Hakim Sahib came out of the gaslight the night seemed even darker. He stepped on a dog. It ran off yelping. He cursed its mother and sister and went on. Rahim was beside him. When he came to the Great Gate he suddenly heard Kulsum's voice raised in grief. He recited from the holy Qo'ran, 'All things come from God, and to God do they return,' and retraced his steps.

The sound of Kulsum's keening woke the traders. Farooq and Anwarul Hasan immediately set out for Phunnan's house. Hammad Miyan called out from his door, 'Arre, bhai, what's the matter?'

'It seems that Phunnan-cha's daughter has passed away,' said Farooq.

Hammad Miyan went back indoors. All of Dakkhin Patti was awake, but pretending to be asleep. Javad Miyan went so far as to scold his kept woman, Rahman-bo, when she wanted to go out, with the words, 'Where do you think you're going? Don't you know there's a *huqqa-pani bund* against Phunnan Miyan?'

When Rahman-bo tried to reply, Javad slapped her twice. She deserved it. How dare a kept woman utter a sound against his will! His grown-up son Kamaluddin, or Kammo, intensely resented Javad beating his mother like this. His second son, Fida Husain, or Fiddu, began to cry. Javad Miyan slapped him too.

Throttle the bastard!'

'Hold your tongue, *heramzade*, or I'll give you a bellyful!'

'Half a yard tall and you've got a tongue on you seven yards long!'

'Are you going to beat me?'

'Aren't you beating my mother in front of me?'

'Yes, take this!'

Javad Miyan started hitting Rahman-bo again. Kammo grabbed hold of his hand. He was a young man. Javad was broad-built but old. He struggled and when he couldn't release his hand he began to curse Kammo's ancestry.

'What's new in that? I am a bastard in any case,' said Kammo, 'but if you say anything more to my mother, I'll bury you alive.'

Rahman-bo was clinging to Kammo, 'Let him go, *matimile*! How dare you hit your father! May your corpse be carried out! *Jharumare*! Are you mad? Arre, I'm telling you let him go!'

Even then Kammo didn't release Javad's hand and so Rahman-bo began hitting him. Further annoyed by this, Kammo finally shoved Javad Miyan away from him. Javad Miyan fell on to a bed and began to curse Kammo from where he lay.

When Thakur Prithvipal Singh heard the news of Razia's death and immediately came to Gangauli he passed Javad's house and heard his curses. Naturally he paid them no attention.

Without asking Hammad Miyan, Phunnan had opened the doors of the Great Gate. When Hammad objected, he went and fetched his lathi.

'So now you've come to this! I'm telling you, Hammad, stay out of my way! This is the gate through which people have come to offer condolences for the death of my father, and my forefathers. Where do you want me to go to receive condolences for Razia's death—Jinnah Sahib's Pakistan?'

Seeing his mood, Hammad retreated, but Naima-bi and Kubara came to their doorway to curse him. Phunnan addressed Naima-bi, 'Oh, weaver woman, if you were a Saiyid you wouldn't swear like that! But talk your nonsense. After all you're a woman. What can I say to you? But just remember that if you don't hold your tongue, I'll beat Hammad into pulp.' Both women shrank back indoors. Phunnan sat down on a bed and lit a beedi. Farooq sat on another bed but Anwarul Hasan didn't sit down by him. He squatted down on the platform by the gate and began to smoke a cigarette. Rahim brought new clay pots and ber twigs were placed in them.

Phunnan Miyan looked around the wide courtyard, which could hold five hundred people. Then he looked at the two men who had come to offer their sympathy. Phunnan was a brave man. He began to play with the ends of his moustache. But tears are not overawed by brave men. When his eyes brimmed over, he turned on to his side so that Farooq wouldn't see that he was crying. Then, when it was no longer possible for him to lay quietly, he began to murmur the lament of Imam Husain's sick daughter Sughra begging her father to take her with him on his last journey.

I'm not asking you to seat me on a camel,
Father, seat me just with our nurse Fizzan.

When Razia's funeral procession set out, Phunnan Miyan, Thakur Prithvipal Singh, Jhinguriya and Anwarul Hasan carried her bier, and the entire family of Thakur Kunwarpal Singh walked behind. Phunnan Miyan led the procession to the northern wall of the Karbala by his family burial ground. The grave was ready. The bier was set down. Maulvi Bedar Husain Sadrulfazil, and every one of the faithful of Gangauli had refused to read the prayers for the dead over her body, and so Phunnan Miyan prayed alone. He didn't remember the prayers for the dead and so he prepared to say his namaz.

'Pure Protector of the World! I don't remember the proper prayers, but what can I do? But accept this namaz which I offer to you, Allah-o-Akbar!' announcing the words 'God is great!' in a clear voice, he said his namaz. Then he started to climb into the grave. But Prithvipal Singh wouldn't let him. 'I'll put my sister down there,' he said.

Naturally, Phunnan couldn't agree. Razia had kept purdah from Prithvipal Singh. So Phunnan climbed down himself. Prithvipal Singh and Jhinguriya lowered the corpse into the grave. Phunnan Miyan drew the shroud from her face and said, 'Eh, beti, what can I do? I don't know how to recite the right prayers for you at all . . . but I can bear witness that you were a beloved daughter of the community, said your prayers regularly and served your husband well!'

He climbed out of the grave. The grave was levelled.

When Phunnan Miyan came back into the village, Badrun's palanquin was setting out. Leading the procession was Moinuddin, also in a palanquin. His wooden leg was unstrapped and lying to one side. Phunnan Miyan made way for the returning wedding procession.

The moment the procession reached Qasimabad, an informer told the Thakur Sahib that Parusaram the Chamar had gathered together men from a religious establishment near the Murdarpur temple and was holding a meeting. The Thakur Sahib hadn't had time to consider this piece of information before news came from Ghazipur that Gandhi, Nehru and all the other senior Congress leaders had been arrested and it was necessary to be on the alert.

The Thakur immediately set out for Murdarpur with eight of his constables but found no one there. Even the saint, Babaji Maharaj, was missing. There was a red book like an accounts book lying in front of the deity. The Thakur Sahib picked it up. It really was an accounts book and it didn't take long for the Thakur Sahib to recognize it. It was Gobardhan's accounts book, the one which held all the details of his far-flung business.

It was already evening by the time the Thakur Sahib reached Qasimabad again. From the direction of Samiuddin's quarters came the sound of Gulabi Jan's lilting voice. The Thakur Sahib looked at Samiuddin, who was unfastening his belt.

'Go, have a look at your daughter-in-law.'

Samiuddin had a look at his daughter-in-law and was pleased by what he saw. In reward for her showing her face he gave her the gold necklace his mother had given him for Moinuddin's wife before she died.

They ate just before ten o'clock. The gaslights were turned out. Gulabi Jan pushed and pulled Moinuddin and sent him into the bridal chamber—behind the 'Curtain of Heaven'—because the ladies from Jaunpur who should have done so had already set off for home with their husbands at the first news of insurrection.

Moinuddin was very shy.

'Even if I want to come to you quietly I can't . . . this wooden leg goes tuk . . . tuk . . . tuk . . .'

He sat down on the bed. Badrun, wearing deep red, was lying flat on her back. Her eyes were closed. Her heart was pounding and the tiny beads of sweat on her nostrils were trembling. A strange fragrance rose from her hair and her clothes were perfumed with attar-of-wedding-night. Glitter sparkled on her brow like a galaxy of stars. Moinuddin saw all this in one glance. Then he took off his leg. He propped it carefully against the wall and bent over Badrun.

'Open your eyes just once, and see what I look like.'

Badrun heard his voice. She liked it too. But she didn't open her eyes. Her heart began to pound even harder because someone had told her, 'Don't show off too much on the first night . . . when you give birth it's so painful it's killing.' And she began to feel a sense of curiosity—how did a boy come into your stomach? But her whole body was as cold as ice and seven or eight days of fasting had robbed her of all strength to resist. It's possible that girls were made to sit on a string bed and fast so that if the bridegroom had only one leg or was very ugly, the bride couldn't resist. At least Badrun couldn't.

Late at night when Moinuddin had worn himself out and gone to sleep, Badrun opened her eyes. She was worn out herself. Despite the numbness in her body caused by fasting, she felt a sweet pain. And yet she opened her eyes. First she looked at Moinuddin's face, and although he was asleep, she blushed. Then she looked at his whole body, bit by bit. But part of his body was leaning against the wall. Seeing the wooden leg, she felt sad.

Just at that moment the constable on duty at the police station fired his first shot.

The Bhars from the Bhar settlement, and the men of Prithvipal Singh and Ashrafullah Khan had surrounded the thana. There must have been some two thousand men. In this crowd there were few people who knew the slogan, 'Quit India'.

There weren't even people among them who knew what 'freedom' meant. These were the people from whom one-and-a-half the amount of land revenue had been taken, from whose fields the grain had been seized, who had been forced to contribute to the war fund, whose brothers and nephews had been killed or were about to be killed in the war, and from whom the police of Qasimabad had been extracting bribes for generations. Among them were Komila Chamar's father, Baburam Chamar, and Gobardhan. But the largest group among them belonged to Phunnan Miyan, although Phunnan Miyan wasn't there himself. Leading Phunnan's group was Harpal Singh, grandson of Thakur Kunwarpal Singh and eldest son of Prithvipal Singh, and standing shoulder-to-shoulder with him was Jhinguriya.

The crowd's demand was that Thakur Harnarayan Prasad be handed over to them. It's obvious that this was impossible. The Thakur Sahib barricaded himself in, and it was he who fired the first shot—the shot which killed Harpal Singh. Gobardhan was also killed in the first round of firing, as was Mumtaz, who had celebrated his fifteenth birthday two days earlier. Phunnan Miyan didn't know that he was among the attackers or perhaps he would have stopped him. Or perhaps he would have recalled some verse of a marsia which described Imam Husain at Karbala fastening a sword around the waist of his eighteen-year-old son, Ali Akbar or his thirteen-year-old son, Qasim—if he had recalled such a verse, it's very likely that he would have recited it softly and given Mumtaz permission to go, and not told Kulsum.

When the crowd saw those three corpses it turned mad. The police station was overrun. The Thakur Sahib and all his constables were tied to a tree and burnt to death, and their quarters were set on fire.

There was no noise from any of the quarters except that of Samiuddin. For a long time the sound of women's screams came from there.

When the crowd had dispersed, a woman picked her way out of the ruins of Samiuddin's quarters. If anyone had been present they would never have recognized her in that miserable condition. It was Gulabi Jan. In her hand was a wooden leg on which she leaned like a walking-stick.

The Tale

The days passed but the pain of the walls and doors of Gangauli did not. The scratches made in the mud walls by the kicks of the leather-soled boots of the government forces did not fade. The vengeance of the leather-soled had not fallen on the houses of the Saiyids but still Moharram was a pale shadow of itself because the hands which beat breasts in mourning, and the hands which decorated and bore the heavy wooden tazias, and the hands which led the processions holding long, stout lathis, and the hands which displayed their skill at lathi-work, were all disabled by fear. The crowds of Hindu boys outside the imambaras were no less, but the light in their eyes was somehow extinguished, and the same boys Javad Miyan or Hakim Ali Kabir used to grow tired swearing at to keep quiet, were themselves silent. The leather-soled had wrung out the bodies of the Bhar, Chamar and Ahir settlements and Barikhpur village like wet cloths and perhaps extracted every single drop of their souls. The Hindu population of Gangauli was also afflicted, but the Muslims to a large extent escaped. According to Abbas, they were saved by the Muslim League. As for the Saiyids, those of Uttar Patti were counted as loyalists due to Deputy Collector Ali Hadi, and because the Hakim Sahib had been responsible for the recruitment of one-hundred-and-eleven men, and had helped raise a large sum for the war fund.

Destruction would certainly have fallen on Dakkhin Patti but was mitigated by the influence of Aggu Miyan, Bashir Miyan and Wazir Miyan, and by the fact that Hammad Miyan took advantage of the opportunity to testify against Phunnan Miyan. Phunnan Miyan was consequently arrested for the martyrdom of Mumtaz. Like all the other 'rebels' he was sentenced. Aggu Miyan and Wazir Miyan tried hard to persuade him to file a plea for pardon, as there was no point in going to jail when he hadn't done anything. But Phunnan Miyan's sense of honour found this suggestion intolerable. He said, 'Eh, bhaiyaa, I am a great sinner. If I have to beg for pardon I'll do so from Allah Miyan. But I'll never ask these *susaran* bastards for it.'

So Phunnan Miyan went to jail. But where could Kulsum go? When she discovered that Hammad Miyan had testified against Phunnan Miyan she stepped into her courtyard. Standing with her face in the direction of Hazrat Ali's tomb at Najaf, she said, 'Eh, Lord, Solver of Problems! You alone make light our difficulties.'

After entrusting her difficulties to Hazrat Ali, she began in a loud, clear voice to curse Hammad Miyan, wishing that worms would eat his body, that there would be darkness in his tomb, and that his daughter, Umme Habiba, would run off with an untouchable. These words reached Naima-bi by way of Saifuniya, and she began to express her thoughts about the relationship between Phunnan and Kulsum, the parentage of their children, and especially about the youth of their daughter Maghfiya, reaching the conclusion that Maghfiya was carrying on with Mohammad Husain, which was why he had given his wife Razia poison and murdered her. 'And who knows if Kulsum isn't carrying on with her son-in-law too. What else? How can any woman like that be decent? She's already had two husbands, she must be on the look out for the third.'

It's quite possible that Kulsum took some hint from these insults of Naima-bi's because three days after the first anniversary of Mumtaz's death, she called for the Maulvi and had him say the necessary words, and Maghfiya became the mother of her sister's four children.

'I told you so,' Naima-bi said to Rabban-bi, 'now if, God forbid, Maghfiya dies, goodness knows who Kulsum will get to be his next wife.'

'And I've heard that Mohammad Husain isn't taking his wife to Calcutta,' added Kubara, 'she'll be looking after Puddan, Dullan, Fattu and Pammu right here.'

'Well, fancy that!' said Rabban-bi, her one eye dancing, 'The things you say! But won't she have a child then?'

'That she will,' said Naima-bi, 'but who's to say whose it'll be? If anyone says anything they'll have their tongues caught, but who doesn't know that since Phunnan Miyan went to jail, Jhinguriya's son has been going to their house every day. He goes to ask after their welfare, and he must be eighteen or twenty years old!'

The fact was that the government had hanged Jhinguriya, but his son, who by chance was not in Gangauli at the time, had escaped being arrested. He knew of the friendship between Phunnan Miyan and his father. That was the reason he went to Phunnan's house every day so that Kulsum should not feel deserted. He would come, squat outside the door and call out, 'Eh, Dullan Miyan!'

The moment he heard his voice, Razia's son Dilshad Husain, or Dullan, would run out.

'Tell me, Miyan, how's your *musalmani*?' At this, Dullan would hold firmly on to the hem of his kurta. He hadn't yet been circumcised. Razia had prayed for something and had promised in return not to have him circumcised until he was twelve. Meanwhile he had seen the fate of several *musalmanis* and was thoroughly scared.

'All right, let it be, bhaiyaa. I won't cut it. Go, go inside and ask your grandmother if she has any work for me to do.'

Dullan considered this chance to escape a blessing, and immediately ran inside. He would pass on Chikuriya's message and pass straight back whatever message Kulsum gave him without altering a word. Even after receiving the reply, Chikuriya would remain sitting there for a short while, drawing crooked lines in the dust or busying himself rubbing chewing tobacco in the palm of his hand, blowing off any excess lime, putting the lime and tobacco between his gums and lower lip, and spitting noisily. And sometimes he would look across at Hammad Miyan's two-storey house which was now complete.

The platform on which the house was constructed was quite high above the ground, and so wrought iron railings had been erected around its edge, in front of the arched hall facing the lane. Gaya Ahir could generally be seen leaning over them. Chikuriya didn't speak to Gaya. He had nothing against him personally. But Gaya was as close to Hammad Miyan as the hair in his nose, and Hammad Miyan had given evidence against Phunnan Miyan. Chikuriya could bear no man of his goodwill.

Chikuriya was not overwhelmed with grief at his father being hanged. He was bound to have been hanged sooner or later. And Chikuriya didn't even know that his father had been killed for undertaking a heroic deed, or that he'd been martyred. He only knew that Imam Husain had been martyred, and therefore he believed that to be a martyr you had to be an Imam Sahib. And he also knew that whatever his father was, he was certainly no Imam Sahib. Anyhow, even Jhinguriya himself couldn't have known as he drew his last breath that he was not simply dying, he was attaining martyrdom. This fact had only been established after he was dead.

When a teacher in the town told Chikuriya that his father had been martyred in the cause of the motherland, Chikuriya emphatically refused to believe it. The teacher was astonished. He delivered a long speech on the subject too. But the speech was beyond Chikuriya's comprehension, and he thought he should say something to the teacher.

So he said, 'Don't say all these things, Master Sahib, if the Imam hears there'll be hell to pay.'

'Imam Sahib?' screamed the sandalwood tika on the Master Sahib's brow, 'What Imam Sahib?'

Chikuriya was absolutely flabbergasted at this question. He wondered what on earth the Master Sahib was teaching his pupils when he didn't even know who the Imam Sahib was! So he said, 'That I can't tell you. But he's a very powerful man. He comes here for ten days. We lift a whole lot of tazias for him, and prasad is given. The men who do lathi-work gather . . .'

He described Moharram in every detail.

'Arre, are you the offspring of an immortal martyr or a Muslim to be talking such nonsense?'

'Hold on there, bhaiyaa. I'm not an idiot. You shouldn't call the Imam Sahib a Muslim. If he was so do you think the Miyans would let us make offerings to him and he would accept them?'

The Master Sahib tried his level best to persuade Chikuriya that the Imam Sahib was a devout Muslim, but Chikuriya knew that he couldn't be. The Muslims were Maulvi Bedar who didn't eat anything touched by a Hindu, or Hakim Ali Kabir who kept bathing in the tank by his Gate for the slightest of reasons to keep himself pure.

The Master Sahib lost his temper. He cursed and abused Muslims. He said that these outcaste aliens had destroyed the land of India. These sinners had demolished countless temples to build mosques. Chikuriya didn't accept this cither as no such thing had happened in Gangauli. The Miyans gave donations to the Dussehra celebrations and Zaheer Miyan had given five bighas of revenue-free land to the monastery of a Hindu holy man.

But the Master Sahib had also studied history. He said, 'Didn't the Emperor Aurangzeb destroy one or two temples?'

'I don't know about Aurangzeb,' said Chikuriya, 'but I know Zaheer Miyan and Kabir Miyan and Fussu Miyan and Anwarul Hasan Raqi. I don't agree with what you say. The people you're talking about—those *saalas* may have been *badmashes*. I'm not talking about the cruelties of the zamindars. But anyone who has a zamindari is bound to be hard. If they're not they can't run their lands, and the Miyans are zamindars.'

'And what about the fact that they're all trying to make Pakistan?'

'I don't know nothing about Pakistan-Akistan. But if Pakistan is no very good thing, then don't let them make it. But I'll have you know that if I back down from what I say then I can't be called my father's son. Now get off.'

But where could the Master get off to? He still had to count the bricks of all the temples which he thought the Muslims had destroyed. And he had to calculate how many scars the Mughals and Pathans had left on the body of Indian culture. This Taj Mahal, this Fatehpur Sikri, this imambara of Asaf-ud-Daula, this tradition of Khayal singing, these swaying mango groves of grafted mangoes—the Muslims really had caused India immeasurable harm, and that was why the Master Sahib was relating the list of their misdeeds.

'I'm no very great man, I'm just a farmer. I know nothing of Pakistan-Akistan. I understand fields and groves. And I have seen that when the Thakur of Barikhpur is cruel he's no better than the Miyans of Gangauli.'

The Master Sahib made his final assault. 'Arre, Phunnan Miyan was responsible for getting Jhinguriya hung!'

'Now look here, Master Sahib! Don't you say a word against Phunnan Miyan. And as for my father's hanging, you were just saying that I should look on him as a martyr. So now what are you saying I should look on him as? All the Bhars of our settlement are ready to die for Phunnan Miyan, wherever his sweat falls. Now you go and do your teaching!'

Chikuriya returned from the town depressed. Until then he had wanted to give his son an education—not in the village school but in the town school, where the boys sat on chairs. But his heart was embittered by his conversation with the Master Sahib. Was that the nonsense taught in the town school? That day Chikuriya sat for a long time before the Shiv lingam beneath the peepul tree, and asked Lord Shiva who had told this mixture of truth and lies to the Master Sahib . . . but the next day when he went as usual to Phunnan Miyan's house he called out in the same affectionate tone as he always had, 'Eh, Dullan Miyan!'

And when Dullan came running out and, as soon as he saw him, put his hand over his *musalmani* as he always did, Chikuriya was convinced that the Master Sahib had been wrong.

So he stretched out his hand and caught hold of Dullan's *musalmani*. Dullan began to shout and scream.

'Arre, what are you doing?' came Kulsum's voice from inside the house.

'I'm cutting Dullan Miyan's *musalmani*,' said Chikuriya controlling Dullan who was writhing like a fish.

From within came the sound of Kulsum and Maghfiya's laughter.

Kuddan came and peeped round the door. Fattu and Pammu came right outside to enjoy the scene and Dullan began to wail.

Chikuriya burst out laughing. He let go of Dullan's *musalmani*. Dullan ran off to the Great Gate as fast as he could, then turned and began to curse Chikuriya's mother and sisters. Chikuriya was rolling around with mirth. And when Maghfiya began to scold Dullan from inside the house, Chikuriya stopped her. Kubara overheard this exchange between Maghfiya and Chikuriya and hurried straight off to Rabban-bi. She didn't even feel the need to call for her palanquin, but glanced around, slipped through the Great Gate and, via Gori-bi's courtyard, the zenana imambara and Aggu Miyan's empty house, arrived in Rabban-bi's house. At that moment Rabban-bi had opened her penbox and was writing to Akbari-bua in the simple coded script she knew. Coincidentally she was in the process of writing about Maghfiya and Chikuriya, and so when she heard from Kubara that the day of judgement was right at hand, she immediately put down her pen and listened attentively. Kubara told a great, long tale about the two. She omitted to mention that Maghfiya had been in purdah and had been laughing at Dullan's helplessness. On the basis of that laughter she built a complete love story about how one night she had seen Chikuriya use his lathi to vault over the wall into Phunnan Miyan's house.

'Eh, Dulhan,' Rabban-bi called out to Sakina, 'give Kubara some paan. Let me write a letter to Ba'ji.'

Sakina opened her betel box. Rabban-bi began writing to Akbari again. In this letter she described the relations between Chikuriya and Maghfiya too. Meanwhile Kubara and Sakina both began to discuss the war and their grown-up, unmarried daughters. Then they began to argue. They had settled that there was only six months' difference in age between Umme Habiba and Salma, but Sakina said that her Salma was younger, and Kubara said her Umme Habiba was. Mothers refuse to let their daughters grow older. The matter of a day's difference in age assumes importance, so that if anyone criticizes their daughter's unmarried state, they can reply, 'But she's no age to be married! The girl of such and such a Miyan isn't married yet, and our daughter is six months younger than her.'

The argument became so heated that Kubara left in a huff.

As long as Hammad Miyan was living in his little apartment, his wife Kubara could never have spoken like that to any Saiyid lady. However, living in a two-storey, brick house makes you a Saiyid in any case. Kubara had become a proper Saiyid lady herself. Even

Hammad's mother, Naima-bi, had become a Saiyid, despite the fact that all the members of her family were still mere weavers and worked on looms in Gangauli itself.

In collaboration with the patwari, Lala Dindayal, Hammad Miyan had transferred to his name all the land owned and cultivated by Akbari-bi, his elder brother (who was the son of a real Saiyid lady) and Saghir Miyan (who was a shareholder in the zamindari and had given Hammad power of attorney). In return the patwari had obtained the field near the pond which he had been wanting for a long time. Taking advantage of the war, Hammad also carried out some further evictions. All together he was now cultivating as much land as five ploughs could turn, and the crop was solely potatoes. He began to be considered one of the rich men of Gangauli although his wealth couldn't compare with that of the Raqi traders. On the other hand, the traders didn't have the status of the zamindars. Nowadays when Hammad went up to town he wore a long silk shervani coat. He had inherited trunkfuls of these coats when his elder brother died. On his head he wore a beautiful, carefully selected cap. He put more effort into choosing his cap than girls must do into choosing their dupattas.

Now the wife of such a splendid Saiyid as Hammad Husain Zaidi, son of Saiyid Abbas Husain Zaidi, and herself Musammat Kubara Begum, daughter of Sheikh Shuja'at Ali Ansari, undoubtedly had the full right to speak sharply to an idle, old and haggard Saiyid woman like Sakina.

However, when Javad Miyan heard that Kubara had spoken harshly to Fussu's wife, he was incensed.

'Now Hammad's wife has got the face to think she can start talking back to Saiyid ladies! May the Lord preserve Saghir and Akbari-bi, thanks to whom Hammad's become rich. But as long as I'm alive, that doesn't mean that his wife can insult Rabban-bi's daughter-in-law.'

Slapping his headcloth over one shoulder, he went off to Hammad Miyan's door. Gaya was leaning on the railings as usual. The moment he saw Javad Miyan he salaamed him. Javad Miyan was after all a member of a zamindar family. But Javad Miyan did not reply. He said, 'Where's Hammad? That *haramzadi* weaver woman's started swearing at Saiyid ladies!'

Hammad was indeed at home. He heard Javad, but didn't come out. However Kulsum and Maghfiya rushed to their doorway and peeped out to watch the fun.

Gaya was at a loss as to what to do. Javad Miyan was after all a

Miyan. So Gaya just stood and said nothing. Javad Miyan became even more of a tiger. 'I'm going now, but if after this that Kubara shows any disrespect there'll be no one worse than me.'

'What'll you do then?' asked Naima-bi, unable to keep silent any longer.

'Eh, weaver woman! What do you expect me to do to you? But I'll tear off Hammad's legs for him.'

'So the government belongs to your father does it, *matimile*? You can't afford to eat bread twice a day, but your tongue's a foot long.' Suddenly she addressed Gaya, '*Matimile*, what are you doing just standing there listening?'

'Arre, what else do I do?' said Gaya helplessly, 'Hit an old man?' He turned towards Javad Miyan. 'Eh, Mir Sahib, that's enough, now go home.'

'So you're eating Saghir Miyan's bread too are you?' said Javad Miyan, pulling himself up to his full height. His pink and white face had turned absolutely red with rage. His veins stood out. 'Don't bark from the house of a bastard.'

The news reached Uttar Patti that Gaya had challenged Javad Miyan. There was uproar. The young men thought that there was no need to get involved in the matter but the Hakim Sahib said, 'No, this concerns the community.'

When he set out from his house the whole of Uttar Patti came with him. The Chamars and Ahirs who were at their doors joined them. The Hakim Sahib drew to a halt outside Hammad Miyan's house.

'What's the matter, Miyan Javad?' asked the Hakim Sahib.

'How can I tell you, Miyan Kabir?' replied Javad Miyan, 'Now the day has dawned that weaver women are showing off in front of Saiyid ladies. Out of respect of the memory of his late father we people keep quiet, and then this Hammad thinks that, God forbid, we are dependent on him for our bread . . . and now this *haramzada* Gaya is being offensive.'

'Don't say that, Mir Sahib!' said Gaya, 'How could I be rude to you? I just said that was enough, and this crowd came here. I'm a servant. I'm here to serve you. Don't speak to me if you don't want to. But don't abuse Hammad Miyan in front of me or I'll . . .'

'Or you'll what?' said the Hakim Sahib hotly.

'Arre, what can I do, Mir Sahib?' said Gaya helplessly. It was obvious that he could do no harm to the Hakim Sahib. Naima-bi had been watching. At this point she began cursing the Hakim Sahib, and Hammad Miyan thought it no longer fitting to remain indoors. He came out with his sixteen-or seventeen-year-old son, Mighdad. Mighdad was quite unlike his brother Abbas. Hammad Miyan had not given Mighdad an education, saying that if he learnt to read and write there would be no one to run the farm. Neither did Mighdad mind. He was always busy looking after the bullocks, or milking the buffaloes or supervising the fields and threshing floors. After he returned from a pilgrimage to Karbala, Hammad Miyan had grown a beard and given up eating any food touched by Hindus. Kubara and Naima-bi couldn't milk the buffaloes and so Mighdad had to do this too and he had first become aware of his manhood as he was doing so.

He was in the middle of the evening milking one day when Saifuniya arrived. Saifuniya used to bother him a lot. The moment she saw him she'd come up with some sharp comment which would hurt him and worry him all night. It came to the point that Mighdad became scared of Saifuniya, and realizing this she began to be more of a tigress. That evening too she had thrown a cutting remark at him. Mighdad burned with anger. He put down the bucket of milk and grabbed her by the throat. But her throat was soft and warm, and he could feel the long eyelashes of her wide eyes brushing against his forehead, and her full, fresh lips were so close to his that he could feel the heat from them. Saifuniya didn't cry out or scream. She began to laugh. There was pleasure and contempt in her laughter. His hair stood all on end, and it seemed as if the whole world was engulfed in Saifuniya's big, dark eyes. Suddenly Mighdad became a man . . . . A young man who ploughs enough land for five ploughs does not leave his village. After he had won Saifuniya, Mighdad no longer felt any ill-will towards Abbas, and he began to pray that somehow Pakistan would be created soon.

'Father and Abbas will happily go off there,' he thought. 'I'll stay here and farm, and Saifuniya will cook the food.'

As a result, he asked Abbas, who'd come back during his summer vacations, the direct question, 'Eh, bhaiyaa, when is this Pakistan-Okistan going to be made?'

'Why?' smiled Abbas, 'Will you vote for the Muslim League?'

'Yes!'

'And if Father tells you off?'

'Is the vote mine or Father's?'

'But you're still a child. You can't even have a vote.'

A very meaningful smile came over Mighdad's lips. How could he tell Abbas that he wasn't a child, he was a man? So he let the matter drop and went off to put out fodder for the bullocks. He was very fond of these animals. He whispered into one bullock's ear, 'Are you listening? Bhaiyaa still thinks that I'm a child. He's an idiot.' He laughed. Just then Saifuniya came in. She used to come every evening to collect some milk for herself. Mighdad would give her a full seer of milk and then add a seer of water to the milk bucket.

'Just let Pakistan be made, then we'll have great fun,' said Mighdad.

'Aren't you having fun now?' complained Saifuniya. She had really fallen for this young man. Despite being four or five years older than him, when she came to take milk in the evening she forgot the age difference and the experiences of other young barber girls. Mighdad really was her first man. Until now men were constantly thinking of how to win her. One or two actually could. But she had won Mighdad herself. She had begun to consider him her own possession and in the lap of twilight she would forget that she was a barber's daughter and he was the son of a zamindar. She didn't think of marriage but she certainly did want to make time stand still, the evenings not to end. Her father arranged her marriage but the very day the groom and his wedding party arrived she disappeared. Mighdad hid her in the storeroom where the straw was kept. The groom's wedding party had to return. When Saifuniya went home Mehruniya and Rahim beat her like washermen beat the dirt out of wet clothes and hang them on the line to dry. But she didn't tell them where she'd been. Every limb in her body ached, but she was happy that she had not once mentioned Mighdad's name. For ten or twelve days she wasn't fit to leave the house. Still, Mehruniya was after all her mother. She didn't leave her daughter's bedside. When one day she could no longer bear to keep quiet she said, 'Don't place any hope in the Miyans!'

This was an ordinary sentence. But in this one sentence was the whole story of the deprivations and disgrace suffered by Mehruniya, her mother Jinti and her grandmother Fakhruniya. Saifuniya was deeply moved by her mother's tone. There was more pain expressed in it than there was pain in her body. But Saifuniya endured this pain too.

'I won't tell!'

'You're thinking, aren't you, what does your mother know? But your mother knows it all. All right, don't tell, but listen to me—it's easy to suffer the pains of the body, but the pains of the heart are impossible to bear. Don't waste your life for a seer of milk.'

After saying this, she started, and wondered why her thoughts had never turned in that direction before. 'Arre, *baap-re-baap*! What a calamity!' She stood up in agitation.

'What's wrong?' asked Saifuniya, herself distressed.

'You should ask what's not wrong!'

Saifuniya wanted to ask something more but Mehruniya had hurried out. She wanted to go faster than the wind but she was forced to stop outside Hammad's doorway. How could she go on? There was a crowd at the door and Mighdad was holding a lathi and staring at Hakim Ali Kabir.

'I would like to request you to go inside,' said Hammad Miyan to Mighdad in chaste Urdu. Ever since he'd inherited his brother's shervani coats he'd started speaking in Urdu. 'Hakim Sahib, you are well-acquainted with the law. If you make a forcible entry into a house, charges of dacoity and rioting can be brought against you.'

'Bring them, then,' replied the Hakim Sahib in his native tongue, 'but I'm not going to stand and see this *haramzada* Ahir bandy words with Mir Javad. Now the days have come when he'll even talk down to me!'

'Now then, *beh* . . .' said Hammad Miyan, aiming a few abuses at Gaya, 'apologize to the Mir Sahib.'

'Huzoor, you are my mother and father. Forgive anything I've said or you've heard,' said Gaya to the Hakim Sahib.

'However, Miyan Javad,' continued Hammad, 'it does not abound to your credit that you become entangled in women's remarks and start swearing like a good-for-nothing. The Lord Almighty Himself said that women are foolish . . .'

'Accha, leave your Persian out of this. And tell Hammad-bi that she can say what she likes within her own four walls, but she shouldn't answer back to Saiyids.'

'Hammad-bi' was a very derogatory term for Kubara. The arrow hit its mark. Hammad Miyan flushed with anger, but controlled it. He smiled and said, 'You are an elder of the community. I cannot reply to your remark.'

Javad went off swearing. The men from Uttar Patti also returned. Hammad Miyan went into his office room followed by Gaya. When Mehruniya entered the room she could hear half a sentence of Hammad Miyan's '. . . there's a quarter bigha of arhar dal, isn't there?' Seeing Mehruniya he paused, 'What is it, *re*?'

'Something terrible's happened, Miyan.'

Gaya understood her tone. 'So I'm off. The job will be done tonight. Salaam!' After offering his salaam by bending his head and raising his hand to his forehead, he picked up the nine-foot-high lathi leaning against the wall and left.

'Haven't I told you not to come here like this?'

'So what am I to do? Should I close my eyes when I see that Mighdad Miyan's fallen for Saifuniya?'

'What nonsense are you talking?'

'Then let it pass. What is it to me? Whatever's happened has happened.'

'Eh, bhai, so why don't you get her married?'

'Can we do that just now? It's not fifteen days since the wedding procession came for her.'

Hammad Miyan stood up and started pacing up and down. There was nothing surprising in the fact that a son of a Saiyid had been ensnared by a barber's daughter. These were the ways of the zamindars. There was nothing much to the Saiyid women, they were just wives. But Saifuniya and Mighdad, this really was something dreadful. For the first time Hammad regretted that his relationship with Mehruniya had remained a secret. And then he didn't even know how far things had gone. If they had gone too far, then? Then what? Even if things had gone too far, he would keep quiet. Naturally he couldn't have any damage done to his good name. He couldn't tell anyone now that he had had relations with Mehruniya. And once things had gone too far there was no question of telling Mighdad. And then who was to know whether Mehruniya had told the truth or not. After all she had had relations with other men besides him. With Sulaiman for a start. Fussu had also been circling around her. Ali Hadi and Wazir used to heave cold sighs for her as well. And could you rely on anything a loose woman like Mehruniya said? He found consolation in this direction. But still the suspicion was wriggling over his entire existence like a worm—who knew, perhaps she was right.

'Do you have any proof that Saifuniya is mine?' he asked Mehruniya.

'No, I haven't,' she replied.

'Saifuniya could be Wazir's, Fussu's, Hadi's or Sulaiman's—any one of them's.'

'But she is someone's, isn't she?' said Mehruniya with such conviction that Hammad Miyan began to tremble.

'Accha, now you go. I'll think of something.'

Mehruniya left. Hammad Miyan went straight into the inner house.

'What was that Mehruniya whispering to you about?' asked Kubara.

'You've made my life impossible. What on earth was the need for you to show off in front of Sakina, you ill-mannered woman!'

Until now Hammad hadn't scolded her. She began to cry and the sight of her tears enraged Hammad further.

'If I wasn't the son of a noble father I would give you such a belabouring now that you would remember it as long as you lived,' said Hammad, his words pouring out in Urdu.

'You've gone senile, *re*!' his mother Naima-bi reprimanded him, 'Now you're going to beat your wife!'

Hammad Miyan felt like throttling the old weaver woman who, by bearing him, had robbed him of the right to look people in Gangauli straight in the eye. But it was not the custom to raise one's hand against one's mother, and Hammad Miyan always attempted to disguise his low blood by respecting all customs and practices. Besides this, he had convinced himself that the lineage of a family depended on the father, otherwise, apart from Hazrat Ali, Imam Hasan and Imam Husain, all the twelve Imams had been born of slave women. But he knew that there was a difference between slave women and weaveresses, and so he was always careful to see that nothing happened which would give one an excuse to say that his low blood was showing. So he swallowed his anger and said nothing. Just then Firoza came out of the kitchen with a bowl of curd. Her foot caught in the hem of her shalwar. She fell, the dish broke, and the curd spread everywhere. Hammad Miyan had his opportunity. He began to beat Firoza. When Naima-bi rushed to her rescue, he flung her away in his anger. She fell and and hit her head against the corner of a bedstead. Blood flowed over her forehead. Umme Habiba, Sughra, Najma and Azra ran to pick up their grandmother. Hammad Miyan left the sobbing Firoza and went outside.

Naima-bi was having her wound washed and bandaged and berating herself, 'Oh, Lord! What else is there left to see? Take me to you, Lord, take me to you!'

When Mighdad came in after giving the bullocks their fodder he found Naima-bi in this state. He loved his grandmother dearly, perhaps even more dearly than Saifuniya. His eyes turned red with a rage which didn't cool for several days. The moment he saw Hammad Miyan lines of anger formed on his brow. One day he commented.

'Let it be, you're my father. What can I say to you? Otherwise you're doing such things that . . .' He left his sentence incomplete.

'How dare you speak like that to me, you ill-mannered layabout!'

'Are you watching, grandmother? He can raise his hand against his own mother and I can't say a word!'

'Get right out of my sight!'

'That I'd do right away. But then who would feed the bullocks, milk the buffalo, look after the land? But you just order me to get out without thinking.'

'Now do you see what happens when you argue with a son as big as you are?' asked Naima-bi.

Mighdad walked out, muttering angrily. When he couldn't settle down outside either he went to the Great Gate. But what was there to see? Only during the ten days of Moharram was there any splendour. And it was still a long time till Moharram. The courtyard was the same, the three-doored hall the same, the rooms the same, the shahnashin the same—but there were no signs of life. The wooden frames which supported the tazias were propped up against the outer wall of the bathroom in the sun, and the bamboo flag pole was hanging above them lengthways, suspended in rope loops.

He went on from there too. He didn't even realize that he was suffering the pain of being separated from Saifuniya for the past fifteen days. All he sensed was that the bullocks seemed like different animals and the buffaloes had started playing up more during milking.

But that evening when he went to milk the buffaloes and feed the bullocks, Saifuniya came and he felt that life had begun to be pleasantly familiar again. Saifuniya was not carrying her milk pan, but she came and sat beside him as she always did.

'Won't you take any milk?' asked Mighdad.

'No.'

'Why?'

'My mother's told me not to. She says I'm not to meet you.'

'Why not? And who told her?'

'Who knows who told her? But she's found out.'

'Then?'

'Arre, then what? The amount I've been beaten, people can't do more than that.'

'Did they beat you a lot?'

'Yes.'

'I'll break the ribs and bones of that *saala* Rahim-va.'

He took her off towards the pile of straw. They both lay down, as they always did. They didn't know the conventions of love. They didn't even know that lovers don't talk. They only knew that the relationship between them was stronger than that of the body.

'Come with me to Ghazipur. I'll take you to the *silema*.'

'*Silema*? What's a *silema*?'

'That I don't know, but I've heard that pictures talk straight out loud.'

'Never!' Saifuniya refused to credit it. 'How can a picture talk!'

'I swear by God, *re*! My brother was telling me and I didn't believe him. But Uncle says that two *silemas* have opened right in Ghazipur.'

'Then take me there and show me.'

'What else was I suggesting? Are you quite mad or what?'

They were both falling into the warm grasp of their dreams. When Hammad Miyan arrived, he too heard a part of their conversation.

'And if anything happens, then?'

'Nothing will happan.'

'How do you know?'

'My brother was telling Shammu-bhai that now you get these thin-skins. I've taken one of them from his trunk. I'll bring it with me tomorrow.'

'But today?'

'Arre, when nothing has happened up to now, why should it happen today?' This argument of Mighdad's silenced Saifuniya.

'But you will show me the *silema*, won't you?'

Hammad didn't think it appropriate to listen to any more. He retraced his steps. It was clear that things had already gone too far, and there was now no alternative but to keep quiet. But he certainly did decide that Mighdad should be married and Saifuniya should be removed from Gangauli.

There was only one way of removing Saifuniya and that was to have her married. But Mighdad's wedding had to be his first priority, and so that night he raised the subject with Kubara. Kubara was highly surprised and said, 'What's the hurry to get Mighdad married? Umme Habiba's sitting there as tall as a palm tree, and you're not worried about her marriage. By God's grace, Sughra is now in her sixteenth year. Azra's in her fifteenth. Najjbo will be of an age to be married in two years. We've got three great mountains of girls in the house, and yet you'll put off their weddings and be sure to get Mighdad married!'

'So what do you want me to do? Give birth to husbands for them myself?' said Hammad Miyan, 'Or marry off my girls to some weaver or cotton-carder? Sometimes you do talk nonsense.'

'But what will people say if there are three grown-up unmarried daughters in the house and you get your son married? And there's no logic in getting Mighdad married.'

'Why?'

'Have you forgotten Abbas?'

'He's in love with some girl. In the first place romance-vomance is no activity for a decent man. In the second the girl is a Sunni. Do you want me to bring a Sunni girl into the house as a daughter-in-law? How will you feel when she walks around in Moharram with her bangles clinking? But just at the moment it's Mighdad's marriage I'm talking about.'

'What is the hurry, after all?'

'How can I explain to you? I think we should work out an exchange with your brother. If he will have his son engaged to Umme Habiba, Mighdad can be married to his daughter. His son's a good boy, by God's grace. He's studied up to BA and has a good job in Lucknow too.'

'But what use is the girl?' said Kubara. 'For one thing she's black. On top of that she's very fat. I'm not going to make her my daughter-in-law.'

'And I suppose our young gentleman is a second Joseph? And I say that after all the girl does belong to our family. If we don't accept her, who will?'

'That's all very well, but . . .'

'I'm not asking your opinion. Just have a letter written to your brother tomorrow.'

Kubara wanted to discuss the matter further, but Hammad turned over and faced the other way and she was left to console herself in silence. Letters were exchanged regarding the engagement, and one day all Mighdad's sisters, except Umme Habiba, laid siege to him and began to quarrel with him and tease him into giving them presents to celebrate his new status. Naima-bi tried to fend them off, but when she saw the way Mighdad turned on his sisters and stormed out she was worried that, God forbid, there was some special reason for it. Then she was comforted by the thought that he was only just entering adulthood and by the grace of God may his enemies not hear of it. Her tiny, old and experienced eyes couldn't see the reason for Mighdad's irritation.

'What is it, beta? Why did you get so angry about your wedding being talked of?' she asked, fanning Mighdad.

'I'm not going to have any marriage-arriage.'

'Why on earth not?'

'Now how can I explain, bhai?' said Mighdad, beginning to lose his temper again, 'I'm just saying that I'm not getting married.'

'That's no reason.'

'Whether there's a reason or not. I've said I'm not doing it, and I'm not.'

Naima-bi began to play with his rough hair, her old fingers picking out the nits. And Mighdad began to think of Saifuniya. Since Hammad had entrusted the job of feeding the bullocks to Gaya, and put Nabi the weaver in charge of milking the buffaloes it was no longer easy to meet her. Only that tiny private apartment of the imambara was left which had been deserted ever since the departure of Najjan Mirasi's family. When even Abbas had forgotten about that apartment, no one else was likely to remember it. Mighdad had secretly tidied and cleaned it and, when no one was looking, even moved a bamboo bedstead into it. They had promised one another to meet there at midday, and so Mighdad was anxious to get away from Naima-bi. Finally, when her grandmotherly gestures of affection became too much, he scolded her. Naima-bi was astounded and hurt. After he left she offered a prayer, 'Oh Lord! If Mighdad's wedding passes off well and he's the father of a son in a year I'll fill the pulpit and provide the feast for Imam Husain on the eighth of Moharram. Eh, Chote Hazrat! Help me! If a boy is born within the year my worries will be over. I am saying this because I really don't know why Mighdad should get so heated over the mention of his marriage.'

Unaware of this prayer, Mighdad was lying on the bamboo bed in the apartment waiting for Saifuniya. It was extraordinarily hot. Time and again he wiped the sweat from his face with the hem of his European-style collared shirt. Then he took it off, made a pillow of it and lay down. But he raised his head immediately. There was a bundle of beedis in its side pocket. He took out the bundle and looked at it. The beedis weren't broken. He again folded the shirt into a pillow, lit a beedi and began to imagine the lines of Saifuniya's body in its thick smoke.

When Saifuniya came he moved over to one side without saying a word. Saifuniya lay down.

'What are you thinking?' she asked.

'Father is getting me married,' he replied.

'Look at that!' she laughed, 'So what is there to get upset about? If he's thought about it, he must be right. Or aren't you ever going to get married your whole life?'

'Of course I'm going to get married!' he said, 'But I'm going to marry you.'

Perhaps this was the first time that any barber's daughter had ever heard such a sentence from the mouth of any son of a zamindar, as Saifuniya couldn't even feel amazement. She laughed and said, 'Are you mad or what? How can you and I get married?'

'What's wrong with the idea?'

'No, no! Miyan, wherever your engagement is being arranged, go through with it.'

'No,' he said petulantly, 'if I get married it'll be to you or no one.'

Saifuniya put her hand over his mouth. His lips thrilled with pleasure, a thrill which passed through his whole body. He turned over and hugged Saifuniya. His embrace was so tight that she began to feel stifled. But the enjoyment of being stifled was so intense that she didn't try to stop him. She just closed her big, wide eyes.

'I've got fifty rupees,' said Mighdad. 'Come on, let's run away to Calcutta.'

'What are you saying?' said Saifuniya without opening her eyes, 'Our link with this village is unbreakable. You get married, I'll still be yours.'

'No.'

Hearing this tiny little word of refusal she was so happy that she burst into tears, and Mighdad began to peck at those teardrops with his lips. But Saifuniya knew that Mighdad would have to marry according to the compunctions of the community.

Only half the sun could fall to her lot, and she had never even wished for the whole sun. For her it was enough that in secret Mighdad would hold her in his arms so fiercely that she would feel stifled and close her eyes, and a crinkle would form in her full, young lips.

For a long while she lay silently and the warmth of her existence dissolved into his.

'But how can you and I be married?'

'I've got ten bighas of land in my own name,' said Mighdad, 'I'll leave my family.'

'And where will we live?'

'In the little place where we used to live before the new house was built.'

'And if the Miyans don't let us?'

'Don't you think about that. You just tell me if you'll marry me or not.'

'That's the problem. I can't say that I will and I can't say that I won't.'

'What does that mean?'

'I'm scared.'

'Of marriage?'

'No.'

'Of Father?'

'No.'

'Then of who? Of me?'

This time she didn't speak. She nodded. Even if Mighdad had wanted to put her in his home as his kept woman she would have been scared. But Mighdad was doing something completely unheard of. So she was very frightened indeed.

'So you're scared of me?'

'Yes.'

'Are you worried that I'll leave you?'

'No. It's not that. But how can I tell you?'

Mighdad released her from his embrace. Saifuniya opened her eyes. Mighdad was looking upset and annoyed. Saifuniya glanced down at her firm body which was clothed in sweat.

'You're angry with me, aren't you?'

'What's the point of being angry?' said Mighdad, 'When you've decided that you're not going to marry me, what can I do? I'm just an idiot.'

'It's not that!'

'Then what is it?'

'You get married . . .'

'No.'

'Chi, chi! Wait, let me finish.'

'All right, go on.'

'I'm saying this—get married to whoever the Miyans are telling you to. Then have two words said by a maulvi with me too, like your grandfather did with your grandmother.'

'No!' exclaimed Mighdad, 'I'm just getting married once, or not at all. Am I the only one left for that fat girl of my uncle's?'

'So you're not marrying her just because she's ugly?' The spell of Saifuniya's dreams seemed about to be broken. 'If that's what it is, then go. I'm not marrying you.'

'You won't?'

'No, I won't?'

'You won't?'

'No, I won't, I won't, I . . .'

Mighdad landed her such a slap that her head turned right back. This slap demolished many barriers. She clung to Mighdad and began to sob like a child, her tears mingling with the sweat of his body.

'I will, *re*! Who else could I marry but you.'

Silence descended on the apartment room. Only this sentence reverberated like a string of a tanpura, and its soft note gradually was absorbed into the existences of Saifuniya and Mighdad until their two bodies burnt in the fire of love. Then Saifuniya left, first opening the door and looking left and right. There was no one in the alley but a pariah dog. She dived immediately into the deep waters of the stillness of the alley. The dog looked at her and then began to sniff around the big door of the zenana imambara.

For a long time after Saifuniya had left, Mighdad continued to lay there, melting in the heat of the fire that he'd felt. He didn't realize that it wasn't easy to marry Saifuniya. His whole body was sticky with the sweetness of her body, and that sweetness had oozed into his veins. He yawned, stretched and got up. After wiping the sweat from his face with his shirt, he put it on and then smiled. He swept and wiped the empty bamboo bed with his eyes, and left the room.

The afternoon was drawing to a close. There was not even the slightest patch of sunlight in the little courtyard. The sun had crossed the tiled roof of the imambara. A kite was perched on the ridge of the roof of the apartment room, preening itself. Mighdad threw an imaginary stone at it and it flew off. A flock of domestic pigeons were sitting on the tiled roof of Anwarul Hasan's house. He threw a clod of earth at them and made them fly away too. Then he shut the door which led into the alley from within and walked into the room to the east of the imambara.

Thirst

Tannu returned as Major Hasan. The softness natural to a Saiyid had disappeared from his face, and he looked as stiff and hard as a shoe which has dried after being drenched in the monsoon rain. In place of the shine of dreams, into his eyes had come a half-scared callousness.

After he'd left Gangauli he had never even thought of Saifuniya once. Now he carried the pictures of several girls in his case. He had forgotten their names. He just remembered their bodies. He had almost married one Italian girl. Now in the crowd of all those Egyptian, African, Moroccan, Sicilian and Italian girls, why should he remember Jinti's granddaughter and Mehruniya's daughter? But when from far off he saw the beautiful minarets of the Brar mosque, the breeze suddenly became heavy with the strong scent of Gangauli. He forgot that he was coming back after spending six years of his life in a wilderness of wounds and screams. He forgot how his conviction that he was alive would tremble at the sound of machine guns and bomb explosions. It had taken him quite a long time to learn that when you heard the sound of aircraft engines you didn't go outside, but hid. He forgot all this at the sight of full, green fields of arhar dal and sugarcane. His heart began to pound. The horse cart was swaying along, the small bells on the harness jingling, and Tannu taking draughts of memories of former days as if they were old wine.

He looked at his watch. It was four o'clock. That would mean that the majlis at the Hakim Sahib's gate would already be over. People would be at Sibtu-da's gate. Young boys would be knotting their handkerchieves to make mice and throwing them at one another. He felt that he probably wouldn't be able to recognize those mice-makers. Who could say which children must have come of an age to make mice? And who could tell who would recite the nauhas? Masen-cha and Masshu-bhai must have given up. They must have left the rows of the young nauha-chanters of the Husainiya Society and be sitting with the old men and practising loud weeping. Shutting his eyes, Tannu could see the floor-covering spread through two connecting rooms of Sibtu-da's house. At the northern end was a chair without armrests draped in white. In front of the chair sat Hakim Ali Kabir, Abbu Miyan and the other old men. Javad Miyan was sitting leaning against the central archway. Right next to him was Fussu Miyan, sitting with his legs stretched out. Mohammad Husain and Masshu Miyan were sitting in the centre of the floor with the young nauha-chanters. The small children were sitting round and about the chair tossing handkerchief-mice around and pinching one another, and kicking up a row and being told off . . . . Tannu now realized that for all of six years he had been pining for Gangauli and its Moharram, and that tomorrow it was the eighth of Moharram. Alim-va would make halva . . .

When he saw the old indigo godown his eyes filled with tears. He could no longer bear to sit in the cart and jumped down. The carter pulled up the reins and came to a halt on that old road.

'You go ahead. I'll follow you,' said Tannu.

The carter clicked his tongue. The horse flicked away some flies with its tail and trotted on, defecating as it did so. The sound of the bells on its harness faded into the distance and the cart disappeared into the sugarcane fields. Tannu rolled up the sleeves of his olive green pullover and set off towards the godown. A cow grazing with its neck bent down raised its head to look at him. Some naked urchins playing near it began to run after Tannu. A young Chamar girl collecting cow dung smiled when she saw Tannu running and said to her mother, 'Just look at that Miyan!'

Tannu heard her voice, stopped and looked at them. Then he came towards them. They both began to feel nervous.

'Whose daughter are you?'

'Parusaram's.'

'So you're the daughter of a Congressman!' Tannu said reprovingly. She shrank away from him. Tannu laughed.

'You're Shabbu Miyan's son aren't you?' said her mother, who had pulled down the end of her sari well over her face.

'Yes.' He took a two-rupee-note from his pocket and stuck it on the forehead of a toddler playing on the ground who was now staring at him. 'I'd heard that Parusaram-va's in jail. So did he send you this boy by post? He doesn't look much more than two years old.'

'Now he's just about two,' said the girl.

The toddler tried to tear up the note but his mother gave him a shove.

'Ha!' shouted Tannu, 'Look at that!'

'For a whole year the Thanedar Sahib let his father . . .'

'All right, all right,' Tannu interrupted, 'there's no need to make up stories.'

But the boy's mother wanted to clear herself. She didn't want Shabbu Miyan's son to get any wrong ideas about her. But Tannu didn't have the time. He went off to the godown. Lovingly stroking its brick walls he climbed up to the third storey and sat down. Before him was Gangauli. His mother—Gangauli.

When evening fell and the village women began to come out towards the fields, he thought it was time he should go. It was growing chiller too. The moon of the seventh of Moharram had risen and on the hillock of earth by the pond he could see the old mango, jamun and peepul trees whispering together. He stopped by the pond for a moment. Everywhere was perfectly still. The water was lying silently staring at the moon. Tannu picked up a stone and tried skimming it across the water. It sank as soon as it hit the surface. He threw a second and then a third . . . one stone skimmed right across to the other side. He smiled. He brushed his hands and took out a packet of Woodbines. There was just one cigarette left. He lit it and threw away the box. Then, without thinking, he gave it a kick. The box flew up and into the pond. Tannu began to sing softly some old nauha—so old that he had forgotten the words and just remembered the tune.

The wind was rustling through the sugarcane fields.

'Now Saifun's not in her right senses . . . ,' came a voice.

Tannu stopped.

'But the thing to think is what can Hammad do now?'

'What is there left for him to do? The poor man tried to sort them out by thrashing them.'

'Someone was saying that one day when Hammad Miyan's temper got out of control Mighdad Miyan punched him.'

'*Chach*! No. That's one of those tales put about by the Miyans of Uttar Patti. I don't credit it.'

Tannu went on. But he had only gone two or three paces before another chain held his feet.

'Who's coming there?'

This was a very sweet womanly voice. Tannu was sad to think that it was a voice which must have grown up when he wasn't there. He was no profligate. The special characteristic of all the sons of Shabbu Miyan, Bashir Miyan and Wazir Miyan was that they were not lechers. It was only the pain of being separated from Gangauli for six years which made him sad.

'It's the wind.' This was a male voice, and he recognized it. This was the voice of Anwarul Hasan Raqi's nephew, Mashiatullah, Masita for short.

'It's not the wind. It's me,' said Tannu.

There was no reply from the fields. Tannu went ahead tearing up a leaf of sugarcane.

Right in front of him was Fussu Miyan's small porch. The light of the petromax lamps burning in the zenana imambara was peeping through the cracks in its closed doors. Two beds were laid out in the hall and next to them several cloth easy chairs. When he saw that hall it became impossible for Tannu to walk slowly any more.

'Fussu-cha, adaab!' he called out from a distance in greeting.

'May you live long!' replied Fussu-cha, 'But where did you disappear to, bhai?' He hugged Tannu. 'But you're just the same as ever. You've not got a bit fatter.'

'Allah Miyan said He'd put all the extra flesh on my Fussu-cha,' said Tannu, rubbing Fussu's pot belly.

In reply, Fussu Miyan began to cry. Really cry. Tannu was taken aback and said, 'What's this, sahib?'

'If your father had lived to see this day, how happy he'd have been!' said Fussu Miyan, pausing to blow his nose. After wiping his hand on the leg of the charpoy, he cleaned his glasses on the hem of his kurta. 'I happened to be sitting by your father's bed when he died. He was remembering you as he passed away. He told me, "Eh, Fussu! God's will be done. Life has not given me enough time. But I'm sure that Tannu won't deny me my wish."'

'What was his wish?'

'He was very fond of my daughter Sallo!' said Fussu Miyan, 'And it was his great desire somehow or other to make her his daughter-in-law. I even told him, "Bhai Sahib, I respect what you say. By God's grace Tannu will come back having seen the world. But why should he be prepared to marry some completely uneducated village girl?" But he said . . .'

'Eh, bhai, is Tannu sitting here?' said Javad Miyan, coming in arranging his beard.

Tannu stood up. 'Adaab, Da!'

'May you live long, son! Hai! If Shabbu had been alive today, how happy he'd have been!'

'You've been keeping well, haven't you, Dada?'

'Why shouldn't I be, son? But there's no cure for old age. Nowadays this *saala* gas is giving me a lot of trouble.' He farted with complete ease. The whole hall resounded.

'That couldn't be any one else but Javad,' came Rabban-bi's voice.

'Well what do you expect me to do, bhai? Not fart? Has anything that wanted to come out ever been kept in? How can I order it to stay in?' asked Javad.

'Adaab, Choti-dadda!' Tannu greeted Rabban-bi.

'How long have you been sitting there outside, son?' she asked. He entered the inner house. Rabban-bi hugged him. Then Sallo's mother, Sakina, immediately cracked her knuckles around his head to ward off the evil eye. Then Salma, young Kubara, Saida, Umme-Laila, Kaniz, Rabab and Mahjabin offered their salaams. He couldn't hug Salma, Kubara or Saida. He held out his arms to them, but stopped when he saw they had grown up. When he had left Salma had been only thirteen or fourteen, and Mahjabin had been in her mother's lap. Now when he'd arrived she was reciting a nauha! In a way six years is nothing at all, but in other ways it is a great deal. In six years girls can completely grow up and little children who urinate into shallow drains at the edge of courtyards begin to race through nauhas.

A small black bag was hanging around Mahjabin's neck over her green kurta. Tannu stole a mouthful of betel-nut, roasted coconut and coriander from it. She began to cry. At first young Kubara tried to console her, but when Mahjabin refused to be consoled, she lost her temper, 'Be quiet . . . or should I give you a beating?'

This scared Mahjabin into silence. The moment she was quiet Rabban-bi began to talk again. Tannu was amazed that so many things could have happened in six years. Mumtaz was dead. Razia was dead. Maulvi Bedar had fallen for Saifuniya and Mighdad had married her. Phunnan Miyan had been sentenced to life imprisonment. Jhinguriya had been hanged. Gobardhan had been shot. Maghfiya was stuck on Chikuriya.

He felt thoroughly disturbed.

'And on top of all this there's been the calamity of Saifuniya . . .' Rabban-bi fell silent as there were young girls present. 'Why are all of you standing on my head? Go and bury yourselves somewhere!' The girls went off whining. They didn't want to leave their Tannu-bhai—he'd come back after such a long time. But who could withstand Rabban-bi's dictatorial commands? After Rabban-bi had packed the girls off, she started again.

'Now where was I?' she asked Tannu.

'You were about to say something about Saifuniya.'

'Yes. Now how can I tell you, my son? It's not a thing to put into words but why should I hide anything from you? This Saifuniya is Mighdad's sister.'

'How on earth can that be, sahib?'

'Why on earth can't it be, sahib?' shot back Rabban-bi. 'In this Kaliyug what isn't possible? And Hammad is sitting there so tight-lipped, that it defies description. Now, son, whether she's a bastard or not, a daughter is a daughter. And now a girl has been born to that brother and sister.'

'But Choti Dadda . . .'

'Just because your Choti Dadda says so, has a lie ever become true that it should do so now? His son has gone and married his own sister, and that Hammad is just worrying about how to be accepted as a Saiyid. He searched high and low and found himself a Saiyid son-in-law from Darbhanga.'

'Is Mighdad so grown up that he can get married? And have fathered a girl?'

'Listen to him! So should Mighdad have stayed as small as he was when you went away?' Rabban-bi burst into laughter. 'Accha, now you tell me, is this war really over or is it still to be finished off?'

'The war is completely over.'

'I had promised that if the war ended and you came back safe and sound I would have a majlis held and have Maulvi Kabban Sahib speak at it. But he's a very big maulvi. I won't be able to get hold of him before Moharram is over. When rajas and maharajas ask him to speak for them, he won't come here. But I have to get him to speak.'

'Eh, Tannu!' said Fussu Miyan as he came in, 'Well then, bhai, aren't you coming for the majlis at the Gate?'

'Let's go!'

It felt very strange to Tannu to tread that familiar road again after six years. The bamboo thickets were just as before, so were the houses of the weavers.

The horse cart Tannu had hired was propped up against the wall on the near side of the Gate. The horse was grazing close by and the ground was wet with its urine. The gaslight streaming through the Gate picked it out clearly.

The majlis had already begun. Shabbar Miyan was speaking. At the sound of his voice, Tannu felt a thrill which made every hair on his body stand on end. His eyes filled with tears. He walked through the gate, wiping them on his sleeve.

The green, folding door of the shahnashin was open. The beautiful wooden tazia draped with black velvet was just as beautiful as it had been when he'd left it. The same old Benares silk dupatta was spread over the crests of the standards. Fussu Miyan briefly saluted the standards and sat down on the floor. But Tannu remained standing, raised his forefinger in witness and said, 'Peace be upon you Prophet of God, peace be upon you the Family of the Prophet, peace be upon you and the mercy and grace of God be upon you!'

Shabbar Miyan was saying: 'This was the task of Husain and Husain alone. When death and destruction were knocking at the door of his camp, and the children, holding empty bowls, were crying out "We thirst, we thirst!" and Zainab, the daughter of Ali, was walking from one tent to another in search of water, it occurred to Husain that before going to the Court of the Almighty he should fulfil all his duties. Accordingly, he said to Zainab, "Sister, how can I go before God leaving Kubara behind unmarried?" And then, looking towards Kubara, living testimony to his late brother, he wept.' Fussu Miyan felt no need to hear more. He began to weep and wail. But the voice of the narrator of the affliction of the Prophet's family seemed to come to Tannu's ears as if from a great distance. He was looking at the floor of the imambara in consternation. Now Muhammad-da was sitting where Gore-dada always sat. The place where Phunnan Miyan used to sit was empty. There was still a gaggle of boys behind the pulpit but, apart for one or two, Tannu couldn't recognize any of them, and the boys he had left sitting behind the pulpit were now sitting with Muhammad Husain in the centre of the floor, and they wore the open-sided black tunics of the Husainiya Society.

When the time came for the nauha to be recited Tannu stood with the members of the society. Masshu and Muhammad Husain smiled at him. Masoom and Maddu made room for him between them. Moonis was right in front of him and Shammu, who was standing next to Moonis, sent Tannu the message of a smile with his shiny, white teeth. Tannu couldn't recognize any of the boys in the centre of their circle but it was clear that they must be members of the family.

'Husain!'

'Husain!'

Tannu noticed that he had not at all forgotten the art of matam. His hand beat his breast in perfect rhythm, and so he pushed out his chest. The matam began in earnest. The round glass lamps, and the crystal pieces hanging below the lotus-shaped candleshades began to quiver. For no apparent reason, everyone began to weep. Shabbar Miyan, Abbu Miyan, Aggu Miyan, Wazir Miyan, Fussu Miyan, Hamid Miyan, Muslim Miyan, Deputy Collector Ali Hadi—in short, everyone present was weeping freely, their faces uncovered. Masshu Miyan sat down in the middle of the matam and began to sob. From the zenana side came the sound of women weeping. Tannu understood the meaning of these tears. He knew that people were not weeping for Husain, but were condoling him for the loss of his father. Accordingly, his arms moved faster and faster. The tone of the matam rose. Moonis began to beat his breast with his left and right hand alternately. Masoom didn't know this art. His right hand was tired out. Gigge, Mannan, Shammu and some of the others were tired too. Exhausted, the boys in the group sat down one by one. But Tannu kept up the matam, and the faithful continued to weep. Gradually the number of those standing decreased, and then Tannu was left alone. His soft, brown hair had fallen over his forehead, and was lifting and falling with the jerks of his neck. He had even stopped calling out 'Husain! Husain!', but his hands continued to beat his chest. Rainbows were forming and disintegrating before his eyes. Then the walls of the imambara bent inwards over him, and the round glass lamps and lotus-shaped candleshades surrounded him, and . . .

When Tannu recovered consciousness he was in the room next to the main hall, and Hakim Ali Kabir was giving him something sweet to drink. Tannu looked around. The room was packed full of people. All the senior gentlemen of both the Uttar and Dakkhin Pattis were gathered there, and children were peeping in through the doorway. Fussu Miyan was rubbing his hands to bring him round. When Tannu tried to sit up, he put his hand on his chest and said, 'Lie down for a bit longer.'

'I'm all right, sahib!' said Tannu, irritable for no reason.

'Go, wash your hands and face and change your clothes,' said Bashir Miyan.

This was as if to say that everything was all right. One by one the crowd began to disperse. The Hakim Sahib wrote out a prescription for medicine which Ubbad Miyan himself brought from his dispensary. Then only the people of the house were left. The gaslights in the imambara were extinguished. Bedding was laid out on the floor-covering and then word came from the inner house that food was ready.

Tannu saw two or three new faces in the house. One was Shabbar Miyan's daughter, Zuhra Parveen or Manno, and two others were Bashir Miyan's daughters, Mahjahan or Munni and Ahmad Bani or Suraiya. Manno and Suraiya were both two years old, and Munni was five.

'Arre, bhai, have some of this qeema!' said Bashir Miyan.

'Yes, I am having some,' replied Tannu.

'Have a little more!' said Sarwari, ladling out qeema on to his plate with a big spoon.

'Where's your son?' asked Tannu.

'He doesn't have holidays now,' said Sarwari as if it was entirely Tannu's fault that he didn't.

'Arre, so why are you telling me off? Scold your husband instead!' said Tannu.

'Eat your food, eat your food!' Bashir Miyan reprimanded his plate.

A kind of stillness descended around the cloth on which the food was spread and people began to eat in silence.

'Eh, Tannu! Did you kill any German-Arman or just came back after letting off some smoke and fireworks?' asked Bashir Miyan.

'War is a very crude thing, sahib!' Tannu replied, 'In it there's no difference between the blood of your companions and pond water. The same way that you get used to seeing the files of court cases, we get used to seeing wounds and hearing screams. Once . . .'

'Eat your food . . .' said Bashir.

Tannu stopped speaking. The only sound in the room was that of people swallowing their food. Everyone was busy eating, their heads bent over their plates. For some considerable time Masoom had his eye on the kidney on Maddu's plate. Maddu was keeping it to eat last. When Maddu bent to pick up a glass of water, Masoom made clean work of the kidney.

This action of his seemed very strange and to Tannu, as if it belonged to the past. He forgot the plates and mugs that he had had to wash himself.

The smell of human sweat, blood and urine which had embedded themselves in his mind left him. He even forgot that he couldn't even recognize those he had killed. A deep unhappiness took the place of all these memories. God only knew how many families were sitting at their evening meal like this, watching and waiting for men who would never return. For some reason he recalled an Italian soldier whom he had lifted on his bayonet. As he died his eyes were filled with a kind of bewilderment. Perhaps he was wondering why he was dying. He had said something too—Tannu couldn't hear or couldn't understand it. There was a red leather wallet in the soldier's pocket. In it was a photograph of a young woman, two children and an old woman. In one pocket were a few grains of wheat. Perhaps they had come from his own land.

'Eh!' Tannu jumped. He saw that Munni was asking him something.

'I'm asking you why you can't see shadows at night?' questioned Munni.

'Look at that! How could you see shadows at night!' said Maddu.

'When all the shadows meet it becomes night,' said Moonis.

'No!' said Masoom, 'Just like we go to sleep at night, all the shadows do too.'

'But it's no crime to evict,' Wazir Miyan was telling Bashir Miyan.

'Bhai, we people have never made evictions,' replied Bashir Miyan.

'And what's the point of evicting anyone,' added Akbari-bi, 'if Hammad is going to get the land . . .'

'Sarwari, eh, Sarwari!' came the voice of Wazir Miyan's wife from the kitchen, '*Naooj*, all these people have gone and sat out there, and where has that *matimili* Latifani gone?'

'Ba'ji, please could I have some water?' Masoom asked Sarwari.

'Arre, bhai Sarwari, isn't there any sweet?' asked Bashir Miyan.

'I'll just bring it.'

There was a ruin in the desolation of Tannu's heart, and every footstep, every sound was a brick in it, and some unseen hand was picking out those bricks and building an outline of Tannu's home. Tannu was drinking in each sound.

The meal finished.

Bashir Miyan and Wazir Miyan went outside. Wazir Miyan wanted to take Tannu with them too, but the ladies wouldn't let him go. The girls besieged him. The old women squatted down on the beds and Tannu began to tell them stories of different lands.

Suraiya dropped off to sleep sitting in his lap.

'Aren't you people coming to the majlis?'

Tannu started at the sound of this voice. It belonged to Abbu Miyan's daughter, Saiyda.

Saiyda was very attached to Tannu. She was almost ten years younger than him. Tannu loved her dearly too. He wasn't as fond even of Sarwari or Afsari who were like real sisters to him. He always used to give Saiyda little childhood gifts. Sometimes this would upset Afsari and she and Saiyda would squabble. Through the terrifying days of war and the long, miserable and scaring nights, when every moment wriggled over his body like a poisonous worm, hissing like a snake, he had never forgotten Saiyda. The first present he had bought in Cairo had been for her.

When he saw her he automatically smiled. 'Arre, you've really grown up!' he said.

'Adaab!' Saiyda came up to him. Tannu held her head to his chest.

'Arre, bhai, and you've grown very fashionable,' he said and for the first time he sensed that despite six years of absence, which felt like six centuries, he had not forgotton the dialect of his own home. His speech was still as strong as before, melting and softening the harsh, inflexible words of town Urdu.

'Look at that! You think as she's studying English so she won't take care to show herself off!' said Rabban-bi, her one eye dancing.

'Has Dada given you permission to study?' Tannu asked in amazement.

'Yes, he has,' laughed Saiyda, 'I'll have you know I passed my high school exams with a first division, and I'm studying in Aligarh.'

'Get on with you, little liar!'

'I swear by Allah!'

'Eh, *behini*, why are you dragging poor Allah Miyan into talk of that wretched English language?' spoke up Akbari-bi. 'I've told Abbu many times. But he just starts telling me that times have changed . . . this has happened, that has happened . . . it's happened, my foot! But the moment she starts speaking that gitir-pitir language, Abbu starts smiling. He thinks his daughter's making a name for herself! A big, grown up girl studying alone in Aligarh. If she didn't study she wouldn't be falling for these fashions. Drown these wretched fashions!'

'But this is a very good thing, Dadda!' said Tannu.

'Accha, let it pass. Our nose has been cut off in front of the whole community. This going to Aligarh—has any girl from any Miyan family from Naunahra, Para, Jangipur, Arzanipur, Devkathiya ever gone to study English that Abbu Miyan's daughter should? Bashir wanted to teach Munni English . . . . I stood up with my shoe in my hand and said, "You just watch out before you start thinking such a thing."'

'You were quite right, Dadda!' said Tannu. Saiyda pulled a face.

'There's no point in taking badly what these folk say,' he said quietly. Saiyda smiled, rubbed her nose in Tannu's hair and ran off.

'Eh, Dadda, let's go off quickly to the majlis,' said Sarwari picking up the books of nauhas. 'We have to hold this majlis just now, and then go off to Uttar Patti.'

'You're behaving as if it's entirely my fault that we're getting late,' said Akbari-bi, getting up. 'Latifani!' she called out to the servant-girl. Then, touching Tannu's head she said, 'We're going to the majlis, so you oil Tannu's hair.'

There was complete quiet once the women had left. Small children were sleeping on beds here and there. In the central arch of the main hall hung a large lantern which spread light over half the courtyard.

Latifani brought the bottle of oil. Tannu straightened the pillow under his head and relaxed his body, but when Latifani put oil in his hair his whole being tingled. The tingling increased. Finally, after two or three minutes, he turned his head. Latifani was a beautiful woman, twenty-four- or twenty-five-years-old.

'Turn down the lamp. The light's shining in my eyes,' he said. Latifani got up, and went to the arch. Her gait was very attractive. When she lifted her arm to turn down the lamp all the lines of her body seemed to draw breath. She came back and began to massage his head again. Tannu held out both his arms as if to stretch, and perhaps by accident they fell around Latifani's neck.

'Let go, someone will see,' she murmured.

'No one will see,' he said, his throat dry, 'everyone's gone to the majlis.' And then it seemed to him as if the walls, the round, white, shiny pillars of the arches of the hall, the lantern, and the trembling shadows of the courtyard were all watching him in astonishment and saying—Tannu, the war is over. This is your home.

He removed his arms from around Latifani's neck.

From Abbu Miyan's house came the sound of a nauha being chanted:

Very frail your feet, on them will blisters form,
In sacrifice, oh seeker of the Najaf road . . .

Tannu could recognize each of the voices reciting the nauha. He asked himself, did I really go to war? Have I really come back after six years? If so, why haven't I forgotten anything? Why do I remember all these things, all these voices? . . .

The nauha had finished. The women were beginning to mourn.

'Husain! Husain!'

'Ya Sayyadi! Ya Abbas!'

Tannu smiled.

No, some changes had definitely taken place. Saiyda was studying in Aligarh; the Saiyid ladies of Gangauli had deserted their centuries-old traditional, simple and moving style of mourning and become entangled in the artificial and ineffectual matam of Lucknow and Jaunpur. In other words, fashion was knocking at the door of the matam of Gangauli. He didn't like this new affectation. He was sure that Dadda and Rabban-dadi and Khurshid-dadi and Muhsina-dadi and Gori-dadi must certainly have said '*Naooj*—dreadful!' under their breaths when they heard this matam, and the tears flowing from their eyes must have shrunk back and dried.

'The majlis is over,' complained Latifani.

'Eh!' Tannu started. He saw that Latifani was trying to force back her small, tight breasts into the cups of her blouse, and their soft, fresh, wheat-coloured skin was shining in the moonlight. He quickly walked out.

In the three-doored hall of the imambara people were already asleep. In a niche a small glass lamp of beautiful design was burning sleepily, and the white flag standing next to the door of the bathroom was billowing gently in the breeze. Both the crests, in the form of open hands, fixed to the top of the pulpit in the three-doored hall were in a deep slumber, the Benares silk dupatta pulled over their faces. On the walls the pictures of Karbala, the camp of Hazrat Imam Husain, and his wounded horse, Zuljenah, were mere dead lines. From the room to the east came the frightening sound of Bashir Miyan talking in his sleep.

Tannu lay down on his bed. He stroked his pillow. Then he touched the satin upperside of his quilt, tickled the side of his cotton mattress and smiled. He smiled because Dadda must still think him a child! That was why she had left Latifani, fresh and sweet like an ear of ripe wheat, alone with him in the stillness of the night and in the light of a dim lantern. Dadda didn't know how hunger increases on the battlefield—hunger for bread, hunger for love, hunger for lust! He remembered the nameless forty- or forty-five-year-old Sicilian woman he had raped. She had not agreed for money—it had been rape. If the Italian army came to Gangauli, would the same happen? Of course it would. His hair stood on end. In the three-doored hall of the imambara on that night of the seventh of Moharram, surrounded by his sleeping relatives, he lay awake and cursed war. He saw that same old Sicilian woman standing leaning on the bamboo pole of the white flag. He saw that she was sitting on the third step of the pulpit and holding a majlis for herself—not in some strange language, but in pure, chaste Urdu, in the tone of Maulvi Kabban! In the flowery vocabulary of Maulvi Ibne Hasan Naunahravi. At that time he had not understood a word she had said. At that time he only comprehended the helpless amazement, deep resentment, contempt and hatred expressed in the language of her eyes (perhaps throughout the world eyes all speak the same language). But now in the three-doored hall of the Great Gate of Gangauli, by the black pulpit, after lying on a warm, soft bed, he could understand the woman's language very well. 'I know, Major Hasan, that you are not just Major Hasan. You are Tannu too, Tannu of the Dakkhin Patti of Gangauli. Tannu, the only son of Shabbu Miyan, the favourite grandson of Akbari-bi. Don't you remember your mother? You must do. If she were alive today she would be a little younger than me. What you think is my skirt are really the wide pajamas of your mother, you mad boy, pull them off . . . pull them off . . . !'

'Be quiet!' he screamed. His eyes opened.

The night was still as dark and as depressing. Two dogs were fighting in the courtyard and around them slept Moonis, Maddu, Haddan, Nassan, Kaisar, Hammad Miyan, Abbas and others. 'God is Great!' muttered Tannu.

'What is it, son?' asked Hammad Miyan.

'Nothing, I was just dreaming.'

'Go back to sleep.'

Tannu turned over. To preserve himself from the thought of that old woman he began to think of Latifani.

But what could he think about her? He didn't know her at all. She too was a stranger to him like that old woman. In the morning when he awoke the floor of the imambara was empty. All the bedding had been rolled away. Lakhna Chamar was sweeping the courtyard and dust was flying through the air. Tannu stretched and smiled to see the familiar ceiling and walls.

'Salaam, sahib!' said Lakhna.

'Salaam. Where's everyone gone?'

'They've all gone to the Hakim Sahib's majlis,' he smiled.

'I've slept too much,' said Tannu.

Lakhna didn't hear this remark because he had already busied himself again with his sweeping. Tannu lay down again. For a short while he turned from side to side and stretched, and then taking out a packet of cigarettes from underneath his pillow, he lit one. He hadn't finished smoking it when a group of boys under the leadership of Masoom came in through the Great Gate.

'Look at this!' said Masoom, 'Here we've finished a majlis and you're still in bed.'

'You recited a nauha?' asked Tannu.

'Yes, I did,' replied Masoom proudly.

'Have Muhammad-cha, Abul Qasim-cha and Masshu stopped

reciting nauhas then?'

'Arre, what are they going to recite?' said Masoom with contempt, 'They still drag the same old tunes on and on. I'll have you know Ba'ji has taught me all the new tunes from Lucknow.'

'Accha . . . !' Tannu sat up suddenly. 'Does Abul Qasim-cha still make you practise down at the godown?'

'What else does he have to do? He went to the war. Accha, eh Tannu-bhai . . . .' Masoom sat down beside Tannu, 'Can you see the people on the ground from an aeroplane?'

Tannu laughed. 'Is that what Abul Qasim-cha says?'

'Yes!' said Masoom. 'He says that once when he flew over Gangauli he saw Khurshid-dadi on her way to the toilet carrying a lota of water, and Maulvi Bedar washing his face in the pond.'

Then all the boys started to beat their chests in matam. And then two boys began to fight and pull each other's hair. Tannu leapt up to separate them and Masoom took this opportunity to roll up Tannu's bedding and put it on top of the pile of bedding behind the pulpit.

'Eh, Masoom bhaiyaa!' Latifani called out, peering from behind the door of the zenana, 'Has Tannu bhaiyaa woken up?'

'Yes, he has!'

'Then tell him his breakfast is ready.'

'I'm just coming . . .' said Tannu.

Latifani stood back from the doorway but did not go inside the women's quarters. She leant against the wall in the half-light of the corridor and began to breathe deeply and to wait for Tannu. And she began to pray that Tannu would come there alone. It's obvious that there was no question of Allah Miyan answering her sinful prayer but Tannu did walk into the corridor alone.

'Come, breakfast is ready,' she whispered.

But Tannu ignored her and entered Gori-bi's courtyard. The custard apple tree standing next to the door of the toilet was laden with fruit. He picked a custard apple and tossing it into the air and catching it like a magician's ball, went into the main house.

'Adaab!' he greeted Akbari-bi.

'May you live long . . . be happy!' replied Akbari-bi.

Tannu lay down on the charpoy on which Akbari-bi was sitting. It was exceptionally cold. He wrapped a light quilt lying at the foot of the bed around him and, turning on one side, began to warm his hands in front of an earthern brazier full of glowing charcoal near the head of the bed.

Saiyda came up and said to Tannu, 'Give me my quilt please.'

Hearing her voice, Tannu turned his head. Saiyda had turned out to be very beautiful. Fair complexioned, with small extremely white teeth, a long neck, black hair and black eyes. Her body was like sculpted marble. He smiled. Saiyda stretched out her hand to snatch the quilt. He wrapped it more closely around him.

'Arre, give it, give it . . . ,' said Akbari-bi. 'She's feeling cold.'

'No, I won't!' said Tannu.

Saiyda held on to his hair with both hands, and he writhed and let out a shriek.

'Have you gone mad, Saiyda!' said Abbu Miyan's wife, arriving on the scene, 'Let go of his hair.'

'He won't give me my quilt.'

'If he won't then let it pass,' her mother said. 'Wrap another one round you.'

'Why doesn't he go and get another one?'

'You are squabbling like a brother and sister right next to each other in age.'

'All right then!' said Tannu, grinding his teeth, 'I'll find a fat, black, hefty husband for you!'

'Aren't you ashamed of yourself to be talking about weddings on the seventh of Moharram?' Saiyda scolded. And then it suddenly occurred to her that Tannu himself was talking about her marriage and so she blushed. Tannu burst into laughter.

'No, son, today's not a day you should laugh.'

Abbu Miyan's wife sat down on the same bed. 'It's so cold today, Ba'ji, that it could kill you. This *nikaundi* wind is blowing through my bones.' She wrapped herself so far within her quilt that it nearly veiled her face.

'Go and have your breakfast,' said Akbari-bi. Then she began losing her temper with Latifani. 'Has your mind collapsed? Have your eyes burst? Cover the teapot!'

Latifani hastily covered the pot with a teacosy.

'Come on, have some tea!' said Tannu to Saiyda.

'No, I won't,' she replied.

'Dadi, should I make some tea for you?' Tannu asked Saiyda's mother.

'There can't be any heat left in the mui tea,' she said. 'If there's a frost like this how will we have the procession tonight?'

'Don't you walk about with bare feet,' Akbari-bi told Tannu.

He sat on a wooden bed and began to eat his breakfast. The combination of savoury bread fried in ghee and scrambled eggs seemed very odd to him. After the first mouthful he looked at Saiyda again. She was leaning against the door trying to work out the tune of a nauha. Her dupatta had slipped down. She was gently patting her chest in matam, and singing softly, and wondering why she should be so happy. She didn't even realize that she had become unhappy after Tannu left. She didn't realize this because ten-year-old girls don't know the reasons for unhappiness. In her trunk was a photograph of Tannu. There were no photographs of Moonis, Masoom, Maddu, Shammu or Gigge—but there was one of Tannu. This picture had also travelled to Aligarh inside the layers of old newspaper which lined her trunk.

She hadn't put it there by accident, but on purpose. And she had put it inside the layers of newspaper because her mother was going to repack her trunk and, for some reason, she didn't want her or anyone else to see that photograph. She didn't even realize why she didn't want anyone to see it. In Aligarh she had not once taken the picture out from the newspaper to look at it. But whenever she opened her trunk for anything it was as if she could see the picture even without removing the newspaper, and for a moment she was lost in thought. What would Tannu-bhai be doing . . . where would he be . . . how was he . . . might he come back soon . . . might he then get married . . . then she would take a whole lot of gifts from him. Thinking of Tannu's wedding never made her happy, but she certainly did think about it, perhaps because girls of good family were too shy to think about their own weddings. But she used to talk about Tannu to her friends at the Waheediya hostel so much that they nicknamed her 'Tannu-bhai'. And now that same Tannu-bhai was sitting opposite her having his breakfast and his dark brown eyes were still smiling mischievously. And she refused to believe that Tannu had come back after an absence of six years.

'Well, bhai, you're having your breakfast late!' said Sakina as she walked in.

'Adaab!' Tannu greeted her, and then turned to Saiyda. 'Have some tea, come and sit here by me.'

'No, I won't,' she replied.

'Eh, daughter, have you gone totally mad?' said her mother, losing her temper, 'Why don't you go?'

Saiyda came and sat beside Tannu. The light, sweet fragrance of her fresh young body mingled with the smell of the bread and eggs. Tannu looked at her as he chewed a mouthful. Her long, tapering fingers were tracing invisible lines on the stool. Her big, big eyes were bent under the weight of their long eyelashes. A sliver of dry neem twig was peeping from her right nostril where her nose had been pierced. Her delicate, slim wrists were bare and her black dupatta had slipped down from her shoulders and was hanging over her elbows.

'Dadi, you should marry her to a man with squint eyes,' he told Saiyda's mother.

'Eh, bhaiyaa, why should she?' smiled Saiyda.

'Your two eyes are as big as four!'

'Are your eyes any smaller than mine?' said Saiyda hotly.

'What need do you have for such big, big eyes, little sister?' he asked.

'Accha, now don't cast the evil eye on her,' scolded Akbari-bi.

'I'm hungry,' wailed Masoom.

'Eh, bhai, this boy absolutely wears me out,' said Sarwari, 'I just stuffed him up to his throat a little while ago.'

'So boys should stop feeling hungry on your orders!' said Akbari-bi. Masoom came and hugged her. She began to play with his hair, 'Are you very hungry?'

'Yes.'

'Come with me, I've kept some moong balls for you.'

Masoom went off with Akbari-bi into the inner room and came out with sweets made of moong dal. Sarwari began to grumble that her grandmother had spoiled Masoom horribly. She was still grumbling when she entered the kitchen where she began to scold Latifani.

'I've come back after six years and you haven't brought any moong balls for me,' Tannu complained with a laugh, 'and you took them out for Masoom straightaway.'

'As if you're going to eat moong balls!'

'Let's go to the majlis,' Masoom said to Tannu.

'Please give me some moong balls too,' said Maddu.

'Eh, bhai, is it a *nikaundi* stomach you have or a furnace? You've only just had breakfast,' said Akbari-bi.

'Masoom had only just had breakfast too,' Sarwari added her bit.

'You can't compare the two. Maddu hasn't been lying sick for five years.' Akbari-bi lost her temper, 'You people are jealous of him.'

'What else? After all he's a step-brother, isn't he?'

Tannu went out with Masoom.

After the majlis, the elders settled down to battle things out. They spoke about the Muslim League, Congress, Pakistan, the Qor'an and Hadith, and Gandhi. Tannu had no interest in these subjects. Several times Abbas tried to involve him in the conversation but each time he avoided saying anything.

Abbas had gained the right to sit in the majlis of the elders and take part in their conversations. He was no child. He was studying at Aligarh University. He was also the one best acquainted with political matters. He had met the Qaid-e-Azam, and eaten with Liaquat Ali Khan.

He had toured with Sir Sultan and Chaudhuri Khaliquzzaman had said that there must be only two or three better speakers than him in Hindustan. His photograph had been published in several Urdu newspapers.

'Abbas' speeches are published in English newspapers.' Hammad Miyan, his father, was constantly armed with the naked sword of this sentence. Whenever any boy or man of the village or community was praised, Hammad Miyan would swing this sentence into action and destroy the opposition! It was true that Hakim Ali Kabir's son, Saddan, had become Deputy Sa'adat ul Husnain Zaidi. It was also true that Moonis was talked about for his intellect. It was true too that Shabbar Miyan and Bashir Miyan and Wazir Miyan and Aggu Miyan practised law and earned money. It was also true that the late Shabbu Miyan's son, Tannu, had become Major Tanvir ul Hasan. But did any of them have their pictures in the newspapers? Did thousands of people gather to hear any of them speak? It was something entirely different to be made a Deputy Collector! Accordingly, Hammad ignored the fact that Abbas had married a Sunni girl and didn't bring her home because she wouldn't remove her bangles during Moharram. Anyhow, Hammad Miyan had heard that now educated girls didn't even wear bangles. He had decided that when he went to Agra to take part in the annual congregations commemorating the Shia martyrs, he would go to Aligarh to see his daughter-in-law. What were Sunnis and Shias anyway? The main thing was that you should have faith in God, his Prophet and his Book. If only that *haramzada* Mighdad hadn't married Saifuniya, Hammad's life would have been very beautiful. He had heaved a sigh of relief after Mehruniya died as at least a great secret had been buried with her. If only Mighdad had been content to make Saifuniya his kept woman! But that faithless boy had married her and only God could understand that Maulvi Bedar, who had read them the marriage vows. The wretch called himself a Maulvi! He couldn't even tell them that the son of a Saiyid couldn't marry a barber's daughter. With Mighdad, Hammad had lost ten bighas of land. Mighdad's separation from the family had been disgrace enough but the biggest trouble had been that without him Hammad's hands had, so to speak, been cut off. Now he had to keep visiting the fields himself. He had to supervise them at sowing and harvesting. The truth was that Gaya Ahir was still with him, otherwise Hammad Miyan would have been left completely helpless. These were very dark days. Only one thing turned out well. Umme Habiba and Sughra were both married into a rather polluted Saiyid family of Darbhanga. Hammad Miyan had thought that no one would bother coming all the way from Darbhanga to Gangauli to see what the in-law's family was like.

The family from Darbhanga had had the same idea. Accordingly, it became well-known in Darbhanga that the girls belonged to the family of Raja Saiyid Munir Hasan, and it became well-known in Gangauli that the boys—Saiyid Badrul Hasan Rizvi and Saiyid Ziaul Hasan Rizvi—were from the family of Nawab Zulfikar Ali. But Maulvi Bedar knew all the family trees of all the Saiyids of Hindustan off by heart, and so when the wedding procession arrived and the poem composed especially for the occasion in praise of the groom was read out and, as was customary, included a few ironical comments on the bride's family, the people of Gangauli fell on Maulvi Bedar and insisted he give a reply. The Maulana immediately composed a verse including the word 'Darbhangis'—men of Darbhanga—and scanning it in such a way that when it was recited the 'Dar' became separated from the 'bhangis.' Now a bhangi is a sweeper, an untouchable, and it so happened that the grandmother of Badrul Hasan and Ziaul Hasan was a sweeper woman. Naturally this verse cut the bridegroom's party to the quick, and so a geneologist from their side recounted to Hammad Miyan the story of the Nawab of Avadh and Inshaullah Khan Insha,* thereby evening matters . . . . However this exchange naturally had no ill-effect on the relationship between the two sides. Hammad Miyan was therefore satisfied with the marriages of Umme Habiba and Sughra. And now, by God's grace, they were both the mothers of a son . . . and right at that moment Habiba's son was peeing in his lap.

Tannu laughed to see Hammad Miyan leaping up at being peed on. He bent down and gave the baby's red nose a little kiss. The baby smiled.

---

* The poet Insha once joked with the Nawab that he was ajnab which has a double meaning—of immaculate descent from both mother and father's sides, and also the offspring of a servant woman. There were doubts over the Nawab's parentage. As a result of this Insha lost favour at court.

'He really is the image of Habiba.'

'You do make some incredible remarks,' said Hammad Miyan. 'In both the eyes and the nose he resembles Miyan Badrul Hasan most exactly.'

Javad Miyan shrugged his shoulders at the sound of Hammad Miyan's Urdu and then he began to stroke his beard with a contemptuous expression. Because of this Urdu of his, Hammad was day by day becoming further removed from the people of Dakkhin and Uttar Pattis. People there would say, 'Bhai, if you go out of the village speak Urdu or English or Persian. What's the point of tampering with the language of your forefathers in your own home?' It was during this period too that Hammad Miyan had become rich. Instead of one, there were two buffaloes tethered at his door, and they were big, hybrid Jamnaparis. That was the reason that the Miyans were not well disposed to him in the first place. One day Rabban-bi actually told him, 'Eh, Hammad! Don't give yourself so many airs that . . .'

However Hammad was not prepared to be at all influenced by these things. He knew that the Saiyids of the village were jealous of him, but he couldn't choose to starve for fear of the Miyans' jealousy. He had even scolded his wife into learning pure town Urdu.

Only his mother had refused to give in, and she had since died. His daughters spoke the language of the home but the moment Hammad stepped indoors they began to speak in rapid Urdu. This harsh tongue sounded extremely ugly and arrogant to them. They were scared to use it to express what lay in their hearts, just as you don't tell a stranger your family secrets. And so when Hammad Miyan was present no one spoke about family matters at all. In fact it sounded as if some ladies who were strangers to one another had met by accident and were talking very politely to pass the time. As a result, the homely atmosphere of the house disappeared. His wife would begin to scold in Bhojpuri: 'I'm telling you this that . . .' Then she would stop and continue in Urdu, 'Have your brains become defective, young ladies?' and then give up. 'Oh, to the furnace with this *nikaundi* language!'

She began cursing Urdu and in her anger would fail to administer the scolding she'd set out to, and the girl who was to be scolded would find this an appropriate opportunity to go into the kitchen or slip quickly into another room. The result was that Kubara was gradually forgetting to tell the girls off and every day Hammad would say irritably, 'Why on earth don't you reprimand those girls?'

Then she would reply, 'What can I do, I don't know your language and you won't let me speak mine.'

At that remark Hammad Miyan would lose all hope of reforming his household. But he was most hurt when he heard Abbas speaking the same rustic dialect. Naturally he couldn't rebuke Abbas, as Abbas was more educated than him and was studying at Aligarh university. But when Tannu began to talk in dialect Hammad Miyan thought there was no harm in correcting him. For one thing he had only studied to FA, and then he was only an army man.

'What is this, Miyan Tannu . . .' he said, 'you've been around the whole world and yet you are still conversing like a peasant? Personally, I would say . . .'

'Why are you always going on "I this", "I that"?' Javad Miyan interrupted in his mother tongue, 'You go bleating on as if you're the only man in the village.'

At that moment Abbas was expounding in favour of Pakistan. He stopped in mid-sentence and gave his father a meaningful look. But he was helpless. He couldn't bring Hammad Miyan back to the winding, innocent and slate-clean lanes of the village.

'I will proffer my vote to the Muslim League,' said Hammad Miyan, ignoring Javad Miyan's remark. He had mastered the art of ignoring what other people said. He took a kind of pleasure in the impotent anger caused by such action and when anyone spoke to him angrily he became even more polite and formal.

'Well, if *you're* going to vote for the Muslim League what is there that can stop them winning?' said Javad Miyan with contempt.

'Why do you keep on butting in when he's talking?' asked Fussu Miyan.

'Accha, now you hold your tongue!' Javad Miyan shot back, 'I am after all a Saiyid.'

Fussu Miyan had spoken softly. Javad Miyan had replied at the top of his voice. Everyone had heard. But everyone swallowed it. Abbas' blood did begin to boil, certainly, but he said nothing because he knew that Javad Miyan was not a bad man.

'Now what do you intend doing?' he asked Tannu, so that the humiliating silence could be broken, 'I think that . . .'

'Not now!' Tannu interrupted, 'I'm very tired, Abbas-bhai! For the time being I'm not doing any thinking. I'll be staying in Gangauli after Moharram. After some days I'll forget the sound of cannon and rifle fire. My nose is full of the smell of pus and corpses. It will take some time to get rid of it. When I'm pure and clean again, then I'll think.' He stood up.

'Where are you off to?' asked Abbas.

'To the Karbala. I'm going to pray by Father's grave.' No one stopped him. Hammad just suggested that he take Gaya with him. Tannu refused. Then everyone went back to discussing Pakistan and Tannu walked out through the Great Gate.

Opposite was the door of Phunnan Miyan's house. Maghfiya had lifted the sacking curtain across the doorway and was peeping out. Pammo was sitting on the threshold trying to recite a nauha, and Dullan was using some neem twigs as a chain, and was beating himself, as men whip themselves with chains during Moharram processions, and looking repeatedly at his naked chest which was covered with red marks left by the twigs.

Maghfiya recognized Tannu. He recognized her too. Maghfiya remained where she was standing and bent forward to salaam him. He went up to the door.

'Eh, Amma, Tannu-bhai has come,' said Maghfiya.

'Where?' Kulsum came running, 'Arre, my dearest, my son!' She immediately put her hands to his temples to avert all evil from him. Tannu went into the house and sat down. Maghfiya brought some finely chopped nuts and spices in a saucer. In the middle was some roast coconut, some small pieces of betel-nut and some cloves. To one side on the edge was a lump of lime and on the other a thick paste of catechu had oozed down towards the betel-nut. Tannu first put the coconut and betel-nut into his mouth. Then he dipped his forefinger in the lime and his middle finger in the catechu. After licking the catechu he began licking the lime, a tiny bit at a time. It was such a long time since he had eaten these things that he could no longer remember how much lime you could eat without burning your mouth. As he did all this, Kulsum's tongue never stopped for a moment. She related the entire history of the previous six years. When she came to describe Mumtaz's and Shabbu Miyan's death she wept too. Then she went on to Maulvi Bedar and Saifuniya, and finished with Saifuniya's marriage to Mighdad.

'And I hear that Saifuniya is Hammad's daughter,' she concluded her recital. 'He's been on Haj and to the holy places, but his son married his daughter and he said nothing. Eh, beta, do you think that God is going to be overawed by his grand new house?' This was a question, but Kulsum didn't wait for a reply. 'I'm just waiting for Maghfiya's father. If he comes back safe and well then I'm going to cut Hammad's nose off with my shoe, and if I don't then my name's not Kulsum! There was a death in our house and not one of them came to give a shoulder to the bier!' Her voice was full of tears and they flowed from her big, big eyes. 'If it hadn't been for the Raqi traders and Kunwarpal Singh the corpse could not have been taken out.'

'Everything will be all right, Dadi,' said Tannu.

'I think that on the Day of Judgement I will catch hold of the hem of Hammad's shirt and tell Allah Miyan . . . this is that Hammad Miyan.'

'Accha, Dadi, I'll just go down to the Karbala.'

'You're going to pray for your father?'

'Yes.'

'Go then, son, when you're here, serve him. This is the only service you can offer him now. You'll be staying a while, won't you?'

'Yes.'

'Then come again, son. These Miyans of Gangauli have cast us out of the community!'

Tannu found these domestic troubles and complaints hard to bear. He had never understood why Kulsum had left her marriage and home for Phunnan Miyan. It was well-known that women want material comforts and so stick to their husbands as closely as possessing spirits and stand in their paths like shadows. But Kulsum had renounced her material comforts and accepted Phunnan Miyan. She had been a wife, and now she was just a kept woman. Whenever Phunnan Miyan wanted, he could throw her out, and no one could touch him for it. And so there must be something called love. Otherwise, what was there now in Kulsum that he would keep her? Her breasts, as firm as unripe guavas, had sagged. Her body had become slack. The light in her eyes was extinguished. But here she still was in this house living as if she was Phunnan's wife. Then it wasn't as if Phunnan Miyan himself was any beauty. He was dark-skinned, tall and well-built, with a round and extremely ordinary face on which grew an extremely villainous-looking moustache.

Pammo came running up to Tannu and hugged him, her muddy hand dirtying Tannu's kurta. Kulsum leapt forward and slapped Pammo as cruelly as if she had been a loathsome worm and not a child. She pushed her twice. Pammo began to cry.

'Take your kurta off, we'll wash it and dry it just now.'

'I'll go and change it, Dadi.'

'No.'

First he took off his sweater and threw it on to a bed. Maghfiya began to examine its knitting. Then he took off his kurta. Maghfiya broke into laughter.

'Eh, bhai, why don't you shave under your arms? Aren't there barbers in the army?'

'Who told you to look in his armpits?' smiled Kulsum. Then she turned to Tannu and said, 'But, eh, beta, do have them shaved . . . they're very unfortunate.'

'Very well.'

Maghfiya washed his kurta. Removed from a young body, the kurta carried the pleasant fragrance of youth. Maghfiya began to think as she washed it of Mohammad Husain, who had not yet been able to give her a single child. Their house in Calcutta was so small that they never had any privacy. And apart from once Mohammad Husain had never tried to obtain any privacy. And that time too he had shaken her to wake her, and then dropped off to sleep himself. She had stayed awake a long time looking at the ceiling, and then begun to cry . . . . She dried the kurta at the hearth and brought it out. There were innumerable creases around the hem. Tannu put it on, went outside and set off towards the Karbala. He could have prayed sitting at home. But he wanted to tell the lanes of Gangauli, and the platforms where tazias stood during Moharram, and the tomb of Nuruddin the Martyr, and the Karbala that he had returned.

At the zenana imambara he caught sight of Mighdad.

'What is it, bhai? You've drowned so deep that no one ever lays eyes on you.'

'Adaab!' said Mighdad, 'I heard that you'd come back yesterday. I really wanted to meet you but how could I? Just now I saw that you'd gone to Phunnan Miyan's so I stood here in case you came this way.'

'Don't you come up to the Great Gate?'

'No, what I say is, bhai, that what skin is it off anybody's nose that I married her? I wanted to and so I married Saifuniya. Did that harm anyone's father? But they all kicked up hell. Don't you think I knew that she was a barber's daughter? But I also knew that I am no Saiyid. But you know Father has forgotton it completely. He's suddenly become a proper Saiyid, and now, since he inherited his brother's shervani coats, he's got even more arrogant. He came to attack me. He said, "Remove your presence from this apartment!" You know he's begun speaking Persian now. I said, "I'd like to see who's going to throw me out of here." When he saw that I wasn't scared he hung his head and quietly went away. Eh, sahib, do you know when Pakistan will be made?'

'Why? Do you intend going there?'

'I'm not going anywhere! They can go as they are ashamed of ploughs and bullocks. I'm a farmer, Tannu-bhai! Wherever my crops are, my land is—that's where I am! I'm asking when Pakistan will be made so that somehow Father can be sent there.'

'Why?'

'Our home is very small.'

'Didn't I send you to the bazaar . . .' came Saifuniya's voice, 'And you're standing there gossiping . . .'

'Arre, Tannu-bhai's come, *re*!' said Mighdad.

Every hair of Mighdad's body was singing. This was the first time the son of a Saiyid was talking to him since he married Saifuniya.

'Come, Tannu-bhai, come and see my little girl for a minute.'

'Let's go.'

The apartment was still as small as it had been six years ago. The guava tree by the door still stood as it had before. The washing line still hung in the same place, and some quilts were airing across it. And in the tiny courtyard on a child's bed lay a flower-like baby girl. Tannu sat on the bed beside the baby.

'Salaam!' said Saifuniya.

Tannu looked at her. She was still just as beautiful. The only difference was that those eyes, which were always smiling mischievously, had become serious.

'How are you?' he asked.

'I'm well, bhaiyaa . . . I told him not to do it, but he wouldn't listen.'

'So have the Miyans managed to do anything to us?' Mighdad flared up, 'That remark deserves a beating. This *behenchod* doesn't understand, Tannu-bhai, that I have married her. Now she is my honour, my self-respect. Fuck those Miyans!'

Tannu took his wallet from his pocket and stuffed a five-rupee-note into the baby's red fist. He held out eleven rupees to Saifuniya, but Saifuniya didn't stretch out her hand to take it. There were tears in her eyes. Mighdad had already beaten her once or twice. He'd used foul language to her several times. But he shouldn't have done so now, when Tannu-bhaiyaa was there.

'Go on, take it, you're Mighdad's wife. Do you think I should be allowed to see your face for free?'

Saifuniya stretched out her hand and took the money.

'This little girl is very beautiful, even more beautiful than you. What have you called her?'

'Ahmadi!' Mighdad said with great pride.

Tannu burst out laughing.

'You're still the same old stupid owl! Is that any name? Such an old woman's name for such a beautiful girl! Wait, I'll give her a name . . . Nazish . . . Shadan . . . no, no, this is the one . . . call her Najam-us-sahar!'

'Call her what?' exploded Mighdad.

'Najam-us-sahar!' said Tannu.

'Najmosar! The only person in the whole village who'd be able to pronounce it would be Father! What does it mean?'

'Not Najmosar, Najam-us-sahar . . . morning star!'

'No, sahib, that name won't do. Tell us some village name. I won't be able to say that name, so how could I call her by it? You call her by it!' he told Saifuniya.

Saifuniya blushed red.

'Arre, say it!' he repeated, 'Just look at this *haramzadi*, Tannu-bhai!'

'How can I call her by the name when I can't say it?' said Saifuniya plaintively.

'Tell us some name, Tannu-bhai, which I can say and she can too,' said Mighdad. 'I'm not going to give my child a name so that my father can call her by it.'

'Accha . . . call her . . . ,' he paused, 'Nikhat.'

'What does that mean?' asked Mighdad.

'Fragrance!'

'That's a good name, isn't it?' he turned to Saifuniya.

'Yes,' she smiled.

'That's the smile that trapped me, Tannu-bhai!' said Mighdad, bending over the baby. Then he bit her nose. She began to cry. Saifuniya rushed to pick her up and began making meaningless noises to comfort her.

'What sort of behaviour was that?' Tannu rebuked Mighdad.

'I'm ever so fond of her little nose, sahib!'

Tannu laughed. He had left Mighdad performing matam with the boys of the Husainiya Society. And now this same Mighdad was the father of a girl and not long hence this girl would begin to recite nauhas, and perhaps then some one else would be forced to leave the familiar alleys of the village and the familiar faces of his home and go to war. So would there be wars again and again? He didn't want to answer this question. It was very difficult to fight without a cause . . . you weren't a human being then, just a murdering machine . . .

'Sit you down, Tannu-bhai, I'll be back in a minute,' said Mighdad.

'Eh!' Tannu came back to reality, 'No, let's go, I'll be leaving too. I'm still here a while. I'll come again another day.'

They both stepped outside.

Gangauli had changed a great deal in six years. He saw several brick houses. Mighdad told him about every house and its inhabitants in detail.

'Wasn't Gulzar the tailor's house here?' Tannu asked on seeing a new brick building just a little ahead of Anwarul Hasan's house. On the lane in front of the arched hall were set out a couple of charpoys. Some young men were sitting on them talking. They saw Tannu and Mighdad approaching but paid them no attention.

'That is his house. He made a lot of money in the war and put it into building it. They say he supplied the army with grain. And this isn't much. Do you remember Razaq-va, he used to sell vegetables? Until only yesterday the *saala* used to wander round with a basket shouting out his wares. Now he has a fine house and he's not Razaq-va any more, he's become Sheikh Muhammad Razzaq Quraishi. All the brick houses you see in the village belong to what you can call the nobility of the war. You're the only people whose mud house has been standing there since God knows when.'

'Salaam, Mir Sahib!' said Gulzar the tailor.

'Have you been well?' asked Tannu.

'I'm an old man now, Miyan . . . my dying day is drawing close. Are these the days to be well? When did you come?'

'Yesterday.'

'Shabbu Miyan died well before his time. If he'd been alive today he'd have been so happy to see you. Shall I have some sharbat-arbat made for you?'

'No, thank you.'

'This is my grandson, Mohammad Siddiq. Faqire's son. He's studying in Calcutta, goodness knows in what class . . .' he said gesturing to one of the young men. 'What class are you in, *re*?'

'B.Com.,' said Faqire's son, Mohammad Siddiq.

'Very well, Haji Sahib!' said Tannu, taking his leave of the tailor.

The Haji Sahib sat down. Mohammad Siddiq took Haji Gulzar to task.

'What is it about these Miyans, that you leap up when you see them?'

'What is it?' replied the Haji Sahib, 'It's the zamindari, what else?'

Tannu didn't hear this exchange because he was busy drinking in each village sound like a man who had been thirsting for centuries. But he stopped when he came to Rahim-va the barber's home. It was no longer a home. It was practically a ruin. There were some half fallen walls and the tazia platform made of thin bricks in front of the shell of the hall looked very forlorn.

'Where's Rahim-va gone?'

'Who knows?' replied Mighdad.

'But . . . ?'

'But what, Tannu-bhai?' interrupted Mighdad. 'I brought my marriage procession to this door. The musicians here weren't ready to come so I gave fifty rupees to call an English-style brass band from Ghazipur. In the procession there was just me and the band and Maulvi Bedar. This even stopped the quarrelling between the Uttar and Dakkhin Pattis. People said that it was a question of the honour of the community. Hakim Ali Kabir told the headman of the barbers that he should either turn Rahim-va out of the village or be prepared to be evicted. So Rahim-va was made an outcaste. Then no one in the village was prepared to sell anything to him. Father had him turned off his fields. Mehruniya died. So then he thought that there was nothing left for him in Gangauli. Then one day he just left. I told him many times—where are you going, stay with us, we'll see to the Miyans. But a barber's after all a *behenchod* barber! He ran away!'

'So who prepares the tazia now?' asked Tannu, gesturing towards the tazia platform.

'Saifuniya,' replied Mighdad. 'Accha, so I'll be off now to get some salt.'

'Fine!'

Mighdad turned into an alley. Tannu lit a cigarette and walked on.

'Salaam, Miyan!'

'Salaam, Mir Sahib!'

'Salaam, bhaiyaa!'

'Have you been well?'

'Will you be staying for a while?'

At each step these voices blessed him like a mother. And he wept inwardly as he remembered those countless people who would not hear these voices, who were strangers, but whom the proximity of death had made friends, sharers of pain, or enemies. He was startled to realize that of the forty-five men from Gangauli who'd enlisted only two were still alive. Himself and Gobardhan's son Narayan—Colonel Narayan. The rest were all dead. He thought that Imtiyaz too must have died in some concentration camp. Kulsum wasn't convinced he was dead because his salary still came every month. But Tannu—no, Major Hasan—knew the meaning of the words 'missing in action'.

For a long while he sat on the dilapidated tomb of Nuruddin the Martyr, thinking that it should now be repaired.

There was something very vulgar in the fact that Hammad Miyan should build a new two-storey house and Nuruddin the Martyr's tomb should look completely neglected and abandoned. And as he was thinking about the tomb of Nuruddin the Martyr, it suddenly occurred to him how beautiful Saiyda had grown. He had never seen such big, beautiful, dark eyes in Africa or in Europe. How mature those eyes have become now that she's a young woman, he thought. He leant against Nuruddin the Martyr's tomb and closed his eyes, imagining Saiyda measuring them with her long, tapering fingers.

'What are you doing here?' Hakim Ali Kabir's voice startled him.

The Hakim Sahib was mounted on a pony. Tannu stood up straight and, as he hadn't followed what the Hakim had said, he smiled.

'I'd just gone to the Karbala to pray. I was on my way back and sat down for a while. Where are you coming from?'

'I've been to Hundarhin to see a patient . . .'

'Eh, sahib, when you don't take any fees-vees why do you go wandering all over the place in your old age for no reason?' asked Tannu.

The Hakim Sahib smiled, 'I wander around to oblige people. Is anyone grateful if they recover after paying a doctor's fees? No, they're not! But they certainly are if they get well without having to pay. My family of patients is like my army. Do you understand? And then I write prescriptions and they are made up at Ubbad's dispensary. And doesn't Ubbad have a family to feed?'

'Is Alim-va cooking halva or not?'

'Eh!' exclaimed the Hakim Sahib, surprised by this question. Then he laughed. 'Didn't you forget the halva majlis even in the war?'

'I kept living on the memory of that majlis, ate all kinds of bad food, and thanked God. Saddan-bhai hasn't come?'

'How could he? He was planning to come but then he was called away. Now I see that in this country the number of Hindus and Muslims is growing. It's getting bigger and bigger, bhai. Will Pakistan be made? You've seen the world. You must know.'

Tannu smiled. 'I went to fight, but it looks to me as if Pakistan will be made.'

'So what's to be done when it's made?'

'Perhaps even Jinnah Sahib doesn't know the answer to that,' said Tannu. 'Who will you vote for?'

'We'll have to vote for the Muslim League.'

'Why?'

'It's a matter of Hadi and Saddan's promotion. Hadi supported the government in '42 and, by God's grace, was made a Collector. If God wills then Saddan will be made a Collector too.'

'Insha Allah!'

'Will you come home with me?'

'You go ahead, I'm going from here to Fussu-cha's house.'

The Hakim Sahib set off and Tannu took the road which the people of Uttar Patti still use today for the procession of the tenth of Moharram. He was not planning to go to Fussu's house. He just wanted to be alone so that he could meet the memories which he had been separated from, and connect broken relationships. There must surely be some relationship between man and the land. Otherwise how could anyone take joy in returning to the mud houses of Gangauli and its people, sweet-smelling like black earth, after beholding the great ruins of Rome and the Pyramids of Egypt. These mud walls were not even beautiful, nor was there anything special in these men of black earth. What was there in these Hakim Ali Kabirs and Maulvi Bedars? What was there in these Phunnan Miyans and Hammad Miyans? What was there in this Jhangtiya-bo, this Saifuniya, Bacchaniya, Rabban-bi, Kaniz and Sakina? But for them people would leave the lively, bustling bazaars of Calcutta, Bombay, Kanpur and Dacca. Tannu didn't think all these things. He didn't have the ability to. He only knew that he was happy to be back in Gangauli. He knew that he had longed to see Rabban's single, old eye, and that he had missed Saiyda—who had quite grown up in six years. He smiled and, leaving the road to Fussu Miyan's house, walked through Sibtu Miyan's house to Abbu Miyan's.

Saiyda was lying in the courtyard. A black scarf was tied round her neck. There was no one else in the courtyard, perhaps no one else in the entire house because he could hear the sound of a majlis coming from Fussu Miyan's home.

'You've not gone to the majlis?' he asked.

Saiyda looked at him and sat up. Tannu lay down on the charpoy next to hers and began to play with the grass-string of the bed. Saiyda lay down again too, turned over to face him, hung her right arm over the side of the charpoy and began to trace lines in the earth of the courtyard floor, and to bother a lone ant which was anxious to go goodness knows where.

'Now you won't go anywhere else, will you?'

'No,' he replied.

'How many men have you killed?'

'I don't recall. And I don't recall how many men I tried to kill.'

'Did you used to miss us there?'

'Ha!' he laughed, 'Is that anything to ask? But why didn't you go to the majlis?'

'Who knows why I didn't!' she said. The ant crawled over her finger. She jerked it away, and the ant ran off quickly in another direction. 'I didn't feel like it, but where did you disappear to? I was waiting for you. You came back yesterday and only remembered the way to this house today?'

'I'd already met you! I'd met your mother, and I met your father yesterday as well. I was on my way just now to pray at Father's grave, and went to Phunnan-da's house. Then I met Mighdad, so I went to his place for a bit. Saifuniya's little girl is very beautiful.'

'We haven't seen her,' said Saiyda.

'Eh bhai, I'd like to know what difference there is between Saifuniya and Naima-dadi?'

'Ubad-da didn't take a wedding procession to Naima-dadi's home. But Mighdad went completely lunatic. He went there with a great noise and show. They didn't want that.'

'Have you seen Abbas-cha's wife in Aligarh or not?'

'I have.'

'What's she like?'

'Very nice. She got such big, big eyes, Tannu-bhai, that I can't describe them . . .' she sat up in her enthusiasm.

'They can't be bigger than yours.'

'Let that be.'

'I swear to God,' said Tannu, 'I've seen a lot of girls with big eyes. But, by God, I've never seen one with eyes like yours. *Baap-re-baap* . . . these eyes of yours! They're so deep that elephants would drown in them.'

Saiyda burst out laughing. Then she quickly stopped herself and began to gently slap her cheeks, '*Toba-toba*! May God forgive me. God's curse is upon those that laugh on the eighth of Moharram!'

'Eh bhai, you've suddenly become a total mullah,' said Tannu. 'Now if someone feels like laughing on the eighth of Moharram, then what's he to do? Gag himself?'

'Why say anything to make anyone laugh on the eighth of Moharram?' She lay down and, turning on her side towards Tannu, began again to draw lines with her fingers on the ground. A lock of her hair fell forward. Tannu stretched out his hand and hooked it back behind her ear.

Suddenly the connecting door between Fussu Miyan and Abbu Miyan's homes burst open. Abbu Miyan's wife was the first to enter, then the other women of the family. But Tannu and Saiyda took no notice of them. They continued lying down and chatting. In no time at all several girls and women had stuffed themselves on to the two charpoys. Even so Tannu continued lying down but Saiyda had to sit up to make room for the new arrivals.

'Eh Tannu!' came Aggu Miyan's wife's voice from the outer hall, 'You're being called for.'

'Very well,' Tannu stood up.

'*Naooj*,' complained Abbu Miyan's wife, 'what sort of behaviour is this? The boy's come home after so many days, and no one lets him sit still! One after another—*de danadan*—people are calling for him. You just sit down, beta!'

Tannu lay down again.

The way Sarwari had pushed herself on to Saiyda's charpoy there was no room left for her to sit.

'What are you doing, Ba'ji?' she grumbled. She got up from that charpoy and went to sit at the head of Tannu's. Tannu's head touched her firm thighs. She began to draw lines with her fingers in Tannu's brown hair. All the women began talking at once about different subjects and to scold the young children. Tannu seemed to be swinging slowly to and fro in the innocent sound of their voices. The touch of Saiyda's fingers seemed to be singing a lullaby. His eyes began to close.

'Eh bhai, is Tannu-bhai here?' called out Maddu from the doorway. Tannu opened his eyes.

'What is it?'

'Look at that!' said Maddu, 'I've been scouring the whole village for you. Come on, Father's sat down to eat and is shouting.'

'Let's go.' Tannu freed his hair from Saiyda's fingers. Saiyda tousled his hair, and he stood up laughing.

He entered his home prepared for a scolding but he wasn't given one. Sibtu Miyan and Shabbar Miyan were present too. Sibtu Miyan was talking to Akbari-bi and Shabbar Miyan was amusing Suraiya and listening to Munni chant a nauha. Munni was putting enormous effort into her lament and the sinews of her neck were standing out.

When he saw Tannu, Masoom moved to one side. Tannu sat down between Masoom and Moonis.

'But bhaiyaa, Shabbar-mamu is absolutely right in what he says.' Wazir Miyan was saying, 'It really is something to be ashamed of that we are the zamindars of this village and there's not one Shia mosque here . . .'

'Yes, bhai Bashir!' said Sibtu Miyan, ignoring what Akbari-bi was saying to him, 'It feels very bad. There should be one mosque.'

'Mamu, it's not difficult to build a mosque,' said Bashir Miyan, 'but . . .'

'No, bhai, no!' said Wazir Miyan, 'That's not the point. This mosque will belong to the Husainiya Society and the construction will be paid for only with money from the Saiyids of the village. It will be paid for with money from all the Saiyids. It will be built between the two Pattis on the edge of the pond. It's a very attractive place. In the monsoon it will look just like the Taj Mahal.'

'Fine, I have no objection,' said Bashir Miyan.

'So will you make the proposal in the society?' asked Sibtu Miyan.

'What proposal are you going to make?' asked Abbu Miyan as he walked in. 'Adaab, Bubu!' he greeted Akbari-bi.

'We're intending to build a mosque, bhai!' said Shabbar Miyan.

'Is there anyone wanting to say namaz who's suffering for lack of a mosque?' asked Abbu Miyan.

'Eh Abbu!' shot back Akbari-bi, 'Now if you start raising opposition to building a mosque, bhaiyaa . . .'

'No, Bubu!' said Abbu Miyan, 'I was just asking out of caution. It's better to have no mosque at all than to have one where a lamp is never lit. Look at this house—Shammu, Gigge, Moonis, Masoom, Maddu, Tannu—by God's grace there are so many boys . . . but which one of them is fond of saying his prayers? So in the end who are you building the mosque for? For jinn and ghosts?'

But despite the opposition from Abbu Miyan, in the meeting of the Husainiya Society on the eleventh of Moharram the proposal for the construction of a mosque was approved. It was also agreed that only contributions from the Shia faithful of Gangauli would be employed in its construction, and that there would be no general collection of funds. The original proposal was amended to replace 'Saiyids' with 'Shia faithful', because Sujjan and Ubbad, both non-Saiyids, had asked if they would be expected to keep on saying their prayers in the Sunni mosque. As a result, the Saiyids conceded their point and made them party to the construction of the mosque too. Sujjan donated four rupees in cash and pledged another twenty rupees. Ubbad gave one rupee in cash and pledged five rupees. Tannu gave six rupees and pledged one hundred-and-eleven rupees. In this way a total of eleven rupees cash and three hundred-and-twenty-one rupees and twelve annas in pledged donations were collected. After each pledge the Shia faithful recited praise of the Prophet in ringing voices. As Maulvi Bedar was the only Maulvi, he dug the first spadeful of earth at the site.

According to ancient custom, on the twelfth of Moharram Gangauli was again deserted. First the Ghazipur caravan departed. Saiyda asked Tannu, 'Tannu-bhai, you will write to me, won't you?'

'Yes,' said Tannu, 'and I'll stop in Aligarh on my way to Delhi too.'

This made Saiyda happy, and she left. Tannu felt sad and went back to his own gate. But what was left there now? There were no pictures on the wall of the three-doored hall. The floor-covering had been taken up. The pulpit had been removed. Two or three charpoys were standing there. He wondered whether he hadn't made a mistake in staying on in Gangauli after Moharram, perhaps he should have gone too with everyone else. He lay down on a charpoy and began thinking of Saiyda, and his unhappiness increased even more when he remembered that he was already engaged to marry Salma. 'Why am I?' he asked himself. 'If I had died in the war, what would have happened? Would Fussu Miyan have kept Salma unmarried all her life? So why should I marry Salma? Will Saiyda write to me?'

'What are you doing, son?' asked Abbu Miyan, as he came in.

Tannu hastily sat up. He stubbed out his cigarette on the wooden frame of the charpoy and dropped it on the ground. 'Nothing.' He stood up. 'I was just lying down for a minute. How deserted it is here after Moharram.'

'Yes, son!' said Abbu Miyan, sitting down, 'These two Pattis come alive at Moharram. But as soon as the Imam goes, the whole house is so empty it's frightening.' He began to weep. 'Eh, Hammad!' he called out after wiping his eyes.

'Yes!' replied Hammad, peering out from his room.

'Just send the huqqa over, bhai . . .'

'I'll just bring it.'

'I hear that your late father arranged your engagement before he passed away,' remarked Abbu Miyan as he lay down.

'Yes, he did.'

'And he revealed his wish at a time when there was no one else by him but Fussu Miyan.'

'What?' said Tannu in surprise.

'What else, son? We should thank God that Fussu was there, otherwise how would you ever have known your father's last wish?'

'What do you mean to say, Dada?' asked Tannu.

'Why are you forcing him to put it more clearly?' said Hammad as he stepped into the courtyard. 'Arre, bhai, if this really was what your late father wanted, wouldn't he ever have mentioned it?'

'But, da . . .'

'What are you iffing and butting about, son?' said Abbu Miyan. 'By the grace of God, you're now a Major, and everyone wants you to marry their daughter.'

Tannu's heart began to beat hard.

'What happened to the engagement you were arranging for Saiyda, sahib?' asked Hammad Miyan.

'Bhai, I haven't decided yet,' replied Abbu Miyan. 'We're not in a tearing hurry like Fussu, and neither is there anything wrong with our girl. It's true that the boy is an engineer, but he's not too good-looking. The other boy is handsome but his only income is his salary. Four hundred rupees salary is not at all bad, but still an engineer is an engineer.'

Tannu's heart began to beat normally again. He again felt unhappy.

'Girls come from all over India to study at Aligarh. So they all say when they come home. And by the grace of God, Saiyda is one in a thousand.'

'What I say is forget the face, it's the income which matters. Take the name of Allah, and accept the proposal from the engineer.'

'We'll put it to the test of the prayer-beads.'*

'And if the prayer-beads forbid the marriage on both sides, then?' asked Tannu.

'What a thing to say! Why on earth should that happen?' said Abbu Miyan, 'But for that reason I'm not having Maulvi Bedar see the prayer-beads. I'm going to have bhaiyaa Nasirul Millat see them. What does Maulvi Bedar know about reading prayer-beads . . . . I keep quiet out of respect for his advanced years, but the fact is he did such a thing that . . .'

Tannu went inside. Gori-bi's apartment was deserted because she hadn't come back to the village even for Moharram. From Mighdad's

---

* Shia Muslims seek the approval of God using prayer-beads.

apartment came the sounds of his baby crying and Saifuniya comforting her. There was still a lot of fruit on the custard apple tree, but he didn't pick any. He went into the main zenana of the family elders. But what was there now? A painful silence all around. A crow was sitting on the handle of the pump preening itself.

Tannu passed through the zenana imambara to the zenana of Sibtu Miyan's house. That was also deserted. The back door was open and voices were coming from Abbu Miyan's house. Abbu Miyan's wife was explaining to someone else's wife what sort of last wish it had been, and what sort of brother the deceased had been. 'The one who was dying, poor man, died. And he's not going to come back now to say that in his dying breath he went and whispered this wish in Fussu's ear. Arre, what sort of last wish is that? Fussu couldn't get a match for the girl, so when he saw a good boy, he immediately dug out a wish.'

Tannu wanted to enter Abbu Miyan's zenana and to breathe in the air of the courtyard, hall and rooms which just a short while ago had been imbued with the fragrance of Saiyda's existence. But it was as if Abbu Miyan's wife's voice had slammed the door of their house. He was left standing like an extinguished candle in the courtyard of Sibtu Miyan's empty zenana . . . . Was it true that Father had made no last wish? If he hadn't then at the very least Tannu could send a proposal for Saiyda's hand and Abbu Miyan could refuse it. If he read that letter of refusal then he could content himself with the thought that Saiyda was a shadow, difficult to touch and impossible not to. This love of his for her felt extremely strange. Until a few days ago he had just known that he was in love with her. He wanted to dream of her and to win her. How odd these love affairs of the home are! So simple and so straightforward that it's difficult to credit them. He remembered each moment of closeness to Saiyda, but he could come to no conclusion. Sometimes her touch told him that she did love him, and sometimes her open informality indicated that she didn't. Saiyda behaved with him no differently whether they were alone or in a crowd . . . in this deserted courtyard the thought of Saiyda vanquished him. He forgot the difference in their ages and persuaded himself that his father had made no dying wish.

'Eh, bhai, what are you doing sitting in the courtyard?' Abbu Miyan's wife asked, peering through the back door.

Tannu replied with a complete lie. 'I was on my way to your house when my head began spinning.' But was this really a lie?

'God have mercy! What's the matter, beta?' she said, immediately upset.

'Nothing, Dadi.' Tannu smiled and stood up, 'I've been wounded many times and I'm weak.'

'Come in. Lie down for a little while.'

'No, Dadi.'

'Accha, there's no need to pretend with me.' She dragged him into her house. First she made him lie down on a charpoy. He recognized the bedding spread on it. Saiyda used to sleep on it. A silky, black hair had come away from the mattress and was lying on it. He picked it up and began to play with it.

'Can I ask you one thing, Dadi?'

'Ask me, beta.'

'Did Father really make a last wish?'

Abbu Miyan's wife was famous for her plain speaking. But perhaps she was unprepared for this question and so she didn't give an answer immediately. She began to make a paan. She put a folded betel-leaf into Tannu's mouth and began to prepare another one on top of a very small betel-leaf.

'You haven't told me.'

'What can I tell you now? Who knows if he said it . . .'

'So it could be that he didn't!'

'What isn't possible? But . . .' she paused, 'whether he said it or not, in the end you have to marry someone. And, God keep her, there's nothing wrong with Salma.'

'There's nothing wrong with her, Dadi, but why should I have to be the one to marry her?'

'Eh, beta, if you turn her down now it'll cause a disgrace and Fussu still has a basketful of girls to marry off.'

'I can't marry every unmarried girl in the village. Why don't they chose Moonis or Shammu or Gigge?'

'The things you say! Are Fussu's girls the only ones left for them to marry?'

'So what?' he fell silent.

'So far, by the grace of God, Bashir is still alive, and may God protect Wazir, Shabbar and Sibtu's lives as well. So who else's last will and testament can Fussu present?'

'I am not going through with this marriage!' Tannu stood up and went out without waiting for Abbu Miyan's wife to reply. He didn't feel like going to Fussu Miyan's house. He found the special hospitality with which Rabban-bi, Sakina and Fussu treated him very odd. When he went there, it was as if an earthquake had struck. Salma would immediately run into the kitchen. Once, when she couldn't find anywhere else to hide, she had disappeared into the toilet without even taking a lota of water with her. Tannu had laughed. Then all of Fussu's girls had besieged him. And Rabban-bi and Sakina had scolded and cursed them into leaving him alone. The first couple of times this had happened, he had taken pleasure in these homely formalities, but then he grew bored. He didn't at all like the fact that when he came in, Fussu Miyan would get up from his bed. Tannu wanted to go there as he always had, lie down on Rabban-bi's charpoy, give her a hug, and make her laugh and scold him. But Rabban-bi could no longer do this. The thought of Saiyda returned. And then he felt a great weight pressing on his heart. He walked out of Sibtu Miyan's door with a bowed head and set off towards the tomb of Nuruddin the Martyr.

It was not easy for Abbu Miyan's wife to swallow Tannu's refusal in silence. All these people belonged to one family but, in spite of sharing each other's troubles, they also used to take a small amount of pleasure in them. There was a deep bond of love between all of them, but that love never came between them and this mean sense of enjoyment. And then the one who had most disapproved of Saiyda's going to Aligarh had been Rabban-bi. So Abbu Miyan's wife immediately ate her paan and went into Fussu Miyan's house through the back door.

'Adaab, Mamani!' said Fussu Miyan.

'May you live long, son,' Abbu Miyan's wife blessed Fussu Miyan before sitting herself at the foot of Rabban-bi's charpoy. Sakina began to make her a paan.

'After Moharram you feel frightened the village is so deserted.'

'Very true, *behini*!' said Rabban-bi. 'May God preserve those that come here.'

'Have you fixed a date for Sallo's marriage or not?'

'Moharram has only just finished, how can a date be fixed! It'll be settled after *Rabi-ul-avval*.' said Rabban-bi, 'I'm thinking that the marriage should be held in the month of *Rajab*, by the grace of God.'

'I've a case coming up in court the day after tomorrow,' said Fussu Miyan. 'When I go to Ghazipur I'll speak to bhaiyaa about it too.'

'But have you asked Tannu or not?' said Abbu Miyan's wife.

'What need is there to ask Tannu?' Rabban-bi replied sharply, 'As yet there's no custom of asking the boys and girls of good families about these matters.'

'You take umbrage at the smallest thing,' said Abbu Miyan's wife. 'Tannu told me just now that he doesn't accept any will or dying wish! "Who knows if he made one or not," he said, "I'm not going through with this marriage!"'

'What! Did Tannu say that?' exclaimed Sakina.

'Of course, do you think I made it up?' said Abbu Miyan's wife, losing her temper. 'Here I am, come running to tell you solely out of sympathy. And you start interrogating me!' She walked out grumbling. After she left a deathly hush descended on the courtyard. Fussu Miyan began to draw on his lighted huqqa. Rabban-bi lay down, but then suddenly sat up again. She said, 'I never expected this of Tannu.'

'Our good fortune has burst, mother!' Fussu Miyan commented, 'Otherwise would Hammad's daughters have got married, and Sallo still be sitting at home?'

'May the good fortune of your enemies burst!' exclaimed Rabban-bi, crackling like lightning, 'Who are you to say it's bad luck or not? Is there no other boy in the world besides Tannu? If he doesn't want to marry, then let him not. I wipe the toe of my shoe on his uniform and belt! Arre, we sat quiet out of respect for his late father's wish. But when that *matimile* wretch has no regard for his father's wishes, what compulsion are we under? Do you think that we can't find a husband for Sallo? God forbid that there should be any such dearth of boys. And that wife of Abbu Miyan came here to make a mockery of us! Doesn't she have Saiyda to marry off?'

'Now what's the point of saying all these things. I'm sick and tired of your sharp tongue!' said Fussu Miyan. 'What harm have Mamani and Saiyda done you?'

'And you can hold your tongue! Whoever wishes my girl ill, may her daughter pay for her mother's bad behaviour!'

She raised both hands to wish ill on Saiyda. 'Oh Lord! Who eases difficulties! I rely on you and have patience.'

The matter would perhaps have gone no further, but the connecting door between the two houses was open and Abbu Miyan's wife was standing behind it. When Rabban-bi raised her hands to curse, Abbu Miyan's wife confronted her in anger. 'Arre, who dares say a word about my girl? I'll cut off their tongue with my shoe!'

'So you're going to cut off my tongue!' exclaimed Rabban-bi, forgetting her curse.

'I'm not saying it to you. But if anyone says anything against my girl I cannot sit quiet. These villagers are burning with jealousy because of her studies. They're all jealous—they say, "Why should Saiyda study when nobody else's girl does?"'

'No, Dulhan, let her study more! She can have a job just like a Christian woman!'

'May her enemies take up employment!'

'And we people are her enemies, aren't we?' said Rabban-bi through clenched teeth. 'But neither has our girl gone miles away to learn English, nor is she going to take up any job.'

'Eh, Amman, be quiet,' said Fussu helplessly.

'You are asking your mother to be quiet,' shot back Abbu Miyan's wife, 'as if I'm the one talking nonsense and she's reciting the holy Qor'an! Arre, if you can't get a husband for your daughter what can I do about it? It's not as if I'm marrying off my girl to Tannu!'

'Is your girl fit to marry into any decent family?' said Rabban-bi, 'She's studying English so why don't you marry her off to some Englishman too?'

'Look here, no good will come of speaking ill of my Saiyda!' said Abbu Miyan's wife, beginning to tremble in every limb.

'What will you do about it?'

'May that tongue rot that says a word against my girl!'

'May your tongue rot!' said Rabban-bi, replying in the same coin.

Abbu Miyan's wife slammed the connecting door shut and chained it.

These doors which connect one home to another are certain to be closed once or twice a year, and then after a few days without anyone's intervention, they open again. Fussu Miyan knew that this slanging match would end with the door being slammed, and so when the door did close he heaved a sigh of relief. Rabban-bi kept on grumbling for some time. After a short while Kubara arrived and then Umme-Habiba. The palanquins of the ladies of Uttar Patti began arriving one by one as well, and Rabban-bi's forehead began to throb. She became convinced that the news of Tannu's refusal had spread through the whole village.

All the ladies condemned Tannu with one voice, saying that he ought to have honoured his late father's dying wish. As it was, it was no good thing for an engagement to be broken. You couldn't tell from their words, but all these ladies were to some extent happy in their heart of hearts that this disgrace had not befallen their daughters. However, no one felt the necessity of asking Salma how she felt.

Like all daughters of respectable families, Salma was an extremely simple, straightforward and rather foolish girl. That's not to say that she was slovenly. She even knew how to crochet a chain, and to embroider cushion covers. All the bedcovers in the house had been embroidered by her. She had no equal in the kitchen because Rabban-bi and Sakina had fed her a distillation of all their knowledge of cookery. She could read Urdu at a great pace, and even tried to write it in a broken sort of way. Therefore, when she was alone thinking about her future, she didn't give her children rustic names, but the sort of names which characters in stories she had read in the magazines in Masoom's room in Ghazipur gave their children—Nazish, Tabanda, Taj, Neelo. She had made up her mind not to call them names like Salma, Ahmadi, Akbari and Sarwari. Then, when negotiations began for her marriage to Tannu, she used to feel happy to think how her grandmother would jump when she called her first daughter Seema or Nazish. '*Naooj*!' the old lady would say, 'What sort of name is that?' But now one word from Tannu had thrown her far away from the magic land of her dreams. In the kitchen she had overheard all that had passed between Abbu Miyan's wife and Rabban-bi. At that time she had been rolling out chapattis. Their voices hit against her soul, and her hands worked the rolling pin mechanically . . . patting dry flour on to the balls of dough before rolling them . . . turning the chapattis roasting on the tavva. Then she jumped, because Rabban-bi had begun to curse her. She was amazed that it should be considered her fault that Tannu had turned down the marriage. 'Yes, how is it my fault?' she said out loud, but of course there was no one there to answer her.

She removed the last chapatti from the tavva and turned the small, round rolling board upside down on the basket of bread. Then she washed her hands and, wiping them on her dupatta, went out from the kitchen into the courtyard. Rabban-bi had taken out her pen-box and was perhaps writing a letter to Akbari-bi. Sakina was sitting scraping potatoes against the rough string of a charpoy. Fussu Miyan had already left.

Salma made her way towards Sibtu Miyan's house down the zenana corridor. She knew that this was not an appropriate time to visit Abbu Miyan's house. Still, she didn't want to stay at home as she didn't want to cry, and so she intended visiting Javad Miyan's house so that she could console herself by talking to Rahman-bo. But just as she turned at the doorway of Sibtu Miyan's house, she bumped into Tannu. Really bumped into him—her head collided with his chest. Tannu held out his hand to steady her. Rahman-bo saw from her back door that Sallo was in Tannu's arms. She silently shut the door. Therefore she couldn't see that Tannu immediately separated himself and headed off towards the men's section of Sibtu Miyan's house.

Rahman-bo went straight to Javad Miyan's bed, where he was lying smoking a huqqa. She sat at the foot of the bed and said, 'Now what can I say! . . .'

'Don't say anything,' interrupted Javad Miyan before she could go further.

'How can I not! I've seen something I'd rather my eyes had burst than I'd seen.'

'What's happened?' said Javad Miyan, sitting up.

'Tannu's not marrying Sallo, and he's going round hugging her.'

'What nonsense are you talking?'

'I'm not talking nonsense-vonsense . . . I've seen it with my own eyes,' she replied. 'These are signs that Judgement Day is at hand. Otherwise everything has happened in this family, but not that. And what I would like to know is, what on earth has come over Sallo?'

'Accha, so you've told me. But if this news spreads now I'll cut your tongue out,' said Javad Miyan.

'You think I'm a troublemaker that I'll go round talking? Whenever I say anything, you're always bent on cutting my tongue out.'

Javad Miyan kicked her. She toppled off the bed. Javad Miyan began swearing at her. In fact he wasn't angry with her. He was annoyed with Tannu and Sallo due to whom he had been forced to listen to Rahman-bo, his kept woman. Rahman-bo got up from the ground and, brushing the dust from her clothes, went off towards the courtyard. Javad Miyan said, 'You keep your mouth shut or I'll scorch it for you.' He came outside, where his elder son Kamaluddin, or Kammo, had set up his school. The young girls and boys of the neighbouring weavers, polluted Saiyids, and poor pure-blooded Saiyids were busy memorizing their two times table, and Kammo himself was sitting on a three-legged stool reading a book. His younger brother Fida Husain, or Fiddu, had taken a deep dislike to the school. He had just returned from the fields and was squatting in a doorway opposite smoking a beedi.

This school had fulfilled a good many minor desires of Javad Miyan's household. For example, Rahman-bo no longer wore patched clothes. From the students' homes came both grain and money. Some fifty boys and girls came to Kammo's school to learn their tables and to read the *Aam Sipara** and the Baghdad Arabic Primer. At a rate of four annas a month per child the fees amounted to some twelve-and-a-half rupees. But the total amount was never collected, and the income

* The thirtieth part of the Qor'an.

from the school was about ten rupees a month. Apart from this, grain was given at harvest time. The weavers used to give some shoulder-cloths and lungis too. Then Javad Miyan had three- to three-and-a-half bighas of land. That's why there was a certain degree of prosperity in his home, the greatest indication of which was that Rahman-bo was longing to arrange Kammo's marriage. She dreamed of a daughter-in-law day and night. Javad Miyan himself wanted Kammo to marry but he was waiting for him to set up his practice as a doctor before finding a match. Javad Miyan and Rahman-bo and Fiddu had kept the news of Kammo's becoming a doctor a strict secret. There was no point in annoying Hakim Ali Kabir before it was necessary. Kammo himself used to keep his homoeopathy book in the cloth-bag of a Holy Qor'an and could sometimes be seen reading it placed on a bookrest used for the Holy Book. Accordingly, in Gangauli it became well-known that Kammo was a very devout man and was always reading the Qor'an all the time; and for the past two years he had ceased to take an interest in the things of this world; the whole time there was just him and the Holy Qor'an. No one paid attention to the fact that during Moharram or the summer holidays, when Saiyda came home, a shine came into Kammo's eyes and he began to laugh and smile when he talked to his mother. And that when Saiyda left he became sad. No one paid attention to this because it was nothing to pay attention to. Where was the comparison between Abbu Miyan's granddaughter, Saiyda and Javad Miyan's bastard son, Kammo! Only Kammo knew that he became sad when Saiyda left. But even he was frightened to ask himself why it was so. Even when he was alone he didn't think about talking to Saiyda. But he certainly had decided that he wouldn't marry, and so whenever Rahman-bo brought up the subject of his marriage he avoided talking about it.

Javad Miyan stroked his long beard when he saw Kammo absorbed in study. Kammo glanced at him once and then returned his gaze to his book. He had no love for Javad Miyan. To some extent he hated him. What sort of a father was he whose son was ashamed to mention his name and whose wife still bore the name of another man? Kamaluddin—father, Saiyid Javad Husain Zaidi, and mother—Rahman's wife, Rahman-bo! What a lineage! He knew that he had no choice over his birth, and in his heart he had no respect for his mother—that is Rahman's wife and Javad Miyan's kept woman—either. But he didn't hate her. Sometimes it seemed to him that he loved her. Those were the times that Javad Miyan used to curse and hit her. At such moments Kammo would resist him and he and his father would abuse each other. And then Kammo would sit on the three-legged stool in the outer hall and wonder why he stayed in the village. What was there in these mud houses and dirty alleys? He wanted people to look at him the way they looked at the sons of other fathers. But in the village everyone down to the Bhangis and Chamars knew that he was a bastard. The pure-bred bones of his father couldn't make him legitimate. And so he was jealous of everyone in the village who was, and he had no friends among the children. He didn't play with Moonis, Masoom, Gigge, Shammu, Mamman—not even with Mighdad. These boys went around in groups, kicked up a noise, got up to mischief, picked mangoes from the orchards and stole sugarcane from the fields—and Kammo watched them all alone. In the whole village there was no one like him except for Phunnan Miyan's boys. But Phunnan Miyan's boys had mixed in thoroughly with the Saiyids and so he didn't make friends with them either. As a result his childhood passed in great loneliness. He didn't know any children's games. Even when he began to grow up, this killing loneliness didn't leave him. All that happened was that he began to spend more time in the toilet and his face began to look yellowish, and black circles began to form around his eyes. Around that time Taqqan Miyan took him to the godown. Then one day Javad Miyan saw him coming out of the godown with Taqqan Miyan. There and then he cursed Taqqan a hundred thousand times and beat Kammo all the way home. He made such a row that the news spread round the whole village that Taqqan Miyan had taken Kammo to the godown. Everyone knew what going with Taqqan to the godown meant. The boys of the village began taunting him, and Kammo stopped venturing outside his home altogether.

But he didn't forgive Taqqan Miyan. One day he took his lathi and attacked him. If Phunnan Miyan hadn't arrived at that moment he might well have killed Taqqan. From that day onwards the boys of the village stopped taunting him out of fear. And that same killing loneliness surrounded Kammo. He was struggling against this loneliness and therefore he didn't know why, when and how he had begun to love Saiyda. It could have started the day Saiyda had crept up to him and tickled him. It could also have begun the day Saiyda walked across from the kitchen to the hall with her shalwar pulled up to save it from the mud, showing her fair, soft calves . . . . He realized he loved her the day she was going to Aligarh. He didn't count her living in Ghazipur as separation. But Aligarh was a completely unfamiliar town. That very day he had even gone to the village school and asked the Master Sahib which country Aligarh was in, and had not been consoled even to discover it was actually in India. And now he heard that Aligarh was going to go to Pakistan. He had no interest in whether it went to Pakistan or not. His only worry was that Saiyda might go to Pakistan with it. However, he couldn't understand—Aligarh wasn't a human being so how could it go anywhere? For goodness sake, how could any village or town move anywhere? But when Kammo asked Abbas these questions, he just burst out laughing. Abbas was educated and so Kammo had to shut up. What reply could village-educated Kammo give Abbas? But he didn't understand how Aligarh could go to Pakistan. Finally, when he couldn't bear it any more, he went to Abbu Miyan's house. Saiyda was very busy. She had pinched crinkles into a starched dupatta, but she couldn't find anyone to help her twist it. So for the first time she was happy to see Kammo.

'Eh, Kammo-bhai, just hold on to this dupatta.'

Kammo silently took hold of one end of the dupatta. Saiyda took hold of the other end. Then she slowly began to twist it. And Kammo was lost in the music of her bangles. And he began to watch the sweet little breasts that were peeping through her fine dupatta.

'If a town wants to move from one place to another, can it?' he asked.

'What?' said Saiyda, folding up the twisting dupatta.

'Aren't people saying that Aligarh is to go to Pakistan? But what I mean to say is that it's not possible.'

'Why isn't it possible?'

'Look. Is a town like a man that it can go where it likes!'

'A genie can go into a bottle,' said Saiyda, 'so why can't Aligarh go into Pakistan?'

'That's all nonsense. I can't believe it.'

After Saiyda took her twisted dupatta and left, there was no reason for Kammo to remain there. He went too. But that question still bothered him. Then once when he went with Javad Miyan to Ghazipur, he asked the same question of Masoom, Maddu, Gigge and Shammu. Not one of them could answer him to his satisfaction. Maddu did however remark that he couldn't say anything about Aligarh going or not, but he had certainly heard something about it from a boy from Aligarh itself at a meeting of the Muslim Students Federation.

'Eh, bhai, that's dreadful!' said Kammo, very upset, 'So will the people who are there go too?'

'If the town goes, how are the people in it going to stay?' Maddu said.

'That's what I'm worried about.'

Accordingly, when he returned to Ghazipur he returned an opponent of Pakistan. He didn't interact with anyone in the village and so he would sit his mother down in front of him and deliver speeches against Pakistan. Rahman-bo heard him out for a couple of days and then got bored. Where did she have the time to listen to such foolishness? So she would depart with the words '*Naooj*, son!', and Kammo had no option but to come into the outer hall and make the boys and girls learn their tables, and then stand the bookrest in front of him and read his homoeopathy textbook and think of Saiyda . . .

'I'm going home,' said one boy.

Kammo started. He shifted his gaze from his book and looked at him. Ghafoor the weaver's lad was standing and all the other boys had stopped studying.

'Sit down and keep quiet!' Kammo scolded him, 'Bastard! You think you can just go home.'

'I have to shit,' he wailed. Kammo's entire school erupted with laughter. But Kammo had no answer to give the boy. Naturally he couldn't stop anyone pissing or shitting.

'Run off, get on with you!'

The boy ran off. The remaining boys returned to their studies. Kammo put his homoeopathy book back in its cloth-bag, hung it on its peg, and then lit a beedi and began to think about the time when he would be a very great doctor.

'Salaamalaikum!'

He was startled at this greeting. Two unfamiliar young men in black shervani coats were standing outside.

'Valaikumassalaam!' he returned their greeting, 'Please come in, take a seat.'

They did come in, both of them! Fiddu laid out a bamboo bedstead for them to sit on.

'We hail from Aligarh,' said one of the young men in the correct Urdu of an educated city-dweller.

'Eh, sahib, are there holidays there nowadays?'

'No, there are not,' said the second young man, also in Urdu. 'We are not on vacation but you must have heard that elections are at hand.'

'That I have.'

'Your respected mother and father are also voters.'

This sentence intoxicated Kammo. For the first time he had heard his mother called 'respected mother', otherwise she was called neither mother nor wife. She was just Rahman-bo. He smiled.

'Accha, tell me this—will Aligarh go to Pakistan or stay here?'

'It is our endeavour that Aligarh be incorporated into Pakistan as it is a beacon of Islamic culture.'

'Beacon?' repeated Kammo in amazement. 'Eh, sahib, I'd heard there was a university there, and you're saying that it's a beacon.'

The young men smiled. They said, 'Please try to see, the reality of the situation is . . .'

'Eh sahib, listen here, what I say is simply this,' interrupted Kammo, 'if Aligarh is to go to Pakistan then say so straight out. Because if it is then my respected mother and father cannot give you their votes!'

'I beg your pardon?' exclaimed one of the young men.

'If Pakistan is not created the eighty million Muslims here will be made, and made to remain, untouchables,' said the other.

'Eh, bhai, it looks to me as if it's been a waste of time educating you. What else? If you people don't even know that Bhangis and Chamars are the untouchables. What sort of Bhangis and Chamars do you think we are? And how can anyone who's not an untouchable be turned into one, sahib? Go on, tell me! I'm listening.'

One of the young men proceeded to deliver a complete speech which Kammo didn't understand in the least because the young man was mentioning matters not one of which had any connection with him or with Gangauli.

'I can't believe all that, sahib!' said Kammo after listening to the whole speech, 'Why should this Gaya Ahir, this Chikuriya or Lakhna Chamar or this Hariya Barhai become our enemies, for no reason, after Hindustan gets free? Is that what you people learn over there?'

'At this moment you may not be able to comprehend this fact, but that is indeed what is going to happen. Cows will be tethered in our mosques.'

'Eh, sahib, if all the Muslims go to Pakistan, what difference does it make if horses are tied in them or cows? It's not as if Hindus are going to say prayers there. It's a fine old bit of nonsense that we all go to Pakistan and then expect the Hindus to look after our mosques.'

At first the young men tried to persuade the peasant in front of them, but then gradually they became angry—and rightfully so. After all there's a limit to everything. One of them said hotly, 'Very well, but don't you complain when the Hindus come and carry off your mother and sisters.'

'Which *behenchod* can carry off my mother and sisters?'

Kammo began to tremble with rage. 'If you people weren't my

guests, I wouldn't rest till I'd torn the legs off you!'

A Chamar was heading towards them, a bottle of kerosene hanging from one hand. He stopped when he heard Kammo's voice.

'Did you hear that?' Kammo asked him.

'What is it, Miyan?' asked the Chamar.

'These people have come from Aligarh to tell me that when Hindustan gets free, you people are going to carry off our mothers and sisters,' Kammo explained.

'Arre, Ram-Ram!' said the Chamar, quite unnerved. He turned to the boys from Aligarh, 'You people know reading-writing and all that. Just ask yourselves whether any man can even look at the sisters and mothers of the Miyans as long as we are alive!'

'Better than you people is this Chamar of ours,' said Kammo, 'who says "Ram-Ram!" just at hearing someone talk about carrying off our womenfolk.'

'I apologize,' said one of the young men, 'that was most certainly not what we intended. We merely wished to express the fact that Hindus cannot be relied upon.'

'But why not, sahib?'

'Now how can I convince you?'

'You expect me to tell you?' said Kammo with a smile, 'Would you like some tea?'

'No, thank you.'

Both the young men stepped down from Kammo's house into the lane. Kammo irritably took down the cloth-bag from its peg. The young men walked on. They unfolded a list of voters.

'We've dealt with Fussu Miyan, and seen Javad Miyan's home too. Abbu Miyan's gone to Ghazipur. So if we just deal with Hammad Miyan we'll have finished off Dakkhin Patti. As for the Miyans of Uttar Patti, their vote is in our pocket.'

'But these weavers?'

'Maulana Azad Subhani and Maulana Abdul Baqi are coming to deal with them tomorrow. I can't bring myself to speak to weavers and Biharis. They're all *saala* mother-borne cunts.'

'Assalaamalaikum, sir!' the other young man loudly greeted the weaver, Haji Ghafoor Ansari, seeing him appear from a nearby house.

'Valaikumassalaam, bhaiyaa,' replied the Haji Sahib, 'have you people come from Aligarh?'

'Yes, we have!'

'I guessed as much as soon as I saw you,' said the Haji Sahib, stroking his beard, and so pleased with his power of recognition that he smiled and asked, 'Will you people be speaking this evening?'

'No,' one of them replied, 'the public meeting will be tomorrow. Maulana Azad Subhani and Maulana Abdul Baqi will grace the occasion with their presence.'

'But why are they bringing their gracious presence here?' asked the Haji Sahib in the same coin, 'We people belong to the Weavers' Association. We can't vote for any Aslim-Muslim League.'

'It is our duty to request you to consider it.'

'It's your duty to say your prayers and keep the fast, bhaiyaa.'

'Pakistan is necessary to safeguard those very prayers,' chipped in one of the black shervanis.

'No, Miyan,' said the Haji Sahib, 'I'm an illiterate peasant. But I think that there's not the slightest need to make Pakistan-Akistan for the sake of our prayers. Lord God Almighty said quite clearly, "Eh, my Prophet, tell these people that I am with people of the Faith." And someone was saying that this Jinnah of yours doesn't say his prayers.'

'False allegations were made even against the prophets, sir!' one young man replied heatedly.

'But the prophets used to do some miracle-aracle to show who was right!'

'Jinnah Sahib's miracle is Pakistan.'

'Well, bless me! I didn't know that Jinnah Sahib had become a prophet.'

The young men stammered and inwardly began to reel off curses against the Haji Sahib. One of them said, 'God forbid! What are you suggesting, sir! That was just a manner of speech. How can there be any question of there being a further prophet after the Seal of the Prophets, Saiydna and Maulana, Hazrat Muhammad-e-Mustafa, peace be upon him!'

'You people raised the question!' smiled the Haji Sahib. Finally he had defeated two university boys. 'Accha bhaiyaa, assalaam-alaikum!'

He walked off quickly. Then both the young men remembered that it was Friday and almost time for Friday prayers. They hurried off too.

But when they slipped into the mosque the congregation was already on its feet. They quickly joined in the rearmost row. One of them joined his hands across his stomach, the other dropped his by his sides. His companion nudged him with his elbow and he too hastily joined his hands.

After the prayers were over one of them stood up.

'Brothers in Islam! Assalaamalaikum!'

'Valaikumassalaam!' replied the brothers in Islam in chorus.

'You must all be aware that at the present time, throughout the country, the Muslims are engaged in a life and death struggle for existence,' began the speech. 'We live in a country where our position is no more than equivalent to that of salt in dal. Once the protective shadow of the British is removed, these Hindus will devour us. That is the reason that Indian Muslims require a place where they will be able to live with honour. I am not suggesting that the descendants of Caliph Khalid-bin-Valid and Muhammad-bin-Qasim, conqueror of Sindh, fear Hindus. However . . .'

It was a very rousing speech. The brothers in Islam even interrupted from time to time to cry out 'Allah-o-Akbar!' As a result, a large section of the traders and weavers decided that they should vote for the League as a religious duty. Haji Ghafoor tried to speak several times but the young men wouldn't allow him the opportunity.

'So you people go ahead and fuck your mothers!' he fumed. In his rage he even forgot that he was in a mosque. The visitors from Aligarh took full advantage of this foul language. Even the men who were wavering became absolutely solid in their conviction.

The Haji Sahib stormed out of the mosque. The speech had been quite beyond his comprehension. He didn't even understand why all of a sudden Muslims needed a place of refuge. And where was the protective shadow of the British that those boys had made such a song and dance about? No Englishman had ever been seen in Gangauli. And why then hadn't the Hindus killed the Muslims before the British came to India? And what about the fundamental question—was life and death in the hands of God or the British and Jinnah Sahib?

'And we'll still be just weavers. Will the Saiyids start marrying their children to weavers in Pakistan?'

'What are you talking about, Chacha?' asked Chikuriya, seeing him muttering furiously to himself. At that moment Chikuriya was sitting at Phunnan Miyan's door chatting to Dullan. Pammo was playing with his moustache, and Sultan Fatima, or Fatto, was telling him about her doll's marriage and complaining that Kaniz Fatima, or Kuddan, had been very miserly with the wedding gifts. Kuddan was sitting on her haunches in the kitchen eating dal and rice.

Kuddan had grown up to be a very beautiful nine-year-old. She had inherited all the charm of her mother Razia. Her features were similar too. Big, deep eyes, the same wheat-coloured, oval face and shining white teeth. She had the same well-shaped body. Kulsum never looked at her to her heart's content, and if she ever chanced to, she would glance down at her heels immediately to ward off the evil eye. And if Maghfiya ever scolded Kuddan, Kulsum berated her. As a result, Kuddan would start laughing and Maghfiya would start crying. So Kuddan thought no end of herself, and when she heard that Fatto was talking against her she shrieked, 'That *matimili* is a complete liar! Don't you believe a word she says. And just you ask her what she brought herself. She couldn't even put together two fistfuls of sugar and then she goes and calls me mean!'

'And I suppose the sweet rice was cooked with sugar you brought!' exclaimed Fatto warmly.

This left Kuddan speechless.

'So who are you going to vote for, *re*?' Kulsum called out to Chikuriya from where she lay.

'We've decided that we should vote for Gandhiji,' said Chikuriya, watching the muttering Haji Ghafoor, who was walking along repeatedly straightening his shouldercloth. 'Who are you going to vote for?' he asked. 'We've heard that the Miyans are voting for the Muslim League.'

'We would never on our lives vote for that *matimili* Muslim League!' replied Kulsum with feeling. 'I'm going to give my vote to my son Muntaz. Both those Aligarh boys came to our house. I told them straight out.'

'Eh, Bibi, where is this Pakistan being made?' said Chikuriya, asking a question which had been bothering him for some time.

'Who knows where the *matimili* thing is being made?'

'If it's made in Ghazipur then I can go and see it!' said Chikuriya, taking out some raw tobacco leaf from a fold in his dhoti. 'I'm thinking that this Pakistan must be some mosque or other.' He was about to rub the tobacco in the palm of his left hand with the thumb of his right, when he noticed Tannu heading towards him. He stood up. 'Salaam, Mir Sahib!'

Tannu smiled, 'What are you doing, *beh*?'

'I was asking the Bibi if Pakistan was some mosque or other.'

Tannu laughed. He had no answer to Chikuriya's eminently sensible enquiry and so, walking inside laughing, he greeted Kulsum and lay down on a charpoy. At the foot of the charpoy Maghfiya was sitting chopping spinach.

'Eh, beta, I've heard that you've refused to marry Sallo?' asked Kulsum, handing him a paan.

'But when did I ever consent, Dadi?' asked Tannu.

'But, eh beta, didn't your father make a last wish?'

'Could he only find Fussu-cha to make his last wish to?' said Tannu, asking the question to which no one in Gangauli had an answer, and which all the inhabitants of the Saiyid homes were considering. There was not a single person in the entire village who could be certain that Shabbu Miyan had made this wish. But not one of them could look Fussu Miyan in the eye and say that the story of Shabbu Miyan's last wish was an invention. The fact was that even when Javad Miyan was reprimanding Tannu he had been sure that Shabbu Miyan had never made any such wish. Now when there was no one in any Saiyid home who could answer this question, how could Kulsum? So she could only say, 'Forget about the wish. But just think, son, what a bad name it brings.'

'Tell me, Maghfiya, bhai,' Tannu addressed Maghfiya, 'is Mohammad-cha sending you rupees-upees regularly or not?'

'And why wouldn't he, beta?' replied Kulsum, 'He definitely sends money, the poor man. But you know that ever since your dada went to jail there's been not one paisa of income. There's only Imtiyaz's salary, and the aziz dulha's rupees to somehow provide us a little food.'

Aziz dulha—dear bridegroom! This title struck Tannu. What women these mothers-in-law were! What names they gave their sons-in-law. Dear bridegroom. Delicate bridegroom. Handsome bridegroom . . . and no one ever asked the bride, 'Tell me, what's your opinion?' He looked at Maghfiya. She was busy cutting spinach just as before.

'Shall I tell you a story?' asked Fatto, sitting down at the head of his charpoy.

'Tell me.'

'Once there was a king . . .'

'Look, Nanna . . .' shrieked Kuddan from the kitchen, 'the *matimili*'s telling stories in the daytime. Arre, Imtiyaz-mamun will forget his way home.'

'Yes, beta!' said Kulsum, 'Imtiyaz is a wayfarer. He'll forget his way.'

'Eh, Tannu-bhai, what's a wayfarer?' asked Fatto.

'A wayfarer? A wayfarer is a man who . . .' he halted in the middle of his answer.

Maghfiya burst into laughter.

'Get on with you, Tannu-bhai,' she managed to say, 'you don't even know a little thing like that.'

'Very well then, you explain,' said Tannu, looking into Maghfiya's eyes. She looked away in embarrassment. Her whole body began to sing. She didn't know the language of the eyes, because Mohammad Husain had never spoken to her in it. Perhaps he didn't know it himself. But at that moment she had immediately understood the language of Tannu's eyes. It seemed to her as if she had known that language for ever and ever, just like the language of her home, and she could speak it fast and fluently. She looked back at Tannu from underneath her long, long eyelashes, but he had already turned towards Fatto.

'We're going to take—Pakistan!' 'Long live—the Revolution!'

Dullan came into the house swinging his schoolbag and shouting slogans.

'I'm hungry!' he shouted after throwing a greeting in the direction of Tannu.

'What are you going to do with Pakistan once you've taken it?' asked Tannu.

'What do I know?' said Dullan. 'But all the boys were shouting it so I did.'

'And you want a revolution as well as Pakistan?' Tannu put a second question. 'Are you a Congress supporter or a League supporter?'

'I'm a Muslim!' said Dullan, thumping his chest.

'You've become a Muslim and you're not even circumcised,' said Maghfiya.

Dullan was thrown into confusion at the mention of circumcision. Taking advantage of this, Fatto piped up with the words barbers used to distract a boy's attention while they cut his foreskin, 'See the golden bird fluttering and flying away.'

'Quiet, you shameless girl!' Kuddan scolded her from the kitchen. 'Are you watching her, Nanna?'

'What is there to be ashamed of in that?' asked Fatto, 'Eh, Tannu-bhai, what is there to be ashamed at circumcisions? You had it done, didn't you?'

Tannu was lost for words, and Maghfiya went into another fit of laughter. Kulsum turned her face away to smile, and then gave Fatto a slap, '*Matimili*, shameless girl!'

'Accha, Dadi, I'll be going now,' Tannu said, getting to his feet.

'Sit down please!' said Maghfiya, fighting to control her mirth, 'No one's going to ask you any more questions.'

'No, I'll be off. I'm thinking of going to Ghazipur.'

'Weren't you just saying that you'd be staying a few days more?' asked Kulsum.

'Yes, but . . .' he fell silent.

'Eh, beta, be strong and do the right thing,' said Kulsum, 'or it'll bring a very bad name.'

'How many people will you tell to be strong and get married?' asked Maghfiya, 'It's a very fine sort of thing to force people to get married whether they want to or not. All out of fear of getting a bad name!'

Tannu was startled by her outburst, and turned to look at her.

'Very well, Dadi!' he said to Kulsum, 'What is it to me! And there are several other girls in Fussu-cha's house besides Sallo. In the end I have to marry someone or the other, so why shouldn't it be Sallo? Isn't that so?'

He didn't wait for Kulsum's reply. When he left the house he was pursued by thoughts of Saiyda. Saiyda! Why am I so much older than you? And why aren't relations between our families good? Why aren't they? . . . He grew irritated. He should at least have told Saiyda how much he liked her. But then, what if she had laughed at him? That is the one thing wrong with these girls of the family. They exist to show affection to everybody. Now how can anyone tell the difference between just a show of affection and real affection?

Gaya Ahir was sitting on his haunches at Hammad Miyan's doorway smoking a beedi. Chikuriya had already left. Mighdad was standing opposite the gate of the zenana imambara playing with his little daughter, whom he had named Nikhat, but whom he called Nakko out of affection. Perhaps long names cannot be spoken by those who love.

In front of the Great Gate some weaver boys were playing with a spinning top and swearing at one another. And at Balli Sain's corner a procession of boys was shouting 'Long live the Muslim League!', 'Long live the Qaid-e-Azam!' and 'Long live the Revolution!', and two women peeping out of two doorways were perhaps laughing at this procession.

Tannu saw that there was no hurricane blowing through Gangauli. Life was just as it had been. Weavers were untangling thread. Women were complaining and arguing and laughing and chatting. Boys were spinning tops and playing hopscotch. Mighdad was kissing his little girl. Gaya Ahir was squatting smoking a beedi. The Hakim Sahib must have been feeling his patients' pulses and swearing at young boys. He smiled at the thought of the Hakim and asked himself why he should bring a hurricane into Gangauli's life which was flowing happily like the Ganga. Heaven only knew how many Tannus had loved how many Saiydas in these village families! Respectable people didn't reveal their love. If you were to rake the ashes of any wife's heart who was to say what spark of love for which Miyan would appear. So what was so special about Tannu's love? It's not as if it'd been touched by the wings of the surkhab bird.* And who was to say that his father hadn't made a last wish? Yes, who knew? Sallo may not have been as sinuous as a Hindi film song, but she was simple and innocent like a folk-song from home. And then was it necessary that . . .

Tannu was startled to find himself face to face with the Hakim Sahib. He saw that he was standing at the Hakim's gate, and hastily greeted him. He recognized the black-shervanied young men from Aligarh. All the men of Uttar Patti were present. One black shervani, a cigarette pressed between his fingers, was waving his arm around and explaining in Urdu to the Miyans where in the Qor'an Allah Miyan had given instructions to vote for the Muslim League.

'. . . and the most important thing is that the map of the world will be marked with the colour of one more Islamic government. And neither is it impossible that the green standard of Islam may be seen fluttering once more on the Red Fort of Delhi. If Pakistan is not created . . .'

Tannu had no interest in whether Pakistan was created or not. He sat down on the foot of a charpoy, began watching the two young men and started to think . . . but the thread of his thought was tangled. He was thinking of everything at once—Saiyda, Sallo, Gangauli, Pakistan, Kulsum and Mighdad.

'We've heard that Jinnah's a Shia!' some unidentified person called out.

'He's a Muslim,' replied the black shervani.

'You must have heard this verse of Iqbal's,' began the second shervani:

For thousands of years the yellow-eyed
narcissus laments its sightlessness!
'Tis hard indeed in the garden
to be born with discerning eyes!

Tannu began to observe the smoke issuing from the young man's

* Brahminy duck—pairs said to enshrine the souls of dead lovers doomed to remain in sight and hearing but separated by a flowing stream.

nostrils and mouth.

'Recite the poetry of Anis to us, Miyan!' said Husain Ali Miyan. 'Ya Ali!' he put his hands on his knees, stood up and left without waiting to listen to any verse of Anis.

'If the line of Prophets and Caliphs was not complete, then I would say . . .'

'What is that to you Sunnis?' the Hakim Sahib interrupted the black shervani, 'Make yourself another Caliph!'

'Look here, sir!' said the black shervani, 'This is no occasion to remember petty sectarian disputes. Hold strongly to the rope of Allah. Today that rope's name is Muhammad Ali Jinnah. He is the strength of Allah. Rise up and proclaim that you want to create Pakistan. Just look at your leader, and then at those Congresswallahs. Whether it's Gandhi or Nehru, they roam around in every back alley. And then there is one man, our Qaid-e-Azam, who is so difficult to meet that even the Viceroy himself has to take an appointment.'

'So if he doesn't meet anyone, then . . .'

'Yes, quite right!' Hakim Sahib interrupted Ubbad, 'When he doesn't meet anyone, then, heaven forbid, he's become Allah Miyan.'

'What are you insinuating?' asked the black shervani.

'I'm not insinuating-vinsinuating anything,' said the Hakim Sahib. 'We people are in any case going to vote for the League, but we're not going to stop from asking one thing. When Jinnah Sahib doesn't meet anyone and neither does Allah Miyan, then why don't we vote for Allah Miyan?'

Tannu burst out laughing.

'You gentlemen can have no reply to this rustic logic,' said Tannu in pure Urdu. 'So why are you delivering speeches to no purpose? This Patti of loyal government Muslims can't vote for anyone but the League. But you will not be able to take the vote of Musammat Kulsum. She will vote for her "Muntaz". She is a totally illiterate woman. She cannot call her son by his correct name, but mispronounces Mumtaz as "Muntaz". He was a very noble young man. How would you know him! He was shot dead at the Qasimabad police station. I was not here at that time but I have heard that he died very bravely. That is to say that when he was sure that he was dying he did not cry for fear of death. They say that he caught hold of the hem of the shirt of a man running away and said, "Eh, bhaiyaa, if you go to Gangauli, tell my mother I'm dead. This *behenchod darad* is going to take my life." Perhaps you will not have understood his language, because you gentlemen have made the Urdu tongue Muslim.

But I swear by God that the language I am speaking now is not my mother tongue. My mother tongue is the one in which Mumtaz sent that message to his mother. Because of his speaking Urdu, Hammad-da is looked down upon by the whole village. After Pakistan is created will you leave this Urdu here or take it with you?

'Look, I'm no politician. But I have seen the field of war. Those who die in battle die a very helpless death. Those who kill become very ugly too, because to save their lives they are forced to regard those before them as enemies and to hate them. It's possible that if any one of those enemies were to meet me here, in Gangauli, I would give him a cigarette to smoke and sugarcane juice to drink, invite him to swim in my tank, and then at night, spread out soft and warm bedding on a charpoy strung as tight as a drum, and talk to him about his country . . . and tell him about mine. But there I killed him. Because if I hadn't he would have killed me. That's why I am afraid. You gentlemen are making people fear for their lives, but it's we people here who will have to cut the harvest of this fear. This is why I am so afraid.'

'You, descendent of Muhammad-bin-Qasim . . .'

'I am not a voter!' Tannu interrupted the black shervani, 'I am a Muslim. But I love this village because I myself am this village. I love the indigo godown, this tank and these mud lanes because they are different forms of myself. On the battlefield, when death came very near, I certainly remembered Allah, but instead of Mecca or Karbala, I remembered Gangauli. And I used to be upset and cry at the thought that I may never again be able to chew sugarcane at the indigo godown, and that I may never again taste the halva of the eighth of Moharram. Allah is omnipresent. Then what is the difference between Gangauli and Mecca, and the indigo godown and the Ka'aba and our pond and the spring of paradise?'

'People like you are selling out the Indian Muslims to the Hindus!' said the black shervani angrily. 'Have you no shame? Are you comparing the Noble Ka'aba with this miserable village?'

'Yes, that's just what I am doing!' replied Tannu. 'And neither am I ashamed to do so. Why should I be? Gangauli is my village. Mecca is not my city. This is my home and the Ka'aba is Allah Miyan's. If God loves His home then won't He be able to understand that we too can love our home as much as He loves His?'

'Eh, beta, you're talking like a kafir,' said the Hakim Sahib, in the same breath shouting out, 'what are you doing, you *haramzade*!' and making a boy about to spit into the tank run off in fear. 'The

Ka'aba's after all the Ka'aba, son.'

'When did I say that it wasn't? But Lahore is not the Ka'aba, is it?' asked Tannu. 'Look, Chacha, you have not seen all that I have, and so you cannot see what I can. Anything constructed on a foundation of hate and fear cannot be auspicious. Even after the creation of Pakistan, Gangauli will remain in India, and Gangauli is after all Gangauli. Then when Gaya Ahir, Lakhna Chamar and Chikuriya Bhar ask you why, when they have never shown you any enmity, you voted for Pakistan, what answer will you give?'

'So then should we vote for the Congress, which is sitting there with its eyes on our lands?' asked Ubbad Miyan.

'Whether you vote or not, it's the Congress which is going to rule in Gangauli.'

'What sort of justice is that?' said the Hakim Sahib.

'And you can take it for granted that the days of zamindari are over too.'

'What else!' said the Hakim Sahib heatedly, 'The zamindaris belong to that Gandhi's father, don't they, so he can break them up the moment he arrives!'

'Don't you listen to him, revered sir!' the black shervani said. 'The Congress will certainly try to break the zamindari system, because most of the zamindars are Muslims. But it won't be so easy for them to do. If they try then the Islamic army of Pakistan will launch an attack on Delhi!'

'You can talk about attacking Delhi because you have never seen war,' said Tannu. His tone became bitter. 'By all means create a Pakistan!' he said as he got up, 'But from time to time send us a letter from there to let us know that all is well.'

Touching the empty tazia platforms he walked out of the Great Gate and into the lane. He was very angry with himself—what need had there been to make a speech? But he really was scared of where this hatred would end. Did Indian Muslims really not belong to this land? Surely the Rajput Muslims of Dildarnagar and Gahmar were formed of this earth. So why were they going to vote for the Muslim League? Why did they feel the need for a homeland? Why were Muslims who had kissed the sandals of Lord Rama, accepting them as footprints of the Prophet, making Pakistan?* And did they really

* One theory of Indian Muslim thought is that there have been 1,24,000 messengers of God, of whom only a few are known. Therefore all sages and prophets can be considered messengers of God and respected as such—including, for example, Rama and Mahavir.

want to create Pakistan? Did all of them, who were going to vote for the Muslim League, know what Pakistan would be, and what it would be like? Pakistan was no God that it could be accepted unseen! It takes several generations for the name of a new country to come easily to the tongue. So what would happen to the generations in between? What would become of these generations suspended in mid-air? The black shervanis had no interest in these questions. They weren't even prepared to consider the fact that man cannot live by hate, suspicion and fear alone . . . . Tannu was trapped in the crowd of his own questions. He began to feel stifled and asked himself, 'What should I do now? Kulsum Dadi wants to vote for her Muntaz. Hakim Ali Kabir for the Muslim League. Which of them is right? 'Oh, dammit!'—he suddenly returned to army language—'Bastards!' He kicked a dog which ran off yelping.

'Cha, I cannot stay here after my leave is over,' he said to Fussu Miyan. 'You speak to Manjhale-Abba and fix a date.'

Fussu Miyan was completely taken aback. He suddenly stood up. His huqqa fell over. Its clay bowl broke to pieces. The embers it contained scattered. Sallo, who was making a doll for her little sister in one corner of the courtyard, was overwhelmed with embarrassment. Sakina instantly began making Tannu a paan. Rabban-bi's only eye smiled.

'But, beta, before the ninth of *Rabi-ul-avval* . . .'

'Imam Husain's daughter was married on the ninth of Moharram, wasn't she?' said Tannu, interrupting Fussu Miyan.

'But what's the hurry?'

'What's the hurry? Arre, sahib, who knows when Pakistan will be made and then the date will be put off till God knows when. So I shall fulfil the wish of my late father before next Moharram.'

'So then why were you telling Abbu's wife that you wouldn't go through with this marriage?' asked Rabban-bi.

'So please could you speak to Uncle,' said Tannu, evading her question.

'No,' said Rabban-bi, 'the marriage may take place or not, but it can't take place before the tenth of *Rabi-ul-avval*.'

'Mother, you . . .'

'There's no need for you to mother-other me!' said Rabban-bi to Fussu Miyan, having pronounced her judgement. Then she turned to Tannu and said, 'Eh, beta, are you going through with this marriage to do us a favour? If that's the case then say so at once! Thank you very much! But we require no favours from you.'

Salma's heart began to pound.

Tannu made a calculation and worked out that his leave extended until after *Rabi-ul-avval*. He agreed. But that night when the whole house was asleep he quietly turned up the wick of the lamp.

Fussu Miyan was snoring loudly. Rabban-bi's nose too occasionally gave forth a few trills.

Tannu took a notepad from his suitcase, and then looked at the smooth, almond-coloured paper for a long time. He was always nervous of writing letters. But by the time he had smoked about two-and-a-quarter cigarettes, he had prepared himself to write the letter. But now the question was how to start it. His mind was overflowing with all the other things he wanted to put in the letter. It wasn't as if he was going to write anything that wasn't true. He was to write only of his own love. And the fire of love makes even the most ordinary words shine like pure gold. Every foolish phrase becomes magic. But still this seemed difficult to him.

Finally, after a great deal of thought, he wrote down:

Dear Saiyda,

Greetings and prayers for you. I am well. I hope that you are well too. I am a rustic soldier. I don't know how I should write this, but I have to write that the date for my and Sallo's marriage has been set. I hope that you will definitely come to take a gift from me. Dadi is well. Dada has gone to Ghazipur. Everyone there is well too. Choti-da is asking me to send you her best wishes. Prayers for you.

Your brother

Tannu.

With this letter, a weight was lifted from his heart. He hadn't wanted to write a letter like this, but he was unable to write any other. How could he write, 'Saiyda, I love you,' because she could answer straight back that there was nothing special in that as every brother loved his sister. Now Tannu didn't know that his picture lay in the bottom of Saiyda's trunk. And he didn't know either that in Aligarh the girls of the Waheediya and Sultaniya hostels had nicknamed Saiyda 'Tannu-bhai'. There were several other things of this nature of which he was also unaware. That's why, when he received Saiyda's letter, he couldn't understand its simple, straightforward Urdu.

Dear Tannu bhai sahib,
Greetings. I received your letter. You all seem well. I am well and I pray to all-merciful God for your welfare and good. You have chosen such a date for your marriage that I shall be unable to attend. Away with you, you've made me cross.
My greetings to everybody there!
Simply,
Saiyda.

Tannu received this letter in Gangauli itself. He didn't recognize Saiyda's handwriting and so he opened the envelope in the courtyard. But the moment he opened the letter his heart began to pound. And it pounded so hard that Rabban-bi heard it.

'Whose letter is it, beta?'

'Saiyda's.'

'What has she written?'

There was certainly meaning in her tone, because Tannu started.

'Nothing,' he replied.

He went out. In the distance a horse cart was approaching. The jingling of the harness bells was running ahead of the cart to the house. Tannu stopped to watch and wondered who could be coming to Gangauli after Moharram.

There was only one passenger in the cart. Tannu came out on to the steps of the outer hall, and then down to the road.

To the right near the bamboo thickets a group of boys, were learning the lesson 'Long live—Pakistan!'—and doing so at a throat-splitting pitch. Tannu looked at the children and smiled. In that procession there were several Hindu boys as well, and they too, just like the Muslim boys, were wishing life to the Muslim League at the top of their voices.

'What sort of Pakistan are they making, bhai?' Tannu asked Kammo.

'Who knows, sahib!' replied Kammo putting his homoeopathy book back into its cloth-bag, 'Who's coming on that cart?'

'What I'm thinking is that this isn't any season for any visitor to come,' said Tannu, looking at the horse cart which was now quite close. 'Eh bhai, that looks like Phunnan-da!'

He ran towards the cart.

'Adaab, Da!' he greeted Phunnan as loudly and with as much force as the boys were shouting the slogan 'Long live Pakistan!'

'Eh, bhai, when did you get here?' asked Phunnan with astonishment and love.

'Stop, you *madarchod*!' he scolded the carter. The cart drew to a halt. Phunnan leapt down. He hugged Tannu and began to examine his body. 'Eh, bhai, what sort of war did you go to fight, ain? You've come back with all your joints intact. Did you do any fighting there or not?'

Tannu laughed, 'How have you turned up all of a sudden?'

'Those *betichods* let everyone go, so what could I do? I told them again and again that there's still time left in my twenty-five year sentence but none of them listened to me.'

The news spread through the whole village that Phunnan Miyan had returned. Practically the entire population came out of their houses. Only the Saiyid gentlefolk of the Uttar and Dakkhin Pattis stayed indoors. Phunnan Miyan met all who came to him, and asked after everyone's welfare.

'I hear that Mighdad-va married Saifuniya?' he questioned in a loud voice which carried to the zenana of Hammad Miyan's house. Hammad Miyan squirmed. 'And Hammad didn't stop the marriage?'

'The things you say!' said Kulsum, 'If he'd been able to he'd have married her himself.'

'*Dhat*!' Phunnan Miyan scolded Pammo when he saw her standing next to him. Pammo had just screwed up her face to cry when Phunnan caught hold of her and lifted her into his lap and then tossed her into the air. Pammo began to cry in earnest. Phunnan Miyan poked his long moustache into Pammo's neck. Pammo tried to stop him. Maghfiya was rolling with laughter.

'Let her be, father!' she managed to say, 'Arre, this is your grandfather, *re*!' she said, caressing Pammo.

But perhaps Pammo didn't believe her. She kept on crying, and Phunnan Miyan kept laughing. Then he threw Pammo down on to a bed.

'Just hand me a lungi,' he said to Kulsum. 'It's been an age since I had a bath at the pond. I'll just take a bath and come back.'

'Why don't you have a bath here!' said Kulsum. She wanted to see him for some time more. She wanted to know if the time spent in jail had changed her Phunnan and if so, how much. It was not a matter of the body, because she had crossed the limits of the heat of the body a long time ago. It was a question of the soul for which she had renounced the life of a married lady and consented to become a kept woman.

'We're going to take—Pakistan!' shouted Dullan, as he came into the house.

'You and whose army?' Phunnan Miyan shot back at him.

Dullan was astounded.

'Won't you greet your grandfather?' said Kulsum.

'Adaab!' said Dullan, offering his salaams.

'Who are you going to take Pakistan with?' Phunnan Miyan repeated his question.

'With the men from Aligarh!' replied Dullan, after some consideration.

'Where did you come across these men from Aligarh?'

'Two of them came here to ask for votes!' said Kulsum, 'They told us to vote for the Muslim League. What are these wretched votes?'

'So what did you say?'

'I said that I'm going to vote for my Muntaz. But when I went to vote Muntaz's name wasn't there, so I brought the papers home. Did you get any news of Imtiyaz in jail or not?'

'Do you think I opened a post office in jail?' said Phunnan Miyan, 'But I think that Imtiyaz must be gone.'

'Eh, God forbid!' said the boy's mother, writhing inwardly, 'How could you say such a thing!'

'All the armywallahs have come back,' said Phunnan Miyan. 'A lot of them have ended up in jail. Someone came back and immediately got involved in a fight, someone else carried off somebody's wife. One man pulled off a theft and another a dacoity. If Imtiyaz had been alive he would have come back by now. The joy of children is not written in our fate. We had just two sons. Both have been killed. Girls can't shoulder our biers. Who's going to lift our corpses?'

'You go and have a bath,' said Kulsum. 'What sort of things are you saying!'

'I met one prisoner in jail. Some Singh or other!' said Phunnan Miyan. 'He was a Communist. He said that God-vod, everything was a lie. I didn't believe what he said. One day when he began squealing a lot I gave it to the *saala* with both hands. But it is something to think about. Hammad has stolen everyone's rights and that's why he's enjoying life. If Allah Miyan did exist, Hammad's bow couldn't have been strung like this.'

He walked out of the house with the lungi over his shoulder. Kulsum noticed that his broad shoulders were drooping. And it also seemed to her that the sparkle was missing from his eyes. Her heart became full. Her big, big eyes filled with tears.

Phunnan Miyan's glance fell upon Hammad, who was in his high porch explaining something to Gaya Ahir. Phunnan Miyan immediately cleared his throat loudly, stroked his moustache and walked past.

'Salaam, Mir Sahib!' said Haji Ghafoor.

'How are you, bhai?' said Phunnan Miyan, 'And, eh bhai, the couple of black hairs left in your beard are still there just as they ever were.'

'The things you say,' said Haji Ghafoor, heaving a sigh. 'I've not grown old but I've been buggered by rising prices!'

At Balli Sain's corner a procession of boys suddenly began shouting slogans:

'Nara-e-takbir!'

'Allah-o-Akbar!'

'Long live . . .'

'The Qaid-e-Azam!'

'Long live . . .'

'The Muslim League!'

'Have all these boys gone mad or what?' asked Phunnan Miyan.

'The amazing thing is, Mir Sahib, that the people who are shouting and screaming are the ones who aren't voters. I'm a voter and no one asks what I think. But whoever you see will be making a speech. And they're all looking for Pakistan to be made. This Jinnah Sahib, now, where's he from?'

'Who knows who he is and where he comes from. I've heard that he was a lawyer in London.'

'So have the British tutored him in all this and sent him here?'

'To hell with all of them!' said Phunnan Miyan. 'If Pakistan's made, it'll be a long way from Gangauli. You go and look after your spinning wheel, and keep your warp straight. Pakistan-Akistan is just a game for filling stomachs.'

Phunnan Miyan went on.

From both sides came the sound of looms—khat! khat! Weavers, sitting in pits up to waist level, were busy weaving long strips of coarse cotton material, shouldercloths and lungis. The weaver women were breastfeeding their children and chatting. Some of them were washing dirty clothes and arguing with one another. Opposite work was in progress at the Shia mosque. The walls had been constructed to their full height. Two boys were sitting on their haunches on the edge of the pond smoking beedi and waiting for fish to bite.

This familiar atmosphere began to make Phunnan Miyan tingle. He began to sing softly:

To stretch fully she failed although she'd raised her hands,
She saw me there, and smiled so fair, and dropped her hands.

But he was singing this verse of a love poem to the tune of a Moharram lament.

Seeing a lot of activity in Javad Miyan's outer house, Phunnan stopped. Javad Miyan's entire body was shaking with peals of laughter, opening out, and throbbing with the pressure of so much happiness. He was talking at the top of his voice to a weaver he'd caught hold of.

'What I'm saying is what's the point of writing prescriptions for five seers of medicines? You can fill yourself up to the throat but a whole cupful of medicine will still be left to take. Real medicine is when the patient eats no more than three little white tablets as thick as a pubic hair, says "Ya Ali!" and leaps to his feet. Taffazul-bo, poor thing, went on taking medicine for a year. Miyan Ali Kabir fed her the whole of Ubbad's dispensary but it didn't make the slightest difference. One day Tafazzul mentioned it to Kamaluddin . . .'—he didn't think it appropriate to call his son Kammo at such moments. By the grace of God, he had qualified as a doctor, and therefore Javad Miyan called him by his full name. 'So Kammo . . . I mean Kamaluddin gave him two doses of his medicine and said give it to her and see what happens. May God curse lying *behenchods*! After three doses she began to eat whole plates of rice!'

'Yes, Mir Sahib, of course she did,' said the weaver, 'God gives some healing hands.'

'I am telling Kamaluddin that he should have a big tin signboard painted like the town doctors do and hang it on the pillar here. It should say "This is Dr Kamaluddin's clinic—cheap and quick cures, your money back and five rupees extra if not satisfied". But so far Kammo hasn't agreed.' The sight of Phunnan Miyan made him even forget that Phunnan had been cast out from the community. He said, 'When did you arrive then, *ji*?'

'A short while ago,' replied Phunnan. 'And what's this function you're holding here? Have you fathered another boy or what?'

'If I wasn't buggered by all this farting, I might well make your words come true,' Javad Miyan smiled. 'I haven't given up any sort of activity yet. What are you listening to, *re* . . .' he scolded his young son, Fiddu, who was standing nearby eating jalebis.

'I'm not listening,' said Fiddu, 'I'm eating.'

'Get off with you, *susar*, or I'll give you two handfuls!' laughed

Javad Miyan.

Fiddu went into the house munching jalebis.

'And how are things?' asked Phunnan Miyan.

'Arre, just come and fill the huqqa!' called out Javad Miyan. 'You tell me, how did things go in jail?'

'Fine,' said Phunnan Miyan. 'Arre, after all I am Phunnan Miyan. I fucked that *madarchod* of a jailor . . . he looked after me like a son-in-law.'

Fiddu put fresh water into the base of the huqqa, and re-set the pipes and bowl. Phunnan Miyan sat down. Javad Miyan pressed the pipes firmly into place in the base of the huqqa. Phunnan Miyan took the first puff. The smoke caught in his throat. He began to cough and his big, big eyes turned red.

'It looks like you've forgotten how to smoke a huqqa,' remarked Javad Miyan.

'That it does!' said Phunnan Miyan, wiping his eyes with his lungi. 'It's not the only thing I've forgotten. Who knows if I still remember how to sleep with my wife or not.'

'Have a try today!' opined Javad Miyan.

Phunnan Miyan burst out laughing and all the walls erected by the judgements of the community came crashing down.

'Eh, bhai, you've been keeping well, haven't you?' came the voice of Rahman-bo. She didn't appear before Phunnan Miyan. When she had arrived in Gangauli as Rahman's wife she hadn't kept purdah from him, but she had done so ever since she'd become Javad's kept woman.

'Arre, why are you hiding from me now?' said Phunnan Miyan, straightening his moustache. 'I'm not capable of carrying off people's wives any more.'

'I'm not so sure of that!' replied Rahman-bo.

'Eh, bhai, why don't you get Kammo married now?'

'Just let his *doctory* get underway,' said Javad Miyan, 'I'm thinking of sending a proposal to Hammad's house.'

'Hammad's no match for you,' said Phunnan Miyan. 'There's no doubt about Kammo's father being a Saiyid, is there? At least his son's in-laws should be Saiyids. God only knows when Hammad became a Saiyid. And if he's a Saiyid, that makes the rest of us absolute Prophets!'

'Have you heard this or not?' asked Javad Miyan. 'There's been a hell of a fuss over Tannu. He went and said that he wasn't going to marry Sallo. It went round the whole village. I caught hold of him by his throat and told him if he didn't marry her I'd tear his legs off. That sort of thing may go on in Calcutta and Lucknow, but it can't happen in Gangauli. I said, if Fussu made a wish, what fault is it of Sallo's? That was enough. Tannu didn't have an answer. So then I was soft on him. Now I've heard a date's been set.'

But if the date for Tannu's marriage put an end to the story, why was the pain in his heart no less? Why was it that Saiyda's big, black eyes always seemed to be watching him?

As the day of his marriage approached, his loneliness of heart increased. He was no poet and could not form his pain into a song of the yearning born of separation. When that pain grew too strong, all he did was to write a letter to Saiyda, and then read it through several times and tear it up.

No one had any idea of the storm that was raging within him, and so wedding songs, musical insults, began to be sung with great contentment in the house.

Make your bid, na!
The kotwal will hear your bid. Make your bid, na!
Five rupees for the elder sister.
The younger sister's priceless. Make your bid, na! . . .

But it was as if these simple songs had quite lost their ability to produce any thrill of pleasure. The girls were dissolving into peals of laughter. Old women were blushing. A great light was burning in Rabban-bi's single eye, illuminating not just the homes of the Saiyid families, but the whole village . . . . But Tannu was in total darkness. He didn't know that his love story was not the first which was to remain unspoken. He didn't know that in respectable families innumerable stories like his had remained untold and perhaps innumerable stories like his remained to be untold. And because he didn't know this he found himself alone, and his shoulders were breaking under the weight of his own love.

He turned over. The sound of women talking was still coming from the inner house. He looked at his watch. It seemed as if its radium dial smiled at him after it told him the time. He saw desolation all around him. He was totally isolated.

After the date for his marriage had been set he had stopped going to the inner house. He spent the winter nights in an outer room. But to pass the nights of the hot weather he had to come outside. A short distance away, under a neem tree, stood Kammo's charpoy. But who could spend time with that blockhead? He was always sunk into homoeopathy. And the time left over he spent thinking of Saiyda, though he alone knew that he thought of her.

'What is it, bhai, are you thinking of some prescription-uscription?' asked Tannu.

'No, sahib!' said Kammo pulling his lungi down over his knees, 'I've been trapped by starting this *doctory*. The Hakim Sahib and Ubbad don't acknowledge my greetings. Now you tell me, did I go from house to house saying, "Eh, people, come to me for treatment. A new age has dawned with all sorts of new diseases. Hakim Sahib is still using the medicines prescribed by Luqman, so how do you expect anyone to be cured?" One day he called me and told me I'd be arrested. And God knows what else he said,' concluded Kammo as if bored. He took out a bundle of beedis from beneath his pillow and lit one. Tannu lit a cigarette.

Tannu also knew that Kammo's practice had created a tumult in the village. For one thing Javad Miyan's tone had become so strident that it was becoming day by day more impossible to bear. He had turned Kammo (whom he now referred to as Kamaluddin) into a minor messiah. He even went to the extent of saying that three of Kammo's pills had reduced the force of his flatulence. Otherwise it had been difficult for his family to sleep at night. However, to Rahman-bo and Fiddo's minds his farts were drumming out with just the same volume, force and splendour, although it was true that he was slightly more circumspect about farting outside the house. So in that respect Kammo had done wonders! But what really made Kammo's practise a success was that his medicines were cheaper than those from Ubbad's dispensary and, most importantly, that English medicines were, after all, English medicines.

However, it's obvious that the medical practice of Rahman-bo and Javad Miyan's bastard son did not please Hakim Saiyid Ali Kabir Zaidi one bit. He was opposed to homoeopathy. The homoeopaths had sat down with a box in every village. They neither knew how to feel a pulse nor take a temperature, but were treating people like nobody's business. And people were even benefitting from them. It was true that the Hakim Sahib himself didn't ask anything from his patients but they did have to pay for the horse or horse cart that brought him. These homoeopaths didn't even ask that. Consequently, the number of the Hakim Sahib's patients was dwindling. He could endure the other doctors from round about but by setting up shop in Gangauli itself, Kammo had broken the Hakim Sahib's back.

'What is it to me? Let the *haramzadas* die!' he had declared and washed his hands off the matter.

But this defeat was a massive one as for some eight or nine hundred years his forefathers had been treating the people of Gangauli and its neighbouring villages. Therefore, he was pained to see his ancestral patients at Kammo's door. But the real disaster came the day when his own daughter, unbeknownst to him, sent her infant child over to Kammo. The Hakim Sahib suddenly aged. The child was not even really ill. She had thread worms and could have recovered just with household remedies. That was why when the Hakim Sahib saw his own daughter feeding her children white pills something inside him was extinguished. He said, 'Very well! All that I needed was to live to see the day that *haramzada* Kammo would be treating my granddaughter.'

'Eh, father, you had gone to Alavalpur, and this *matimili* wouldn't stop crying. There was no way I could quieten her, so I sent her there, and took some medicine.'

'All right, beti!' said the Hakim Sahib without raising his eyes, 'But I was going to return from Alavalpur, wasn't I?'

Fakhrun had no answer to this, and so she began beating her son, Bikku, who was at that moment standing at the door of the hall peeing, and squirting his stream of urine all around the place. The Hakim Sahib left the house without scolding her. Fakhrun was left gaping, because this was the first time that she had ever beaten Bikku and the Hakim Sahib hadn't scolded her for it.

Ghani the weaver was sitting on his haunches next to the tank smoking a beedi. He leapt to his feet the moment he saw the Hakim Sahib. The Hakim Sahib sat down, making a cushion of his rolled up bedding, and began to draw on the lighted huqqa. Ghani hurried to fill a fresh bowl of tobacco and, blowing on the embers on top, fitted it on to the huqqa.

'Badruniya's a lot worse,' said Ghani.

'So what can I do, *beh*?' asked the Hakim Sahib. 'Why don't you take her to Dr Kamaluddin.'

'Please just take a look at her.'

'I'm not going to, you *behenchod*! I give you land. Every highday and holiday I give you money. I give you the wood and bamboo to build your house. If you die I give you the land for your grave. And then you go and get yourself seen to by Doctor Saiyid Kamaluddin Zaidi! The day has dawned when Rahman-bo's boy is handing out medicine in Gangauli!'

'I wouldn't have gone, *malik*!' said Ghani, 'But Hammad Miyan made me.'

'So go and tell Hammad that Badruniya's worse. What have you come here for? I don't have any prescription for raising the dead.'

Ghani began to press his feet. Slowly the Hakim Sahib lay down. Ghani kept telling him about Badruniya's illness and the Hakim Sahib kept trying to chew the ends of his finely-trimmed moustache.

'Get her married off quickly,' opined the Hakim Sahib, 'what are you standing staring at me for?'

Even after this Ghani kept pressing his feet. The Hakim Sahib silently smoked his huqqa, inwardly reprimanding his daughter Fakhrun—when people heard that even Hakim Ali Kabir's granddaughter was being treated by Kammo, who would ever come to him? It was not a question of income, because medicine was not his profession. It was a question of honour and prestige. If Hammad had sent Ghani to Kammo, then it meant that there was some dirty conspiracy of the men of Dakkhin Patti in his becoming a doctor. If there wasn't he would never had had the courage to put up a board saying 'Dr Kamaluddin' outside his house.

'Ya Ali!' he groaned and sat up. 'What can I do now?' he asked Ghani, 'Send for Sukhram-va's mother and get her to massage her stomach.'

Ghani left.

The Hakim Sahib sat down by the tank and began to wash to prepare himself for prayer.

'Eh, bhai, Anwarul Hasan was saying that there've been riots in Calcutta,' said Maulvi Bedar, as he set foot through the Great Gate. 'There's been a great deal of bloodshed.'

'Why have there been riots?'

'Arre, must have been something to do with that Akistan-Pakistan!'

Maulvi Bedar lay down on the same charpoy on which the Hakim Sahib had been lying to smoke his huqqa.

'Lord God Almighty!' exclaimed the Hakim Sahib, 'You've made me forget whether I've washed my mouth out or not . . . . Arre, arre, arre! What are you doing, *behenchod*!' he scolded the son of his ploughman who was playing marbles on the tazia platform. 'Where is this Harnaraina! Eh, . . .!'

'I've heard that these *haramzade* Hindus are creeping into Muslims' homes and murdering them,' remarked Maulvi Bedar.

'And I suppose the Muslims are great saints, are they?' commented the Hakim Sahib, as he cleared his nostrils. 'But who cares about the facts?' he said sitting on the prayer platform. Then he said, 'God is Great!' and began to spread out his prayer-mat.

'No, these Congresswallahs have completely turned the heads of these Hindus,' said Maulvi Bedar.

'God is Great!' said the Hakim Sahib, beginning his prayers.

Maulvi Bedar began to murmur a poem of praise by the pre-Islamic Arab poet Umar Ulqais, and to think about land disputes. He had been itching to get his hands on the land by the Mangare pond for a long time. But at the same time he was scared of the Hakim Sahib, and so he didn't want to involve himself in the dispute openly. Phunnan Miyan and Hammad Miyan also had their eyes on this land. The Maulvi was of the opinion that if the other three got entangled with one another, he might get the land. To prevent each other getting hold of it, they may be forced to hand it to him as a compromise.

'I've heard that Hammad is going to get Bafatiya to sign over that piece of land to him,' Bedar told the Hakim Sahib, once he'd said his prayers and was telling his prayer-beads. 'And Phunnan has told Bafatiya that if . . .'

'It looks like Phunnan is anxious to go back to jail,' said the Hakim Sahib, 'that land is mine. To hell with Hammad and Phunnan!'

'That's exactly what I say!'

'Hammad and Phunnan will never be able to get hold of that land. I'd rather anyone else got it. Why don't you take it? You've got fields around there.'

'No, bhai! I'm a single man not about to get involved in this quarrel.'

'Have you forgotten how Phunnan's disgraced you? Is that anything to forget?'

'No, it isn't but . . .'

'In this age,' said the Hakim, 'so many things have begun to happen together that a man goes mad thinking what to forget and what to remember. That Kammo, the bastard, has become a doctor. I told Ali Hadi to get him some government job so that we could somehow get the nuisance away from here. But he's turned into a real Lord Sahib now, hasn't he? If he'd got a government job he wouldn't have cut off my nose with his case of homoeopathic medicine.'

'But, eh bhai, his medicines are working,' said Bedar Miyan. 'You've been treating my piles for an age. I've just taken his medicine for six days and the bleeding's completely stopped.'

'Ha! And I suppose he cured your late father Ali Muhammad-cha's piles as well!' remarked the Hakim Sahib. 'Do piles change with the times now? Ali Muhammad-cha's piles belonged to the old times and yours to the new?'

'Eh, bhai, that's unfair of you,' said Maulvi Bedar, rather irritated, 'people are going to go to the man whose medicine does them good.'

'Arre, so am I standing begging in front of anyone?' said the Hakim Sahib, his old face flushed with anger. Even after Bedar Miyan left he muttered angrily for some time. The little girls playing hopscotch in the courtyard ran off home in fear. The Hakim Sahib lay down.

'Arre, just bring a fresh bowl of tobacco,' he called out.

'What was this Bedar saying, bhai sahib?' asked Husain Ali Miyan, walking over picking his teeth with a neem twig, and sitting down on a cloth chair.

'He came to rob me!' said the Hakim Sahib. 'He's worried about taking the land next to the Mangare pond. But eh, Hussu! He may have passed the highest religious degree from the Sultanul-Madaris college in Lucknow, but does that mean he knows about landowning? I just told him, "You take the land," and he didn't have an answer.' He smiled.

'But I've heard that Phunnan is keen to get his plough on that land,' said Husain Ali Miyan.

'How is he going to plough it?' replied the Hakim Sahib, 'I'll have him bound over to keep the peace. And Hammad doesn't have the courage. You've been to persuade the Lala, haven't you?'

'The Lala's arse has been split open by the Congresswallahs,' said Husain Ali Miyan. 'What can the *saala* do now? But what times have come, that's what I say! Sukhram-va's son Parusaram-va has become a political leader the moment he's stepped out of jail. He's roaming around wearing a Gandhi cap and making speeches everywhere that the times have changed, now the zamindars' force and cruelty won't work!'

'Why don't you call that *behenchod* Sukhram-va and explain matters to him?'

'Arre, he's the father of a leader, sahib! He's not going to listen to us any more.'

'Fuck that leader's mother . . .' Seeing Tannu approaching he swallowed the rest of his curse like spittle, 'Where did you disappear to as completely as a moon that's set?'

'I just went to Ghazipur,' said Tannu after greeting both of them.

'Everyone's well, aren't they?' asked Husain Ali Miyan.

'Yes. Chachi was a little unwell, but nothing to worry about. They've all come here. Only Manjhale-Abba and Chacha have still to arrive, and they'll come by Thursday.'

'If they're not coming till Thursday, why are they taking the trouble of coming at all?' commented the Hakim Sahib. 'The wedding's on Friday and Manjhale-Abba's not coming till Thursday! Here, have a smoke!' He turned the pipe of the huqqa towards Tannu.

This was a sign that now Tannu had begun to be numbered among the respected elder members of the community.

Tannu laughed. 'Adaab! I can't smoke huqqa. The smoke's very bitter. I wrote to Saddan to come for the marriage but that Man of God hasn't replied.'

'Arre, beta, how can I tell you how caught up he is . . . .' The Hakim Sahib proceeded to deliver a speech on the difficulties of being a Deputy Collector. And on top of that, the Congress had made the business of government even harder by turning the heads of the lower castes. 'Only God can understand this Gandhi. But Saddan wrote to me that he'd try his very best to come. Still, if these riots spread, how can he come, poor boy? What I'm asking, beta, is have people suddenly gone mad or what? Without any reason they're fighting and dying . . .' He paused at the sound of the horn of a motor car. 'Eh, bhai, whose motor is that speaking?'

'Anwarul Hasan's wife is ill,' said Husain Ali Miyan. 'I heard that Dr Trilokinath was on his way from the town. It must be him that's come.'

'What need was there for Trilokinath?' asked the Hakim Sahib. 'Why didn't they show her to that bastard Kammo?'

'I can see that in a few days' time if you hear Kammo's name you'll start throwing stones,' remarked Husain Ali Miyan.

The Hakim Sahib was boiling with anger, but at that point Ghani appeared, and immediately began reciting a paean of praise about the splendour of Trilokinath's 'motor'. 'It's so impressive, Miyan. It looks just like the tazia of the great platform!'

'Repent, *behenchod*! Repent!' The Hakim Sahib burst out at Ghaniya.

'God save us! Did you see that, Tannu? This *behenchod* compared a motor with a tazia!'

'Eh, bhai, there's something very splendid in the village,' remarked Bedar Miyan as he walked up.

'So you've been to look at the motor,' said the Hakim Sahib.

'It's very handsome,' said the Maulvi, 'and Naraina's sitting on a chair talking to the Doctor Sahib in English.'

'So the day has dawned that low wretches like him are sitting on chairs! Arre, Lakhna!' called out the Hakim Sahib, 'Put all the chairs indoors. It's like saying that people should burn their food first and then cook it. Now it's come to this. Low castes are sitting on chairs and respectable people have to hide their faces.'

'Eh, Nana, Ba'ji's got a bad pain in her stomach,' called out Fakhrun's middle daughter, Bunni, from the doorway of the inner house.

'Send her off to Kammo at once!' replied the Hakim Sahib angrily. He had decided not to treat Fakhrun's child. 'When is this Naraina going?'

'I've heard that the government has cancelled all the army men's leave,' Husain Ali Miyan informed him.

'Why's that, bhai? Is there going to be another war?'

'There are a lot of riots going on. I've heard that all the Muslims in Bihar have been slaughtered.'

'You're hearing a lot these days. Arre, you can't rely on any of these newspapers. How can you believe that all the Hindus are slaughtering the Muslims for no rhyme nor reason?'

'They are killing them because of the vote for Pakistan.'

'Eh, bhai, that's nothing to kill for,' said the Hakim Sahib. 'It was our vote and we put it where we wanted.'

'That's all very well,' said Maulvi Bedar, 'but there's certainly some trouble or other in this Pakistan. From the day this Jinn-va came out with the idea of this accursed Pakistan, I've had a feeling about it. Now look. There've been riots in Calcutta, in Chapra. In a few days they'll be riots in Ghazipur.'

'We'll witness whatever God chooses to show us,' said the Hakim Sahib, 'now we've given our vote to Pakistan.'

'That I know. The road connecting east with west will pass through here,' said the Maulvi Sahib.

'What are you worried about?' asked the Hakim Sahib. 'You've no one before you and no one to come after you. If Pakistan is made, what's it to you, and if it's not, what's it to you? If you'd have married Saifuniya then you could have worried.'

'Lord God Almighty!' remarked Bedar Miyan, considerably out of sorts, 'Is that *haramzadi* the only one left for me to marry!'

'Don't call her a *haramzadi*,' said Husain Ali Miyan, 'If Mighdad hears, there'll be hell to pay.'

Right at that moment Mighdad stepped inside the Great Gate. He greeted no one. A farmer's lathi lay over his shoulder, and his face was caked with dust from the fields. His dirty feet were peeping out from his canvas shoes. He had given up wearing pajamas, saying that they weren't clothes fit for farmers, and had a grubby dhoti tied round his waist.

Laying his lathi on the tazia platform, he mopped his forehead with his shouldercloth and came up to the platform in the courtyard near the three men.

Silence descended on Uttar Patti.

'I've come to say that the land by the Mangare pond is mine, and if any mother's darling has the courage he can come to throw me out and plough it.'

'Who gave you the right?'

'You're elder to me,' said Mighdad, 'so I can't say it to you. But I swear by the Chote Hazrat, that I'm the one who's going to plough that land. And I've said the same thing to Hammad Miyan!'

'Are you listening to what this *haramzada*'s saying?' chipped in Bedar Miyan. 'He's your own father, isn't he? And you're taking his name!'

'I don't know about his being any father of mine,' said Mighdad. 'He's a zamindar and I'm a cultivator. And you should also know that Phunnan-cha and Parusaram-va are both with me.'

He picked up his lathi and walked off in silence.

If the Hakim Sahib had called for him and told him that he wanted the land by the pond, then perhaps Mighdad would not have taken it ill, and have borne it quietly. But he wasn't going to be pushed around by anybody, whether it was the Hakim Sahib or Hammad Miyan.

'So what did Hakim Ali Kabir say?' asked Phunnan Miyan.

'Arre, what could he say?' replied Mighdad. 'I just told him that the land was mine and I was going to plough it.'

'It is my opinion that the days of Hammad Miyan's cruelties and excesses are over,' said Parusaram in correct Hindi, pushing his Gandhi cap to a slightly more rakish angle. 'The man who owns the land is the man who tills it, who labours upon it. By putting your hand to the plough you have broken your connections with the zamindars. You are the farmer-god!' He joined both his hands together in respect before Mighdad.

'Eh, bhai, what's all that you're saying!' remarked Phunnan Miyan in amazement, 'Since you've become a Kangressi you've forgotton your own tongue.'

'Arre, so what else can I do, Miyan?' Parusaram smiled, reverting to Bhojpuri, 'How can you speak village language to the citywallahs? After all I have to fight an election. And will our aili-gaili language work in the Parliament in Delhi? So I'm learning to speak the way the citywallahs do.'

Neither Phunnan Miyan nor Mighdad could comprehend why the language which was of use in Gangauli couldn't be of use in Delhi. And their surprise about this made them forget to wonder how Parusaram could go to the Parliament in Delhi. Phunnan Miyan busied himself lighting a beedi.

'So I'll be off now, then,' said Parusaram.

'Just tell me one thing,' said Phunnan Miyan, 'I've heard that in Bengal, Bihar, Punjab and God knows where else, all the Hindus and Muslims are at each other's throats. You belong to Gandhi's party. One of these days ask him what's happening and what he wants you to do about it.'

'It's not easy to meet the Mahatmaji.'

'No! Arre, you are in his party, aren't you?'

'I am in his party, but . . .'

'*Dhat*!' exclaimed Phunnan Miyan, 'If I didn't meet the men from my group just for a day there'd be an uprising. So when Gandhi doesn't meet you why do you accept him as your leader?'

Parusaram had no answer to this simple question. He really didn't know why he had accepted Gandhiji as his leader. Perhaps for his Gandhi cap! Perhaps more than Gandhiji he needed the Gandhi cap, due to which government officials had begun to fear him, and due to which his status had increased and income too. He did no work and was comfortable. Before he had worked night and day and known no comfort. Now he was a leader. He delivered speeches, was a member of the District Committee. He sat with Brahmins, Thakurs and Kayasths.

He could approach the Collector to get work done, the same Collector his elder brother still worked for as a gardener. The thanedar would salaam him. He had given up smoking a huqqa made out of a hollow coconut shell, and had begun to smoke cigarettes instead. And, most importantly, at all times he now wore clothes as shining, bright and white as an egret's plumage. He bore a watch strapped to his wrist and a fountain pen in the top pocket of his kurta, and a beautiful pair of wide-framed spectacles was constantly perched on his nose. The pace of change was so rapid that he never had the opportunity to consider why he accepted Gandhiji as his leader and why riots were breaking out in various places.

'Adaab, Da!' said Tannu as he joined them, 'How are things with you then, bhai Parusaram?'

'Fine, Major Sahib!' replied Parusaram. 'These communal disturbances are a worry though. I cannot comprehend why men are going mad . . .' He was very fond of this speech of his. He had already delivered it at several meetings and it had gone down well everywhere. Therefore, he rattled off his favourite speech to Tannu as well.

'Did you hear that, Da!' Tannu smiled, 'He speaks so well and clearly. Absolutely no mistakes in pronunciation.'

'Yes, he's fit to sit with Hammad now.'

'Well, I'll be off then!' said Parusaram, returning to his native tongue and adding to Mighdad, 'Don't you worry. That land is yours and you'll get it. I've told that *susar* of a patwari that if he tries to double-cross us I'll put my stick up his arse.'

'Get off with you!' laughed Phunnan Miyan, 'Your wife must be waiting for you.'

Parusaram left.

'How is Nakko, *ji*?' Tannu asked Mighdad.

'Shitting a lot, sahib. It looks to us as if she's teething.'

'Any news of Mohammad-cha?' Tannu asked Phunnan.

'Not a word,' came the answer, 'and I can't think what to do. This is the way things are without a Pakistan. If the *behenchod* is ever made I can't but believe there'll be bloodshed in Gangauli. That *madarchod* Matadin-va has already started filling people's ears round here. I've heard there was a meeting in the Salimpur orchard last night. He suggested attacking Gangauli, Alavalpur, Hundarhi and Salimpur all at once and murdering the Miyans. And then he said they would go to the houses wherever any Chamar or Lala or Bhar had been kept by a Miyan as his woman and carry off the girls from there.'

'Who gives you all this news?'

'Ashrafullah told me himself.'

'I suppose the Hindus went and invited him to their meeting?'

'You're just splitting hairs!' exclaimed Phunnan, irritated. 'If you don't believe me then listen to this. Chikuriya went to that meeting. This *saala* Matadin-va gave a speech. Fuck the mother of . . .' His eyes fell on Dullan, who had come outdoors and was standing near him. 'What are you doing here, *beh*? Go to school!' Dullan slipped away after this scolding, and Phunnan Miyan turned to Tannu again. 'So Pandit Matadin gave a speech. He said that Muslims were unclean aliens and should be thrown out of India. And this is the *behenchod* I gave land to build a temple, as well as half a bigha of land to support himself with. And this *saala* is giving speeches, forgetting that in the end Phunnan is a Muslim. If I come across him anywhere I'll tear the *saala*'s legs off him!'

'But what did he say in the speech?'

'Don't talk about that *madarchod* to me. How can I tell you? If I hadn't given the land in the name of the temple, I would fuck the mother of that *bhonsriwale*. But because the temple's name is there in between my hands are tied. After all it's a house of God. He told a whole lot of stories about Lahore and Calcutta—how ten Muslims had raped each Hindu woman. If I lay my hands on him!'

'What will you do?'

'I'll just ask him, so Muslims raped Hindu women, but just you tell me if Hindus are ringing temple bells by despoiling Muslim women. But anyway that's a different matter. At that meeting there was a crowd of Hindus from all round the neighbourhood. When they heard all he had to say they said straight out that it couldn't be true. So then Matadin went and appealed in the name of a cow. That *behenchod* Fakir-va the butcher slaughtered a cow yesterday. The cow was a stolen one, and so the story got out. When those poor people heard Matadin-va talk about a cow, they had to keep quiet. But even then Chikuriya didn't give in. He went and asked, "Eh, Panditji, who did that land belong to that was gifted to you?" And the Panditji couldn't find a way out of that one. Then Chikuriya really went after him saying that there wasn't a Hindu doctor anywhere nearby. If anyone was taken ill, what would happen? Who had the money to go and bring a doctor from the town? That was all that was needed to cause an uproar. The meeting finished . . . . When is Bashir coming?' he changed the subject.

'Tomorrow or the day after.'

From the inner house came the sound of women singing:

Look, here comes mum-in-law
Full of joy and fun
In her front's a little pond
At her back a wrestler's bum
Drinking sharbat she's got drunk
She'll be pissing chul . . . chul . . . chul . . .

The song was drowned in peals of laughter. Then another song raised its head.

Mother-in-law,
Your palanquin's
In the gram field!
Mother-in-law,
You were caught
Among the mangoes!
Making eyes at the gardener!
What a man-eater!
What a trouble-maker!

'It sounds like Sakina has come back from Faizabad,' remarked Phunnan Miyan.

'I've heard, sahib,' said Mighdad, 'that some holy man or the other has arrived from somewhere. He's going round from village to village stirring up the Hindus.'

'Hindus aren't such cunts as to be stirred up by the likes of him,' said Phunnan Miyan.

'The fact of the matter is, Dada, that this coalition government that's been formed . . .'

'Salaam, sahib,' said Chikuriya, walking up.

'What's the matter?' asked Phunnan Miyan, realizing that something was the matter. 'Come over here!' he said, taking Chikuriya to one side.

'Lathis are about to go to work between the Khan Sahib of Salimpur and the Thakur Sahib of Barikhpur.'

'What?'

'There's going to be an attack on the Khan Sahib's home tonight. A whole army of Ahirs have set up camp. The Thakur Sahib's mango grove is absolutely full. The holy man is there. And the Thakur Sahib has sent word to the Hakim Sahib that this is his opportunity. So the Hakim Sahib is going off to Ghazipur this evening.'

'So the Barikhpurwallahs think they've seen the day that they're fit to launch an attack on Salimpur, do they? Are any of your men there or not?'

'Ten of them!' replied Chikuriya, 'But if lathis are lifted in the name of Hindus against Muslims, there'll be problems.'

'Nothing'll be achieved by making it Hindu-Muslim!' said Phunnan Miyan, stroking his moustache, 'Are you a Hindu or Muslim?'

'I'm a Hindu, Mir Sahib, but . . .'

'Forget the ifs and buts. Will you fight beside me or will you be a Hindu?'

Phunnan dismissed the matter with a toss of his head. But the fort-like residence of the Khan Sahib of Salimpur was unnaturally hushed, and fear had performed its ablutions and was saying its prayers in its strong and beautiful mosque.

Barikhpur was full of activity. And amidst this activity the three or four Muslim families there were standing in amazement wondering what on earth was about to happen.

A few Muslims went and sat in the mango grove to hear stories from the holy man. They were instantly recognized.

'. . . then Lord Krishna said, "Oh, Arjun! I am Myself, and there is nothing else but Me." Today that Divine Flute-Player is calling to every Hindu of India, saying, "Arise, and remove these unclean Muslim aliens from the holy banks of the Ganga and Yamuna . . ."' The holy man was not delivering a religious discourse!

'If we're removed from here then where will we have to go?' one middle-aged Muslim asked a Hindu. They had both played together as children. They were close friends.

'That's what I'm thinking too,' came the reply. 'But if it's the order of God, then you'll surely have to go. They're making Pakistan, go there.'

'You tell me to go there. Say somehow I manage to get together the money for my fare, still how can I take my fields to Pakistan? I ask you, haven't my ancestors and your ancestors always gone together with the ancestors of the Thakur Sahib to attack Salimpur? So why isn't anyone today asking us to come with them to attack the fort?'

'Look at this, people!' said a young Hindu from another village, 'This *behenchod* Miyan is squealing right here!'

'Are you insulting us, Bafati-chacha?' asked a young Chamar angrily.

'No, bhaiyaa!' said Bafati, trying to prevent a fight, 'I was just asking where we would have to go.'

'Go to Pakistan, you *behenchod*!'

'I've spent my whole life here. Now, when I've not long in this world, should I go to Pakistan? I won't go!'

'Swearing at your elders and betters!' said the middle-aged Hindu, 'Don't you have any shame?'

'. . . the faith is in danger. Raise up Ganga water and vow to wash clean the pure land of India with Muslim blood!' The holy man had worked himself up to a climax, 'See, how these unclean Turks have insulted our mothers in Calcutta, Lahore and Noakhali . . .'

'Say—Victory to . . .' came a lone voice.

'Bajrangbali!' resounded the whole village.

Then the crowd rose to its feet. The holy man went off in the darkness to another village, and once he was gone the crowd was forced to think for itself. It thought that Muslims are Muslims and the only difference between the Muslims of Salimpur and Barikhpur was that the Salimpur Muslims were rather far away and those of Barikhpur were nearby. Therefore, raising the slogan of 'Victory to Bajrangbali!' the crowd set off towards Barikhpur.

When this news reached Thakur Prithvipal Singh he was unnerved. It was one thing to launch an offensive against the Khan Sahib of Salimpur and another to murder the barbers, weavers and one or two Pathans of Barikhpur. What harm had they ever done? They had always lived and died with the other people of Barikhpur.

'Save us, mai-baap!' said Bafati, as he collapsed in the Thakur's courtyard. Hindus from some other village were chasing after him. They stopped when they saw the Thakur Sahib. One of them lit a beedi.

Thakur Prithvipal Singh recognized Bafati. How could he not recognize his Bafati, the vegetable-seller?

'Victory to Bajrangbali!' came a shout from somewhere nearby.

'Who beat you?' Prithvipal Singh asked Bafati. His body was shaking with rage.

'I didn't recognize those people, sarkar!'

The flames of torches were setting fire to the night. It was ablaze.

'And now they're all going off to burn our houses. They were saying, "Go to Pakistan." I said we won't go. Then they just went mad.'

The Thakur Sahib rushed over and picked up his lathi. No one in the Thakur's household asked a single question. Every lathi was silently raised.

And when that crowd, coming to announce its dark decree in torchlight, reached those few Muslim homes it halted in amazement.

'Why have you people stopped, bhaiyaa?' asked Prithvipal Singh, 'Come on with you!'

The crowd could not comprehend why the Thakur Sahib wanted to save Muslims. The holy man had said that the puris cooked in the mango grove had been provided by the Thakur Sahib. And didn't the Thakur Sahib know what treatment the Muslims had meted out to Hindu women and children? Therefore, one of them said, 'These are all Muslims, sahib!'

'You think you know more than I do?' asked the Thakur Sahib.

'The best thing for you people is to go back! Did Bafatiya, and Dildarva and Kalua rape the Hindu women of Noakhali? If you people are so brave and so worried about the honour of the Hindus you should go to Calcutta and Lahore! What is there here that you should attack these people?'

'We've come here to burn down their houses!'

'Yes, yes! Why not! Come and try it! Just let me see which mother has given birth to a son with strength enough!' Prithvipal Singh turned to the men of his house. 'See what's going on! Beat the *behenchods* and make them run!'

Seeing the lathis raised in the hands of the Thakurs the crowd split like an old sheet and tore apart. Later the few Muslims in the village came to the Thakur Sahib's house. Bafati said, 'If you allow us, we'll go to Bahadurganj or Mau Mubarakpur!'

'I'll fuck the mother of anyone who mentions leaving this village. Look at these *bhonsriwalas*! They want to go to Mau Mubarakpur to get buggered!"

By morning the story of the events of the previous night had travelled all over the surrounding countryside. The simple, straightforward farming community couldn't understand, even after tours by several holy men, why Bafati of Barikhpur, Ghurau of Alavalpur, Ghasita of Hundarhi—in short, their own Muslims, should be punished for the sins of the Muslims of Calcutta. How and why should they rape Muslim girls who as infants had pissed in their laps? Neither could they understand why and how they should set fire to the houses of Muslims whom they had been living with for centuries. How could anyone kill the Mullah who, after saying his prayers in the mosque, would come out and blow over the heads of all the children, Hindu and Muslim, to ward off evil . . . . The farmers could understand that the crops of disputed land should be looted. A couple of murders over land was nothing to worry about. But to murder someone or burn his house down simply for the crime of being a Muslim was beyond their comprehension.

The Thanedar of Qasimabad wrote to the Superintendent of Police that it was impossible for him to prevent communal riots with the force at his disposal. This was entered in the police station records so that it became a registered fact and could be of use later. The Superintendent of Police wrote to the Deputy Inspector General, who informed the Home Minister. Then the Thanedar of Qasimabad thought that he should have a word with the Saiyid gentlemen of Gangauli—he had his horse saddled and rode to the village. The Hakim Sahib had gone to Ghazipur and so he pitched camp in Hammad Miyan's house.

The Great Gate was just opposite, and from the inner house came the sound of women's songs. The outer courtyard was full of people. The relatives from Ghazipur had also arrived.

My bridegroom will ride
over the high hills of Shimla . . .

The Thanedar Sahib bathed by the brick-built well and had a cup of tea. Then he spent five or six minutes arranging his moustache. Casting a last look at himself in the mirror he left Hammad Miyan's home and went through the Great Gate.

Hammad Miyan immediately rose to welcome him. The Thanedar Sahib greeted Bashir Miyan and the others and sat down on a chair. Phunnan Miyan regarded him with loathing and then, in a very relaxed manner, lifted one buttock and farted. Several young boys, busy running around the place, stopped in their tracks at this thunderous release of air. Then they burst out laughing and ran indoors.

'Phunnan-nana farted just as loud as a Shab-e-Barat firework!' Sarwari's son Waseem informed his aunt Munni. Munni grinned showing her crooked teeth.

'And you came straight home to give the news!' Sarwari scolded Waseem, suppressing a smile with difficulty. Then she turned to Afsari, 'Eh, *behini*! Hurry up! Father's already ill-at-ease.'

'Eh, beta, just take this paan outside,' Umman-bi told Maddu.

Just at that moment the curtain over the door lifted and a woman with four children came inside. The eldest girl must have been about ten. Her hair was neatly tied and she had a side parting. The woman also had a side parting and was wearing a beautiful sari.

'Salaam, Ba'ji! Salaam, Khala! Salaam, Dadi! Salaam, Bubu . . .' she said, greeting all the ladies one by one. All the ladies gaped at her. Afsari looked into her big, big, dark eyes with her own little ones.

Crooked-toothed Munni's eyes fixed on the stranger's pearl-like teeth.

'Perhaps you don't recognize me,' said the stranger.

'Who are you?' rang out the voice of Saiyda's mother. 'No, wait a minute. Let me see you!' She looked her up and down from head to foot. 'Well I never . . .' she said waving her forefinger around her nose, 'It's that wretched Bacchaniya, Jhangtiya-bo's daughter. Have you just got a litter of children or did you get married?'

'I got married right after I left,' replied Bacchaniya in almost correct Hindi.

'And where did you learn to talk like a whore, then?' objected Saiyda's mother.

'How come you remembered Gangauli all of a sudden?' asked Sarwari.

'There's so much killing going on. Whoever you meet is murdering someone. So I told Saghir Fatima's father, "Let's go to Gangauli."'

'Just look at the arrogance of this girl!' burst out Saiyda's mother angrily, 'Saghir Fatima! Couldn't you find any other name?'

In a short while Bacchaniya was absorbed into the community. The tales of riots were concluded, and the stories of life began—these are the stories which never end. The drum began to play again, and insults were sung. Barber women bustled around and lidded trays of paan were handed to servants and boys who came calling out for them.

Amidst all this uproar Saifuniya was confined to her tiny apartment. She listened to all the roars of laughter and all the songs and all that was said, and fed Nakko, and felt angry, while Mighdad squatted in the middle arch of their room and smoked a beedi.

'I'm saying you should go to the Lawyer Sahib's,' said Saifuniya.

'I've told you not to make any noise!' retorted Mighdad angrily. 'I thought that Tannu-bhai would definitely have called us.'

'No one can fight the community,' said Saifuniya, accepting defeat. 'What can the poor man do! Do you expect him to leave the community for your sake?'

'Didn't I leave it for you?'

'With us it was different.'

'All right, don't go on.'

'Look at that! No one can talk to you any more.'

'It looks to me as if you're bent on a shoe-beating.'

'By my life, you must go to the Lawyer Sahib's.'

'I've told you time and time again, don't swear by your life, you *behenchod*!' Mighdad threw down his beedi and landed Saifuniya a slap. She fell to one side. Nakko slipped from her lap on to the floor of the courtyard and began to scream at the top of her voice. Mighdad walked out of the house, cursing. He was extremely angry with Saifuniya. Why on earth did she keep swearing by her life over the smallest things? 'What am I going to say to the people there? Am I supposed to say enough is enough, let us come back . . .' But Saifuniya had sworn by her life and so he had to go to Bashir Miyan's.

He crept through the Great Gate like a thief.

'Adaab!' he said, intending to use a normal tone of voice. But it came out almost like a scream, or at least it seemed to him that he had spoken very loudly. Even his soul was drenched in sweat. Hammad Miyan came and stood in front of him and said in Urdu.

'Why have you come here?'

'I've come to give my salaams to Bashir-bhai.'

'That's enough, why not forgive him?' said Bashir Miyan. 'He's a young lad, he made a mistake . . . so will you take his life for it?'

'Arre, sahib, he'd come after me to kill me!'

'But he didn't, did he?' said Abbu Miyan. 'Go on, apologize to your father!' he ordered Mighdad.

'What for, sahib?' asked Mighdad. 'I married her, I didn't do anything unclean.'

'Accha!' exclaimed Maulvi Bedar, 'So you're telling us about Muslim law!'

'And you got there quickly enough to read them their vows!' said Hammad Miyan, suddenly remembering the language of his forefathers in his rage.

'And what sort of Maulvi are you anyway, *ji*?' questioned Phunnan Miyan. 'Up to this day has a brother ever married his sister?'

'What are you saying?' asked Mighdad, putting his hand on Phunnan Miyan's shoulder.

'Sit down over there . . . over there . . .' said Phunnan Miyan shaking off his hand. He could not forgive Hammad. 'Who doesn't know that Saifuniya is the daughter of Saiyid Hammad Husain Zaidi?'

'You're lying!' said Mighdad, blood coming to his eyes.

'Ask your father!'

'What is this stupidity, Miyan Phunnan?' said Bashir Miyan.

'You're asking that of me?' replied Phunnan Miyan.

'Come here, Mighdad,' Bashir Miyan called to him.

'How can I come now, sahib!' Mighdad was like a young peepul tree felled to the ground. He turned to Hammad Miyan and screamed, '*Abeh*, why don't you say whose daughter Saifuniya is, you *betichod*!'

'How do I know?' replied Hammad Miyan.

'Eh, bhai, has Hammad suddenly remembered the language of his forefathers?' remarked Javad Miyan.

Mighdad was standing to one side panting under the weight of disgrace. Tears stood in his large eyes. From the inner house came the sound of the songs of professional musicians, girls laughing, women talking, the din of children. Perhaps a young girl was crying.

Mighdad suddenly recalled that when he had hit Saifuniya Nakko had fallen into the courtyard.

'I'm asking who is Saifuniya's father,' he implored the flagpole hanging in its rope loops against the wall, the naked frames of the tazias and the green door of the shahnashin. When he received no answer he turned to the Hakim Sahib. 'Eh, Kabir-cha! Take the land by the Mangare pond, but please tell me who Saifuniya is to me.'

The Hakim Sahib did not reply. No one replied. Mighdad grabbed Gaya Ahir's tall lathi from his hands.

'Mighdad, what are you doing!' cried out Bashir Miyan.

Mighdad gave no answer. He hit the green pillar of the three-arched hall with all his might. The pillar cracked. He threw down the lathi. Then he addressed the whole community, his chest thrust out.

'Saifuniya may be anything of mine. But Nakko is my daughter! Do you hear me? Nakko is my daughter!'

He walked out of the Great Gate with his head high, but then returned immediately to say, 'And if anyone lets a word of this pass his mouth, and if Saifuniya finds out, I'll take the man who opened his mouth and push Gaya Ahir's lathi up his arse!'

He left.

Rain clouds were bending over the village. The evening had turned black. Mighdad looked up at the sky, and strode off towards his apartment. But the rain came and came with such force that he was drenched before he reached home.

From the main house came the sound of women rushing in out of the rain. Mighdad collapsed on to a bamboo bedstead. Nakko was deep in slumber. Saifuniya was cooking.

'It looks like Tannu bhaiyaa or Sallo *behini* must have scraped food from the pot for it to rain like this!' she remarked. She wanted Mighdad to know that she hadn't taken the slap amiss. It was always like this after they'd argued. Then for a moment or two it used to be just like the days when she would go to take milk from him.

She was very surprised when Mighdad didn't reply. She skilfully turned over the chapatti on the tavva, began to knead another ball of dough and then gave Mighdad a second opportunity. 'Did you go there?'

'Yes.'

Her hands, which were rolling out a chapatti, stopped dead. She looked at Mighdad with her big, big, black eyes and her brows, joined in enquiry, which came even closer together. There was a new kind of gentleness in Mighdad's tone. Another type of love.

'This rain is going to ruin the whole wedding and wedding procession,' said Saifuniya. 'I heard that Bacchaniya's come back from Calcutta?'

'Safir-va was at the gate!' said Mighdad, 'Why don't we go to Calcutta?'

Saifuniya took the chapatti from the tavva and laid it in the basket of bread. She dropped another chapatti on to the tavva. Then, after putting another ball of dough on the rolling board, she said, 'Calcutta's come to mind again? And someone was saying that there and God knows where else, all the Hindus and Muslims are fighting each other. Are these the days to leave your home? And even if there wasn't any fighting, I wouldn't leave the village.'

'I'd be very happy working in a jute mill.'

'And what would happen to the fields?'

'We'd give them to some sharecropper.'

'What strange things you're saying today.'

After that evening the same question raised itself in Saifuniya's mind every day—what had happened to Mighdad? He was scared even to touch her. She felt that his love for her was no less but whenever she tried to lie with him he'd find some excuse to move away or to make her move away, and then he'd talk and bring the conversation round again to Calcutta.

He even began to avoid going to the bazaar. He just went as far as his fields, came back and talked nonsense to Nakko and began to worry about something.

'Calcutta must be a very big city?' Mighdad asked Safir-va one day, looking at the golden watch strapped to his wrist, on which a little second hand was continually turning round and round. 'Don't you feel uncomfortable in those pantaloons?'

Safir-va laughed. 'The things you come out with! So many people are going round in pantaloons.'

'Can you get fields to farm in Calcutta?'

'There are no fields in Calcutta.'

'How can that be?'

'You don't find fields in cities, sahib!'

'How can that be? Aren't there fields in Ghazipur?'

'What sort of city is Ghazipur? Every single locality of Calcutta is two or three times as big as the whole of Ghazipur.'

'It can't be as big as that.'

'I swear by the Chote Hazrat!' shot back Safir-va.

Mighdad was speechless.

'But if there are no fields-vields, where do people get food from?'

'Grain comes in from here and there.'

'I'm thinking of going to Calcutta.'

'The Miyans will have to leave the village in any case.'

'Why's that?'

'Arre, do you think that the farmers will let the zamindars stay here once zamindari's abolished? After all the cruelty they've done? Not that there isn't oppression in Calcutta. The millowners are capable of causing any calamity. But our union keeps the *saalas* in control. Once . . .'

Safir-va told a story about a strike which went entirely over Mighdad's head.

'Now that's too bad of you people!' he said, 'You're working in their factory and refusing to give free labour like the tenants do here.'

'Why should we give free labour, sahib!' said Safir-va excitedly, 'Should we workers mix our sweat and blood, so the millowners can lay around enjoying themselves?'

'Eh, bhai, you're talking like Pandeji.* Have you become a Communist?' asked Mighdad in astonishment. 'Pandeji was here only yesterday. He took a rupee from me. I'm thinking of going to Calcutta.'

'Nowadays is no time to stir outside your home. There's so much bloodshed going on. There's even more since Pakistan's been made. What atrocities are taking place. Now they're stopping trains and killing people. No less than a lakh or a-lakh-and-a-quarter people must have been killed.'

'But what is this fighting all about?'

'It's a gift from these *behenchod* British. As I see it, it's in our best interests to go to Pakistan. Just think that in Delhi—where tens of millions of Muslims lived—there's not a sign of one left. All the Hindus have put Muslim girls into their houses as kept women. I'm still here because I'm scared for Saghir Fatima's sake, otherwise I would have gone to Pakistan long ago.'

'But I can't go.'

'Why can't you.'

'Not with ten bighas of land here.'

'Are your fields more important than your life and honour?'

---

* Sarju Pande—a communist leader of that area.

'They aren't and they are.'

But one day Safir-va did set off for Pakistan with Saghir Fatima. Bacchaniya wept bitterly as she left. Rabban-bi tried to persuade Safir-va that one didn't desert the door of one's ancestors. But he wouldn't listen. The train stopped somewhere between Delhi and Amritsar. Bacchaniya and Saghir Fatima were left this side of the border. Safir-va carried the corpses of his younger children with him into Pakistan.

In all directions such great cities were ablaze that Bacchaniya and Saghir Fatima fell into that fire like straw and were immediately consumed. Delhi, Lahore, Amritsar, Calcutta, Dacca, Chittagong, Saidpur, Rawalpindi, the Red Fort, the Jama Masjid, the Golden Temple, Jallianwalla Bagh, Hall Bazaar, Urdu Bazaar, Anar Kali . . . Anar Kali—the Lahore bazaar named after the Mughal Prince Salim's beloved, who died cruelly and tragically on the orders of the Emperor. Now Anar Kali was named Saghir Fatima, or Rajni Kaur, or Nalini Banerjee—Anar Kali's corpse was in the fields, on the streets, in mosques and temples, and on her naked body were the marks of nails and teeth. And men carefully collected strips of blood-soaked skirts, shalwars and saris and put them away in boxes of memorabilia as keepsakes.

Four-year-old Sakina was petrified with fear,
The sweet child cried out and held her mother near,
'I am close to death, someone call the Great King here!
Oh, listen people, someone call my father here!
Oh, listen people, where's my brother Ali Akbar to be found?
Where's my aunt's beloved nephew? Who will bring him safe and sound?
His bride is being robbed, where is Qasim, Hasan's kin?
Where's now the brave Abbas? I am sacrificed for him.'

Sajjad lay all alone unconscious on his bed,
Half beyond her wits, Sakina to the hero fled,
With her tiny little hands she shook his arm and said,
'My mother's veil's been seized, rise up, brother, from your bed!
I am very, very scared, hold me close against your breast!
Don't let them take my pearls, hide me close against your breast!'

The listeners began to weep out loud.

Wazir Miyan lay the book of marsias down upon the pulpit. Then he himself put his handkerchief over his eyes and began to cry. He stepped down from the pulpit. Everyone stood up.

The nauha began to the rhythm of the cries, 'Husain! Husain!'

'Sughra, Medina's been despoiled!'
Screamed Zainab and beat her head,
'Sughra, Medina's been despoiled!'

Medina was Delhi. Medina was Lahore. Medina was Hindustan. Medina was Pakistan—and Medina was being looted and despoiled.

The Saiyids began to cry more and more loudly. The chandeliers and lotus-shaped candleshades began to tremble to the rhythm of the matam. The petromax lamp hanging in the doorway of the hall watched silently and its gas hissed out in long breaths.

'I had a letter from Tannu today,' Fussu Miyan told Phunnan Miyan when Javad Miyan began to distribute the blessed sweets after the matam.

'What does he say? Is he all right?'

'Yes. And here's something strange—after going to Pakistan, Safir-va's suddenly become Saiyid Safirul Hasan Zaidi!'

'Eh, bhai, what fault is it of Safir-va's? After all here Hammad became Saiyid Hammad Husain Zaidi.'

'Safir-va didn't have your name put down as his father, did he?' asked Ali Mehdi Miyan, laughing.

'Leave jokes until after Moharram!' Javad Miyan reprimanded Ali Mehdi Miyan, 'Here, take your share.'

'Do you get letters from Saddan?' Fussu Miyan asked the Hakim Sahib.

'What need does he have to write to me?' replied the Hakim Sahib.

'He shouldn't have gone,' said Shabbar Miyan, 'I tried hard to persuade Miyan Tannu too.'

'You wasted your time!' said the Hakim Sahib. 'We're no longer the fathers of our sons, now our sons all think they're fathers to us. I told Saddan countless times, "Son, what need have you to go to Pakistan?" And he would say that the roads for the progress of Muslims were closed here. Now if he would only take his wife and children too I could rest content. Eh, Bashir! This Pakistan was made to separate Hindus from Muslims. But as far as I can see it's separated husband from wife, father from son and brother from sister. Saddan's gone there and so he's a Muslim. I'm still here—does that make me, heaven forbid, a Hindu?'

'Accha, now let's be off to the majlis!' said Javad Miyan, 'It looks like this Pakistan is doing Imam Husain's work, making people grieve.'

'Answer that, Miyan Abbas!' said Shabbar Miyan.

'He's got no answer, poor man,' said Abbu Miyan. 'His Jinnah Sahib has washed his hands and gone, leaving the Muslims here to go, God forbid, to hell. All very fine, I must say. The Muslims here give their votes for Pakistan, and when Pakistan is made Jinnah says they can be sent to the devil.'

'And your Aligarh is still in India, hero Abbas!'

No one in the whole village knew how happy Kammo was that Aligarh was still in India. And no one knew why Tannu had gone to Pakistan—not even Saiyda. And without Tannu this Moharram seemed very strange to her. The war was different—men return from war. But no one came back from Pakistan. Did that make it a land of the dead?

'Eh sahib, if all the Hindus had voted for Pakistan, what would Jinnah Sahib have done then?' Kammo asked Shabbar Miyan.

Shabbar was saved from having to reply to this as just at that moment Mighdad came running like a mad man through the Great Gate.

His punishment for the sin of his marriage to Saifuniya had been that he had been stripped of his right to sit on the floor of the imambara. Saifuniya didn't know a single nauha, and so Mighdad himself would softly sing marsias morning and evening, and on the ninth night he would buy a paper tazia from Maddu Miyan and stand it in his courtyard. Therefore, when he ran straight through the Great Gate, people were shocked.

'Eh, Chacha!' he implored the Hakim Sahib, 'Please come for a moment and take a look at Saifuniya!' Then he paused, scared that the Hakim Sahib was after all a Saiyid, and might not come. So he turned instead to Kammo, 'God knows what's wrong with her . . . just come and see.'

But how on earth could Kamaluddin go! He looked at Javad Miyan. Meanwhile the Hakim Sahib spoke up, 'What's happened to her?'

'I don't know, sahib! Her hands and feet have gone suddenly cold!'

The Hakim Sahib stood up to accompany Mighdad. But Saifuniya didn't wait for him. All the Hakim Sahib could do was to cover her face with a sheet.

Nakko was sitting next to Saifuniya giggling. Mighdad picked her up and held her tightly against his breast, then he sat down by the edge of Saifuniya's charpoy and began to sob like a little child, 'I didn't slap you today, so why are you angry with me?'

The Hakim Sahib quietly left their apartment.

'She'd dead!' he announced to the Saiyids gathering for the majlis in his imambara. It immediately occurred to Hammad Miyan that he could now marry Mighdad off into some reasonable family and their lands could be worked jointly again.

'I think that we should go with the shroud!' he suggested.

'Yes, of course!' they all said.

The majlis was therefore speedily concluded and the congregation went off to Mighdad's small apartment.

'Mighdad! Eh, Mighdad, my son!' called out Hammad Miyan.

Mighdad came out. Nakko was in his arms. She was very happy to see so many people outside her house. Mighdad stepped down from the doorway and stood before them.

The sound of women's voices was coming from the zenana imambara nearby.

'Take courage, beta!' said Abbu Miyan.

'Who can interfere with the will of God!' remarked the Hakim Sahib.

Meanwhile two women, wrapped in shawls, arrived from the direction of the zenana imambara. One was Mighdad's mother and the other his sister.

'I don't need your sympathy!' Mighdad's voice carried to all those assembled, and they were all startled by it. 'I went to wed her alone, and I can bury her alone.'

'Janab-e Fatima, said, "O, Father of Hasan!"' This was the voice of Sallo, reciting a Hadith in the zenana imambara. '"Carry out my bier at night under the cover of darkness and permit not those who have caused me hardship and pain in this life to be present at my funeral . . ."' Sallo's voice was drowned in the loud weeping of women.

'Have you gone mad!' said Aggu Miyan, 'Stand to one side. Let your mother pass!'

'Now she's dead you've come, now that you don't have to give the money for seeing the bride's face,' Mighdad said to his mother. 'All right, go inside! Look at your daughter-in-law! And you . . .' he turned to his sister, 'Take your gift from this bridegroom!' He threw Nakko into her lap. Nakko began to scream.

The wheel of zamindar tradition turned. The barbers came. The shroud came. Ber leaves came. Camphor came. A grave was dug a short distance away from the family cemetery, and the Saiyid gentlemen set out carrying the bier of the barber's daughter . . . Hammad Miyan was the first to shoulder the bier.

'I've heard that they're building goodness knows what at the Qasimabad police station,' Abbu Miyan told Phunnan. 'Jawahirlal is coming the day after tomorrow to do something or other . . .'

'They're building a martyrs' memorial,' said Phunnan Miyan with pride.

'Panditji isn't coming!' Deputy Hadi Miyan contradicted Abbu Miyan, 'The news is that Balmukund Varma's coming.'

'Who's he?'

'A very big leader.'

'I'm hearing his name today for the first time.'

'Have you been invited?' Abbu Miyan asked Phunnan Miyan.

'Do you think it's Muntaz's wedding that invitation cards are being distributed? I'll go just like other people are going.'

But on the day of the meeting Phunnan Miyan began getting ready from early morning, and from early morning Kulsum began to weep. Phunnan Miyan even told her, 'You good woman, this is no occasion for weeping . . . heaven knows who, but an important man, is coming to praise your son!' But Kulsum couldn't understand this. She continued to weep, and Phunnan Miyan went back to his preparations.

He'd even quietly gone and had some new pajamas stitched for the occasion.

He went off to Qasimabad smartly turned out. Thousands of people had gathered there and the speeches had already started. Balmukund Varma was praising the martyrs of the 1942 movement. Phunnan Miyan was drinking in every word like drops of blessed sharbat. But when Balmukund Varma had spoken for a long time and still had not mentioned Mumtaz once he became distressed.

'. . . immortal is that village, and fortunate those mothers and fathers who offered such sons as Haripal and Gobardhan in sacrifice to the Motherland! Blessed is this pure soil of Qasimabad, which bears the mark of the blood of Gobardhan and Haripal upon its brow . . .' Babu Balmukund Varma's voice trembled with fervour. The entire audience was entranced and everyone held their heads high with pride.

But it became impossible for Phunnan Miyan to endure any more. He stood up in the middle of the speech, looking strangely comical in his shervani coat. The shervani had belonged to his father and was made of the finest, delicately embroidered, Kashmiri wool.

'Eh, sahib! A son of mine was killed here too. It looks like no one told you his name. His name was Muntaz!'

Having finished what he had to say, Phunnan Miyan turned to look at the crowd. His head was held higher than anyone's.

Introduction

I, Saiyid Masoom Reza Abidi, son of Saiyid Bashir Hasan Abidi, am deeply worried. I am constantly asking myself where I belong—Azamgarh or Ghazipur? Is my home in Gangauli, a village of Ghazipur district, or in Thekma Bijauli in the district of Azamgarh—a village I have never seen. Even though I accept that my paternal grandfather, Mir Ali Mohammad Sahib Bijauli, belonged to district Azamgarh, I do not thrill at the name of Bijauli. To me Azamgarh is just one of thousands of towns in India, and Bijauli just another village. What if my grandfather did come from there? I belong to Gangauli. I know only Gangauli. I know nothing of Bijauli. I don't even know what the house there is like, which is called my ancestral home. What colour are the doors of its imambara? Which marsia is recited at which majlis, and who recites it?—In other words, I have no spiritual bond with that house in Bijauli. To me Ghazipur is not just another town, and Gangauli not just another village. They are my town and my village. You must have understood what I am trying to say—and my grandfather did not come to Ghazipur armed with a sword!

You must be wondering why there is an introduction in the middle of the story. This is not a different story, but now with every line it is becoming more difficult to tell, because I am speaking of my village and my people, and I love them. This love has become a barrier in the way of what I am trying to say, and at this moment the story of half the village has reached a very delicate point. I knew that this point would be reached, and that's way I chose to describe, not the entire village, but just the part of the village which I knew well. It's essential for a storyteller to be well acquainted with those whose story he is telling. I know all these people, but still I am breaking the rules of storytelling and writing this introduction. The fact is that now our story has come to a place where one age ends and another begins. And doesn't every new age demand an introduction?

That is why I considered it necessary to tell you that my grandfather belonged to Azamgarh, but I belong to Ghazipur, to Gangauli.

Gangauli is the home of my father's mother. It's possible that my father's loyalties were split between Bijauli and Gangauli, but mine are not. I belong solely to Ghazipur. I belong to the indigo godown which Mr Gilchrist constructed. I belong to that pond which, like the Ganga, holds Gangauli in its lap. I belong to the processions of the fifth and eighth of Moharram. I belong to the sound of the looms working night and day, never stopping. I belong to Gaya Ahir, Hariya Barhai and Komila Chamar. My paternal grandfather may have come from Azamgarh—but then everyone's paternal grandfather and great-grandfather must have come from somewhere.

I am not hurt because Safir-va became a Saiyid in Pakistan. He must have done so. And who can say that there was no blood of some purest of the pure Zaidi Saiyid in his veins? But I am concerned about Sallo and her daughter Shahida whom Tannu left here and whom Rabban-bi continually curses. Hearing Rabban-bi's curses, Sallo beats Shahida—and the question is, what sort of mother will Shahida be when she grows up? The question is, when Saddan has married again in Pakistan, what will become of the Hakim Sahib's litter of grandchildern here? . . . There are other questions of this nature too.

The Jan Sangh says that Muslims are outsiders. How can I presume to say they're lying? But I must say that I belong to Ghazipur. My bonds with Gangauli are unbreakable. It's not just a village, it's my home. Home. This word exists in every language and dialect in this world, and is the most beautiful word in every language and dialect. And that is why I repeat my statement—because Gangauli's not just a village, it's my home as well. 'Because'—what a strong word this is. And there are thousands of 'becauses' like it, and no sword is sharp enough to cut this 'because'. And as long as this 'because' is alive, I will remain Saiyid Masoom Reza Abidi of Ghazipur, wherever my grandfather hailed from. And I give no one the right to say to me, 'Rahi! You don't belong to Gangauli, and so get out and go, say, to Rae Bareli.' Why should I go, sahib? I will not go.

This introduction was necessary to carry the story forward.

Vali Manzil, Badar Bagh *Rahi*
Masoom Reza
Aligarh

Loneliness

'What a world of loneliness lies upon Husain this day!' Husain Ali Miyan had only recited the first line when the whole majlis dissolved into tears. Even Hakim Ali Kabir, who never wept, was crying. Phunnan Miyan's white moustache was wet with tears. Fussu Miyan wept so loudly that Shahida, asleep in his lap, woke up with a start, and seeing her grandfather crying, began to cry herself. Besides Hammad Miyan and Haqdar Miyan, everyone was weeping, because the cut umbilical chord of Pakistan was around their necks like a noose, and they were all suffocating. Now they knew what 'a world of loneliness' meant! For the Hakim Sahib it meant his only son being in Pakistan, and himself being in India with his daughter-in-law and grandchildren, leaving him clucking like a chicken which has been stopped from laying and lost its feathers. But the Hakim Sahib didn't have much opportunity to think because Kammo's medical practice had become such a runaway success that most of his time was taken up with cursing him, and mocking homoeopathy. Sallo's loneliness had bitten deep into Fussu Miyan, and Phunnan Miyan had felt himself completely isolated from the day of the inauguration of the martyrs' memorial at Qasimabad. When he had told the gathering that his son too had been martyred there, he had himself been startled by the loneliness of his voice. That one moment had produced a boundless emptiness . . . the universe began to echo, as if there was no one else but himself for a vast distance . . . . In short, with independence several kinds of loneliness had been born, from the loneliness of the bed, to the loneliness of the heart. Every individual in the Uttar and Dakkhin Pattis had found himself suddenly alone. Old age, youth and childhood, wedded life and widowhood, friendship, enmity and inter-Patti rivalry—all these conditions of man were alone too. Every emotion was alone. The relationship between day and night and night and day had been broken. The days could be got through much as they used to be—the same curses and abuses, the same disputes between the Pattis . . . the same tingling sensations of touch . . . the same shadows of meaningless smiles, the same fields . . . the same threshing floors . . . . But the nights became intolerable. There was a desire to dream, but what was there safe to dream about? What could Nakko dream? Or Mighdad? Or Hakim Ali Kabir? Or Phunnan Miyan? It was possible to go alone to the mosque inhabited by jinn, or the burning ghat, but no one could tread alone the crooked pathways of dreams. And the atmosphere was such that the blood of one's veins was wandering hopelessly in Pakistan, and the relationships and mutual affections and friendship upon which society was based were breaking, and in place of confidence, a fear and deep suspicion was growing in people's hearts. They say that the amarbel creeper sucks dry even the greatest tree . . . . The splendid great tree of the gatherings at the Saiyids' gates was withering day by day. Several new centres of power were being established in Gangauli. It was obvious that people would gather where a huqqa was passed round, where paan was distributed, and tea made; but, as long as they just heard that their zamindaris were going to be taken from them, the Miyans kept laughing and making fun of whoever suggested such a thing. How on earth could zamindari ever be abolished? This was not a concept they could grasp. Neither could the men who tilled their lands, the old farmers in the village, believe that zamindari could come to an end. They used to enjoy listening to what Parusaram had to say, but the fear that had been sitting in their hearts for centuries held them back. Zamindari was as strong as religion. Their personalities were in its grasp. They wanted zamindari to be abolished so that they could own the land they tilled, but they didn't have the courage to make this wish consciously. Therefore, when one night at midnight a drum beat out and it was announced that zamindari was no more, the old farmers, like the zamindars, couldn't accept it. The zamindars collected funds and held meetings. The meetings passed 'resolutions'. The Miyans opposed Parusaram tooth and nail. Only Hammad Miyan supported him openly, while Phunnan Miyan repaid him for his friendship. Parusaram became an MLA, and was accorded a splendid welcome procession in Gangauli. He came to the Gate of the Miyans to offer his respects. That day Hakim Ali Kabir, Abbu Miyan, Sibtu Miyan, Fussu Miyan and Husain Ali Miyan—in short, all those living in the Saiyid households—realized once and for all that zamindari had been abolished. Orchards and fields spreading over huge distances—that great universe—contracted and was contained in a few documents. Documents are, after all, only paper. No society can be based on them. The land which the zamindars traditionally cultivated themselves, but had given out to sharecroppers, was taken from them too. Apart from Hammad Miyan no zamindar had land left equivalent even to the hub of the great wheels which had been their zamindaris.

In a few moments all the zamindars collapsed like the tomb of Nuruddin the Martyr.

Moharram was celebrated with great zeal. 'Zamindari bonds' were sold at forty rupees each. Halva was distributed at the majlis of the eighth. The pulpit was filled with sweets offered by Saiyid ladies for prayers granted. The majlises where bread was distributed were held. Respected and elderly ladies prayed with all their hearts for the British to return. At every namaz ill-wishes were heaped on the Congress party.

'Arre, may leprosy strike those *matimile* Congressmen! May their last rites never be performed . . .'

But neither the Saiyids' prayers nor their ill-wishes were granted. The Miyans, who for centuries had made Gangauli their home and had lived and died there, realized that they no longer had any links with the village they had called and believed to be their own. Whether to create Pakistan or not had been of no meaning to them, but the abolition of zamindari shook the very foundations of their souls. They left their homes, and when their homes were lost, what difference was there between Ghazipur and Karachi?

'At least there's an Islamic government in Karachi.' Ashrafullah Khan Sahib at first stood firm at Salimpur. One year he even held the majlis where bread was distributed with the same old munificence; but the very next year he denounced the custom of preparing tazias as idolatry. Accordingly, he left the wooden frames of his tazias, the platforms on which they were placed, his mansion and the beautiful mosque built in its courtyard, and went to Pakistan. But for the Saiyid gentlefolk of Gangauli it was not easy to go to Pakistan. It was their fate always to be in a minority. Pakistan belonged to the Sunni Muslims, and what hope could Shias have of Sunnis? And so they stood firm in Gangauli, holding to their breasts whatever land belonged to their wives and to the widows of the family.

But the amount of blessed food distributed after each majlis declined. The covers of the tazias became old and began to split. The paper tazias offered for fulfilment of prayers were no longer so tall. The Orphan's Share was no longer auctioned. The Gates of the Saiyids began to look deserted. All thought of lifting the Great Tazia on the tenth of Moharram was given up. Neither were there any bearers willing to carry it, nor spare money for repairs. Only Hammad

Miyan's tazia, decked out in gold and silver thread, was taken out in procession like a bride. It was a modest, but very beautiful tazia, with a black velvet covering very finely embroidered with gold and silver thread.

After returning from its procession around the village on the fifth night, the tazia was taken into the shahnashin and the smoke of fragrant incense wafted all around it like temple dancers.

'I'm not staying here!' said Maulvi Bedar, perhaps to Hammad Miyan's tazia, but it didn't take the slightest notice. The standards too stood there just as disinterested as before. The white flag next to the bathroom fluttered once, but no one paid it any attention as they were all looking at Maulvi Bedar.

'Well, I'll be . . . !' said Phunnan Miyan, 'We people with wives and children aren't going, so what need is there for you to go? If you die here you can be near your ancestors, and if you die there who knows what *susar* will be buried next to you!'

'No, I'm not staying!' said the Maulvi, 'The Sikhs have taken control over Delhi's imambara!'

'All the mosques in Amritsar and Jalandhar have been turned into temples, bhai!' someone said.

'Arre, so what's so dreadful in that?' said someone else. The fact was that the petromax light had run out of fuel some time ago, flared up and died. The hall was in pitch darkness, but the Maulvi's words had so shocked people that they no longer noticed.

'How can you say there's nothing dreadful about it?' spoke out Maulvi Bedar, recognizing his own voice.

'Muslim emperors demolished temples to build mosques and used the idols of gods and goddesses to make their toilets . . . .'

'Eh, bhai, and what were the Hindus up to when they were doing that?' asked Phunnan Miyan, lighting a match for a beedi. For a moment a flickering, frightened light illumined Phunnan's face, and Hammad Miyan saw that Fussu Miyan had fallen asleep, his face uncovered, and his pot belly rising and falling with his breath. The match went out and only the glow of the end of Phunnan's beedi was left, but that too was dimmed by ash.

'Why didn't people catch hold of those *behenchod* emperors and kill them . . . . Just look! The emperors knocked down the temples and it's us who are being buggered for it . . . . Wonderful!' Phunnan drew deeply on his beedi. His face glimmered in the light of its stub.

'You can say what you like,' remarked Maulvi Bedar, 'but I'm not staying here.'

'What will happen to your imambara then?' asked Ali Kabir Miyan.

Maulvi Bedar had no answer to this question. The fact was that Ali Kabir Miyan had not been the only one to ask it—several centuries and several generations had asked it too. Maulvi Bedar hesitated. He felt as if he was cheating Imam Husain.

'I will establish an entire series of ten majlises there!'

'By all means!' said Phunnan Miyan, 'But what will happen here? Who will make offerings in this imambara?'

'This is why we always told you to get married,' said Fussu, who had been woken up by Shahida. At the mention of marriage, Maulvi Bedar began to swear and curse like he always did, and for a few moments the Saiyid gentlemen of the Uttar and Dakkhin Pattis were transported back to the time when zamindari had not been abolished, when Karachi was in Hindustan, when Saddan's wife lived with him and when Tannu couldn't have left his wife and gone to Pakistan because Pakistan didn't exist.

'Eh, Kammo bhaiyaa!' Rafiq the barber called out, standing beneath the silent petromax lamp which hung in the lefthand archway of the three-arched hall. 'Please come quickly! Anwarul Hasan's little girl's been taken sick.'

Kammo stood up and began feeling around for his sandals. Javad Miyan loudly cleared his throat, making the whole imambara echo. The sound came down on Hakim Ali Kabir's being like a brick wall, and he was crushed as flat as a parantha.

'As far as I can see, one day we'll all have to go to Pakistan,' the Hakim Sahib remarked some time after Kammo had left. 'What's left here now? We had just the zamindari, and that's gone. Leave alone having to support grandchildren . . . how can one live?'

Fussu Miyan tickled Shahida and she burst into a fit of giggles. Her childish laughter made the darkness tremble.

'I'm thinking of going to Ghazipur,' said Abbu Miyan, 'it's very difficult to stay on in Gangauli.'

'But, uncle,' said Fussu Miyan, 'there's some verse or the other which goes, "I agreed to go to Delhi, but what will be there to eat?" We've got two or three bighas of land, haven't we, here and there? What's there for us in the town? I'm not going anywhere.'

'Who's asking you to?' said Abbu Miyan, 'Live here and pay your respects to weavers and traders!'

'Eh, Hammad, aren't you repairing the imambara this year?' the Hakim Sahib asked Hammad Miyan. 'Earth's falling from the ceiling!'

'Recall the Prophet's kin imprisoned in the dungeons of Damascus, and be silent,' said Phunnan Miyan. 'What need is there to repair it? If people could have their way they'd turn this imambara into fields as well. Haven't you seen what a fine crop of maize is growing in Akbari-bi's courtyard? There's profit in a house collapsing, bhaiyaa! You get three bighas of land, complete with a surrounding wall.'

Hammad Miyan began to feel highly uncomfortable at this, because since the abolition of zamindari, Akbari-bi's family had ceased to come to the village. Consequently their house collapsed. And once it had, Hammad Miyan ran a plough over the area and converted it into arable land. In other words, the zenana imambara, which once used to shine like a dewdrop on the green leaves of the voices of the Saiyid ladies, now stood on the edge of a field of barley. And it was as if the stillness were asking—'Arre, bhai, where's Sarwari or Qamarjahan Begum? Why hasn't Umme Laila come? Where has Baqri gone? Where are Suraiya and Munni? Why aren't the voices of Moonis and Masoom and Maddu to be heard?'

In the zenana imambara a kerosene lamp was dozing in a niche, waiting for the Saiyid ladies to arrive. And the Saiyid ladies were attending a majlis in Uttar Patti, in which Deputy Ali Hadi's eldest daughter, Shadab Fatima, was reciting a nauha of the poet Nazm Afandi to a completely new tune. The ladies were sitting and weeping, completely indifferent to the verses being recited. In each one's lap was a Sakina and a Ruqayya, in every home was a Kubara. In every home was a Zainab. In every home was a Bano—and in every home there was mourning.

Saiyda's mother listened to Shadab Fatima's nauha and began to think that Saiyda's voice was better than hers. By the grace of God, Saiyda's face was also better than Shadab Fatima's. So why was it that Shadab Fatima was married, and Saiyda was still sitting unwed? Had all the decent young men been consumed by fire? If she found one with a good family background, he turned out to be useless, and if a boy turned out to be of use, there was something wrong with his family.

All the engineers and doctors and well qualified boys, whose proposals of marriage had once beaten a path to Abbu Miyan's door, had gone to Pakistan. Now all around there was desolation. Her daughter's unmarried youth was hovering and playing round her head like a mischievous spirit because Saiyda herself did not feel the great dearth of young men.

She had completed her Bachelors in Teaching and, despite

expressions of disapproval from the 'noble' ladies and gentlemen of the area, had taken up a job. To begin with even Abbu Miyan had been very much against this. He had stopped speaking to Saiyda—but then that had been before the abolition of zamindari. People round and about had made up a lot of stories about her. She'd fallen for several men. She's had a couple of abortions. Saiyda's mother kicked up an almighty fuss, but in the end Abbu Miyan had forgiven his daughter. Then even her mother went to a majlis wearing a suit of new mourning clothes paid for out of her earnings. All the ladies admired its material, and the young girls more or less fell on her—where had it come from? How many yards were there? . . .

Most of the young girls in the Saiyid households could only ask the price of material, and dream of it night and day. Their eyes began to ache from such dreaming, and they suffered so much that they came close to tears, and whenever they saw a new type of material they fell apart. These new types of material and new cuts of clothes came to Gangauli only with Saiyda, and so the young girls waited for her the whole year, and when she came the senior ladies put their noses in the air. The ladies who were fond of nauhas even went to the extent of refusing to recite nauhas with Saiyda. But the young girls hovered round her like bees round a honeypot and began to ask themselves why their fathers didn't send them to Aligarh to study. But the day Saiyda's mother wore the mourning suit Saiyda had had stitched for her, even the senior ladies couldn't help being attracted.

Rabban-bi's single eye began to dance.

'Tell me, where did you get that material from in Gangauli? It's from your daughter's earnings!'

Earnings!

Daughter's earnings!

Saiyda's mother writhed in anguish. If she'd not been sitting in a majlis, and if the shahnashin hadn't been opened, she would have tangled with Rabban-bi.

'Oh, Lord! You are witness to the kind of people who are tormenting my daughter!'

'How am I tormenting her,' asked Rabban-bi, 'that you're raising your hands to curse me? If she's not earning what is she doing, reading the Qor'an?' At that precise moment Shadab Fatima began reciting a nauha, and Rabban-bi covered her eyes with her handkerchief. Saiyda's mother started to weep—thinking about when her daughter would get married and to whom. 'I hope to God that Allah Miyan hasn't forgotten to make a partner for her . . . .'

'Eh, bhai, let's be off quickly and hold the majlis at the other Patti,' the Hakim Sahib's daughter suggested as soon as the majlis was over. All the ladies hastily readied themselves. Passing from this passage to that alley and through that backdoor the women began to cross the boundaries of the Patti.

In the old days it had taken two hours for them to move from the floor of one majlis to the floor of another. The palanquin bearers used to come. Voices called out for them. Beedis were smoked. Only then would one lady take her seat in her palanquin. Consequently the majlises would continue until dawn. But now there were no palanquin bearers and so all the majlises were over by ten o'clock, and then the ladies were left alone to pass the night which loomed before them like a mountain, and until morning they were tormented by many fears.

They couldn't imagine how to get through the mountainous nights of Moharram. You could count it a blessing that there were marriageable girls in every home, and that there was a dearth of young men. The ladies, therefore, passed the nights thinking about their daughters—otherwise they would have gone mad. But suddenly everything had stopped dead. And since every home was now empty of even cousin-brothers, the poor young girls too had nothing left to think and dream about. Even the gossips were quiet. When there were no young men, who could they say a girl was having an affair with?

'. . . quoth the Lord of the World, "Oh my dear one, tell them that God is only with those who show patience."' Sitting on a tin chair with no armrests, Sallo began to recite from a printed book to open the majlis. But the light was inadequate. How could anyone recite by the light of an oil lamp? The wretched lampflame was just like a stubborn child that keeps dodging its face around to avoid being washed, and is then beaten by its mother when she can stand no more. So Sallo began to stumble. Rabban-bi endured this for a while but then it became impossible for her to keep quiet. She said, 'Eh, girl, what's come over you today?'

'What can I do, bhai?' said Sallo irritably, 'Is there any light to read by?'

'God curse this Pakistan!' said Sibtu Miyan's wife.

'Why? How is it any fault of Pakistan's?' said Sumari who was going to leave for Pakistan after Moharram as her son Dilshad had become Saiyid Dilshad Husain Zaidi and was earning five hundred-and-twenty-five rupees a month in Karachi.

'If we don't blame Pakistan, who are we to blame?' asked Sakina, 'If that wretched Pakistan hadn't been made, zamindari wouldn't have been finished. Gandhiya said, "All right, Miyans, you've made your Pakistan, now go to hell . . . zamindari's over."'

'But haven't the Hindus lost their zamindaris too?' pointed out Shadab Fatima.

'When did those wretches ever have land to speak of?' Sakina shot back at her.

'Arre, why have you gone quiet, *matimili*!' Rabban-bi scolded Sallo, 'Do you expect us to wait up all night to hear you read . . . who do you think you are, Maulvi Ibne Hasan?'

Sallo began to recite again. Then she began to see her Shahida as she read the name of Muslim's fatherless daughter, Ruqayya.

She held the book to her face and began to cry, and then climbed down from the chair. Kubara told Umme Habiba to recite a nauha but by then Manno had already stood up holding her notebook.

Seeing the notebook in Manno's hands, Sibtu Miyan and Abbu Saiyid's wives prepared themselves to cry hard—this niece of theirs was about to recite her first nauha. The young girls of the Dakkhin and Uttar Pattis all stood around Manno. A few married ladies joined them, but when Manno opened her notebook, the girls and ladies standing to accompany her were left speechless.

'*Naooj*! What is this *nikaundi* language, bhai?' blurted out Umme Habiba, when she couldn't restrain herself any longer.

'Hindi!' replied Manno.

'Lord in heaven, have mercy!' exclaimed Saiyda's mother, gently slapping her cheeks in repentence, 'Have they started writing the name of Allah and the Prophets in that wretched Hindi now?'

'I've heard of Urdu, Arabic-Persian . . . but what's this language that's come up now?' asked Rabban-bi.

'Bashir-bhai's daughter Suraiya has written out the namaz in Hindi and learnt it off by heart,' said Manno.

'Now there's no reason,' said Sakina, 'that you should do what your cousins do.'

'Recite, bhai, recite!' Saiyda told Manno, 'Come on, I'll read with you!'

But the whole majlis had become a mockery. The nauha was the same, the words were the same, the tone of voice was the same. Just the unfamiliarity of a script had annoyed the ladies. As a result, tears rose in no one's eyes, and no one raised their voice in grief. Rabban-bi was left picking her smallpox-scarred nose. Umme Habiba sat down contentedly on the floor and began to feed her infant daughter, Farzana. Sallo's daughter Shahida pinched Umme Habiba's elder daughter and when she started wailing, Ummè Habiba slapped Shahida. Sakina rushed to pick up Shahida and Rabban-bi began to rant against Umme Habiba's elder daughter.

Manno stopped reciting in irritation. The majlis was over. To pretend nothing untoward had happened, Kubara-bi began to distribute the blessed sweets, and the weaver and untouchable women crowded around her. She began to abuse them. In the middle of all this clamour, the oil lamp gave a hiccough, then its breath gave up and it died. Darkness engulfed the imambara.

'*Naooj*! Is the imambara the only place that Hammad can't find oil for?' commented Saiyda's mother. Saiyda heard her mother's comment, and began to feel distressed. She knew that Kubara-bi was bound to answer back, and then they would argue. So first she tried to find her sandals in the dark, but when she couldn't she set off for home in her bare feet. After all, how far was it to go? When she reached home Abbu Miyan was lying down reading a magazine. As soon as he saw her he sat up, 'Bitiya! Give me a word which has eight letters, and ends with "ity".'

'There are lots of words like that but . . .'

'There you go, arguing again!'

'Nobility, insanity . . . there're not just one or two words.'

'If I can just solve this puzzle, our troubles will be over.'

'The things you say!' said Saiyda, suddenly feeling pity for her old father, 'I tell you to let Gangauli burn and come with me. But you won't agree, and just sit down to solve puzzles!'

'How can I let Gangauli burn, bitiya! Do you want me to set fire to the doors of my forefathers? If I could just find a young man and see you married, I'd rest content. But it takes money to have a daughter married, and where will we get that from?'

'I don't want any marriage-varriage,' retorted Saiyda angrily.

Whenever her marriage was mentioned she became annoyed. She felt a great weight of disgrace. It seemed to her that she was not fit to be accepted by another, and then she would remember Tannu and become extremely sad.

She quietly slipped into bed. Dogs were barking in the distance and close at hand. She hid her face in her pillow. Abbu Miyan was working out loud on his crossword puzzle—across and down, down and across. He didn't even stop when Saiyda's mother came home.

'That's enough, are you going to spend your whole life doing crossword puzzles? I say that you've turned completely senile.'

'What's the matter?' asked Abbu Miyan with great affection.

'What's wrong with Abbas . . . his family's only a touch polluted.'

'A touch polluted?' said Abbu Miyan, 'Nobility, insanity . . . there's a prize of 1,00,000 rupees for this. If I win it I'll do no end of good things.'

'You've got to win it first!'

Abbu Miyan gave no reply. Saiyda's mother grumbled into silence. Saiyda began to cry and to think about the picture which she once kept in her trunk and which one day, weary of Sallo's loneliness, she had given to her. At night, before she went to sleep, Sallo would quietly take the picture out of her trunk, put it in her bodice, and then take a lantern and pot of water with her into the toilet. Squatting in the toilet she would look at the picture for a long time, and make heaven knows what complaints to it. But one day Rabban-bi found her out and said, 'Eh, Sallo! What are you doing in the toilet for so long?'

'Eh, Amma, have you gone mad?' said Fussu Miyan. 'Are you going to stop her pissing and shitting now?'

'Of course! I'm her enemy, aren't I?'

Hearing this conversation from the toilet, Sallo began to breathe fast and to think that Saifuniya had been more fortunate than her—at least she had lived happily with her husband. 'And I've heard that Kaniz Fatima's got married. It's an irony of the Lord's that Dullan, Fatto and Pammo can call out for their father, and it's our Shahida's fate just to have a granny and grandad.' In fact the problem was that Shahida had grown old enough to ask questions.

'When you have a father why don't I?' she had asked.

'You have a father too.'

'Where is he?'

'In Pakistan . . .' then Sallo had told her the names of all the girls whose fathers were in Pakistan in the hope that it would console her. But Shahida wasn't content and said, 'Mighdad-cha's Nakko is better off than me. Why didn't her father go to Pakistan? I don't know how to, or I'd call my father back here.'

'He's just waiting for your letter. Why don't you write to him to come?' said Rabban-bi, 'Now sleep, or are you going to keep squealing all night?'

'She's done nothing to be scolded for, Dadda,' said Sallo.

'Eh, Dulhan, just look at this *jharumari* daughter of yours!' Rabban-bi called out to Sakina. Sakina rained abuse on Sallo, and Sallo just stared at her mother dumbfounded. She couldn't understand how it was her fault that Shahida's father had gone to Pakistan, 'I didn't send him there . . .' She became so enraged that her whole being seemed to melt, and to cool her temper she began beating Shahida. 'Take that!' she said, slapping her on the small of the back, 'And this! How many fathers will you take!' Sallo beat her as if she were carding cotton. 'This *matimili* won't die and give me some peace!'

'Accha, that's enough now,' Rabban-bi scolded her.

'She's my daughter!' shouted Sallo, looking straight into Rabban-bi's one eye. 'If I murder her it's no one's business but mine! And what can I call the man who beat this calamity into my stomach and left me . . . ' She became hysterical and began to sob bitterly. Fussu Miyan rushed to call for Kammo. Kammo took his black case down from its peg, tied a lungi round his waist and hurried over.

He felt Sallo's pulse, and then listened to her heart beat through his stethoscope for a long time. Then he touched her stomach and pressed it here and there. It was clear that he had no idea what was wrong with her, but these were all the tricks of his trade and he had to perform them. If he immediately opened his homoeopathy book, targeted the symptoms and shot four pills into his patients, who would ever come to his shop? He'd begun administering injections too, and would manage the occasional minor operation. Accordingly, he now used to take his patients' pulse like the town doctors with a stethoscope hanging round his neck. Then he would examine their bodies thoroughly. The patients would imagine that the doctor was trying his hardest, although all Kammo was doing when he was examining them was wishing that Saiyda would fall sick and Abbu Miyan would call for him so that he could hear the beating of her heart, touch her skin which was as soft as cream, and press her gently concave stomach. But Saiyda just didn't get ill. And then Javad Miyan and Rahman-bo were insisting that Dr Saiyid Kamaluddin should get married. Phunnan Miyan had sent someone to suggest a match with his daughter Kaniz Fatima, or Kuddan, but Javad Miyan had rejected the proposal. Was there no one better than Phunnan's daughter for his son to marry? What did Phunnan possess that he could dream of making Kamaluddin his son-in-law?

He was right too. What did Phunnan Miyan possess? Javad Miyan now lived in a brick house, with a buffalo and a hybrid Jamnapari cow tethered at his door. He also had a pair of bullocks ten-hands high which flicked away flies with their tapering tails. In the evening cloth chairs were set out beneath the neem tree at his gate, and several Saiyid gentlemen of the village assembled there to smoke the huqqa and have a cup of tea, their gatherings continuing until deep into the night.

Javad Miyan would lift one buttock to fart as thunderously as before, and his Kammo would sit in his surgery examining cartload upon cartload of patients until he was exhausted. Then, when he lay down, Rahman-bo would bring a bottle of Jaunpuri jasmine oil, sit down at the head of his bed, massage his head with oil, and talk about his marriage.

'I've told you that I won't get married!' one day Kammo rebuked Rahman-bo.

'Whyever not?' retorted Rahman-bo with spirit, 'Eh, beta, how long do you expect me to go on torturing myself? I can't handle all the housework on my own any more.'

'I have told you to employ a housemaid, but you pay absolutely no attention,' said Kammo in Urdu.

'All right, there's no need to use big Arabic-Persian words like Hammad. When I die you can keep a servant. As long as I live there'll be no servant-arvant in this house . . . . Have you seen a girl you like, or . . .'

'Even if I had seen a girl I'd liked,' said Kammo, 'would you make her your daughter-in-law?'

'Why on earth not? So tell me, who is she?'

'I'm not saying.'

'Tell me, by the milk I fed you!'

'Bhai, you've gone completely mad.'

'No, I haven't. Tell me!'

'Will you marry me to Saiyda?' he asked.

Rahman-bo was stunned. Saiyda! . . . That was a very high wall to climb. An elephant dead's still worth a fortune! God knows what sayings came to Rahman-bo's mind. She stared at her son's face.

'Go away, I'm feeling sleepy!' said Kammo, 'And don't talk to me about getting married any more. I want to marry Saiyda and I can't marry her. I can't marry her because you are my mother.'

His last sentence was very harsh. Rahman-bo was infuriated.

'Of course, beta! What else? Saiyid women have a different sort of uterus, don't they?' She began to cry, 'Why didn't you abort yourself when you came into my stomach? You could have asked your father where he was sending you and told him you weren't going to stay in the stomach of a Pathan woman!'

When Saiyda came to Gangauli that Moharram she asked Rahman-bo, as she always did, 'Bua, when is Kammo-bhai getting married?'

But Rahman-bo didn't answer as she always did, 'What can I say, beti, he's just not prepared to get married. I am tired out with telling him!' This year Rahman-bo kept quiet, and turned the conversation round to the subject of Aligarh.

And the same day Fiddu told Saiyda why Kammo wasn't getting married. He said, 'I swear to God, Saiyda-ba'ji, bhaiyaa told mother straight out that he wanted to marry you.' Saiyda was stunned, and could only say, 'Get on with you, liar!'

'I swear by the Holy Qor'an, Ba'ji!'

Saiyda was left speechless.

But this news did give her a thrill. She was not insensible to the expression of desire. She had seen the eyes of several of the university teachers light up in several different ways. But all of them wanted to travel to America or England at their in-laws' expense, and indeed they did. And so she was always left alone, with the love she had never articulated, and which had still not acknowledged its existence even to her. So she was thrown into confusion when she heard from Fiddu of Kammo's love. She also felt like weeping with self-pity—what a lover to be linked with . . . who'd been just Kammo all his life, but for the past few years had become Kamaluddin, and whose mother lived with Javad but was still known by the name of her husband, Rahman.

However, despite all this, Saiyda did change in that she began to observe Kammo closely. So closely in fact that Kammo was unnerved and when, out of affection, Fiddu told him what he had said to Saiyda, he turned quite pale and began to avoid her, and to pray that Moharram would be over quickly and she would go back to Aligarh . . .

He was inwardly repeating this prayer as he felt Sallo's stomach. 'Oh, God! May Moharram be over quickly. May there be no summer vacations, and no Moharram for three years!'

'Ouch!' groaned Sallo. Kammo had pressed her stomach rather too hard.

'Is there anything to worry about?' asked Fussu Miyan.

'No!' Kammo replied, opening his case and feeling amongst his bottles of medicine. 'It's hysteria. I'll give you some medicine.' He took out several bottles, glanced at them and put them into their compartments. 'The real cure for her is Tannu . . . but if Allah wills she'll recover.' He placed small amounts of glucose powder on small squares of cut white paper with a strangely fashioned ivory spoon, and then tapped out four pills from a bottle on to each piece of paper. 'Give her one now,' he said, carefully folding the squares of paper, 'then one in the morning, one at lunchtime, and one in the evening. I'll come and see her again in the evening.'

'Any thing she shouldn't eat?' asked Sakina.

'No.'

He picked up his case and left. After folding up his lungi to knee level, Fussu Miyan lit a beedi and began to think about Tannu, Pakistan and India's Congress government. He didn't have a good word or thought for any of them. It had become almost impossible for him to bear the weight of his daughters: Kubara, Saida, Umme Laila, Kaniz, Rabab and Mahjabin. Leave aside Kubara and Saida, even Umme Laila was already of an age to knock at the door of marriage, and Kaniz was just about to be. What would become of these girls? He had straight out cursed his wife, using a number of abuses as fat and flabby as himself, for producing girl after girl and making a mess of their upbringing. If only the good soul had borne him one son! Now he'd even given up going to his wife for fear that she'd immediately produce another girl from somewhere for him to put up with.

'Eh, are you listening?' he said to a dozing Sakina.

'What is it?' she said sharply, 'Go to sleep.'

'What I'm saying is what's wrong with Abbas and Mighdad?'

Sakina was wide awake. 'What did you say? I'm not talking about their family . . . but they're both widowers and Abbas is too old.'

'We can't afford to look at age any longer . . .'

'Then marry your daughters off to Hakim Ali Kabir! Send them to hell, what is it to me?'

'If we don't marry them to Abbas and Mighdad we'll have to go to Pakistan to find boys for them!'

'Accha, now don't you take the name of Pakistan in front of me. If you've got a great desire to see it, go, but I'm staying right here with my girls,' said Sakina hotly as she turned over.

But the idea of marrying his daughters to Abbas and Mighdad had driven itself into Fussu Miyan's brain like a nail. If he tried to remove it, parts of his mind started coming away with it too. Therefore he steeled himself and the very next day laid siege to Abbu Miyan. Abbu Miyan was shocked by his suggestion.

'It's not as if I'm happy with the engagements, Mamu,' said Fussu Miyan, 'but I've no alternative. What can I do? A married daughter is any day better than an unmarried one. And I still have to find boys for Umme Laila and Kaniz.'

'Marry them to Kammo and Fiddu!' pronounced Abbu Miyan in a

tone as distasteful as cold tea. 'There's at least no doubt about Javad-bhai being a Saiyid.'

'Uncle, what are you saying?' asked Fussu Miyan in disbelief.

'Your uncle is saying what's right!' said Abbu Miyan, 'Has Hammad become fit to take our daughters in marriage?'

'Then what do you want me to do? Murder my girls?'

'You're talking as if you're the only one with unmarried daughters,' said Abbu Miyan. 'But I will not give my daughter in marriage to the child of that son of a weaver woman.'

'How can you compare Saiyda with my daughters?' asked Fussu Miyan, 'Saiyda, by the grace of God, is educated and earning three hundred a month. The problem is my illiterate girls.'

'Bhai, if you insist, then I'll mention the matter to Hammad after Moharram.'

'And if he gets any proposal before then?'

'Do you expect me to talk about marriage today, the eighth of Moharram?'

Fussu Miyan had no answer to this. How could he say that a marriage should be arranged on the eighth of Moharram?

'I leave that to you, I'm off.'

'*Abeh*, Fussu!' Shabbar Miyan called out as he walked up. 'Adaab, bhai jan!' he greeted Abbu Miyan, 'Where are you off to, bhai?' he asked Fussu.

'To have something to eat,' said Fussu Miyan, with his customary smile.

'He doesn't worry about anything but his stomach,' smiled Shabbar Miyan, wiping his rimless spectacles with the hem of his shirt. 'What happened to that land you were after, sahib?' he asked Abbu Miyan.

'I managed to get it somehow,' replied Abbu Miyan. He didn't think it appropriate to go into detail. The lengths he'd had to go for possession of two bighas of land were best not spoken of. He'd had to part with four pieces of Saiyda's mother's jewellery. The Tehsildar Sahib's wife had been very taken with the gold choker set with precious stones. He didn't in any case wish to recall those pieces of jewellery because, apart from Saiyda's trousseau, there was no jewellery left in the house except for rings set with turquoise, rubies and white Najaf stone. And they were only silver.

'I've heard that you've bought a house?' he changed the subject.

'Yes, I have! I saw the time was right, so I bought it. Bashir Sahib's house is in a very dirty locality. I bought that same house by the mahua grove,' said Shabbar Miyan.

'You were right. Now you should buy a motor.'

'I don't want to buy secondhand. You've seen Bashir Sahib's car—always breaking down.'

'I see that Bashir and you have altogether deserted Gangauli.'

'It's very expensive to come here, sahib! Don't ask how we manage to come! You have to get the whole house together. Then there's altogether a different sort of pain in seeing the conditions people are in here. Someone was telling me that the Hakim Sahib's in debt to Parusaram-va's father, Sukhram-va. What have things come to?'

'But how did that *behenchod* Parusaram-va lay his hands on so much money?' asked Fussu Miyan.

'Arre bhai, he's an MLA! How can he be short of money? And the Chief Minister thinks a lot of him.'

'Parusaram is coming!' called Dhaniya Chamar from outside. Even after the abolition of zamindari he still stuck to Abbu Miyan.

'He's coming, is he!' said Abbu Miyan, his eyes dancing.

Parusaram was sitting comfortably on a chair, smoking a Capstan cigarette, and flicking the ash on to the floor. Two or three of the village's Chamars, and two or three Ahirs were squatting on the ground. One was rubbing chewing tobacco in the palm of his hand. After giving a pinch of tobacco to each of his companions he put the rest in his mouth.

Parusaram was wearing a homespun khadi kurta over a spotlessly white khadi dhoti. Sandals were on his feet and his briefcase lay on a chair. Seeing Abbu Miyan, he stood up. All the people sitting on the ground stood up too.

'Adaab, Mir Sahib!'

'When did you come?' Abbu Miyan asked as he sat down on a chair.

'Just today,' replied Parusaram, taking a seat too. All the others squatted down on the ground.

'And how is your Lucknow?'

'There's great work afoot, sahib!' said Parusaram. 'This committee, that committee. This meeting, that meeting. And on top of that these Hindu-Muslim troubles have driven me up the wall. Then when I am tired out and come here for a few days' rest, these people make me run around.'

'Now look, Miyan, what fault is that of ours?' said one of the Chamars to Abbu Miyan. 'You gave us the land we plough. Now what can we say about that *susar* patwari . . . he has the pen, he can put land in whosoever's name he likes . . . but we're not going to let go of our land. You are our mother and father, you tell us what to do.'

'What land are you talking about?'

'The fields by the Mangare pond,' said a young Chamar.

Abbu Miyan's mind was working fast. He couldn't understand why Parusaram had deserted the members of his caste and joined hands with the Ahirs. He'd also known these Ahirs for a long time—they were hardened criminals, every one of them.

'Why have you people come to me?' he asked, 'What can I do now?'

'I don't want any of these petty disputes in my area, Mir Sahib!' said Parusaram. 'You're one of the responsible individuals of this area. You're an elder of the village. You give a decision.'

'We'll accept the Miyan's judgement,' said the elder of the Ahirs.

'Did you hear that?' Abbu Miyan said to Parusaram, 'I should judge! Arre, who am I to judge anything?'

'I've persuaded these people to give up the land by the school,' said Parusaram.

'No, that can't be!' said a Chamar.

'If it can't, there'll be bloodshed!' said an Ahir, thumping the ground with his lathi.

'I'll consider it!' said Abbu Miyan and stood up. 'You sit here if you like, I'm just going over to the Gate for a majlis.'

'No, I'll be going too,' said Parusaram, also standing up. Abbu Miyan went back indoors. Parusaram took his leave of the Chamars and Ahirs and went off towards Hammad Miyan's house. Hammad Miyan was waiting for him, and smiled as he saw him approaching. Then he peered through the Gate. The imambara was empty; the congregation still had to gather. He sat down.

'What happened?' he asked Parusaram.

'One group or the other will back down. I've left it up to him to deal justice.'

'Fine.'

'And, Mir Sahib, that . . .'

'Yes, yes!' said Hammad Miyan, 'I've told you that the Gate is yours. As soon as Moharram's over you can establish your office in the rooms adjoining it. There are tables and chairs there already.'

'Yes, it's been very difficult functioning from where I have been. I'm considering constructing a house if I find any convenient land. I've already purchased a jeep, otherwise all this coming and going was very difficult.'

'The police are after Abbas.'

'Arre, Mir Sahib, how can you say such a thing? Could the *behenchod* police dare even to look in his direction? I've spoken to the Collector Sahib and told him that Abbas is my man and shouldn't be bothered in any way.'

'Yes, bhai, it's only Abbas that's been worrying me.'

'There's no need, sahib. You can rest assured of that.'

'And here that *behenchod* Ramzaniya the weaver has built his lavatory right opposite the tazia platform. Now I ask you . . .'

'I spoke to the thanedar about that only yesterday.'

At that moment Hammad Miyan's glance fell on Gaya Ahir, who was coming through the gate.

'Salaam!' he greeted Hammad Miyan and Parusaram.

'What's up, *re*?' asked Hammad Miyan.

'Ramzaniya's lavatory's been knocked down and Dukhiram's wings have been clipped too. The Thanedar Sahib's come himself to say so.'

Parusaram lit another cigarette, and stretched his legs out further. His eyes began to smile.

'So now I'm off to the town,' said Gaya.

'Yes, but be sure to come back by tomorrow,' said Hammad.

'Bhai, bring a tin of butter and a packet of Lipton Green Label tea from Rafiq Traders,' said Parusaram putting his hand into his pocket and taking out a red leather wallet containing several denominations of notes.

'He'll bring them!' said Hammad Miyan, 'Put your money away.'

'No, Mir Sahib!'

'Let it be,' Hammad rebuked him gently like an elder. Then he said to Gaya, 'Take ten rupees more from the Bibi,' and turned again to Parusaram. 'What difference is there between your money and mine?'

'I know, it's not that but . . .'

'What are you standing there listening to? Go.' Hammad told Gaya.

Gaya dusted off his feet with his shouldercloth and put on his stout leather shoes. Then he picked up his lathi and called out to Umme Habiba's daughter, Naushaba.

At this time Naushaba was very busy trying to sing a nauha to a new tune. She was very annoyed by Gaya's summons, but what could she do? 'What is it?' she questioned him from her bed.

'Go and ask the Bibi for ten rupees and give them to me. I'm going to the town.'

Naushaba melted at the name of the town. Her doll didn't have any mourning clothes. She persuaded Kubara to give her two rupees extra, brought the money outside and walking with Gaya to the gate, said, 'Bring two rupees worth of black chiffon.'

'Write it down on a piece of paper for me, I can't remember these English names.'

Naushaba wrote the name of the material on a piece of paper, gave it to Gaya and said conspiratorially, 'Be sure to bring it, my doll hasn't got any black clothes.' Having sent Gaya off she lay down again and began practising the nauha. 'The cruel one stabbed him through the heart, Ali Akbar's youth was ended . . .'

'Eh, beta Naushaba!' said Kubara, sitting on the bed opposite and opening her betel-box, 'Just go and roast some dhaniya mixture. Your grandfather must be just about to demand it.'

'I'm reciting a nauha,' said Naushaba obstinately. 'Ask mother.'

'What illness are you the cure for?' Umme Habiba called out from her room where she was quietly trying on a bra which she had asked Saiyda to bring her. After trying it on in a closed room, she would take it off again so that her mother wouldn't see. But she thought that this new bra was far better and more comfortable than the old-fashioned hand-sewn bodices with their irregularly sized cups. There was no bother of tying anything!

'What are you doing, hiding in that room?' asked Kubara.

'Shall I tell you?' asked Naushaba.

Habiba's heart stopped. Thrusting the bra into the bedding, she rushed outside and immediately slapped Naushaba several times. When Naushaba began to cry, she breathed a sigh of relief and began to curse her.

'Lazy, *matimili*! Go and roast the dhaniya, you faithless girl!'

'Hai! Hai!' said Kubara, trying to protect her, 'Have you gone mad? What has she done to deserve a beating?'

'She's become very insolent, Mother! You don't know her. She's made her father's life as impossible as chewing gram with your nose.'

'She's only a child.'

'Razzo's younger than this backward girl. But look at him!' said Umme Habiba. Naushaba always hated being compared with her brother. For one thing he was very small, and for another he was definitely not good, he was a menace. He was only five years old but only Naushaba knew in her heart exactly how good he was. Once when her cousin Mehrun was bathing, the little wretch had peeped into the bathroom and then came running with the news, 'Eh, Ba'ji, Mehrun-ba'ji's got two big boils on her chest, just like mother!' Naushaba being his elder sister tried to explain to him. 'Get away with you, you mad thing! Those aren't boils, they're milk.'

'They're not milk, stupid!' said Razzo, 'Where's your milk?'

'I'll kill you, Razzo!' she ran to hit him and he raced off. The matter was forgotten. Then, one scorching afternoon, he came and told Naushaba, 'Eh, Ba'ji! Father's beating mother.'

'Get away!'

'No, I swear to Allah! Come and see. The door's shut and he's sitting on top of her. And I don't know what sorts of things he's saying, and mother's making all sorts of bleating noises.'

Upset, Naushaba went up to the door and peeped through it too. Father had really put mother in a bad way. She began to cry to see her mother in that state. She howled. Her grandmother came. There was bedlam in the house. Instead of being angered by what she said, her grandmother turned her face aside and smiled. The maidservants went off to one side together. To send off the Tempter Satan her grandmother recited a quotation from the Qor'an to the effect that Allah alone was the Almighty and All-Encompassing One, and everyone dispersed. After a short while Naushaba's mother slipped out of the room like a thief, caught hold of her by the hair and began to beat her.

It was natural that when Naushaba was compared with that lying little Razzo, she became furious and, without intending to, was ccrtain to do something or other which would make her mother beat her. She stared at Umme Habiba. 'What are you staring at me for?' said her mother, 'I'll tear your eyes out!' Kubara managed to distract her. Naushaba quietly slipped out. Day by day she was beginning to hate her mother more and she had some very substantial plans in mind for Razzo. She had decided to make a regular study of black magic.

The majlis at the Great Gate was underway. Naushaba saw that Razzo, enclosed in a shervani coat up to his neck, his head covered by a cap, was sitting with his grandfather on the floor of the imambara. He had covered his eyes with a handkerchief and was pretending to cry. Naushaba's blood began to boil and she swore to herself that she would have Razzo beaten into the ground by her husband.

Razzo had no idea of the plans Naushaba had in store for him. He was peeping at Maulvi Bedar from underneath his handkerchief and laughing at him. The Maulvi was sitting in the pulpit and reciting goodness knows what in his off-key voice.

'Why is Bedar-nana shouting so much, grandfather?' he asked Hammad Miyan.

'Be quiet! You don't talk in a majlis,' replied Hammad Miyan. Razzo fell silent and began to look at Fussu Miyan whose belly was quivering as he wept. He was very fond of Fussu Miyan's stomach and therefore was very jealous of Shahida, who could lie on it whenever she liked. He'd thought of a way of capturing Fussu's belly. He'd decided that when he grew up he would marry Shahida and then he could enjoy himself lying on Fussu's stomach and making and smoothing out waves in his paunch.

'Ya Husain!' Shabbar Miyan's son Allan stood up holding a book of nauhas. The members of the Husainiya Society formed rows and began to beat their chests, providing a rhythm for the poem. Allan began to sing a nauha by Fazl Lakhnavi. Fussu Miyan slid over towards Abbu Miyan. Nearby Shabbar Miyan and Sibtu Miyan had covered their faces with handkerchieves and were waiting for some verse which would provide them with the opportunity to weep loudly. But the nauha was very flowery and contrived, just like a Lucknow love poem. A pile of words, with every verse missing the listeners' hearts by yards, leaving the Miyans standing with their handkerchieves over their faces and nothing to cry about.

'Whose nauha did you begin with, *ji*?' Abbu Miyan asked Allan after reciting the salaam.

'Fazl Lakhnavi's.'

'He's a fine poet!' Masshu-bhai said sarcastically.

'Whether the name he calls himself by is fine or not,' remarked Phunnan Miyan, 'he's no poet. What sort of nauha is it that can't make you cry?'

'Don't read any of this Azl-Fazl's poetry on the eighth or ninth,' said Fussu Miyan.

Then they began to discuss the old school of nauhas, whose very words were damp with tears. Even before you began the recitation, the congregation would be weeping inconsolably, and then there were these modern nauhas which anyone might mistake for love poems if they didn't keep their ears open.

Abbu Miyan walked with Hammad Miyan up to his door discussing these matters.

'What's the matter, bhai? Aren't you ever going to get Abbas married?' he suddenly asked.

'The young gentleman is willing,' said Hammad Miyan, 'but I can't see any suitable girl.'

'Really, and is there any lack of unwed girls in the Saiyids' homes these days?'

'Do you have any girl in view?'

'Arre, if there's no one else, then marry him to Fussu's daughter,' said Abbu Miyan. 'And you need to tie up Mighdad too. How long will he wander around like a young bull?'

'He's ready to come to blows at the very mention of marriage,' said Hammad Miyan. 'But Fussu Miyan's girls . . .'

'What times are you living in? Now what does Fussu have that he can afford to look at a boy's breeding?' said Abbu Miyan, 'Blood and breeding was an affectation of the zamindars, don't you see? If you give the word, I'll have the marriage vows read tomorrow.'

'But Fussu Miyan . . .'

'He's not a fool to start iffing and butting.'

'Look, I have no objection to the match. She's a girl of our own home, well brought up and, by God's grace, has an attractive appearance . . . But I have already rejected several good proposals. You know what a dearth of young men there is these days. I shall speak to Abbas.'

'Have a word with Mighdad too,' said Abbu Miyan. 'Aren't you going to the majlis in the other Patti?'

'Why not?'

When Hammad Miyan reached the Hakim Sahib's Gate, he was surprised to see Fussu Miyan discussing current affairs with Abbas. Abbas was enjoying the conversation. When Shabbar Miyan, Deputy Ali Hadi and occasionally Maulvi Bedar interrupted, Fussu Miyan began to speak even more excitedly. Parusaram too was half-sitting, half-lying, on a chair drawing on a cigarette.

Seeing Abbu Miyan they all rose to their feet.

'Eh, Parusaram! I can't get involved in that dispute,' said Abbu Miyan. 'Why should I get on anyone's bad side?'

'That's all very well, Mir Sahib, but if you're summoned to a court of law, then what will you say?'

'What do I have to do with any court of law?' exclaimed Abbu Miyan. 'What do you say, bhai Hadi? Will they accept the patwari's papers in court or ask me when this dispute began? And if they call me I'll tell them straight that after zamindari was abolished I've forgotten all about land dealings.'

'So, bhai, can I cash your zamindari bonds?'

'No one has any bonds any more!' said Abbu Miyan, 'All that's over and done with.'

'Come on, bhai,' said the Hakim Sahib slowly and deliberately, 'we should get on with the majlis.'

Everyone was just getting up when a constable arrived with a summons. Sukhram had filed a claim against the Hakim Sahib for non-payment of debt.

'What's the summons for?' asked Abbu Miyan.

'It's to give evidence in some case,' the Hakim Sahib replied very casually, and no one noticed that he had suddenly aged. It was as if his whole body had become lined. Waves of darkness passed through his eyes. He went into the imambara, leant against the pulpit and sat down. That night, for the first time, he wrote to Saddan.

From Gangauli.

Most dear Saddan, light of my eyes and joy of my life, my prayers are with you.

I trust your dear family is well and in good health. Through God's grace upon the Prophet's Family, everyone else is well too. Your family here is also living in ease. Therefore there is no need for you to be worried on their account . . .

The letter went on, but he couldn't bring himself to write that Pakistan, the Congress government and Kammo had destroyed him. He could not write that he no longer had the strength to bear the responsibilities of Saddan's family. And when he couldn't write that, then how could he write that he was in debt to Sukhram and that Sukhram had filed a claim against him. Therefore, he wasn't able to finish the letter. He lay down just there, on the platform for saying prayers. His eyes closed and until dawn he dreamed terrifying dreams.

He had already sold his late wife's jewellery. There was no question of his selling the jewellery of his widowed daughter. How could he go and hold out his hands to request favours from his daughter-in-law? He didn't even have the kind of hands that would raise themselves to ask for favours.

But for the Hakim Sahib the mourning of the ninth of Moharram was transformed into the joyful celebration of 'Id. He was returning from the majlis at the Gate of Dakkhin Patti when he heard the bells of a horse cart.

He turned round to look and couldn't believe his eyes. In the cart sat Saddan. His son Saddan! He stopped. His eyes filled with tears. Saddan jumped down from the cart and said, 'Adaab, Father!'

'May you live long!'

That was all they said. Then they both set off for Uttar Patti in silence, while the news of Saddan's return flew around the village. Some believed the news, others didn't.

'Arre, are these Pakistanwallahs fools to let people come back!'

'Now we'll find out what sort of calamity this Pakistan really is.'

'But Saddan took his time coming back.'

'Arre, it's no game to come back from Pakistan! It must have cost him a basketful of money.'

'So why doesn't Mohammad Husain come back?' Kulsum asked this exceptionally reasonable question and Phunnan Miyan, lying on a bamboo bed and smoking a beedi, had to look away. The creation of Pakistan had wrought no particular change in his life. His life had in fact improved somewhat. He was as close to Parusaram, MLA, as the hair in his nose. Now the Thanedar of Qasimabad paid court to him. Once Phunnan twisted three hundred rupees from the thanedar to have his transfer stopped—and it had been too. How could the Superintendent of Police refuse Parusaram? And when any of the Miyans began to sigh over the change in Parusaram's fortunes, Phunnan Miyan would display his irritation at the prejudiced tone of the speaker and say, 'Eh, bhai! Who are you to meddle in Allah's factory? He is feeding gram halva to his own donkey.'

But the departure of Salimpur's Ashrafullah Khan 'Ashraf' for Pakistan had come as a great shock to Phunnan. He had only one complaint of Pakistan—it had left him on his own. Dust had begun to blow through his empty home, and he would remember Kuddan, Dullan, Fatto and Pammo and weep when Kulsum wasn't looking, and begin to think that if Imtiyaz hadn't gone to the front, and if he hadn't let Muntaz leave the house that night, his home would still have seemed full even after Mohammad Husain's and Razia's children had left. By now his sons would have produced so many children that his courtyard would have seemed small.

'How can Muhammad Husain come, poor man?' said Phunnan, throwing away the stub of his beedi. 'He can't just come on his own, can he?'

'Who knows what Kuddan's husband is like?' said Kulsum, 'Little Kuddan's got a baby girl in her lap too, by God's grace. Without children the house seems so empty.'

'If you like, we could have another go!' said Phunnan Miyan, smiling, 'Who knows, we might be able to do it!'

'Accha, be quiet will you. You're an old man but you haven't lost your fondness for flirting.'

For a moment Kulsum suddenly became young again, Phunnan Miyan's white moustache turned black, and the line of antimony around Kulsum's eyes, which had not been put there for some three years, began to stand out. For that moment their loneliness ceased to exist. They rid themselves of their memories. It escaped their minds that there had been a war in which Imtiyaz had been killed, or a movement in which Muntaz had been shot. They even forgot that a place by the name of Pakistan had been created which had snatched Maghfiya, Kuddan, Dullan, Fatto and Pammo from them.

'I feel like carrying you off a second time!' said Phunnan Miyan. 'Will you run away with me?'

'Where will you take me?' asked Kulsum, joining in the game.

'Calcutta!' replied Phunnan Miyan. The red veins in his eyes stood out further. Trams began to run through his mind. Motor cars began to race. Country folk couldn't remember the name of any city but Calcutta. Whoever you looked at was longing to go to Calcutta.

'It's a very big city. I'll take you to see the sea.'

'What's the sea, *ji*?'

Phunnan Miyan deliberated—really, what was the sea?

'You know our pond!' he said, 'Well, if there's a stream one or two hundred thousand times as wide as that, it's called a sea, and lots of great big ships sail on it.'

'And aren't people afraid of the water?'

'What is there to be scared of?'

'Baraina-bo was saying that Abbu-bhai took a proposal for Kubara and Saida to marry Abbas and Mighdad,' said Kulsum, returning to everyday life.

'Baraina-bo's turned senile,' replied Phunnan Miyan, 'Hammad's a living fly, who could swallow him?'

'That I don't know,' said Kulsum, 'but she says that she was cleaning the room next door when it happened. She heard it with her own ears, and I've heard that Kammo's cradling a desire to marry Saiyda.'

'Then Imtiyaz and Muntaz died for nothing!' Phunnan Miyan sat up. 'They could have married three or four Saiyid ladies! What it means is that all that showing off of the zamindars is over! His blood is pure, his is not! Come on, I'll have the marriage vows read and we can produce two or three legitimate children . . . without children this *behenchod* home is like a graveyard.'

'Eh, Miyan, are you there?' came Chikuriya's voice.

'What is it, *re*? I'm coming,' said Phunnan Miyan. Then he turned to Kulsum, 'I'm just going to Barikhpur.'

Chairs were standing in the sun opposite Javad Miyan's porch. Fussu Miyan was sitting there smoking a huqqa which was hubble-bubbling away, while Javad Miyan expounded on current events. Saddan was also sitting there, smoking a cigarette and smiling at Javad's speech.

'Adaab, Da!' he said, standing up to greet Phunnan Miyan.

'May you live long!' Phunnan replied, 'When did you come?'

'Today.'

'Have you met Doctor Kamaluddin or not?'

'He's gone to Chavanpur to see a patient,' said Javad Miyan.

'He's begun to attack over a long range,' said Phunnan Miyan, continuing to address Saddan. 'Nowadays Javad prays night and day for people to fall ill! How's your Pakistan? Do you see Tannu from time to time?'

'Yes, why not? I met him at 'Id.'

'At 'Id!' said Phunnan in astonishment, 'You both live in Karachi, don't you?'

'Yes, we do.'

'And still you're saying that you haven't met since 'Id!'

'Karachi's not Gangauli, sahib!'

'Accha, it's not Gangauli, it must be Calcutta, then. But . . .'

'Arre, Da, what world are you living in? If I leave my house at eight in the morning I'm lucky to get back by eight in the evening. Now, when do I have time to meet people?'

'Very well, beta,' said Phunnan Miya, 'but this Karachi seems a very uncivil city.'

Saddan laughed in reply. How could he explain to this Phunnan Miyan?

'How much are you earning?'

'The same thousand, eleven hundred.'

'Eh, beta! I'm longing for someone to come from there and say that he's earning just one or two hundred. But no one stops at under a thousand. Do you grow money there or what? You'll be staying here now, won't you, for some days?'

'How can I, sahib? I was suddenly ordered to go to East Pakistan, and I left. I only just managed to get permission to travel overland and to come home for four days. I'll leave the day after tomorrow.'

'Then I should take a good look at you now. Who knows if your government will ever let you come back home again? There's no relying on it. Are you taking your bride back with you?'

'This time I can't but I've asked for a visa for her. Then I'll come and take her there.'

'And if your government doesn't let you come?'

'Then I'll think of some other way.'

'Where's your other wife?'

'In Karachi itself.'

'Does she have children, by God's grace, or not?'

'Three.'

'Well, that's no bad account. Three here and three there. Accha, so I suppose people there must spend their time fasting and praying?'

'Why?'

'Arre, bhai, it's an Islamic government. How can you ask why!'

'So you think an Islamic government means fasting and praying!'

'Have you people changed the meaning of Islam?'

'Islamic government means, Dada, that Muslims get jobs.'

'Really! I never knew that the Prophet of God made all that effort and noise just for Muslims to get jobs. You've really set my mind at rest today. Maulvi Bedar had been driving us mad with his talk. Now, son, you just explain that point to the Hakim Sahib too.'

'Maulvi Bedar is going to Pakistan,' explained Fussu Miyan.

'Grandmother's calling you,' said young Rabab, who was dressed in a black kurta. After giving Fussu Miyan her message she hung round Phunnan Miyan's waist. Phunnan picked her up and threw her over his shoulder like a travelling cloth merchant lifting a bolt of cloth.

'Go on then, beta,' said Fussu Miyan, 'your mother must be waiting to give you tea.'

Saddan stood up. Sakina had arranged a splendid tea. Rabban-bi opened her basket of complaints, lamenting that Saddan had completely forgotten his own home. Not for one moment did it cross Saddan's mind that he was in a foreign country. How could Gangauli be another country! All these faces, plants and trees, these ponds and this indigo godown, these imambaras and tazias . . . and this Karbala, and these bundles of marsias wrapped in red cloth, lying on pulpits . . . all these things could only belong to his own village. He had become a citizen of a Pakistani city, but he was still the same Saiyid Sa'adatul Hasnain Zaidi of Gangauli. That was why he was called a refugee in his own country, Pakistan. In so many years he had never once asked himself who or what he had taken refuge from. The years passed by, but when Moharram came he grew sad. At the majlises of

Maulana Saiyid Muhammad Dehlavi and Rashid Turani he would miss the majlises of Abbu Miyan and Maulvi Bedar. He would remember Husain Haidar Miyan's soz recitations, and Masshu-bhai's nauhas. On the majlis of the fifth he would miss Muhammad Husain's, and on the Evening of the Bereaved Masshu-bhai's falling down in a faint. Consequently, when he came face to face with Muhammad Husain at a majlis in Karachi, he asked as they parted, 'You're here so who'll faint on the majlis of the fifth now . . . ?' These memories were of no particular importance, they were extremely foolish memories, but still Saddan embraced each one of them again and again and wept. He yearned for Gangauli and now that he actually was sitting in Gangauli he couldn't believe that he was there. What was Rabban-bi saying? Her voice seemed to be coming from a great distance.

'You've stayed there quite long enough, now come back.'

'Sorry?' he said with a start.

'What do you mean sorry?' said Rabban-bi, 'Come back now!'

'Where?'

'To your home, where else?'

He laughed. 'Now that place has become my home.' He was happy that he'd not forgotten his own Bhojpuri tongue and was speaking it with ease. 'I've built a house there, a little one.'

'I'm not talking about that home,' said Rabban-bi, 'I'm talking about the home your grandfather and great-grandfather, and their grandfathers and great-grandfathers built. What'll happen to this home when Kabir dies?'

Yes, what would happen to this home after Father died he asked himself, surprised that he had never paid the question any attention. What would happen to this house, and these tazia platforms, and their wooden tazias? What would be the fate of these drums and cymbals beaten before the majlises? What would befall these crests and embroidered hangings once Father had passed away . . . !

'What can I do?' he asked, unnerved by this flood of questions.

'What can't you do!' replied Rabban-bi. 'You can come back! Come and tell the government here, "Sahib, I'm not happy there."'

'It's not that easy.'

'Accha, what I'm saying is when you people gave your vote and made Pakistan why don't you give that same vote and unmake the *matimili* place?'

'Eh, bhai, you're not eating anything,' said Sallo.

'I am, how much do you think I can eat? Do you want me to say anything to your father from you?' he asked Shahida.

'What would this *nikaundi* girl know about her father?' sighed Sakina, 'May God pay him back . . . he's made our daughter so unhappy.'

'Do you know my father?' asked Shahida.

'Yes, I do!' replied Saddan.

'Then please ask him what sort of father he is, and tell him too that we miss him and Mother hides in the toilet and looks at his picture and cries.'

'Be quiet, you *matimili*!' Sallo scolded her.

'Why should I be quiet? Am I lying?'

'Come on, I'll take you to your father,' said Saddan.

'I'm not going,' Shahida refused point blank.

'Why?'

'I'm not leaving Nana and Nani and big Amma.'

Rabban-bi signalled to Sakina. Sakina found some excuse to leave. Then Rabban-bi found some occasion to disappear into the kitchen. Fussu Miyan said he was going to fetch Sallo's medicine from Kammo and would just be back. Sallo was at a loss to understand why everyone should suddenly have found work to do. She didn't realize that the family had given her an opportunity to talk about Tannu, and even if she had what could she have done? She could never have talked about him.

It wasn't that she was angry with him. Wasn't it enough that he hadn't taken a second wife as Saddan had? But she wouldn't have mentioned him out of shyness. Saddan guessed this and so he broached the subject himself. 'Does Tannu write to you?'

'He doesn't know the code writing I do.'

'Eh!' exclaimed Saddan in astonishment, 'You must know how to write Urdu, don't you?'

'I can just read printed Urdu, but I can't read handwriting.'

'He must be writing letters to Shahida, isn't he?'

'Not one!' replied Shahida. Sallo was saved the trouble of answering.

'That's really very bad of him,' said Saddan. 'I went to Pakistan but I didn't forget my children. We don't have the power to come and go as we choose, but what does it cost to write a letter? The next time I see him I'll pull him up.'

'What's the need?' responded Sallo. 'I've got through my life so far, and I can get through the rest in the same way. We're not naked and starving. May God grant Father long life!'

'That's all very well, but . . .' Saddan left his sentence unfinished.

But this half-finished sentence pierced Sallo's heart. This 'but' was very pointed . . . . May God indeed grant your father long life, but no one can live for ever . . . and after that what will happen to you? What will happen to this seven- or eight-year-old, beautiful and lively daughter of yours? You don't even have a brother. This girl will be grown up in three or four years time and then what will you do? Kubara, Saida and Umme Laila are unable to get married and an educated and beautiful girl like Saiyda is still sitting unwed. So what can fate have in store for your Shaddo? From the pole of this 'but' flew the flag of all these questions, writhing in the face of the wind.

Sallo burst into tears.

Discomfited, Saddan walked out.

He took a round of the whole village. It had changed a fair bit. The alleys had been given a pukka brick surface. Here and there the village council had installed street lighting—kerosene lamps which burned at night. A good many brick houses had also been built. Outside the Uttar and Dakkhin Pattis the village had been transformed. Even the half of the village within the Uttar and Dakkhin Pattis had been transformed. The former owed its transformation to its new-found splendour and a certain bustle and activity, the latter to its desolation.

On one side new houses were being constructed and on the other old houses were falling down. No new addition had been made to any of the Saiyids' houses. Like the clothes of the body the cladding of the walls was old and torn. Here and there it had been patched but it seemed as if these walls no longer had the strength to support the weight of the roofs. These houses could no longer face the monsoon. They would collapse and in all probability the young unmarried women, together with the old people and children, would be lost beneath the rubble.

Saddan couldn't decide whether he was pleased or saddened by Gangauli's growth. Should he be scared of the lights provided by the village council or by the darkness of the Saiyid homes? He began to feel afraid of the familiar bazaars of his Gangauli, and ran back home. At home preparations were underway for the evening's majlis. Deputy Collector Ali Hadi was lounging in a chair in his sitting-room, his legs stretched out, looking through marsias. The Hakim Sahib was squatting by the side of the tank seemingly in consultation with the algae-green water. The water of the tank seemed, like him, to be old and decaying.

'Eh, sahib, why are you sitting here?' asked Saddan.

'What difference does it make whether I sit here or there?' replied the Hakim Sahib, 'I am as deeply disgraced here as there.'

'You seem to be worried?'

'No, son, I'm very happy. I had just one son . . . he went to Pakistan. I had just the zamindari . . . and you can say that's gone to Pakistan as well. Arre, the things I no longer have, haven't they gone to Pakistan? What do I have left? One widowed daughter, her three fatherless children, one daughter-in-law—and she's as good as a widow! Her three children who're as good as fatherless. Yesterday I was handed yet another treasure! Sukhram's filed a complaint against me. Now where can I get the money to pay him his loan back? I had a few patients coming to me, then Kammo started his doctoring. I'm at a loss, bhai, what can I do? How will I fill the stomachs of nine souls?'

'Look, God willing, from now on I'll send you something.'

'That was what you said when you left for Pakistan,' remarked the Hakim Sahib. 'Take your wife and children.'

'Then you come too.'

'I'm not leaving.'

'After all, what are you going to do here?'

'So the thought has finally struck you?' The Hakim Sahib stood up. 'You're asking, aren't you, what I'll do here. Then listen—I will not desert the graves of my family. I am staying here to die.'

To see his young daughter Sakina bibi, the blessed Imam
from the battlefield came.
The wives who stood at the threshold waiting, each one
into the women's tent came.
Sakina addressed the ladies saying, 'The Imam of Ali has home
returned.'
Those who, thirsting, went down to the river, thirsting still
their death have earned.

She raised her sweet young hands to offer
Prayers for her father dear,
Seeing his body, disfigured with wounds,
She prayed his every pain to bear.

To meet his young daughter Sakina bibi . . .

This was the voice of Husain Haidar Miyan reciting a soz in the imambara.

'Eh, Saddan! Isn't your daughter's name Sakina?' asked the Hakim Sahib wryly, 'Come on, the majlis has started.'

Father and son sat down on the floor of the imambara, each in his own place. Saddan began to stare hard at every standard's crest and hanging. A strange deathliness overshadowed them. The covering of the pulpit was torn in places.

After the soz, Deputy Collector Ali Hadi Miyan climbed onto the pulpit. After picking up the bundle of marsias he spent four or five minutes selecting one. Then he stared down at the audience over the top of his spectacles. After reciting two quatrains and a few verses of a salaam he commenced the marsia, 'In this world there is no wealth as priceless as a son . . .'

The Hakim Sahib turned to look at Saddan. He was sitting with his head bowed.

Mir Anis had fallen in the Hakim Sahib's esteem recently. 'If his son had gone to Pakistan . . . then if he'd written that verse . . . I'd know what use that "wealth" is to me. This is the "wealth" which is forcing me to go on my knees to that *haramzada* Parusaram to beg him to have his father withdraw the case against me. I'll even mortgage this house to him . . . but he shouldn't drag me to court . . . ' The Hakim Sahib suddenly began to weep.

'This then is the hope that keeps the aged young . . .' recited Ali Hadi Miyan.

'. . . that blasts men in their old age!' thought the Hakim Sahib. His 'hope' was there, just opposite him . . .

Saddan's daughter Sakina slowly crept up to him and sat in his lap. Saddan poked his nose into her neck, tickling her, and she wriggled. Then she lay in his lap and began to fold a black handkerchief into a mouse.

New and Old Lines

'No, bring the price down a bit. You're asking for a l-o-t of money,' said the customer.

'And don't you see what a strong pair of shoes these are?' said Fussu Miyan, banging the soles of the shoes together, 'Get on with you . . . wear your old peasant shoes then! How would a monkey know the taste of ginger! These come from a British company. They were stitched by the British and not one stitch is broken!'

'No, Miyan, I'm not saying that they're not good, they are. But how can I wear thirty rupee shoes?'

'If God's given you the money, whyever not?'

'Couldn't you bring the price down just a bit?'

'As you're the first customer of the day, I'll cut it by four annas. Give me twenty-nine rupees and twelve annas. But not one pie less. For your sake I'm selling them at cost price. I swear by Allah, that four annas was all the profit I was making!'

The customer paid for the shoes. Putting his old shoes in the shoe-box, he pulled on his new purchases. He was embarrassed to be wearing shoes worth thirty rupees. Then he stood up.

'These shoes will let your in-laws know their son-in-law's coming two miles off,' remarked Fussu Miyan, adding the rupees to the takings. The customer left the shop smiling. Fussu Miyan listened to the departing squeaking of the shoes and smiled to himself. These shoes had been lying in Khalil's shop in the town for four years and no one had cast a glance at them. Consequently, when he'd gone to pick up some things during the wedding season, he'd bought the shoes for eleven-and-a-quarter rupees. He'd thought that if they didn't sell he'd give them to Mighdad and could rest content that he's spent eleven-and-a-quarter rupees on his son-in-law.

It so happened that immediately after Mighdad had remarried, he'd fallen out with Hammad Miyan again, and this time he'd come with his wife to live in Fussu Miyan's home. Abbas and Kubara had tried their best to bring about a reconciliation but Fussu Miyan had prevented it.

Mighdad's arrival had solved many of his household problems. For one thing he now had grain in abundance, other expenses being met by this shoe shop which he had opened in the imambara room. All he had to do was to close the shop two days before Moharram and transfer the goods into a storeroom. Then the room was whitewashed, the floor-covering was spread out, a canopy hung under the roof, and the chandeliers and shining, coloured glass balls took their proper places . . .

Three or four years ago when he had followed Bashir Miyan's advice and decided to open this shop, the Miyans had laughed at him—first he'd swallowed a living fly by giving his daughters into a low-bred family and now he was opening a shoe shop! Fussu instantly referred to the historical fact that Hazrat Ali himself had stitched shoes.

Gradually the shop began to make money. At first he had been embarrassed to speak to the customers, and what customers were they? The same people who had spent generations respectfully salaaming him and his forefathers—the village weavers and traders, the Chamars and Ahirs. Fussu would state the price and then when the customer began haggling, he would lose his temper. But then he slowly mastered the art of selling by swearing to the price at which he'd bought the goods, and business picked up.

Now he no longer had to mix with Javad Miyan and neither did he have to stop sitting at his own door for fear that if anyone joined him he would have to offer a huqqa to smoke, and betel-nut, and neither of these came free. The days were gone when several types of scented huqqa tobacco were prepared at home, and kavam tobacco was offered with betel-nut.

Besides Hammad Miyan and Javad Miyan no one had the courage to sit at their own doors, but his new business had at least made Fussu Miyan fit to sit at his door after he'd closed his shop in the evening. A small durbar began to assemble there. The people who could not sit at Javad Miyan's or Hammad Miyan's door began to appear at Fussu Miyan's durbar. Neither Hakim Ali Kabir nor Abbu Miyan could share either Hammad Miyan's company or that of the father of Doctor Kamaluddin. The abolition of zamindari did not mean that they had to mix with low-bred men and bastards. Abbu Miyan had rented the men's part of the house to Kammo as he no longer needed it and Kammo did need two large rooms. He himself sat in one, and his dispensary was in the other. There two employees spent the entire day folding little paper packets of powder until they were tired out. They were both the sons of Saiyid gentlemen. Kammo reprimanded them for the smallest reasons and they would listen in silence. One day he caught one of his employees, Zaigham, kissing and fondling Dilruba the sweeper woman right in the middle of the dispensary. For Kammo this was intolerable, and so there and then he threw out Zaigham Husain Zaidi, otherwise known as Ballan, son of Husain Ali Miyan. Ballan pleaded to be taken back but Kammo wouldn't listen, and so he had no alternative but to leave. A short while later Husain Ali Miyan arrived and he too tried his best to persuade Kammo to change his mind. In front of Kammo he cursed and upbraided Ballan, and Ballan begged for forgiveness. Kammo's heart softened and Husain Ali Miyan was immensely relieved that an income of thirty rupees a month had been saved.

But Abbu Miyan was not Husain Ali Miyan. Once he had rented out the gentlemen's part of his house he refrained from even glancing in its direction. He began to leave and enter his house by the back door. Therefore, the day Fussu Miyan set out chairs on the platform outside his door, Abbu Miyan arrived and thereafter became a regular evening visitor. Fussu Miyan would read out political developments by the light of a hurricane lamp, and the men gathered outside his door would seriously consider the future of the world. When the gatherings dispersed late in the night, Abbu Miyan would go home and, unmindful of Saiyda's mother's grumbling, would start work on the Urdu crossword puzzle in *Shama* magazine and pray that just once he would win the top prize. But every time the prizes were given to those with up to four errors in their solution, his would have five. In fact his solutions contained innumerable errors. Even Saiyda's mother, who used to refer to these crosswords as her husband's second wife, used to pray, 'Oh Pure Protector of the World, make Saiyda's father win the prize this time, for the sake of the martyrs of Karbala, for the sake of Hazrat bibi . . .'* And as the date of the results approached, both husband and wife became progressively more restless. Saiyda's mother always tried to disguise her uneasiness and Saiyda's father to display his.

'If we win this time then we'll go to Karbala!' he would say.

'You are talking big,' his wife would say with some irritation.

'I'll have a velvet-covered quilt made for you.'

---

* Hazrat Fatima, the Prophet's daughter.

'Just sometimes talk about finding a y-o-u-n-g m-a-n for Saiyda.'

This was the point arguments began. They started calling each other names. The conclusion reached by Saiyda's mother was that Abbu Miyan had ruined her life and such was her forbearance that she had tolerated it.

In reply Abbu Miyan expressed similar thoughts about her. And then they would both stop talking to one another—until the next edition of *Shama* magazine arrived. Abbu Miyan would open it with great expectations, and Saiyda's mother would sidle up to him. Abbu Miyan would compare his solution with the correct one. How many mistakes were there? One . . . two . . . three . . . . After this he would count under his breath and then announce that he just had one mistake too many—otherwise he would have won twenty-one thousand rupees. Anyway . . . next time they'd see. Then he would prepare a solution to the next puzzle, and everything would be repeated. But the necessities of life do not wait upon crossword puzzles. Daily necessities were becoming more and more costly. Income was stagnant. He received four hundred rupees a year in a grant from a religious trust. Of this sum, one hundred rupees was spent at Moharram. That left three hundred, that is an income of twenty-five rupees a month plus fifteen rupees rent. A total monthly income of forty rupees was not sufficient to provide a respectable existence, and Abbu Miyan was not prepared to take assistance from Saiyda. He was a respectable Indian father. It was remarkable for him to have tolerated her being in service. There was absolutely no question of his relying on her earnings. Gradually all his wife's jewellery was sold. The land he had acquired with such difficulty was lost to him in a case in the High Court. The land was lost, but the gold choker he'd given the tehsildar wasn't returned. In these circumstances what support was left him but prayer and crossword puzzles?

'Are you making any arrangements for Aziz Fatima's wedding or not?' Saiyda's mother asked one night, 'If we people don't attend there'll be a lot of complaints. It's their last daughter's wedding.'

'Why shouldn't we go? Of course we'll go,' replied Abbu Miyan. 'Can't you take out one suit of clothes from the ones put by for Saiyda's wedding and give it to Aziz Fatima?'

'Just *one* suit?'

'Give her a tray of jewellery too.'

'Has the day finally come when we're selling our daughter's trousseau?' She burst into tears.

'What are we to do?' asked Abbu Miyan, 'It's the times we live in.'

'And am I to wear these worn-out old slippers to the wedding?'

'No, I'll bring you some from Fussu's shop tomorrow.'

The next day after breakfast when he left home by the back door and made his way to Fussu's shop, he found it very crowded. He replied to Fussu Miyan's greeting with a prayer for his welfare and sat down to one side.

'Eh beta Mahjabin, see, Dada has come. Bring him some paan,' called out Fussu Miyan before saying to a customer, 'I can't bring the price down more than that. If you don't like it then go to the town and have your pocket slit by the city shopkeepers.'

'These shoes look very nice!' said Abbu Miyan, running his hands over the pink leather of the shoes under discussion.

'All these people want shoes for free, Mamu!' said Fussu Miyan.

Mahjabin walked in carrying Mighdad's infant son Dilavar Husain. Dilavar Husain held two paans in his fists and was attempting to put first one and then the other into his mouth. Mahjabin was holding both his hands and doubling up with laughter.

'You're a real little *badmash*, bhai,' said Fussu Miyan, extracting a paan from his hand. Dilavar Husain lost his temper. He pissed and the stream of urine splashed against Fussu Miyan's spectacles. The whole shop dissolved with mirth.

Wiping his face with the hem of his shirt, Fussu handed one paan to Abbu Miyan and put the other in his own mouth.

'Paan just doesn't taste the same since Mother died,' he remarked after chewing once or twice.

'One by one everybody is going. There's just me left now,' said Abbu Miyan. 'And is this world worth living in any longer? What I say is that my sister was lucky to leave this world. Now we'll see when my number comes . . . Bhai, I need two pairs of shoes.' He saw that all the customers had left, and immediately came to the point. 'One for me and one for your aunt.'

Fussu took down pairs of shoes and spread them out before him. Abbu Miyan selected two pairs.

'How much are they?'

'Now, I'm not making any profit on a sale to you,' replied Fussu Miyan, 'yours are seventeen rupees and Mamani's are twenty-one. Together that makes thirty-eight rupees.'

'Fine.' Abbu Miyan stood up holding both boxes. 'So I'll be off now, I'll give you their price in February or March. At the moment I don't have the money.'

He had already said this once before when he'd taken shoes—one pair for Saiyda and one for her mother. Fussu hadn't demanded payment, but if this became an established practice it could become very difficult. However Fussu also knew that he couldn't snatch the shoes from his uncle's hands. Abbu Miyan took the shoes and left, and Fussu Miyan noted down another sum owing. Apart from Hammad Miyan and Javad Miyan practically all the Miyans owed him money, and he couldn't demand payment from any of them. How could he make demands on the same Husain Ali Miyan who couldn't even afford repairs to his purdah wall! Everyone was in the same circumstances. In every house there were piles of trunks and chests. At every Saiyid lady's waist hung a weighty bunch of keys—but the trunks they opened were empty. There was no need for the locks, but the women held tightly to their bunches of keys because they were all they had to remind them of their days of prosperity. This key is for this trunk, and that key is for that chest. This key was for such-and-such a chest and this key for such-and-such a chest. 'Is' and 'was'—how strange these two words are. One is alive and the other as heavy as a corpse. Each key fastened to the bunches of keys was a corpse, and the ladies of the Uttar and Dakkhin Pattis clung to these corpses. The jangle of these keys kept them alive. Otherwise the light in their eyes would have been extinguished, and their backs would have doubled under the weight of the youth of their daughters wasted in spinsterhood. And so they spent their time cursing their daughters and their daughters wandered from room to room to conceal themselves—for the houses were just as large as they had always been, and the ghosts of memories danced in them night and day.

'Javad-cha has sent a proposal from Fiddu through Phunnan-cha!' Husain Ali Miyan said to his wife one night.

'Have we sunk to this?' replied his wife angrily, 'Has the time finally come when bastards call for the hands of Saiyid ladies?'

'Yes!' answered Husain Ali Miyan, 'And I'm accepting, saying that God has made us all . . . if he's a bastard, what fault is it of his?'

'If you've accepted then why ask me?'

'I'm asking because Javad-cha has brought a proposal for Zaigham.'

'From Zainabiya?'

'Yes!'

'Hold on to both proposals with all your might! Some one might steal them!' she exclaimed and, facing in the direction of Mecca, cried out, 'Oh, Pure Protector of the World! Take me to Thee! What is there left for me to witness now? For the sake of the martyrs of Karbala!'

'What I'm saying is do you want the girls to be comfortably off or do you want to marry them to some good-for-nothing but pure-blooded young men, even if it means that they spend their lives weeping? If anyone were to go by the letter of the law, then we're all illegitimate. At our wedding, when the Maulvi Sahib came to ask you if you accepted the marriage did you say yes yourself?'

'What does it matter if I didn't?' replied his wife, 'My aunt answered for me.'

'The Maulvi Sahib was asking you,' said Husain Ali Miyan. 'It wasn't your aunt being married that she should pipe up. But in your own wedding it was she who said yes!'

'What are you saying!' exclaimed his wife, her heart pounding. All the walls of her chastity seemed to be tumbling down.

'What I'm saying is that everyone's a bastard. The only difference is that someone's mother is a Saiyid lady and someone else's Rahman-bo. You people had it written in your fate to bear bastards. If that *haramzadi* hadn't started living with Javad-cha, she would have borne bastard children to Rahman.'

'Eh, bhai, you don't say things like that.'

'I am telling you all this to show that there's no harm in Fiddu and Kamila getting married. And for the same reason I'm thinking that we should accept Zainabiya for Zaigham.'

'Why don't you marry your daughter to Kammo?'

'To that Lord Sahib?' said Husain Ali Miyan, 'He'll only marry Saiyda, and she wouldn't touch him with her shoe. I've heard that she's changed her man for the second or third time down there in Aligarh. When I went to Ghazipur, to Shabbar's place, they were saying that now she's fallen for some Sikh.'

'How would they know what's going on in Aligarh?'

'Manno's studying there! So Shammu went to drop her and stayed at Ali Mehdi's house. He saw the whole spectacle with his own eyes. She goes to the club, speaks English, plays English games. What need does she have to get married? She earns three hundred rupees and makes another three hundred on top of that. Abbu-cha is poor in any case. For a start he lost his zamindari and on top of that he's got this zamindari of Saiyda too.'

'Arre, don't say such things about anyone's daughter,' said his wife. 'You've a young grown-up daughter yourself.'

'No one can say a word against my daughter, *ji*!'

At that moment their daughter Kamila was standing by the bars of the window, apparently unconscious of the gaze of Barkat, or

Muhammad Barkatulla Ansari, the son of Rehmat the weaver. Barkat, who was studying in Aligarh, was singing some Hindi film song in the most unmannerly way. His voice was reaching Kamila, but every time she looked at him he would look away in embarrassment. This performance had been going on since the previous year. It had so happened that Kamila had been returning from the majlis at Abbu Miyan's house. Night had fallen. A dog had ran at her. She had exclaimed 'Ya Ali!' and bent to one side, only to find herself in Barkat-va's arms. This sensation had been most pleasurable. Then Barkat-va had walked her home. Husain Ali Miyan's wife had even given him a paan and talked to him about Saiyda. The next day Kamila happened to be standing by the bars of the window when her eyes met Barkat-va's. Barkat-va had turned to a young child and made a few strange noises. She had smiled. Then it so happened that whenever Barkat-va came near the window he would bark like a dog. Neither had Barkat-va spoken to Kamila, nor Kamila to him. It was just that they were aware of each other's existence. Perhaps for them this was a great deal. Then Barkat-va left and Kamila began waiting for the summer holidays.

Barkat-va too missed Kamila the whole year in Aligarh. Obviously there was no question of their writing to one another. But he had resolved that this time he would definitely speak to Kamila. Then God ordained that when he was feeling the pain of separation most acutely, his grandfather should pass away. He had no special affection for his grandfather. The old man did nothing besides swear, hawk, spit out thick phlegm, and say his prayers. Even so, Barkat-va came running home and at the first opportunity he went to stand in front of the window and bark like a dog. Kamila came immediately and then the same performance was repeated. All his plans came to nothing. In Aligarh he'd told his friends great stories about his love affair with Kamila, emphasizing that his beloved was a pure-blooded Saiyid. But now his tongue wouldn't work. Thousands of romantic sentences he'd learnt off by heart were wriggling in his brain like worms but they could find no escape because some *saala* film song was stuck to his tongue. The appearance of Phunnan Miyan forced Barkat-va to move away from the window.

'What are you doing here?' asked Phunnan Miyan.

'Nothing, sahib!'

'Tell your father that if he wants to stay in this village then he'd better set his brain straight. Now he's reached the stage he can attack Abbu-bhai. I'll tear the legs off him and throw them away. Tell that husband of your mother that whoever's lost his zamindari has lost it for good, but that Phunnan Miyan hasn't lost his zamindari!'

'If you've fought with Abba why are you shouting at me?'

'Abba!' said Phunnan Miyan, absolutely beside himself. 'If you start calling your father "Abba" then what on earth will respectable people call their fathers?'

The fact was that Phunnan Miyan's blood had been boiling since the previous night. The first news Kulsum had given him when he'd returned was, 'Rahmat-va went after Abbu-bhai after lunch because his chicken went into their house and began to peck at some coriander and Abbu-bhai's wife threw a stone at it. Its legs broke. That was all, and Rahmat-va went after them. He shouted all sorts of things. I could hear him from here. It's a good thing that Abbu-bhai didn't stir out of his house, otherwise, God forbid, Rahmat-va would have killed him.'

'That *behenchod* has risen so high, has he?' said Phunnan Miyan, picking up his lathi. 'I'll drive a plough right up his backside! What does he think, that Abbu-bhai has no one to stand by him?'

Outside Rahmat's door Phunnan Miyan delivered such curses that the whole village was stunned into silence. Women stopped their ears. He was using the most impossible abuses. Several people told him that Rahmat-va had gone to Muhammadabad, but this did nothing to assuage his anger.

Some young weavers wanted to oppose him, but the elders of the community prevented them. Even after the abolition of zamindari, Phunnan Miyan was still Phunnan Miyan. Behind him now were some two hundred or more lathis. Gradually all the weavers went back indoors. Phunnan Miyan also returned, and that is why blood rushed to his eyes the moment he saw Barkat-va.

Barkat-va thought it wise to beat a retreat. Inwardly he cursed Phunnan Miyan a thousand times as his own blood had begun to boil at hearing Phunnan's insults. He consoled himself with the thought that if he hadn't been a university student he would certainly have settled matters with that old Miyan.

Phunnan Miyan walked through Husain Ali Miyan's gate. Husain Ali Miyan was lying on a string bed smoking a huqqa. Phunnan Miyan lay down on the bed next to his and Husain Ali Miyan turned the huqqa round to face him. Phunnan Miyan drew on it two or three times and then turned it back to face Husain Ali Miyan.

'What have you decided?' asked Phunnan Miyan.

'I'll not have my children married into a polluted family,' replied Husain Ali Miyan.

'Have you gone mad?' said Phunnan Miyan. 'Are these any times to put on airs about being a Saiyid? Arre, Miyan, consider it a blessing that you can lead a decent life.'

'But it would be like swallowing a live fly, just thinking about it makes you want to vomit.'

'Bhai, you're not going to like it,' said Phunnan Miyan, 'but with my own eyes I've just seen Kamila peeping and peering at Rahmat-va's son Barkat-va!'

Husain Ali Kabir shot up, boiling with rage.

'Lie down, lie down! There's no need to flare up at me. She's my daughter as much as she's yours. What I'm saying is that these are delicate times. Who knows what will happen when! And who says that you people are such great Saiyids? Your forefathers came from Chavanpur and who doesn't know about the Saiyids of Chavanpur? There's no way you're more of a Saiyid than I am.'

'Of course the people of Gangauli dropped straight down from heaven!' said Husain Ali Miyan. 'You're older to me, so don't force me to open my mouth.'

'No, bhaiyaa, you are the offspring of Hazrat Ali himself!' said Phunnan Miyan, 'Why are you losing your temper? Don't marry Kamila to Fiddu, by all means. And when, God forbid, she runs off with Barkat-va, just tell the village that his father's a pure-blooded Saiyid.'

'Is this the way you're blackening my girl's name?' said Husain Ali Miyan. 'Very well . . . what can I do now? The peg we were so proud of has been cut. You couldn't have spoken like this if zamindari was intact today. Then Javad-cha could never have sent a proposal to us. But still I'm telling you to get out of my house.'

'If Kammo sacks your beloved son, Saiyid Zaigham, then what will you do?' asked Phunnan Miyan as he put on his shoes.

'Now that's coercion.'

'As long as zamindari existed, what coercion was there that you didn't use? Do you think I don't know that you had fallen for Rahmat-va's sister? And what gave you the power to fall for her? If you hadn't been a zamindar, and he had, then wouldn't he have fucked your sister? Yesterday was your time, today is his. That's why I'm telling you to quietly marry Kamila to Fiddu and Zaigham to Zainabiya and not to talk to me about blood and breeding. My blood's a great deal stronger than yours, do you understand? Maulvi Bedar's is strong too but he went to Pakistan. Don't you imagine that he went to Pakistan because the Sikhs had taken over the imambara in Delhi and the mosques of Amritsar had been turned into Sikh temples. All that happened the year Pakistan was made. So why didn't he go straightaway then? He went to Pakistan because he no longer had any way to survive in Gangauli. What was there to depend on? No family or children, he didn't know how to plough and hadn't the courage to open a shoe shop like Fussu, and so he said that he wouldn't stay in a country where Sikhs had seized an imambara. Abbu Miyan is about to meet the same fate. He's a guest in Gangauli for just a few days more. But you'll keep on with this lame farming. You can't leave your land and go to Pakistan. And now to go on living in the village a man needs fifty to a hundred lathis behind him, because if those lathis aren't behind you, they'll come up in front of you and start beating a tattoo on your skull. Do you understand? Phunnan Miyan would have gone to Pakistan but he didn't because there was no one here who could so much as lay a finger on one of his short hairs. I'm not just one Phunnan Miyan! I'm one hundred, two hundred lathis, and don't you forget that you owe Parusaram's father money. Kabir Miyan's home would have been auctioned if Kammo hadn't intervened. He said that as long as he was alive Kabir Miyan could never go and beg from Sukhram-va. He straight away took out a basketful of rupees and paid Kabir Miyan's debt. Kabir Miyan's darling son Saddan had just showed the old man his thumb and gone back to Pakistan. He'd said that the sum wasn't big, but here in India he couldn't do anything. I told him, "Eh, bhaiyaa! If you want to send two or three lakhs from Pakistan then I'll have them." Then he didn't know where to look! Someone was saying that you're in debt to Sukhram-va too!'

This was the last straw. Husain Ali Miyan broke. The marriages were settled.

The news that engagements had been agreed between Fiddu and Kamila, and Zaigham and Zainabiya spread through the Uttar and Dakkhin Pattis like wildfire. The Saiyid gentlefolk no longer had the strength to be shocked. Arre, if Maulvi Bedar could go to Pakistan, then anything could happen. If any of the Saiyids chanced to walk by Maulvi Bedar's house they tried to avoid looking at it. Such a big house, standing empty and gazing up at the sky. Then the rains challenged it. But there was no one to save this poor old house. Still, it stood besieged by wind and rain because, unlike Maulvi Bedar, it could go nowhere. Its foundations were in the earth. It began to sway, crushed by its wounds, and then collapsed like a courageous soldier.

Parusaram bought this ruin from the Custodian of Refugee Property and before one's very eyes a new house was constructed. But this brick-built house seemed completely out of place in that environment. A jeep may have stood in its garage, but it had no history and therefore the neighbouring decrepit, mud-built houses looked upon it with contempt.

When Parusaram came to Gangauli he held court in the evenings. His court was the biggest in the village. It was attended by the most wealthy and by the impoverished Saiyid gentlemen. These people sat on chairs, smoked cigarettes and listened to the radio. A short distance from them gathered the village's poor, who squatted on the ground, just as they had in the days of the zamindars, chewed tobacco and smoked beedis. Fate had decreed that they should sit on the ground. Their only consolations were that one of their number now sat on the Miyans' chairs and the Miyans came to his door. The other difference was that now they could smoke beedis in front of the Miyans.

But Sukhram-va never learnt to sit on a chair. He would squat on its seat just as if he were on the ground, and when any of the Miyans arrived he would panic and leap to his feet, unable to think where it was proper to put these guests. The more he flattered them, the more the Miyans became embarrassed, and when Parusaram said that such-and-such a thing couldn't happen in his village or in his area, the Miyans found their entire being trembling with emotion.

For some time there had been talk in the village that Parusaram and Hammad Miyan had fallen out. It had so happened that one day Parusaram's wife had visited Hammad Miyan's house. She had learned how to wear fine saris and her body was ornamented with very delicate, beautiful and expensive jewellery. She didn't know how to wear lipstick and so it was plastered over her lips. It was winter and she had wrapped an expensive shawl round her shoulders.

She came indoors and sat on a bed. Kubara was intensely irritated to see this sweeper woman sit down on one of her beds like this. She made some remark. And Parusaram's wife was not one to keep quiet either. After all, she was the wife of an MLA! She directed some harsh words at Kubara, saying, 'Even now you people's heads aren't straight!'

'Arre, who do you think you are to look at our heads?' replied Kubara-bi, beside herself with rage, 'It was by our votes that Parusaram became an Emallay, and now think you can lord it over us! If I hear one more peep out of you, *matimili*, I'll tear out your tongue with my shoe! *Matimile*! *Khahanpiti*! Get down from my bed!

You've polluted my sheets, you *jharumari*!'

Parusaram's wife, Ramdaiya, understood this much—that her husband had become an MLA by vote, and votes were asked for every five years. And Kubara-bi didn't look as if she were about to die. And an election was just around the corner. Therefore she attempted to swallow all this. She said, 'I'm not going to fight with you. You're elder to me . . . but I didn't say anything that you should . . . '

'All right, let it be, don't blather on!'

Ramdaiya swallowed this humiliation and left but the moment Parusaram came home she filled his ears with the story. Parusaram asked her what need there was for her to go to Hammad's house, and gave her a thorough beating. The next day he even went to Hammad Miyan's house and apologized. He stood outside the door and asked forgiveness from Kubara too, saying that his wife was just an uneducated woman. Kubara did forgive her, but it was as if a crack had formed in Parusaram's heart. As a result, every task that Hammad Miyan put his hand to went wrong. And the day of judgement finally dawned when Gaya Ahir was booked under Section 109 of the Criminal Procedure Code. Hammad Miyan rushed off to the police station, but the thanedar gave him short shrift. Then Hammad began to suspect what was going on. When he came home he scolded Kubara roundly, 'Even if she did sit on your bed, what rubies of yours were stitched there?'

'What are you saying?'

'Peasant!' shouted Hammad Miyan, boiling with wrath, 'It's not possible to live in this village for one day if you argue with Parusaram . . . Do you understand?'

'But that day he came and said he was sorry, and I forgave him too.'

At this, Hammad Miyan seemed to ignite, 'You can take your forgiveness, put honey on it and lick it night and morning to cool your liver!' He walked out, muttering angrily, and for a long time paced up and down in his room. Then he sent one of his men to find out whether Parusaram was at home or not. He was indeed at home. Hammad Miyan opened his trunk, took out a shervani coat, put it on and set straight off for Parusaram's house.

It felt odd to be going to Parusaram's house because he was going for the first time. He was extremely angry with his wife for compelling him to make this visit. But when he entered the Great Gate which had once belonged to Maulvi Bedar it was as if someone had tied an oil press to his feet. Just opposite sat Mighdad saying, 'Bhai, I am a farmer. I was ploughing the land before, and I'm ploughing it now.'

'But, Mighdad Miyan,' said Parusaram, 'Hammad Miyan is your father, after all's said and done.'

'But he's a Saiyid. Now what can I say about my own father? Let it pass, don't force me to open my mouth.'

'What I'm seeing, Parusaram bhaiyaa, is that these zamindars' tempers haven't improved even after zamindari's gone . . . the land's not gone to the cultivators and the thumb of the zamindars is still on our head. That's why I say that we should join Pandeji's farmers' association. Now take Hammad Miyan. Gaya does all the work for him, but still he holds land enough for three ploughs to cover. Gaya should be cast out of the community—deny him the right to share our huqqas or water!' said one of Parusaram's close confidants.

'Gaya went to jail to smoke a huqqa and take water!' said another.

'But . . .' Parusaram's glance fell on Hammad Miyan. He stood up. The others present remained seated.

'Please come in, Mir Sahib! Why are you standing there?'

'I have a minute's work with you.'

Parusaram walked up to the gate. Hammad Miyan began to trace lines on the old wooden door with his thin cane.

'What orders have you for me, Mir Sahib?'

'I never expected you to take a woman's quarrel this far. There's a difference to be made between friends and enemies, bhai! When all the Miyans were against you I gave you support and today my man is in the police lockup!'

'How can that be, sahib?' said Parusaram, 'I'll call that *behenchod* thanedar here this minute . . . . I hear that Pandeji's been coming and going a great deal among the Miyans lately. You tell me, isn't that too much? The government's given so many agricultural loans here . . . pukka roads have been built from both sides so that you people reach the town in half an hour. Every lane in the village has been paved with brick. There are two schools . . . more than that what can any government do? And then you people know how delicate the position of Muslims in India is now, due to the creation of Pakistan. Association with a man like Pandeji is the sort of thing which the Jan Sanghis and Mahasabhawallahs take advantage of to say you're anti-Indian. I don't want any Hindu-Muslim riots in my area. Then you know what sort of man Pandeji is. A real wolf in sheep's clothing. The leader of a band of dacoits.'

'How can you accuse us of such things?' said Hammad Miyan, 'However, if our men start getting locked up what else can we people do except side with Pandeji?'

'Arre, sahib, why are you going on and on about Gaya?' said Parusaram in annoyance, 'If that's how it is then go and tell Pandeji to get him out of jail for you!'

'Now you're really going too far!' said Hammad Miyan, 'Someone comes to tell you his troubles and you start taunting him with Pandeji.'

'Do you want to go and join Gaya?'

Hammad Miyan was stunned. Parusaram's tone was as hard as a well-oiled lathi.

The men sitting on the chairs guffawed with laughter. At that moment Sukhram-va came out of the house. Seeing Hammad Miyan, he rushed up to him. 'How can you be so rude, Parusaram! Offer the Miyan a seat.' He addressed Hammad Miyan, 'Please, Miyan, why are you standing here!'

'I'll come again another day,' replied Hammad Miyan. 'This time I'd just come for some work.'

Hammad Miyan returned a worried man. He had come to fully understand the saying 'to live in the river and be the crocodile's foe'. Now the question was whether to bend his knee or fight. He decided to fight. That very day he went to Ghazipur and put the problem before Bashir Miyan and Wazir Miyan. They were stunned as well. It was settled that Hammad Miyan should take a letter to Lucknow and meet Ali Zaheer. Accordingly, Hammad Miyan went to Lucknow and did meet Ali Zaheer Sahib. Ali Zaheer phoned someone or other he didn't name, and then some other unnamed person. Gradually the message reached Ghazipur that Gaya was innocent. The president of the District Congress Committee told Parusaram that Hammad Miyan was one of the Chief Minister Dr Sampurnanand's own men and should be taken good care of.

'That's all very well,' replied Parusaram, 'but then he should also take good care to remember that he is the Chief Minister's man. His home is a den of Pakistanis. He's always stirring up the Muslims of this area. And on the other hand he's patronizing criminals.'

Then telephone lines began to buzz.

In the meantime Hammad Miyan had a shopkeeper in the town file a case of non-repayment of debt and fraud against Parusaram. A loose woman of Devkathiya filed a report of assault and rape against him and Hammad Miyan himself presented a petition saying that his life was in danger from Parusaram, and requesting that he should be placed under a personal bond. There was tumult in the village. The upper castes sided with Hammad Miyan. The Raqi traders sided with

Parusaram and the low castes. The Ahirs were divided. One group following Phunnan Miyan stayed with Parusaram, and the other went over to Hammad Miyan with the Thakurs of Barikhpur. The crops in several fields were looted. There were several fights.

'Go and tell the Miyan to get himself to Pakistan!' was the message sent by Parusaram.

Hammad Miyan laughed off this threat. Parusaram may have become an MLA, but it was Hammad Miyan who knew the art of arguing a court case. Parusaram's lawyer proved that the woman who had made the allegations was of easy virtue, but a medical investigation had already been conducted. Hammad Miyan had prepared a cast-iron case. Instead of bribing the doctor he had considered it appropriate to ensure that there had really been a rape. Accordingly the state prosecutor was compelled to raise a point of law and ask in which law it was written that a woman of easy virtue could not be subject to rape? The defence lawyer could offer no reply.

Parusaram was convicted.

That day the Thakurs of Barikhpur hosted a splendid party. The town prostitutes came. Thakur Prithvipal Singh invited Phunnan Miyan too. Kulsum did her best to stop him going but he took Chikuriya with him and arrived in Barikhpur. Prithvipal Singh gave him a hearty welcome. When the subject of the court case arose, Phunnan Miyan said, 'Arre, Prithvipal, don't you know that the goldsmith needs a hundred taps, and the ironsmith just one blow? If I get him in front of me once I'll give him such a going over that he'll never get up. I've not forgiven him. Because of him I went to jail. I can't forget that.'

'Let it pass, Mir Sahib! It's not good to harbour grudges for too long,' said Prithvipal Singh.

'If Thakur Kunwarpal Singh were alive today, he would have said that the men these days are not made of the same earth they used to be. Arre, sing you people . . . *behenchod*, what are you sitting around for?' he scolded the prostitute, Hira Bai of Ghazipur, who was playing with the bells tied round her ankles.

'And haven't you invited Mir Hammad Husain Zaidi, the bridegroom of this whole wedding party?' he asked Prithvipal Singh.

'He's not fond of singing and music,' replied Prithvipal. 'Arre, bhai, why are you sitting around?' he rebuked Hira Bai too. The musicians struck up. Hira Bai cleared her throat and began to sing a ghazal by the poet Ghalib:

'My Beloved merely taunts and creetisizees,
It's futile then to speak of my hearrt's pain . . .'

Phunnan Miyan didn't give her a chance to go further. He began screaming, 'Arre, why are you defiling Ghalib's bones! Don't sing him! Arre, sing some folk-song!'

Not one of the people gathered there understood why Phunnan Miyan was getting so angry. Prithvipal's son, Jaipal Singh, was also there. For amusement and personal interest he'd chosen to study at Aligarh and was in the final year of his engineering course. But even he couldn't understand. Hira Bai was left completely speechless. Just a few days ago she'd sung this ghazal for the friends of Seth Nasrullah and they had been thrilled. In his excitement Nasrullah had pulled his lungi up to the top of his thighs and Khamosh, that young man with the great big eyes and the attractive olive-coloured skin, had begun to sway in appreciation. That young man was a very good poet himself and so what was this old man with the moustache screaming for? God preserve us from these peasants!

'You explain to her!' Prithvipal told Jaipal.

'What is there to explain?' Jaipal replied.

'Arre, then when will all your reading and writing be of use?'

'Sing a ghazal by Dagh, if you know one!' Jaipal told Hira Bai, 'And if you don't then sing the qavvali from that film *A Night in the Rains*!'

Phunnan Miyan put aside the idea of slapping him in the face. Thakur Kunwarpal Singh hadn't been educated but he didn't make any mistakes in pronunciation. Still, what was the point of saying anything to Prithvipal when he couldn't even correct this prostitute's pronunciation?

'Did Hakim Ali Kabir give you a prescription telling you to be sure to sing and dance for a living?' he asked, staring at Hira Bai.

'I go to the Civil Surgeon when I'm unwell,' replied Hira Bai, highly offended.

'Accha, then sing to us about your "hearrt's pain" then! Just get it over and done with quickly!' Phunnan Miyan leaned against a cushion, and prepared to endure the performance.

The singing and dancing went on late into the night and Phunnan Miyan kept cursing himself and the times he lived in. Around half-past-two he took his leave. Prithvipal Singh did tell him that it was very late and there was no need for him to go, but Phunnan didn't agree.

'Your Chachi will be worried,' he told him.

With Chikuriya he set out for home. All around the night was completely still. A strong, cold wind was blowing. Phunnan Miyan wrapped the old army coat round him tightly and in a loud voice began to curse the weather. The wind was piercing him to the bone and he felt intensely aware of his age. As a result he began to miss his sons acutely. His eyes filled with tears. He stopped cursing the weather for fear Chikuriya might guess he was crying. He only looked up when lathis began raining down upon him.

'This is unmanly work!' he said as he fell, 'If you gave me fair warning, I'd know you were a man!'

A lathi fell on his shoulder. 'Get off, you eunuch!' he said with enormous contempt. Then it seemed that the night penetrated his eyes, and mixed with his blood, and then he himself became part of the night.

Phunnan Miyan was dead!

Chikuriya died with him.

The blood of both mingled, but this mixture did not produce a third colour. Because the colour of their blood was the same.

That same night an incident occurred in Gangauli. Hakim Ali Kabir went outside to the commode. He slipped, fell and broke his leg. He screamed and screamed until he lost consciousness as his wife, with her daughter and children, had gone to Naunahra to express their condolences over someone's death, and his old maid Fizza had become completely deaf, and his young granddaughter, Sarwariya, was sleeping the deep sleep of youth because Zaigham had completely worn her out. She was dreaming of a little baby.

In the morning when she went to find the Hakim Sahib, she discovered him lying in the toilet. She shuddered and stepped back because he was wrapped in a layer of buzzing flies. Then she screamed. She rushed off and called out to Husain Ali Miyan. Within minutes the entire population of Uttar Patti assembled. The Hakim Sahib was taken from the toilet, and his body washed. Sarwariya blushed several times as she changed his clothes because the thought of Zaigham kept reoccurring to her.

Husain Haidar hurried off to call Kammo. Kammo examined the Hakim Sahib very intently with his stethoscope and then gave his opinion that the Hakim Sahib's leg was broken. He had no idea at all how to set bones, but obviously he couldn't reveal this. At this point Javad Miyan came to the rescue since in his youth he'd been involved in countless brawls and set a number of bones. So the Hakim's Sahib's bone was put back in place and Kammo, that is Doctor Saiyid

Kamaluddin, sat down to take the Hakim Sahib's pulse. This pulse seemed to him to be behaving very strangely.

Gradually the medicines began to take effect. Then, just at the moment the Hakim Sahib began to regain his senses, the news was brought that Phunnan Miyan had been murdered. All the Miyans rushed off. Naturally Kammo couldn't leave his patient and so he sat where he was. In the room next door Zaigham stayed put too. But, there being no point in sitting idle, he kept pressing Sarwariya's breasts and pinching her thighs. Lifting the hem of her kurta he stroked the soft skin of her stomach, as pale as a frangipani flower, and Sarwariya kept making delightful, soft little sobs and saying, 'Bhai, someone will see! Kammo will see!'

When the Hakim Sahib opened his eyes a wave of pain passed through his body. Then his gaze focused on Kammo.

'Lord Almighty!' he groaned and broke within.

'Don't move,' said Kammo.

'Are *you* treating *me*?' said the Hakim Sahib in disbelief, 'I'm not going to eat any of your sugar pills!' He sank in this sea of disgrace, 'Look, Kammo, at the state in which you've put me! The government took my land . . . you took my patients . . . what reason is there for me to live any more?'

'Some people murdered Phunnan Miyan last night!' said Kammo.

'It's what the damned man deserved!' said the Hakim Sahib, 'Still, this is Hammad's handiwork!'

'Take this,' said Kammo, holding out one dose of homoeopathic medicine.

'I've told you, haven't I, I'm not taking it,' said the Hakim Sahib. 'I've a great deal of pain in that leg.'

'Eh, Sarwariya!' called out Kammo.

'Yes!' said Sarwariya, entering the room adjusting her dupatta.

'Where's Zaigham?'

'With Bhai.'

'Call him here, I'm going now. And see, I'm leaving four doses of medicine here. Give him one every half an hour.'

Kammo left. When Zaigham entered the room the Hakim Sahib's eyes were wet with tears.

'Are you in a lot of pain, Bade Abba?'

'No, son, I'm just thinking that the only thing left for me to see was the day that Kammo treated me! It seems as if the Lord has carefully gathered every misfortune for me.'

'Allah tests His virtuous servants, sahib!'

'Arre, what sort of virtuous servant am I, bhai? I'm not Imam Husain to be killed and thank God for it! I've spent a lifetime in prayer and fasting and what have I got in return—Doctor Kamaluddin feeling my pulse! Eh, beta, is there no justice left before God?'

'Please don't talk, rest.'

'Yes, yes . . . that's what Doctor Kamaluddin said as he left.' The Hakim Sahib smiled.

'He set the bone . . . but he didn't see that my liver is entirely bad and there's inflammation in my stomach! All the organs of the body are one. It's not as if the liver's separate and the stomach's separate! So if you treat the liver alone you send the stomach to hell! No one can write a correct prescription without understanding the whole body. That's why so many people are lying sick nowadays. They haven't recovered from one disease before they've gone down with another . . . Saddan says, "Why should I send money to my father? Why doesn't he come to Pakistan?" But how can I go? Only yesterday my late father came to me . . . He said, "Eh, my son Kabir! Are you leaving us and going to Pakistan?" I told him "Eh, Baba! How can you say such a thing . . . whether zamindari's gone or not, whether the sick come to me or not, I'm not about to go and leave you . . . I'm not Saddan . . ."'

His eyes closed. The walls of time and space collapsed. All the elders of the community gathered round his bed. But his closed eyes were seeking Saddan. And his tongue, about to fall silent, was calling out to his grandsons and granddaughters, 'What are you doing, *beh*? Did you see that, Bibi? This little pig pissed! Don't you recognize him, Father? Arre, this is Saddan's son! Greet your great-grandfather, lad! Eh, Father! You know those lands you left, they're not ours any more. Gandhi said that they belong to the Chamars and Bhars. I kept on saying that I'd inherited them from my father. But no one listened . . .'

'Bade Abba . . . Eh, Bade Abba . . .' Zaigham began to call out to him.

'. . . zamindari has gone for sure, but the village has completely changed. All the alleys are paved with bricks and a pukka road has been built from here to Ghazipur. Now no one can have any trouble coming here in the rains or at Moharram. I've heard that on the tenth of Moharram this year, Imam Husain came and sat in Maulvi Bedar's imambara and wept a great deal. He seemed very angry. He said to me, "Maulvi Bedar went and left me and you didn't stop him?" I said, "Oh, Lord! I tried hard to persuade him . . ."'

Husain Ali Miyan, Husain Haidar, Hammad Miyan and the women of Uttar Patti had surrounded the Hakim Sahib's bed. Sarwariya was weeping bitterly. Husain Ali Miyan began to read the chapter of the Qor'an recited to the dying. Zaigham and Kammo together turned the bed so that the Hakim Sahib lay with his head towards Mecca.

Fussu began to weep loudly.

'. . . I couldn't desert the Lord and go to Pakistan . . . Eh, Baba! You bear witness, I forgive Gandhi . . .'

'There is no God but Allah and Muhammad is His Prophet . . .' recited all those present.

'Eh, Saddan! You deserted me, I'm telling you, you left your father . . . left him . . . so should I leave my father? Worthless son . . .' The Hakim Sahib suddenly fell silent. Abbu Miyan covered his face with a sheet. Kamila began to scream and cry.

Exactly at that moment Fiddu entered and whispered into Fussu Miyan's ear, 'Come home quickly! Saida's had a son.'

Fussu Miyan cast a glance at the corpse and quietly went out.

Outside the morning was most beautiful. In the courtyard a cock was chasing a chicken and a crow was sitting on the ridge of the roof, calling out to heaven knows who. A flock of sparrows flew past Fussu Miyan's shoulder. At the edge of the pond two or three naked children were throwing water over each other, and to one side a young woman was sitting scouring pans with her sari lifted up to her knees. Stirring up the dust, a jeep was heading over the winding road paved with river pebbles. Opposite, near the tank, thick smoke was pouring out of the chimney of a brick kiln. A young child, a schoolbag over his shoulder, ran past at great speed.

Fussu Miyan watched him until he turned to the left and disappeared from sight.

Glossary

achcha	lit. good, well, really
adaab	lit. respect. A greeting conveying the sense of 'I am showing complete respect.'
Ahirs	a caste which specializes in keeping cattle
amarbel	a parasitic creeper, *cuscuta reflexa*
anna	one sixteenth of a rupee
Asharh	fourth month of a Hindu calendar. June/July
ashrafi	a gold coin
badmash	bad character
ba'ji	elder sister
balushahi	a type of sweet
Baqra 'Id	the festival marking the anniversary of Abraham offering the sacrifice of his son to God
behenchod	lit. sister fucker. Similar words used are, *betichod* (daughter fucker) and *madarchod* (mother fucker)
behini	lit. little sister
ber	Chinese date or *zizyphus mauritiana*, used in many folk rituals
beta	son (also daughter when used affectionately)
Bhangi	a caste of Harijans, whose traditional tasks included removal of nightsoil
Bhars	a low caste mainly working as labourers or in the houses of zamindars
bhauj	brother's wife
bhonsrivala	lit. cuntwallah—one who comes out of a cunt
bibi	honorofic for a woman, e.g., Hammad uses it to address his wife
bigha	just over half an acre
Bismillah	ceremony when a child reads his or her first words from the Qor'an
bitiya	lit. little daughter
-bo	a suffix meaning 'wife of'
-bua	a suffix meaning 'aunt'
-cha	a suffix, short for chacha or uncle, used for those

	who are not literally uncles, but of the same age
Chamars	a Harijan caste, traditionally leather workers
champa	generally frangipani or *plumeria* species but here a bush with greenish white flowers, *artabotrys odoratissimus*
chiraunji	the tree—*chironjia sapada* and its nut
Chote Hazrat	Hazrat Abbas, half-brother to Imam Husain
chowk	a raised oblong platform on which tazias are placed during Moharram
chowkidar	part-time village policeman
crore	ten million
-da, -dada, -dadi	suffixes of respect for elders
dahi bade	fried lentil or gram-flour cakes, soaked in water, squeezed and then served in yoghurt
dal	lentil
darad	pain
dhaniya	coriander
Diwali	Hindu festival of lights when Lakshmi, the goddess of wealth, is worshipped. Gambling is traditional
dulhan	lit. bride, the title given to the wife of a son of a family in her in-law's home
dupatta	length of fine cloth women use to drape over their heads and/or shoulders
ghazal	a short poem made up of couplets
girai	a small, slippery river fish
harami/ haramzada/ haramzadi	bastard
haramzadgi	behaving like a *haramzada*
harsingar	*nycthanthes arbor-tristis*, a shrub with small, white scented flowers
havildar	a military or police rank equivalent to sergeant
Hazrat	a title of extreme respect
huqqa-pani bund	being ostracized from the community—lit. being refused water and a smoke from huqqa of the community
huzoor	a term of respect
'Id	the festival at the end of Ramadan, the Muslim month of fasting
ikka	a horse cart
imambara	lit. house of the imam, hall where tazias are kept and majlises held during Moharram
Insha-Allah	God willing
ishq-e-pechan	*antigonon leptopus*, coral creeper

jamun	the tree—*syzygium cumini* or *eugenia jambolqna*
jharumare/i (m/f)	a term of abuse—fit to be beaten with a broom
kabaddi	a team game
kadamba	the tree—*anthocephalus cadamba* or *a. indicus*
kajal	collyrium
Kaliyug	the present, the fourth last age of the Hindu concept of time—a time of sin and destruction
Karbala	the place where Imam Husain was martyred. The name of burial grounds where tazias are buried every year on the tenth of Moharram
Kathak	a school of North Indian classical dance
katha	catechu
khadi	homespun cloth, symbol of the independence movement and one of the ideals of Mahatma Gandhi
khahanpiti	a term of abuse—widow
khasdan	a container for folded betel leaves
khichra	meat, wheat and various types of lentils all boiled together—speciality of tenth of Moharram
lajwanti	the touch-me-not plant
lakh	one hundred thousand
lathi	staff—especially for fighting with
lota	small pot for carrying water
lungi	length of cloth wrapped round waist, and reaching the ankles
madrassa	religious educational establishment
mahua	the tree—*bassia latifolia*
mai-baap	mother-and-father—the role of a ruler
majlis	assembly for ritual mourning of the martyrdom of Imam Husain
mamani	maternal uncle's wife
mamun	maternal uncle
mang-patti	lit. ask-for-a-card, a card game
marsia	poem narrating the events of Karbala
matam	the act of mourning—especially breast-beating
matimile/i (m/f)	a term of abuse—may you be mixed with earth
mehr	wedding settlement given by the husband to the wife at the time of marriage
Mirasi	class of professional musicians of low social status
Moharram	first month of the Muslim calendar. The month Husain was martyred at Karbala, therefore a month of mourning, especially for Shias
mui	a term of abuse used by women meaning wretched
musalmani	here 'foreskin' otherwise penis

mutah	temporary marriage, allowed in Shia law
naooj	an exclamation used by women
nauha	a short lament, chanted to the accompaniment of breast-beating
neem	the margosa tree, *azidarachta indica*
nikaundi	wretched, stupid
paan	betel-leaf, *piper betel*
pakkar	the tree—*ficus infectoria*, a relative of the banyan
panchayat	village council; here a council of elders of a particular caste
Pathans	Muslims originally from the NWFP or Afghanistan
patwari	the village official who maintains land records
peepul	the tree—*ficus religiosa*
poth	Benares silk woven with motifs in gold thread
prasad	offerings made to a god and then distributed to devotees
puri	deep-fried round bread
qamiz	shirt; rather long, quite tightly fitting garment worn by women
qavvali	songs, generally religious songs sung by Sufi mystics to help attain spiritual realization
qeema	minced meat
Rabi-ul-avval	month of the Muslim calendar; Shias do not carry out any joyous work before the ninth of this month; second month after Moharram
Rajab	a month of the Muslim calendar
Raqis	Muslim traders
rishi	Hindu sage
roghani roti	bread made from ghee mixed with dough
saala	sister's husband; also a term of abuse
Sadrulfazil	the final degree from Lucknow's Shia religious college, Sultan-ul-Madaris
Saiyid	a descendent of the Prophet, through his daughter, Fatima, and son-in-law, Ali
salaam	a greeting; a poem in praise of Imam Husain
sangi	mixed silk and cotton brocade fabric woven in Azamgarh (eastern Uttar Pradesh)
sarkar	lit. the man heading a work, a term of respect used by the humble to someone in a position of power; the government
seer	about a kilogram
seth, sethji	a form of addressing a wealthy businessman or trader
Shabaan	a month of the Muslim calendar

shahnashin	lit. seat of the king. The raised platform in an imambara where the tazias and standards are carefully arranged
shalwar	loose baggy trousers
sharbat	a sweet, cooling drink
Sheikhs	the second of the four 'noble' classes of north Indian Muslim society
shervani	closely fitting men's coat
soz	lit. burning, chanting of some verses connected with the events of Karbala to a raag of classical Indian music
susar(an)	father-in-law(s); also a term of abuse
tabarruk	blessed food
tamami	cotton cloth embroidered with fine gold wire
tapovan	a forest hermitage where austerities are performed
tavva	small, round, slightly concave griddle
tazia	replica of the tomb of Imam Husain at Karbala
tehsildar	an official responsible for maintenance of land records and collection of land revenue from a tehsil, the administrative area below a district
Thakurs	a dominant caste; traditionally Kshatriyas or warriors
thana	a police sub-district; the chief police station of that sub-district
thanedar	the officer in charge of a thana
tika	a small mark (of vermilion or sandal paste) on the forehead, worn by Hindus
ustad	Urdu equivalent of guru
-va	suffix attached to names, indicating familiarity
zamindar	tax-framers; their word was to a large extent law, and they kept a proportion of the land revenue they collected
zamindari	the land held by a zamindar